I0822567

A Cent A Story!

A Cent A Story!

The Best From *Ten Detective Aces*

Garyn G. Roberts

Bowling Green State University Popular Press
Bowling Green, Ohio 43403

Note: The following stories are facsimile reprints from the original *Ten Detective Aces* pulp magazines. Effort has been made to retain the advertising of the time, as well as the fiction.

Library of Congress Catalogue Card No.: 86-070384

ISBN: 0-87972-353-X Clothbound
0-87972-354-8 Paperback

**For the Pioneers of the Pulpwood Pages—
Swashbucklers in Their Own Write**

Ray and Pat Browne

Gary Hoppenstand

(Friends and Scholars Extraordinaire)

Dad, Mom and Tom

Renee

(Very Special People)

Acknowledgements

Many thanks are extended to Robert and Phyllis Weinberg for their invaluable insight and assistance, the fine folks at the Popular Press, and family members and friends for their support and faith in this project.

Contents

Of Dragnets and Detective Aces: Early Beginnings for the Hero Pulps

Garyn G. Roberts

THE POPULAR MYSTERY STORY has manifested itself in a variety of forms and variations for almost 150 years. Though tales of intrigue and suspense have been part of humanity—as in the case of Homer's *The Odyssey*—seemingly as long as have been human beings themselves, the mystery tale did not solidify itself in popular consciousness until the advent of Edgar Allan Poe's detective hero, C. Auguste Dupin, who first appeared in "The Murders in the Rue Morgue" in 1841. The first identifiable formula of the larger mystery genre was that story of the "Classical Detective," as in the case of Poe's Dupin and Sir Arthur Conan Doyle's master sleuth, Sherlock Holmes, who debuted in "A Study in Scarlet" in 1887. Dupin, and especially Holmes, set the mold for the great consulting detectives to follow like Agatha Christie's Hercule Poirot and Miss Jane Marple, Dorothy Sayers' Lord Peter Wimsey and John Dickson Carr's Bencolin and Dr. Gideon Fell. These Classical Detectives were towers of intelligence and the keepers of an otherwise helpless cast of characters. The detective story and a wide multiplicity of characters proliferated with the advent of the mass media.

America's first mass medium, the dime novel, emerged with mystery fiction, and would not have succeeded as a commercial endeavor had not the mystery been a staple source of material. The Mystery and the Western were the two genres of fiction that allowed the dime novel to survive from 1865 until about 1912. At that time 1912, when several events heralded the demise of this medium, including a change in postal rates, the pulp magazine arrived to fill the void. With the advent of the pulps, the mystery story exploded into a kaleidoscope of formulas and sub-formulas. The "Hard-Boiled Detective" emerged in *Black Mask Magazine* and heroes like Carroll John Daly's Three Gun Terry Mack and Race Williams, as well as Dashiell Hammett's Continental Op and Sam Spade, and Raymond Chandler's Philip Marlowe, boasted individual moralities in societies and settings where everyone was corrupt. In 1931, Walter B. Gibson, friend and biographer of the Great Houdini, produced *The Living Shadow* under the pseudonym of Maxwell Grant. It was the start of one of the most popular of mystery heroes—the "Avenger Detective." The Shadow lived in the pulps as a top flight resident for more than 300 novels, and spawned a variety of colorful imitations like the Spider and Secret Agent X. *Weird Tales*, "The Unique Magazine" and landmark publication in fantasy and weird fiction produced a fare which included several enduring "Psychic Detectives" or ghost chasers. William Hope Hodgson's Carnacki the Ghost Finder, Seabury Quinn's Jules de Grandin, and August Derleth's Solar Pons combatted forces and puzzles more threatening than death itself because the antagonists could control the world beyond. G-Men wrestled with the devils of the "Gangster Story," and "Magician Detectives" and "Gentlemen Burglars" each had stories of their own. More than any other medium and time period, the pulp magazines of the 1920s and 1930s spawned a proliferation of enduring popular mystery fiction.

Of the detective pulps *Black Mask* under the discerning eye of Captain Joseph T. Shaw was and is the most revered. It was *The* magazine for aspiring and veteran mystery writers, and a story published here put the author in the company of the legendary Dashiell Hammett and a host of other memorable figures. *Black Mask* was single-handedly responsible for the birth, development and refinement of the Hard-Boiled Detective, a Mystery formula which from that time forward has rivaled the Classical Detective story for preeminence. With the introduction of the archetypal Shadow in 1931, the Avenger Detective soared, and suddenly there were three major schools of mystery fiction.

In the midst of the emergence of *Black Mask* and *The Shadow* and their many imitators, a small detective pulp debuted which would in its own way substantially mold the form for detectives to come. It was Harold Hersey's presentation of *The Dragnet*. At first, the magazine and its stories were very average, and easily forgettable. "The first issue, dated November 1928, was not a detective magazine at all but featured stories about modern gangsters and organized crime."[1] The magazine limped on, and it appeared that *The Dragnet* would not be long for the literary world. Nineteen-thirty, however, saw a turnaround, and the beginning of better stories and profitability for the pulp. A.A. Wyn and Magazine Publishers, Inc., bought out *The Dragnet* and renamed it *Detective-Dragnet Magazine*. Under Wyn, the magazine "...emphasized stories of detectives and law officers fighting and winning."[2] In 1931, Editor Harry Widmer "... veered away from the detective tales into sheer melodrama of a type that harkened back to the days of the dime novel and looked forward to the single-character magazines."[3] From 1932 to 1936 stories sizzled from the pulpwood pages of Wyn's magazine. Early in 1933, the title was changed for the third and last time. The publication was now called *Ten Detective Aces,* and for his dime, the reader got ten fast-paced mysteries, complete in each issue. As the magazine subtitle boasted, the reader paid only "A Cent A Story!"

As Will Murray notes, *Ten Detective Aces* looked forward to the single-character magazines. In fact, *Ten Detective Aces* nurtured many of its writers and their detective stories to the point that these same authors left the magazine to script whole novels about mystery heroes who had magazines of their own. The detectives that appeared during the height of *Ten Detective Aces,* that period from 1932 to 1936, were Hard-Boiled, Avengers or a mixture of the two. This was a reflection of and subsequent tribute to, the Hard-Boiled tradition set forth by *Black Mask* and the success of the pulps' first great avenger—*The Shadow.* The devils and their deviltry that the detectives of *Ten Detective Aces* faced were those associated with the Hard-Boiled and Avenger formulas, and in some instances imitations of the hideous crimes against humanity upon which the newly emerged and immensely popular "Weird Menace" formula was based. In 1936 the heyday of *Ten Detective Aces* was ebbing. Norvell Page went on to script novels for *The Spider,* and produced a number of marvelous Weird Menace tales for magazines specializing in just such a formula. Lester Dent evolved from an already impressive career to become the force behind *Doc Savage.* Paul Chadwick became the major talent behind *Secret Agent X,* and Frederick C. Davis, along with Emile C. Tepperman, became the pulpsmith largely responsible for the success of *Operator No. 5.* Tepperman wrote for several other hero pulps as well. G.T. Fleming-Roberts went on to do *The Ghost* and *Captain Zero. Ten Detective Aces* carried on until its last issue in September 1949. By the time of its demise, which was by no means untimely since many pulps died about this same time because of a variety of reasons including the advent of television and the paperback book, *Ten Detective Aces* boasted an incredible array of authors and stories. Many of these wordsmiths began their careers in this magazine, and there honed their abilities. The list of those who published here is impressive, not only in quantity but in quantity of significant, enduring authors. *Ten Detective Aces* was one of the longest running, important detective pulps ever.

The first story in this collection of reprints from that magazine is Harry Widmer's "The Corpse Laughs," and it is perhaps the closest *Ten Detective Aces* ever came to printing a Classical Mystery story. While Widmer's contributions to the magazine were primarily editorial, "The Corpse Laughs" is a weird saga much in the tradition and flair of John Dickson Carr. It is fitting that the first story in this collection is by the editor who brought *Ten Detective Aces* into its heyday. The next selection is Paul Chadwick's "Fangs of the Cobra." Chadwick's detective in this story is Wade Hammond, a sort of Sam Spade/Richard

Wentworth (aka the Spider) conglomerate. Hammond was one of the most popular, enduring detectives ever to come from a Wyn magazine. It was because of the success of Chadwick's Hammond that Wyn commissioned the author to script another magazine for Magazine Publishers, Inc.—*Secret Agent X*. In selecting "Fangs of the Cobra" for this collection, a dilemma emerged. Many of *Ten Detective Aces*' contributors turned out consistently entertaining and imaginative mysteries, but there was no problem in selecting one favorite from each author—with one exception. What should be the Wade Hammond representative, "The Corpses' Carnival," "Fangs of the Cobra" or "The Steel Corpse"? "Fangs" was chosen because it is Chadwick and Wade Hammond at their best. The situation reemphasizes what Gary Hoppenstand has maintained for years—that a Paul Chadwick Wade Hammond collection in book form is long overdue.

Norvell Page's Ken Carter is the hero of "Satan's Hoof" which is reprinted in this book. Ken Carter, and the situations he finds himself in, evidence major characteristics of Page's Spider novels that followed. R.T.M. Scott based his early adventures of the Spider on his earlier Secret Service Smith stories. When Norvell Page took over the writing responsibilities for *The Spider*, it is apparent that some of Ken Carter was reborn. The Ken Carter stories, full of vivid color and heinous crime, were, along with Paul Chadwick's Wade Hammond, *Ten Detective Aces*' response to the "Weird Menace" formula. Carl McK. Saunders presented the paradoxical situation of a sort of Hard-Boiled story with a police captain hero. The stories of John Murdock were Saunders' contribution to *Ten Detective Aces*, and "The Wax Witness" exemplifies what those were all about. Standard fare for the magazine, the exploits of Murdock ran for several years during its height—no mean feat when viewed in terms of the competition. "The Tank of Terror" features Lee Nace, one of several scientific detectives created by Lester Dent for *Ten Detective Aces*. By this time, Lynn Lash and Mel Cross had appeared in the magazine for a couple of years, and the adventures of Lee Nace were extensions of the exploits of these earlier Dent characters. Stories such as "The Tank of Terror" were predecessors of what was to come in *Doc Savage*.

Assuredly, the most famous of the detectives to arise from the pages of *Ten Detective Aces* was Frederick C. Davis' Moon Man. The saga of the Moon Man ran for thirty-nine episodes between 1933 and 1937, and his story was probably the most inventive. Stephen Thatcher was a police chief's son, a cop himself, and the alter ego of the Robin Hood figure known as the Moon Man. The selected tale, "Mark of the Moon Man," is a classic from the Davis series because it was the first of the "Red" stories.

Much like the "Hand" stories of the Shadow, the "Red" stories of the Moon Man referred to the criminal element that was the focus of these adventures. "Mark of the Moon Man" introduces the Red Six. When a member of the criminal group is killed in this story, the group reappears as the Red Five in the next story ("Crimson Shackles"). By the third adventure of the "Red" stories ("Blood Bargain"), the villains are narrowed to the Red Four. And so it goes. In the fourth "Red" story ("The Black Lash"), the Moon Man confronts the Crimson Trio. Frederick C. Davis produced *Ten Detective Aces'* most enduring detective even before he became renowned for his Operator 5 stories under the pseudonym Curtis Steele. Wooda N. Carr notes, "But oddly enough, Mr. Davis was never acquainted with other writers who were doing a pulp type of story. He never read a Doc Savage or Spider novel, and even quit reading *Operator No. 5* when he was no longer associated with the stories."[4] "Mark of the Moon Man" is Frederick C. Davis and *Ten Detective Aces* in top form.

The last four tales selected for this collection from *Ten Detective Aces* present four distinct, memorable mystery heroes. "The House of Kaa" by Richard B. Sale is exemplary of the author's Cobra stories and in many ways foreshadows the later Avenger and Weird Menace formulas. The title character of "The Whisperer Prowls" is the contribution of Alexis Rossoff to Wyn's magazine. Another mysterious, dark figure of the night, Rossoff's Whisperer appeared before and is not to be confused with Street and Smith Publishers' hero of the same name. Some of G.T. Fleming-Roberts first work in the pulps appeared in *Ten Detective Aces.* His "The Death Master" features a detective named Jerry Thacker and showcases the talent of Fleming-Roberts that became a hallmark of his work for *The Ghost, Secret Agent X, Captain Zero* and other pulps. Emile C. Tepperman's Marty Quade rounds out the collection in "Killers' Club Car." Quade is more of the Hard-Boiled variety than anything else.

Ten Detective Aces was the birthplace of many of the established traditions of pulp detective fiction. While it was not single-handedly responsible for the creation of an enduring mystery formula, as was the case of *Black Mask* and the Hard-Boiled Detective formula, it was more instrumental than any other publication in the creation of novel length hero pulp stories. A comprehensive history of detectives in the pulps is incomplete without reference to *Ten Detective Aces.* With an appreciation of the stories in hand and an anticipation for prime mystery fiction, you the reader, are ready for the best from *Ten Detective Aces.*

Notes

[1]Will Murray, "The Dragnet," *Mystery, Detective, and Espionage Magazines,* Michael L. Cook, ed. (Westport, Ct.: Greenwood Press, 1983).

[2]Ibid. [3]Ibid.

[4]Wooda N. Carr, "Introducing the Moon Man," *The Night Nemesis,* Garyn G. Roberts and Gary Hoppenstand, eds. (Bowling Green, Ohio: The Purple Prose Press, 1984).

The taut, bitter-souled guests at that isolated, storm-swept mansion were all potential killers. The gunman—the gambler—the surgeon—and the show girl. Every one of them had been on trial for murder—and had been acquitted. They lived in luxury by the strange will of a strange old man. Then one of them died laughing —and no one knew the joke.

CHAPTER I

A MERRY MURDER

FOOTBALLS of fate they were. Life had kicked them around. Death had reached for them—and missed.

There was Doctor Rhoden; the surgeon who cringed at the sight of a scalpel. There was Sam Shalk; the gunman whose stomach turned at the sound of a shot. There was Boxcar Walters; the gambler who wouldn't bet on the coming dawn. And there was Nita Neale; the show girl who shuddered at the glare of a spotlight.

They all were of New York's six million. The doctor was from Park Avenue. The gunman came out of Hell's Kitchen. The gambler was from the lower East Side. And the show girl came out of the West Fifties. Only in its most ironic mood would Fate have drawn them together under the

The Corpse Laughs

And None of the Death Cheaters Knew the Joke!

Thrilling Mystery Novel

By HARRY WIDMER

Author of "Jig-Saw Murder Puzzle," "The Armor Room Mystery," etc.

McKee barked: "You'll get that filthy mouth of yours nice and bloody."

same roof. Yet Fate had done that very thing.

A palatial mansion facing Long Island Sound housed them. They were gathered in the luxuriously furnished library, sipping demi-tasse. The incongruity of the scene must have angered the elements. For a terrific storm beat down on the isolated mansion. Telephone and light wires were down. Candlelight, flickering and eerie, illuminated the library and corridor.

Standing in the corridor was Jack

McKee, a young attorney at law. He watched the candlelight play on the faces of the ill-assorted foursome in the library. But his mind was only partially upon them. For he shot expectant glances to the huge door at the far end of the corridor. Suddenly he stiffened.

The brass knocker on the great door banged above the howling fury of the wind-lashed night. Echoes, muted by tapestry and thick rugs, died on the high walls of the cavernous entrance hall.

Jack McKee strode rapidly down the corridor. Guttering candlelight glazed the starched bosom of his dress shirt. He hunched the collar of his dinner jacket closer to his neck. The damp chilliness of the night penetrated the dismal hall.

A butler slid noiselessly into sight. Jack McKee waved him away. Eagerly he released the bolts on the massive door, swung the panel inward.

Lightning glared, ripping the heavens wide open with its brillance. McKee squinted, made out a tall, slender girl silhouetted against the dazzling light. Then blackness swallowed the sky. Rain beat against McKee's craggy face. A mighty gust of wind whipped the door from his hand, licked the flame from every candle in the hall. Thunder, like a giant clearing his throat, blasted across the heavens.

A warm wet body stumbled against him, clung desperately. The damp odor of a stuffy automobile interior reached his nostrils, then gave place to a fragrant whisp of elusive perfume. It was the tall girl. Her face was close to his. Warm breath fanned his cheeks.

"Bill—"

Thunder rumbled in tremendous volume. McKee pulled the girl into the hallway. His groping hand found the door, flung it shut with a bang that rivalled the thunder. He dug out his cigarette lighter, thumbed the wheel. Yellow flame fanned the girl's face. That face was strikingly attractive. Not pretty, McKee thought, but those full red lips, gleaming teeth, and black flashing eyes had something that a cute, dollish face lacked.

"You're all right now," McKee said.

"Of course," the girl's voice was a bit jerky. "Sorry I was such a chump. The ride through the storm—"

"I know," McKee nodded understandingly. "Glad you got here safely." He smiled slowly. "I'm McKee—the fellow your managing editor talked with."

Putting out her hand, the girl said: "I'm Lona Colin. The *Star-Herald* appreciates your giving us first crack at this story."

"You will tell the truth. I'd like to answer the district attorney's attack through your columns."

The butler moved quickly about the entrance hall relighting the candles.

"Wires are down," explained McKee. "In fact, both the light and telephone wires went down just after you phoned two hours ago. I'm sorry you weren't able to make it for dinner."

"I am, too," said Lona Colin. "It was a keen disappointment to miss having dinner with your — er — guests."

McKee put his lighter away, nodded soberly. "We call them—guests, too. But the district attorney calls them —death cheaters."

Lona nodded. "And he calls this mansion Chair Haven—the home of acquitted murderers."

McKEE'S face tightened grimly. But only for a moment. Then the stern lines softened. "You'd better get that wet wrap off, Miss Colin." He took a portable typewriter case from her hand, then peeled the wrap from her shoulders.

His eyes glowed admiringly as they fell upon Lona's superbly-arched back. Her gown was cut to the waist in the back, breast high in the front, and fitted her body like a coat of shiny black lacquer. She wore long black gloves, and black slippers with rhinestone heels. Her black hair was parted in the middle and fell to her shoulders in shimmering waves. Jack McKee, had never seen a newspaper writer like this one.

"To begin with," said McKee, "I'll present the death cheaters to you. I want you to know them so that you can truthfully tell the public and the D. A.'s office that we are harboring unfortunate men and women—not murderers that we snatched from the electric chair. The fact that we were successful in court proves—"

A medium-sized, distinguished-looking man in a tailored tuxedo came down the wide staircase and approached them. He was older than McKee. A white cardboard box lay in the crook of his arm.

McKee smiled genially. "Miss Colin, may I present Mr. Berwind, my senior partner?" There was pride in McKee's voice. "Stephen, Miss Colin of the *Star-Herald*."

Stephen Berwind bowed. "I am pleased that our cause is to have so charming a champion." He opened the white box. "A slight token of our esteem," he said.

Cradled in the box was a delicate, and unusually-colored orchid. Lona caught her breath. "What an exquisite flower! I've never seen one quite like it."

"Allow me?" Berwind took the orchid and a straight pin from the box, and attached it to the front of her gown.

Lona's murmured, "Thank you," was smothered in an ear-splitting thunderclap.

Both men offered an arm simultaneously to Lona. McKee was on her right. Berwind on her left. She hesitated for the barest fraction of a minute. The uncertain and flickering light of the candles masked whatever fleeting expression crossed her face in that moment of hesitation. Then, without a glance at Berwind, she slipped her gloved hand under McKee's arm, and smiled up at him. The young lawyer was taken aback. He didn't want to offend his friend. And he didn't want to offend the girl. Then all three became rooted woodenly to the floor.

Thunder, like a sharp gun-clasp, crashed down upon them. The silence that followed was almost as terrific as the thunder itself. Suddenly that silence was shattered by a wild shriek.

McKEE jerked his head toward the library. "Quick, Stephen, Sam Shalk must have thought that thunder was a gunshot. He might—" McKee didn't finish. Whirling, he flung himself headlong down the corridor. Berwind and Lona Colin rushed after him.

At the library door McKee slid to a stop, took in the scene at a glance. Sam Shalk, the gunman, was sitting on the edge of a big, winged chair. He was angrily waving the others in the room away from him. His voice was harsh:

"I'm all right! Gimme air! Mind your own damn business. I'll yell if I wanta. Scram! A bunch of lyin' gutless rats—that's what you are! Beat it."

McKee stood transfixed in the doorway. He sensed, rather than felt, Lona brush his left arm. And he, somehow, knew that Berwind was standing taut-muscled on his other side. All three had heard Sam Shalk's rasping tirade. And they listened as he went on:

"Me—I'm through lyin'. I was double-crossed, so I'm gonna say a mouthful. An' when I'm finished, I'm gonna laugh at all of ya. Nothin' can happen to me—now!" His harsh laughter filled the high-ceilinged library.

McKee touched Lona's gloved arm, whispered: "Shalk was on trial for murder. The grind and the shadow of the Death House unnerved him. That sharp thunderclap made him think of a gunshot. He'll quiet down in a minute."

But the little pinched-face Sam Shalk showed no intentions of quieting down. "The law said I killed a guy in a night club," he ranted on. "But they couldn't make it stick! An' that's where I've got the laugh on the law—*because I did kill that guy!*"

A composite, horrified gasp went up to the ceiling. McKee twisted around to Berwind. Jumbled thoughts crowded his brain, but words absolutely refused to cross his tightly-clamped lips. McKee looked like a man whose world had been roughly kicked out from under him.

Sam Shalk lurched to his feet, knocked over the coffee table in front of him. "I killed him—an' I'm tellin' the world. The law can't do nothin' to me—now! It said I was innocent—an' it can't put me up again for that murder! It can't—"

The whole situation seemed so funny that Sam Shalk doubled with laughter. No sound came from his grin-creased mouth. He just shook. His mouth twitched, as if from successive bursts of unrestrained laughter. He flung back his head like a man who reaches the highest pitch of humor. And in that posture, he swayed forward, and banged his head on the floor.

McKee rushed over, dropped to one knee beside the now still form of Sam Shalk. Suddenly McKee stiffened, drew his breath sharply. He coughed to clear his throat, said huskily:

"Sam Shalk is—"

Thunder cascaded down the heavens making a frightful din. But the words of McKee's that it swallowed were unnecessary. For Sam Shalk, the gunman whose stomach turned at the sound of a shot, was dead.

CHAPTER II

A Cup of Horror

McKEE got to his feet. He was groggy from the great mental blow. He went over to Berwind, stood silently before him, then said:

"This is terrible, Stephen. It takes the wind right out of our sails. Our whole cause—"

Berwind took his upper lip in his teeth, shook his head. "We did our best, Jack. Sam Shalk's case was clear and aboveboard. The testimony held under the D. A.'s legal bombardment—"

McKee's fists clenched and unclenched nervously. "But our firm's reputation. Our trust as administrators of the estate. Think, Stephen, we cheated the law!" Anger edged his voice. "We took a murderer from justice and—"

Suddenly McKee reached out both hands and braced his partner's sagging shoulders. "I'm sorry, Steve. Buck up. We'll straighten this thing out somehow." He patted Berwind's back. Together they went over to the corpse. McKee murmured: "What a horrible death. Even now he looks as if he is going to start laughing again." McKee raised his voice slightly. "Doctor Rhoden, will you please step over—"

The man he addressed was short, of slight build, and had a head of unruly gray hair. He sat huddled over in his chair. His shoulders drooped, weighed down by more than the burden of his fifty-odd years. His writhing, thin-lipped mouth made words:

"You don't need me to tell you that he is dead. Didn't you hear that thunder? It was the voice of God! The murderer got what he deserved. God has spoken. You don't need me. Shalk is dead! I won't go near him! I won't—"

Doctor Rhoden slumped back in his chair. His head bowed, rested on the immaculate bosom of his dress shirt.

McKee went swiftly to the doctor's side. Almost afraid of what he might find, he gingerly lifted the doctor's wrist, felt his pulse. Then a sigh of relief vibrated McKee's frame. "Fainted," he announced. "The strain was too much for him. Doctor Rhoden has been dragged through the blackest pit in hell. A severe shock might—"

The sight of Lona Colin standing in the doorway cut short McKee's words. The girl had not moved since he had left her. When she found McKee's eyes upon her, she turned and disappeared down the candlelit corridor.

The weariness in McKee's face gave

place to desperation. Twisting through the chairs in the library, he bolted after her. He caught up with her halfway down the corridor.

"Miss Colin, it's only fair that you hear what I have to say."

Lona stood perfectly still, her hands balled into little fists at her sides. She said nothing. McKee gestured toward a chair. Lona sat down without a word. McKee drew up another chair and faced her. He leaned forward earnestly.

"Miss Colin, to understand the meaning of this so-called 'Chair Haven', I'll start right at the beginning. And it starts with a fine old gentleman named Tully Laborden—God rest his soul." McKee turned in his chair and nodded toward a large portrait on the wall. "That is Old Tully."

A strong, kindly face looked down upon them. There was a world of character in that face. McKee went on:

"Old Tully was a wealthy financier. He was unjustly accused of murder, and brought to trial. Stephen Berwind and I defended him, won an acquittal. But Old Tully lost his business, his contacts, everything during the long trial. A murder trial places a blot on a man's character that can never be fully erased. Even though he is acquitted, there will always be a shadow of doubt in the minds of some people. Old Tully left the courtroom a broken man.

"For three years he learned just how bitter and cruel the world can be to a man who is down and out. But Old Tully came back. He amassed millions. And when he died, he left an unique will. This will provided for the maintenance of Chair Haven. Old Tully wanted to provide a refuge for unjustly-accused men and women who faced the world broken and penniless. He didn't want any human to go through the hell he had been through."

Lona's face had softened, and her mouth had lost its taut line. Her eyes were glued to the runner underfoot. McKee, encouraged, went on:

"The will named the firm of Berwind & McKee to act in capacity of executor and administrator. It was up to us to decide who should and who should not be admitted to the life-long ease and luxury of Chair Haven." McKee's jaw muscles bulged. It took a lot out of him to say: "We made a bad job of that."

McKee grasped the arms of his chair in the gesture so many business men use to terminate an interview. "But I blame myself more than Stephen. I buried myself in the administrative end, and left Stephen to shoulder the court battles. Stephen is a splendid attorney, but a little too easy going. He's like Old Tully. As for myself, I would move heaven and earth to acquit an innocent man—and exert the same effort to convict a murderer .... Well, that's all, Miss Colin."

THE girl still kept her eyes on the runner. Her voice was low, but very distinct, brittle. "That's the way I feel about it." Then she asked: "What do you want me to do?"

"Just give me a chance to straighten things out, read over the testimony of Sam Shalk's murder trial. The mistake must be found, so that we can guard against making it again. Old Tully Laborden's will was never meant to shield murderers."

Lona rose to her feet, shrugged her creamy shoulders. "Anyway, I couldn't phone. The wires—"

"Yes," admitted McKee. "But I couldn't stop you from leaving."

The girl looked steadily at McKee. "I know you are sincere in respecting Old Tully's last wish—but why so much fuss and secrecy about Sam Shalk? He's dead—and a confessed murderer. Nothing you can do will change that. It is bound to come out."

For a long moment McKee was silent. Finally, he said: "I see. Your mind is very keen, Miss Colin. Yes, Sam Shalk's confession means that we are shielding another murderer."

Then McKee said bitterly: "And won't the D. A. get a laugh out of that!"

"I remember the case," said Lona quietly. "Sam Shalk and a gambler named Boxcar Walters were accused of killing a man in a night club. Shalk's confession means that Boxcar Walters is a murderer, too."

McKee then remembered that he had not seen Boxcar Walters in the library when Shalk died. Without a word, he strode to the library. At the door he missed Lona, turned and looked back. Lona was talking to Jill, the trim little serving maid of the mansion.

Going into the library McKee saw the gray-haired Doctor Rhoden standing beside Stephen Berwind. They were looking down at the laughing face of the dead gunman. Ten feet away, and leaning over the back of a chair stood Nita Neale, the blonde show girl. Her superb figure was tightly sheathed in a chartreuse evening gown. A satin slipper of the same color beat a rapid tattoo on the polished floor.

There was a strange, almost wild expression, on Doctor Rhoden's face. McKee quickly crossed to his side, placed an arm about those pitifully drooping shoulders.

"Easy does it, doc. You don't have to stay here. Why don't you go to your room, make yourself comfortable, and smoke a cigar? Stephen and I will take care of things here."

Doctor Rhoden might not have heard, for all the heed he gave to McKee's words. Instead, he just stood there looking at the laughing corpse. The gruesome sight seemed to fascinate him. Then suddenly he flung his arm across his eyes as if to blot out the horrible vision. His thin lips writhed, letting hushed words slip out:

"He looks like—like *she* did . . . . Hands—claws . . . . Body—twisted . . . . Oh, God!"

McKee felt himself go suddenly cold. He knew what the doctor meant. His arm tightened about the quivering man. "Pull yourself together, doc. Do you mean that Sam Shalk was—"

DOCTOR RHODEN did pull himself into a semblance of his long-lost self. His gray head nodded curtly. "Yes. Sam Shalk was poisoned—murdered!" Then he went to pieces again, a trembling shell of what was once a prominent, successful surgeon. He sank into a chair, and buried his face in his hands.

Nita Neale said: "It's stopped raining."

McKee flashed her a scowl, then glanced toward the doorway. Lona was standing there. How long she had been there and how much she had heard, McKee didn't know. He went over to her. "Miss Colin, I'm going to get to the bottom of this. It means everything to us. The police, of course, will be notified when the telephone connections are set up. I'm not going to let you leave. You can help me with your knowledge of murder cases, or you can—"

"I'd like to help," said Lona. "But first, tell me about that poor old doctor. Why—"

McKee drew her out of the doctor's ear-shot, then said: "Please excuse my pulling you around, Miss Colin. But I don't want the doctor to overhear me. Not so long ago he was one of the country's leading surgeons. And like a great many men whose profession claims most of their time, he married a frivolous girl. They could not adjust themselves, and many arguments resulted.

"Then one morning, the young wife was found dead. She had swallowed some strychnine. Whether she had taken it by mistake—on purpose—or whether he had given it to her—was a matter of guesswork. The law claimed that he had poisoned her. But after a lengthy trial, he was acquitted. Since that day he has avoided everything connected with medicine and surgery."

Suddenly McKee spun on his heel and went back to the man who had died laughing. On the floor beside the corpse was the overturned coffee table and the demi-tasse cup and saucer. The fragile china had shattered. A damp blotch stained the rich burgundy rug. McKee remembered how Sam Shalk had lurched out of his chair, knocking over the table. Without a moment's hesitation, McKee took out his pocket-knife and cut the stained piece right out of the rug. Vandalism it might be—but murder was murder.

Then McKee put the knife and the piece of rug in his pocket. Stephen Berwind looked on in silence. He nodded his agreement to McKee's action. Even the elements took cognizance of his deed. For thunder rolled like a mighty snare drum. The orchestra of heaven swept on with its frightful symphony.

McKee started toward Lona Colin. He stopped. The chartreuse-gowned Nita Neale had dashed over to her, flung satiny arms around her neck. McKee heard Nita Neale's low-pitched voice:

"I'm so glad another woman is here. That—that laughing face—is horrible!"

The startling contrast of the two young women momentarily held McKee in his tracks. Lona, dark-haired, in her lacquer-like dress, held herself with a majestic grace. Nita, blonde, voluptuous, her chartreuse dress designed to attract men's attention, was typical "Broadway." McKee had heard Nita's words. But her face, showing over Lona's shoulder, gave the lie to those words of friendship, for that face was hard with hate.

Nita Neale stepped back as McKee approached. Lona gave a little cry of dismay.

"My orchid is crushed. What a pity."

McKEE saw that the beautiful flower was a mashed pulp hanging limply from the front of her dress. He glanced sideways at Nita. The show girl's face was etched with the deepest concern. She said:

"I'm so sorry. Terribly stupid of me—"

Lona touched her arm. "Think nothing of it, please."

McKee's eyes glinted in the candlelight. He was getting fed up. "Has any one seen Boxcar Walters?" he butted in bruskly.

At that name, Stephen Berwind glanced up. "What about Walters?"

McKee pointed toward the corpse, said: "Sam Shalk's confession proves that Boxcar Walters is a murderer, too. Walters had a hand in killing that circus performer at the night club. And Walters has not been seen since Sam Shalk was poisoned." McKee turned to Doctor Rhoden who still slumped in his chair. "Say, doc," he asked, "have you seen anything of Walters?"

The doctor raised his tragedy-laden shoulders, shook his gray head as if to clear it of a haze that shrouded his thoughts. "Er—Walters? Why, no—I haven't seen him."

"Thanks, doc." Then McKee turned back to Berwind, and found him taking the crushed orchid from Lona's dress. Berwind was saying:

"I'll get another from my botanical garden on the roof. No trouble—I assure you."

McKee took Berwind's arm. They walked to the door of the library. McKee said low-voiced: "Take a look around for Walters on the way up, will you, Stephen? We've got to get this thing cleared up. Be careful. Walters is a killer. And don't forget—he was once a gambler."

Berwind patted McKee's arm with his open palm, then disappeared down the candlelit corridor.

Thunder rolled in terrific volume. The mighty orchestra of heaven seemed to be serenading distant worlds. Lightning must have been criss-crossing the night in vivid patterns. But those in the library could not tell. For the windows were heavily curtained.

Doctor Rhoden, his face in his hands, mumbled: "The voice of God is angry tonight. He is crying out against the fiend who uses poison! .... Hands—claws .... Body—twisted—" Rhoden fiercely clamped both hands over his mouth to stem the rush of words.

Show girl Nita Neale glared at the doctor. "The old fool gives me the willies."

The big, dark eyes of Lona Colin were also centered on the doctor. But those eyes were soft with a light of understanding. Then she lifted her gaze to Jack McKee, and said quietly: "I can understand your sincerity better now."

"Thanks," nodded McKee. "I certainly need your help in working this thing out. But first I'm going to find Boxcar Walters. And I think I know just where to look for him."

McKee quickly left the library. In the corridor he snapped the electric switch, and found the wires were still down. He turned sharply to the left, passed the chairs where he and Lona had talked about Old Tully Laborden. And on the opposite wall, McKee caught a glimpse of old Tully's smiling face. He stopped before the portrait.

And somehow that smiling face straightened McKee's shoulders, raised his head, and made his chin just a trifle more aggressive. It was as if Old Tully clapped McKee on the back, and murmured a word of understanding and encouragement. For McKee walked swiftly along the corridor to a door bearing a small metal sign: Medicine Room. Without a moment's hesitation he went in.

A heavy-set man whirled around to face the door. The man was busily engaged in pouring government bonded rye into a leather-jacketed flask. And by the way he was pouring, McKee knew that generous samples of the whiskey had gone down the heavy man's hatch.

"Well, Boxcar," asked McKee, "what are you doing in here?"

For answer, the gambler held aloft the shiny flask. Then he added: "The storm is getting on my nerves."

McKee ran a quick eye over the large assortment of bottles on the white shelves. Many had a red death's head on their labels. This miniature hospital had been fitted out for Doctor Rhoden in the hope that he would recover from his aversion to medicine and surgery.

"The storm is getting worse," said McKee significantly. "By the way, where is Sam Shalk?"

The gambler shrugged. "I wouldn't risk a plugged nickel on betting where he is. Maybe you'll find him in a dark hall, making a play for that cute little maid."

McKee's voice took on an edge. "Sam Shalk told us that he killed that man in the night club."

Walters almost dropped the flask. "The dirty welching rat! I could kill him, and laugh!"

"That," said McKee grimly, "is just what I want to talk to you about."

"Huh—"

"A laugh!"

CHAPTER III

Death Collects a Debt

McKEE marched Walters into the library. Candlelight washed their faces in yellow waves as they progressed across the big room. Lona Colin heard them first. She turned to look, her body rippling like black oil. Her dark, flashing eyes were not on Walters, but on McKee.

Nita Neale's chartreuse slipper missed a beat on the floor. She drew back quickly as Walters passed her. Walters caught the movement, looked her up and down, then smirked.

Doctor Rhoden took his hands from his face, drawing them down over his features from forehead to chin. And that downward motion seemed to slit his eyes, pull down the ends of his mouth. That mouth opened traplike on one word:

"Murderer!"

Walters let a nasty curse grate between his teeth. Then he stopped, shrank as if a giant hammer had nailed him to the burgundy rug. He saw the sprawled body of Sam Shalk. He stared for moments, then turned to McKee, asked: "The punk roll sixes?"

Without answering, McKee took Walters closer to the body. "Look at his face," he said.

Walters did. Then he chuckled, saying: "Cards on the table, McKee. Why that punk can't even keep a straight face. What's the game—statues? I'd like to sling around that bleached blonde—"

"All right," butted in McKee. "Get Shalk up. Tell him he can't keep a straight face."

"Sure"— Walters leaned over, grabbed Sam Shalk's wrist. He let go, yelled, bounded back away from the corpse. He licked his lips, gulped: "Why—he's—he's—"

The chartreuse-wrapped Nita Neale gave a short bark of a laugh. "Good, Walters—but not good enough!"

It took Walters several moments to answer. His eyes suddenly blazed. "What the hell are you driving at?" he demanded hotly.

"Your act!" derisively rasped Nita.

"Why, you dirty little tramp, I'll—"

McKee's fists closed on Walters' coat lapels, lifted him clear off the floor, shook him. He shoved his face down to Walters', said: "You'll get that filthy mouth of yours nice and bloody."

The gambler fumed, but kept his mouth shut. He was big and heavily built. But McKee topped him by a head and a half. McKee was wiry, tough. He hadn't let an office job soften him. For a moment it looked as if Walters was going to get nasty. Then he shook himself free and settled back on his heels.

Lona Colin's luminous dark eyes still rested on McKee.

From his chair, Doctor Rhoden pointed a bony finger at Nita Neale, then levelled it at Walters. He muttered: "Those two are always fighting. They fought the first time they laid eyes on each other. He told her that she had a slick way of getting rid of competition. Ever since that day—"

"I know," said McKee. "But that's all over now. Walters is through here." McKee turned to Walters, stepped close and neatly frisked him. Then he said: "Empty out your pockets on that table."

Walters gingerly edged around the corpse, and did what he was told. A whiskey flask came out first, then two handkerchiefs, a pack of cigarettes, mechanical pencil, keys, a roll of money, handful of change, and a couple of match books.

Lona Colin stepped forward, her eyes swept the articles on the table. She said to Walters: "The papers were right. You never carry cards or dice. Superstition certainly gets you gamblers."

"You mean tinhorns!" jeered blonde Nita Neale. She put a cigarette between her red lips, talked around it. "He hasn't used cards or dice since the night he killed—"

"Miss Neale," cut in McKee sharply, "if you don't mind, I'll take charge of matters here."

NITA NEALE was a swish of chartreuse as she turned on a high heel, walked over to a chair and sat down. She crossed silken legs, got her cigarette going, and leaned back to watch the proceedings. Her eyes fell on Sam Shalk's laughing face. She shuddered, hastily averted her gaze.

The dark, exotic Lona Colin was now looking at Walters. Her black eyes were unfathomable.

The long finger of Doctor Rhoden was still pointing at Walters. His thin lips silently worked over the words: "Murderer!"

McKee squarely faced Walters, asked: "Have you seen—" A blast of thunder swallowed his words. More thunder rolled across the night, making a frightful din. McKee waited until it chased itself into space. Then he started again: "Have you seen a man laugh, Walters?"

"Huh? . . . . Why, sure."

McKee took a zipper pouch from his pocket, opened it halfway and took out a brown Dunhill, then put the pouch away again. He held the pipe-bowl in the palm of his hand, pointed the stem at Walters. It looked like a gun. He went on:

"Sure you've seen a man laugh. You've seen him double up and shake till his sides almost burst open. You've seen him laugh so hard that not even a whisper came from him. You've seen a man like that, haven't you?"

Walters chuckled. "Sure. But what's the game we're playing?"

"Good, Walters," said Nita, "but not good—"

The gambler gave her a dirty look, pursed his lips and drew in his breath.

McKee's neck got red. "Listen, Walters," he angrily pushed out words, "I'm not kidding. Try something like that again and I'll lace into you. This is murder! A man just died—died laughing! Get that? *Sam Shalk died laughing!*"

"He was poisoned—" chanted Doctor Rhoden.

Nita Neale was sitting on the edge of her chair. She jabbed her cigarette toward Walters. "And if he makes a noise like that at me again—"

"Shut up!" barked McKee. "All of you—shut up! I'm trying to conduct an orderly—"

"Perhaps you'd better let me take charge," said Stephen Berwind from the doorway. The senior law partner came into the room, holding an orchid in his hand. "No reflection on you, Jack," he said. "I'm more accustomed to handling matters like this."

McKee looked at the orchid. "Which Stephen?" he asked.

The distinguished-looking lawyer knitted his brows. "What do you mean?"

"Orchids—or murder cases?"

Berwind flushed redly, drew himself up. "I resent that."

McKee made a nervous gesture with his hand. "I'm sorry, Stephen. I'm really sorry. Not myself at all tonight. Do forgive me."

Lona Colin moved over to Berwind, said quickly: "Nice of you to go to the trouble for me. My, this orchid is more exquisite than the last one."

The lawyer smiled. The angry flush ebbed from his face. He nodded. "Thanks. I cross them myself. Quite a hobby of mine." Then he looked over at McKee. "It's all right, Jack. I'm jumpy myself."

Lona took the flower from his hand, saying: "I have the pin right here. I'll attach it. There. How does that look?"

"Splendid," said Berwind. "Glad you like it."

McKee went over to a low, three-cushioned divan, plunked down on it. He waved Berwind over to Walters, said: "Let me know if I can help, Stephen."

Berwind fixed Walters with a frown. He shot: "Where were you when Sam Shalk died?"

The gambler frowned back. After a moment, he asked: "What time did the punk die?"

McKee put the empty Dunhill into his mouth, sucked on the stem. Lona Colin slid down onto the cushion next to him. She leaned very close, said softly:

"I'm sorry to be the cause of so much trouble."

McKee patted her gloved hand. "Many thanks for stepping into the breach between Stephen and myself. I'm afraid I lost my head." McKee suddenly realized the room was silent, sensed eyes upon him. He glanced up to meet Berwind's friendly question:

"Where did you find Walters, Jack?"

"In the medicine room."

Berwind smiled tightly. "So"; he whirled back to Walters. "The medicine room!"

"There's poison there," intoned Doctor Rhoden. "It is a place of evil."

"The whole thing is a cinch," cut

in Nita Neale. "Walters put the poison in Shalk's coffee cup!"

The corpse on the floor laughed silently, eternally.

McKEE lowered his voice for Lona's ears alone, said: "It's not so much of a cinch as she makes it. And I don't like the way she and Rhoden are ganging up on him."

The girl nodded, but said nothing.

Berwind sang out: "What were you doing in the medicine room?"

"Filling my flask. Needed a drink. This damn storm—"

"Is not driving us all to drink!" crackled Berwind. "Pretty thin, Walters. Go on—tell me about it."

"Not much to tell," said the gambler. "I was filling the flask when Mr. McKee came in. He asked where Shalk was. I said he was probably in a dark hall making a play for that cute trick of a maid."

Nita was a flash of chartreuse coming out of her chair. She slid around behind it, putting it between herself and Walters. Then she said: "You'd better tie Walters up before he kills the rest of us. Send for the police."

McKee got on his feet, put his pipe away. He walked toward Berwind, said quietly: "There are several things we have to consider. First, I've never heard of a poison that can produce a laughing death. Secondly, Walters knows next to nothing about medicine. Then there's one angle that we both have overlooked."

"What's that?"

"The maid, Jill. She served the demi-tasse tonight."

"Oh!" said Berwind. "And I haven't seen Jill since she served."

"And there's something I want to ask Walters about that." McKee turned to the gambler, asked: "What did you mean about Sam Shalk and Jill?"

WALTERS shrugged. "Nothing, except he was always making passes at her. She's just a kid with a lot of nutty ideas about romance—so the punk didn't get nowhere. He thought all janes were like—" Walters flicked his eyes toward the voluptuous blonde.

McKee checked Nita's flow of filthy abuse by yelling: "Leave personalities out of this! Another wisecrack and I'll lock every one of you in your rooms until the police come. Take your choice, Answer my questions—or let the state troopers dig into you!"

A vast silence answered him. McKee went on:

"I don't want to rub an old sore, but it's necessary to remind you three that you have at one time or another been on trial for murder. You all are potential murderers. Every one of you had the opportunity to poison Sam Shalk's demi-tasse." He flung his arm in Lona Colin's direction. "Miss Colin is the only one of us above reproach. Mr. Berwind had the opportunity. Little Jill had the opportunity. Damn it! I had the opportunity myself!"

Sam Shalk, on the floor, seemed to laugh at that.

McKee pulled out his pipe and pouch, filled the bowl, then put both back into his pocket again. He swung around to Walters. "Let's get this straight. Do you think Shalk annoyed Jill to the extent that she would want to kill him?"

The gambler replied immediately. "Well, a punk like Shalk would make no bones about callin' a spade a spade."

McKee frowned. "All right. All right. Now, another thing, Walters, do you admit having a hand in the killing of Julius W. Richards in the night club?"

"Sure. That circus slicker was getting wise to my little game. Me and Sam—well, what the hell! The law can't do nothin' to me now."

McKee looked over at Lona Colin. She took her dark eyes from Walters and met McKee's steady, grim gaze. McKee said:

"This is what old Tully Laborden's will has done. Your paper—"

Walters broke in with: "How about

a little drink from my flask? I've talked myself hoarse."

McKee looked undecided. Then he went over and picked up the flask, unscrewed the cap, walked back and handed it to Walters. After Walters took a deep slug, McKee said:

"Before Sam Shalk died he said that he was double-crossed. You were his partner. What did he mean? Was it about the night club killing?"

Walters shrugged, chuckled.

Nita Neale let out a shrill scream. "Look! He—he—"

Doctor Rhoden's face drained of color. He staggered to his feet, cried out: "God in heaven—"

Stephen Berwind clutched the back of a chair. His lips skinned back over his teeth, but no words came.

The black eyes of Lona Colin were riveted on Walters. Her head swayed back and forth. A hand stole to her throat, seemed to push out the words: "He's laughing!"

And Walters was laughing. But no sound came from his twitching lips. He lurched forward, caught himself, clapped his hands to his stomach, doubled over in the manner of suppressing great mirth. He straightened, threw back his head hilariously. He sat down on the floor, rolled. Suddenly he stopped and lay as if he had tired of laughing. His face looked like the theatrical Mask of Comedy.

Then the orchestra of heaven rumbled a mighty march, as if escorting Walters's soul into the Great Guess. For Boxcar Walters, the gambler who wouldn't bet on the coming dawn—was dead.

CHAPTER IV

Killer's Carnival

McKEE tore his eyes from the distorted face of Walters. He shook himself like a great dog. His eyes flicked to the flask that had fallen from Walters's hand. He snapped out a handkerchief to pick it up with. Then he stood stock still. The eager blaze went out of his eyes. He crammed the handkerchief back into his pocket. He glared down at the flask.

It was covered with a coarse-grained leather jacket. Finger-prints were impossible. He stooped, picked up the flask, and sheathed it in his hip pocket. Then he ploughed across the room. In the corridor, he turned around, said:

"Stephen, will you come out here please?"

When Berwind crossed the threshold, McKee reached into the library and closed the huge double doors. The doors were wooden with frosted glass panels forming the upper half in a Gothic arch design.

McKee asked: "Did you see anyone handling that flask, Stephen?"

"No, Jack. I was watching you and Walters."

"Thanks, Stephen. Will you go back in and send Miss Colin out?"

Lona moved through the door like rippling black liquid. She adjusted a shoulder strap. Looking steadily at McKee, she shook her head slowly.

McKee nodded grimly, his face wrapped in a frown. He stood motionless for several seconds, the frown deepening. Then he swept it from his face with a faint smile. "All right, Miss Colin," he said. "Thanks. Will you please ask Miss Neale to step out?"

Nita Neale eased through the doorway, closed the panel behind her. Her hands on the knob were dead white against the brilliant chartreuse of her gown. Then color flowed into her hands. Her lips twisted crookedly. She said quietly:

"Don't expect me to be brokenhearted. It's the damned best thing that could have happened. I hated that louse—"

"He's dead," said McKee, scowling. "It's gonna be tough on hell."

McKee stepped closer, loomed darkly over her. "Which one of them monkeyed with that flask?"

The blonde shook her head. "I didn't see anyone near it."

At that moment, the butler approached to a respectful distance and rooted himself there. McKee turned, asked: "Yes?"

The butler said: "I found the kitchen door open, sir. The kitchen was flooded. I closed the door, sir, but thought you might want to know about it." The butler touched his chin, as if debating whether to put his thoughts into words.

McKee smiled. "What is it, Riggs?" Riggs had followed Old Tully Laborden like a faithful dog through the millionaire's years of despondency.

"Only this, sir: Miss Jill hasn't been in the kitchen since she served demitasse."

"Keep a lookout for her, Riggs," instructed McKee. The butler marched off. McKee turned back to Nita to find that crooked smile still on her lips. He scowled darkly, said: "Please send Doctor Rhoden out."

NITA swished around, went into the library, closed the door and leaned against it. McKee took to pacing the hall. He shot many a worried glance up at Old Tully's portrait. Suddenly he stopped, swung about at Nita's voice coming through the door. She was saying:

"The postmaster wants to see you, doc. Two stamps—and perhaps a special delivery."

McKee ground out a savage oath. He was still growling to himself when Doctor Rhoden dragged his feet into the hall. McKee asked point-blank:

"Did you see anyone go near that flask on the table?"

Doctor Rhoden's high forehead wrinkled in thought. He seemed to be turning those thoughts over in his mind, arranging them carefully. Finally, he spoke up: "Yes. That newspaper woman went over to the table and remarked that Walters did not carry cards or dice."

"That's right!" said McKee, but his voice lacked the enthusiasm of an eager manhunt. "Then what happened?"

"Why—Miss Neale had sharp words with Walters."

Abruptly, McKee left Doctor Rhoden and went into the library. He stood just inside the double doors, a mutinous scowl on his face. He spoke harshly: "Everybody go to their rooms." He turned to Berwind. "Please back me up on this, Stephen. I'm going to stop this killing. The surest way is for all to go to their rooms and lock the doors. And you, Miss Colin," he faced the dark-haired girl, "will do us the honor of remaining overnight."

"I'm right with you, Jack," agreed Berwind.

"I will show Miss Colin to her room," said McKee. He went into the corridor, picked up her portable typewriter case, and waited.

Lona came out very cool and aloof. "It seems that you have made up my mind—"

"This way." McKee took her arm and led her along the candlelit corridor to the entrance hall, then up the stairs. The others trooped up behind. The second landing was "L" shaped. McKee's room was directly opposite the head of the stairs. Next to it, was Stephen Berwind's room. Berwind smiled all around, went in and closed the door. The next room up was Boxcar Walters'.

Then the floor formed the top of the "L" with two rooms at right angle to the others. The first of these belonged to Sam Shalk. The second to Doctor Rhoden. Doctor Rhoden said: "Good night," once to include everybody, then went into his room.

Starting down the other side of the "L" was the guest room. McKee took Lona Colin to this room, and paused a moment before it.

Nita Neale's room was next in line. Hand on the knob, she turned and shot Lona a nasty glance. "Better lock your door, dearie." She flung into her room, banged the door shut. The lock snicked.

Lona looked up at McKee. They were now alone in the corridor. She asked: "What murder case was Nita Neale connected with?"

McKee took his eyes from Nita's door and put them on Lona's upturned face. That pretty face might as well have been the wooden door, for all he learned from it. McKee frowned, put the portable case on the floor, and jammed his hands into his pockets.

"Nita Neale used to be a show girl," he said. "In one of the Night in Vienna editions. Nita and another girl were making a strong play for the backer of the show. The other girl must have had more of what it takes, for she was shutting Nita out of the race. Well, anyway, one of the scenes in the show called for a mass fencing act. As Fate would have it, Nita and this other girl were fencing partners. The spotlight following the star across the stage struck Nita's face . . . .

"The next instant a girl screamed, fell to the floor. She was Nita's partner. And she carried Nita's foil to the floor with her, embedded in her breast. The girls wore only tights, so there was nothing to stop the blunt point penetrating to the heart. The little rubber cap on the tip had been knocked off. That is very likely. I've seen it happen many times at the Fencing Club."

Lona Colin stood transfixed during the recital. A gasp escaped her parted lips. "How horrible—"

McKee took his hands from his pockets, rubbed sweat into a handkerchief. "It was horrible. But Nita claimed that the spotlight blinded her." McKee shrugged slightly. "It may have. Who knows? The law said it was murder. The backer of the show dropped her flat. I listened to her story personally, then advised Stephen to defend her. I may have been wrong. Perhaps she should have gone to the electric chair. I don't know." He shrugged again. "Then the first day she came here, Boxcar Walters told her she had a slick way of getting rid of competition."

"Walters deserved to die!" said Lona vehemently. Taking up her portable case, she stepped into the room. Candles had been placed there by the butler.

"By the way, Miss Colin, our maid seems to have disappeared. I believe you were the last to see her."

Lona frowned. "I asked for a hot drink. She never brought it."

"Thanks," said McKee. "Good night."

TWO corpses grinned up at McKee. He stood there in the library and frowned down at them. He thought: *Rats—both of them. Killers. But they didn't deserve to die like this. No one on God's earth deserved to die like this.*

McKee speared the Dunhill between his teeth, but didn't light it. He sucked on the stem, walking back and forth across the room. He took the piece of rug and the flask from his pocket. McKee thought of Doctor Rhoden, swore, and put them back into his pocket.

He took to pacing again, a scowl carved on his face. Suddenly he stopped, took hold of Sam Shalk's body and lugged it to the chair he had been sitting in. Next he placed the coffee table before it. Then stood off and studied the tableaux. Sam Shalk's death mask laughingly mocked him.

McKee quit the library, closed the door, and ploughed down the corridor to the kitchen. It was a large room, white and ghostly in the flickering candlelight. Beside a fat, white chunk of a refrigerator sat Riggs, the butler. His head was pillowed in his crossed arms on a white, slab-like table. Before him was the remnants of a midnight snack. He was snoring loudly.

Not disturbing him, McKee pulled aside the shade on the door and looked out at the night. The rain had stopped. Thunder rumbled distantly. Intermittent lightning laced the sky. McKee went out, closed the door quietly behind him, and stood against the house. Water dribbled down from the eaves. He focused his eyes on the ground, waited for another lightning flash. It came.

Small, high-heeled footprints had churned up the soggy ground. The next flash showed footprints leading off in the general direction of the glass-tented hot-houses. McKee pushed himself away from the wall and sprinted toward the hot-houses. Mud sucked at his racing feet.

At the door of the first hot-house, he pulled out his pipe and held it like a gun. Taking a deep breath, and doing a lot of hoping, he opened the door, stepped in. Lightning glared, boldly silhouetting him on the hard-packed ground. He grinned. That pipe did look like a gun.

Nothing happened. But the lightning had pointed out a puddle of water inside the door where someone coming out of the rain had stood. The hard-packed earth yielded no more prints. Then a blaze of lightning turned the night into day. McKee saw what he had been looking for—footprints in softer earth near one of the glass walls.

Down the shrub-lined aisle McKee went. He dropped to one knee, took out a book of matches, then put it away. He looked about him. No sound came from the weirdly-contorted shrubs. Sweat poured down his face. Hot-house was right—damned right! The sultry, storm-charged air outside didn't help matters any.

McKee deliberately took out his matches again, struck one aflame. He looked at the patch of earth. It was richer than the plots bordering it. And that richness showed two excellent footprints. McKee's match seared his fingers, went out.

"Jill," he muttered. "Jill made those prints." He scratched another match, and found out why Jill had used this particular spot to stand in. It was not because a shrub had been recently removed from there, but because this glass wall afforded an unobstructed view of the house. Taking care not to gash the prints with his own leather heels, he stepped into the plot and pressed his face against the glass wall.

He made out the kitchen door. Then his eyes cruised past the darkened dining room to the library. He could see faint cracks of light there from the glimmering candles. Suddenly he stiffened. More light was washed into the library. And it came from the corridor. Someone was entering the library.

McKee spun around, and in his hurry tripped over the board separating the plot from the aisle. He barked his knee on the hardpacked dirt, sprawled flat. His pipe flew from his fingers, clattered against the board on the opposite side of the aisle and bounced back. He scooped it up, crammed it into his pocket. He got to his feet, stiffly. The banged knee made him hobble.

Like a huge, ungainly bird, he hopped back across the soggy ground. Fuming, dusting off his trousers, and trying to be quiet, he finally made the kitchen door. Riggs was still snoring lustily. McKee awkwardly tip-tapped across the linoleum. The thick-napped rug of the corridor muffled his advance and made the going faster.

HE paused a moment at the library door, whipped out his pipe again, and swung in one of the big doors. An amazing sight drew his eyes, shut out everything else. Sam Shalk was still sitting in the chair; still laughing. But it was the dead gunman's shirt-front that held McKee's eyes.

Underworld slang calls a dress shirt a "tombstone front." And Sam Shalk's shirt was exactly that. For an epitaph had been inscribed upon it. In big red letters it ran:

HERE LIES A KILLER

McKee found the red-lettered shirt rushing across the room to meet him. In truth, McKee was stumbling toward the corpse in the chair. He had been pushed. As a rule McKee could take a shove and still stay on his feet. But the game leg broke the rule. It buckled under him. He went down heavily.

Breaking the fall with his outstretched arms, he rolled over. The library door closed with a clack. Whoever had been standing behind it and shoved McKee, was now ducking low. No silhouette showed on the frosted glass panels. No running sound came from the corridor.

McKee scrambled to his feet, flung himself at the door, ripped it open. He launched black scowls up and down the corridor. No one was in sight. He hopped and skipped to the staircase, strained his neck to listen. The house was silent save for a faint droning sound. He cocked his head at a sharper angle. Then he swore. Riggs's snoring in the kitchen was making that droning sound.

McKee made better time going back to the library. His sore leg was loosening up a bit. He went in, closed the door, missed something, and started to look around for his pipe. It was nowhere in sight. He got down on his hands and one good knee, dragged himself around the floor.

He pulled up short before the grinning face of Sam Shalk. Mumbling to himself, he leaned closer to inspect the tombstone that was the gunman's shirt. A delicate, fragrant perfume reached his nostrils. He glared at the red epitaph, then muttered:

"Lipstick . . . . Well—that's something!"

REACHING out his hand, he scraped some of the lip rouge off Shalk's shirt with his fingernail. He smelled it, tasted it, let it linger on his lips. He wanted to remember it. And to be sure, he reached to his white vest and plucked out one of the pocket linings. He wiped the little blob of cosmetic off his fingernail onto the lining, then stuffed the lining back into place.

In this half-kneeling, half-crouching position, McKee spotted his pipe. The Dunhill had skated under the chair the corpse was sitting in. McKee went around the chair, still on his hands and one knee, and picked up the pipe. Then he thrust one hand against the back of the chair to help draw himself up to his feet.

Suddenly his hand jerked from the chair as if stung. He barked an oath. His forefinger was bleeding. He pushed it into his mouth, sucked it, spat blood on the burgundy rug. Visions of diabolical poison crowded his brain. He fumbled a match book, feverishly got one alight, and scrutinized the wound with it.

His finger looked all right, felt all right. He raised the match to the back of the chair, and saw a sharp steely point jutting through the upholstery. He took out his own pocket-knife and went to work. In several minutes' time he had dislodged the sharp blade from the chair. It was a six-inch throwing knife minus the crossbar at the hilt.

McKee scowled darkly at it. For this slim blade upset every one of his half-baked theories. It meant that someone had tried to knife Sam Shalk. It meant that two people had tried to kill the gunman. Two people had sought his life at precisely the same moment. One a knifer. The other a poisoner.

Thunder marched across the heavens with a mighty tread. The storm was marshalling its legions for a second onslaught.

McKee hefted the knife. His face hardened. His jaw jutted. He barged angrily out of the room.

CHAPTER V

A Curious Clue

STEPHEN BERWIND said: "Yes, Jack. I threw that knife at Sam Shalk. I wanted to shut him up. Guess it was a crazy thing to do. Thank God I missed him."

McKee was pacing Berwind's room, balancing the knife in the palm of his hand. He wasn't paying much attention to Berwind. He knew he was lying. Berwind was obviously trying to shield someone. That someone was the bee in McKee's bonnet.

In midstride he stopped, looked hard at one of the volumes on Berwind's shelves. The back of the book was caked in places with dried mud. McKee moved away from the shelf, asked suddenly:

"Funny about Jill. Any idea where she could be?"

Berwind frowned, said slowly: "It is funny about Jill. I'm going to take a look around for her."

With a flip of his hand, McKee sent the knife spinning to the table top in front of Berwind. The point stuck; the blade quivered evilly in the candlelight. Berwind looked up quickly.

McKee growled angrily. "Listen, Stephen—" Then slowly he relaxed. The anger went out of his voice. "Gee, Stephen, why don't you take a poke at me? Why don't you ask me who the hell I think I am? I fly off the handle—"

"Forget it, Jack. I understand. But please believe me when I say—"

"You can help a lot, Stephen. And you're shielding someone."

"Please believe me—"

"You're shielding someone. Forget your gallantry, Stephen. We are dealing with murderers. We can take only one side. The side of the law. You're too easy, Stephen. The law—"

"I have nothing more to say, Jack," Berwind said quietly.

For several seconds McKee stared at Berwind. Then he shrugged, walked slowly to the door. There was no anger in his eyes. He was hurt, deeply. He opened the door, went out, closed it, and found himself face to face with Lona Colin.

THE dark-haired girl drew back. "Oh! So sorry. I thought this was the room I'm using."

McKee closed Berwind's door, said: "There is a bath adjoining your room. Why did you leave it?"

"My wrap," replied Lona, nodding to the garment draped over her arm. "It was in the hall downstairs where you took it off."

"I see. Sorry. I'll show you to your room again." He started down the corridor, taking her arm. "By the way, Miss Colin, I have some typing to do. Mind if I use your machine?"

Lona looked up into his face. "I'm afraid I can't oblige you. I was stupid enough to misplace the key to the carrying case."

"I could force the lock," offered McKee. "You'll need the machine yourself, anyway."

The girl frowned. "That would be simple—but the machine is not mine. I wouldn't want to wreck someone's else case. Really doesn't matter. I can remember every detail of these murders. They're so vivid!"

McKee shrugged. He bobbed his head toward the panel of her door. "Let me have your lipstick and I'll put an X on your door so you won't go astray again."

Lona made her lips pout, said: "PULL-ease!"

"What's the matter?" McKee asked.

"I'm superstitious. I don't like an X to mark the spot."

There was just one thing left to do. McKee did it. He took Lona in his arms, crushed her close, and kissed her full on the mouth.

The girl struggled free. A torrent of anger welled within her. Then the anger ebbed, washing her face a chalk white. She said throatily: "I thought you would value it more than to do it —like that." She turned and went into her room. The door closed quietly. The lock clicked.

McKee found his blood running hotly. He shook himself; tried to get his mind back to the murders. With an effort he tore his eyes from Lona's door. He walked the length of the hall, and stopped. He ran his tongue across the rouge imprint of Lona's lips, tasted it.

He shook his head slowly. Taking out a handkerchief, he wiped his mouth, then compared the red smudge with the one on his vest pocket lining.

Lona's lipstick on the handkerchief was lighter in color.

McKee found himself smiling. "Not her," he murmured. Then he scowled and took to pacing the corridor. Suddenly he brought himself to a stop. He saw Nita Neale pause in her doorway and look across at Stephen Berwind's closed door.

Nita's voluptuous body was draped in a lacy negligee. Candles burning in her room shone behind her. Then she saw McKee. She jerked her head around in startled surprise. For a moment it seemed that she was going to slam the door. Instead, she smiled and stepped out into the corridor.

McKee went over to meet her. His right arm went around her waist. His left lifted her chin. He bent and kissed her. Nita seemed to melt, flow against him like a warm liquid. This time it was McKee who struggled to free himself. He did so gently, firmly.

Nita's eyelids were lowered. Her eyes were pools of blue lustre. She said softly: "I have been waiting two months for you to do that." She went over to her room, stood in the doorway.

"I'll," McKee said, "be seeing you later."

Nita smiled, slowly closed the door. She did not lock it.

"Damn!" swore McKee. "Damn!" He savagely jerked out his handkerchief, rubbed it roughly over his mouth, then compared it with the lip rouge in his pocket. Nita's was more orangy in color.

Then McKee did some strong and fancy swearing. His face was like a thundercloud. His brows were knitted, worried. He stuck his pipe into his mouth, fanned the tobacco with a match. The strong aroma took the sweetish rouge taste from his mouth.

He ranged glances up and down the hall. All doors were closed. At the far end, near his room, three candles glowed mournfully. He thought of the three samples of rouge, and scowled darkly.

"Not Lona," he said to himself. "And not Nita. Then who the hell is it?" He put the smouldering pipe back into his pocket, and deliberately approached Stephen Berwind's room. At the door, he paused, put the knob in his sweaty palm.

McKee lurched, stifled a cry of pain. He let go of the knob and steadied himself against the wall. He looked over his left shoulder and saw a long, slender blade speared through the sleeve of his dinner jacket. The steel had creased his arm near the shoulder. He could feel blood coursing down his arm.

His eyes narrowed on three doors from which the knife could have come. The nearest was Nita Neale's. The next was Lona Colin's. And the third was Doctor Rhoden's. McKee strode quickly to Doctor Rhoden's door. Remembering that the doctor had not locked the door, McKee turned the knob and ploughed in.

CHAPTER VI

SCARLET FINGERS

DOCTOR RHODEN was rocking back and forth in an old-fashioned rocker. A cigar spiked from his too-thin face. Blue-gray smoke spiraled from the cigar. Rhoden was staring at the smoke. He kept on rocking, staring at the smoke.

McKee was in the room for several seconds before Doctor Rhoden looked in his direction. Then Rhoden almost fell out of the rocker. He got to his feet, steadied himself. McKee asked:

"Surprised to see me, doc?"

"Why—why—"

"All right, doc, save it. We're going down to the medicine room—"

The doctor blanched. "I won't go near—"

"Right now," cut in McKee. "I don't want to get rough—but I'm not fooling. Come on." He took the doctor's arm and forcibly pushed him out of the room. "Quiet," warned McKee.

They moved quickly along the corridor, down the stairs and through the downstairs corridor. McKee purposely avoided looking up at the smiling portrait of Old Tully Laborden, founder of the Death Cheaters' home.

In the medicine room, McKee closed and locked the door. The same candle that Boxcar Walters had used was still burning. Its yellow glow bathed the taut-lined face of the doctor. He was trembling violently.

McKee pulled the slim-bladed knife from his arm and tossed it on a table. Doctor Rhoden stared at the bloody steel with horrified eyes. Then McKee pulled off his jacket, and tore the sleeve of his shirt away from the wound.

The doctor took a grip on himself, reached for a labeled bottle.

McKee patted down air with his right hand, said: "Never mind the fancy names, doc. Just hand me that peroxide over there. Cotton, too . . . . Look. The knife must have been pretty clean. The peroxide doesn't bubble up much. More cotton." He wiped away the peroxide froth, and applied a fresh dose.

Doctor Rhoden squared his chin. A light of new determination glittered in his eyes. "You know," he said forcefully, "I don't mind this room so much now. The thought of aiding others has brushed the nightmare from—"

"Fine, doc. You can bandage this up now." He gestured toward the knife. "Somebody is sailing them around like paper airplanes. Got any ideas, doc?"

Finishing his bandaging job, Doctor Rhoden stroked his pointed chin. "It seems that some one made a mistake of three inches." His eyes gauged McKee's back. "A fortunate mistake—for you."

McKee looked searchingly into Rhoden's eyes. Then he pulled on his tuxedo jacket, saying: "Thanks, doc. You can go to your room if you wish." He unlocked the door, went out, waited for the doctor to come out, then locked the door and put the key in his pocket.

Stephen Berwind, wearing a green slicker and carrying a long flashlight, came down the stairs. McKee called out to him:

"Wait a moment. I'll get Riggs to help you." McKee strode back to the kitchen. Riggs was washing the dish he had used for a snack. Going up to him, McKee whispered: "You and Mr. Berwind are going to search the grounds for Jill. Stay close to Jill—search her for a lipstick." Without waiting for Riggs to ask a lot of questions, McKee swung out of the kitchen.

He called, "Good luck," to Berwind, then went up to his room, closed the door, and stood with his ear to the panel. He heard Riggs's voice mingle with Berwind's and the doctor's. Then the big front door banged as Berwind and Riggs went out. McKee darted across his room to the window and peered into the night.

RAIN was slanting down in sheets. Lightning blazed and danced all over the sky. Thunder was only a deep-throated rumble in the distance. McKee went back to the door, heard Doctor Rhoden pad down the corridor to his room. Waiting several minutes, McKee stepped noiselessly into the corridor. He went straight to Sam Shalk's room, quietly let himself in.

Sam Shalk's taste must have been in his mouth. McKee grimaced at what a gutter-born gunman could do to fine old furniture. Frowning, he went directly to the secretary. There was absolutely no correspondence there. McKee doubted that Shalk had known how to write. The contents of the drawers were press clippings and pictures of the night club murder case. Sam Shalk's dark face smirked from many a front page. Then McKee came across the picture of the murdered Julius W. Richards.

"Well!" he muttered. "Well!" Then he hastily thumbed through the clippings. Near the bottom of the pile, he plucked out a folded sheet of white stationery. On the paper was a crudely printed warning.

KILLER—

I HAVE SWORN TO WRITE YOUR EPITAPH.

There was no signature. McKee pursed his lips in a soundless whistle. He put the picture and warning into his coat pocket. Leaving Shalk's room, he slid quietly down the corridor and into Berwind's.

Once inside the door the first thing he did was to take down the volume with the dried mud flakes on its leather backbone. Gold-stamped letters said the author was DuMolin. The book was written in French. McKee took down the book next to it. This one was by Moris, and was in Latin. Carrying the two volumes to an easy chair, he first tackled the one by Moris.

McKee knew Latin from his legal schooling. And with this Romance language basis, DuMolin was not so difficult to follow. The puzzled frown on McKee's forehead gave way to wide-eyed amazement, then darkened to a black scowl. His pipe found its way to his teeth, but he read on without lighting it.

He closed the books with a snap, got on his feet, and put the books back into their places. So preoccupied was he that he let Berwind's door slam shut behind him. The bang brought him out of his reverie. He glanced quickly about him, then swung along the corridor and climbed the stairs to the third floor.

The third and top floor was a huge storeroom on one side, and the two servants' bedrooms. Riggs, the butler, was also cook. Old Tully Laborden would have no other. McKee darted into Jill's room, made a swift examination of the bureau and bathroom, which netted him exactly nothing. For there was not a sign of a lipstick or lip rouge in the maid's severely neat room.

McKee climbed still another flight of stairs and let himself out into Stephen Berwind's roof botanical garden. The entire garden was walled and roofed in glass. It was jet black now. Rain slammed at the roof and cascaded down the walls. Thunder was still rumbling. And lightning flicked on and off like a dim electric bulb loose in its socket. McKee scratched matches, moved along closely examining the earth beneath the grotesquely shaped plants.

Suddenly he stopped before a rich-looking plot. Then he blew hard on the match, dropped it. He ducked across the aisle, and wedged himself between two plants, stood there sweating in the lose, hot air.

The lightning stopped blinking.

McKee waited, focusing his eyes in the direction of the door. The door hinges creaked. And McKee felt another presence in the botanical garden. But the jet of the night was impenetrable. Seconds later the door creaked again. McKee thought he heard a stifled gasp.

THEN lightning blazed in a dazzling burst. Every plant, shrub and flower in the garden stood out vividly. And so did the beautiful figures of two women. Nearest to McKee was Lona Colin. And standing in the doorway was Nita Neale. The lightning burned out as quickly as it had blazed. Inky blackness swallowed the garden.

A shrill scream of terror shattered the close, oppressive silence. A woman's tortured soul pored out of that scream. The door banged violently. Frantic footsteps beat down the stairs. Then silence again.

McKee ventured: "Lona?"

And out of the dark came a half-whispered: "McKee?"

"Right. Jack McKee. Stand still, Lona. I'll come to you." He stepped out from between the plants, walked till his outstretched hand touched the silky smoothness of her shoulder. She closed swiftly, clung to him.

McKee's arms were straight at his sides. He said, gently: "Let's go to your room, Lona. We can talk there."

The girl said nothing. Together they groped to the door, went inside and down the staircase. Halfway down the steps Lona shuddered, said:

"That scream—"

"Nita Neale," replied McKee.

"But what frightened her—"

McKee frowned. "This whole thing gets crazier every minute."

No more was said until they were in Lona's room. McKee closed the door, strode over to the girl. He raised his head in the general direction of the roof. "Up there was the second time tonight you've mistaken me for Stephen Berwind."

Lona started, but still did not speak.

"The first time," said McKee, "I was standing with my hand on Berwind's doorknob. The second time you heard me bang out of his room and tramp upstairs." McKee pointed to his left arm, grimaced. "The first time—I got it there."

Lona's shoulders quivered. Her full lips quivered, but no words came from them.

Crossing the room, McKee picked up the portable typewriter case, snapped it open without a key. He looked inside. There was a typewriter there. But wedged in beside it were three long slim steel knives without cross-pieces at the hilt. He closed the case, put it down.

Lona laid a hand against her creamy white throat. "Were—were you hurt?"

"Just a flesh wound," said McKee. He faced her squarely. "Now let me tell you some things. You're not from the *Star-Herald*. And you're not Lona Colin. But you do look like this picture." He took the newspaper photograph from his pocket and handed it to her. "This is Julius W. Richards—your brother."

LONA held the picture in her two hands, stared dully at it.

McKee's voice became very gentle. "You called him 'Bill'. That is the name you used when you first came into the house and were frightened at the thunder. You had always depended on him. You were scared, and naturally thought of your brother."

The girl nodded. "You don't miss much, Jack McKee."

McKee went on: "You must have waylaid the real Lona Colin in some fancy way, then came on in her place. When you got here you chucked a knife at Sam Shalk. Circus training with your brother, I guess. But you missed. Later you went down, couldn't find the knife—but did make a tombstone out of Shalk's shirt front." McKee took out the warning he had found in Shalk's room, showed it then put it away again.

He scratched his chin, looked reflectively at her small hand bag.

The girl said quietly: "You needn't. The lipstick has been disposed of. It's the shade I use in daylight."

"Damn!" muttered McKee.

"That's why you kissed me," said the girl.

McKee didn't answer. He wrapped his face in a scowl.

"Well," shrugged the girl, "what are you going to do with me?"

"Nothing," McKee said. "You haven't killed anyone. I can forget this scratch on my arm." He made a wry face. "And that shove you gave me downstairs."

The dark-eyed girl smiled warmly. "I like you a lot," she said earnestly. "But—" her voice hardened to a steely rasp— "—there is one man you've forgotten."

"Who?"

"Stephen Berwind! He knew that Shalk and Walters killed my brother. He freed them—gave them life!" The girl flung herself at the door, whipped it open. Crossing the threshold, she snatched a slender blade from the long black glove on her left arm.

The sight of the knife coming from that left-hand glove stung back into McKee's memory. And the thought didn't make him feel so good. For his mind flicked back to when he introduced Stephen Berwind to Lona Colin in the hallway downstairs. Berwind had given her an orchid, then offered his arm to her. She had refused him. Why? Because Berwind had been on her left. And her left-hand glove had held the knife she had thrown at Sam Shalk. McKee realized that the girl's preferring his own arm hadn't meant a thing, personally.

McKee's thoughts had flicked back with the split-second speed of glancing light, but his body had been lurching forward after the girl. He reached the doorway, pushed himself away from the frame with his right hand, and skidded into the corridor. The girl was ahead of him.

Both Doctor Rhoden and Nita Neale must have been eavesdropping, for they stood near their doors with a guilty and scared look on their faces. Their eyes were riveted on the running figure of the girl.

Suddenly she tripped, her high heel catching in her long dress. She sprawled headlong. Her unprotected head thudded against the frame of Berwind's door. She shuddered, curled up a little, and lying flat on her stomach became very still.

McKee dropped on his knees beside her, lifted her head from against the woodwork.

"Water!" he barked fiercely. Then he took out a handkerchief and patted blood from her glossy hair.

Nita stood frozen before the open door of her room. Doctor Rhoden had advanced down the corridor. He shot a glance into Nita's room, then darted in. In a moment he hurried out with a glass of water and bent down over the Richards girl.

McKee snatched the glass from his hands, raised the girl's head. Suddenly McKee stopped, jerked the glass up before his glittering eyes. In the bottom of the glass he made out a faint crystalline sediment.

Slowly McKee got to his feet. His eyes were humid, and a dark shadow crept down across his face. He sent a malignant glare cruising from Nita Neale to Doctor Rhoden.

A door slammed downstairs. Berwind's voice sang out: "Hey, Jack! I have Jill down here—and is she going to upset somebody's apple-cart!"

CHAPTER VII

THE DEATH CHEATERS

McKEE took Nita Neale and Doctor Rhoden by the arm and led them to the top of the stairs. He called down: "Stephen, keep a close eye on these two. I'll be right down."

He put the glass of poison in his room and locked the door. Then he lifted the unconscious girl in his arms and carried her into her room. He gently placed her on the bed. Going into the bathroom he ran cold water on a towel. Laying the wet compress on her head, he went out into the hall, picked up the knife she had dropped, came back and put it in the typewriter case.

By that time the girl was sitting up on the bed. McKee went over, steadied her, asked: "Still wobbly?"

"A little." She brushed a damp strand of hair from her face. "Guess I'm not much of a success as a murderess. Failed three times."

McKee grimaced. He was thinking of how close she came to being a laughing corpse. He nodded toward the door. "When you're ready we'll go down. What is your first name?"

"I'm ready now. Grace." She flicked at her face with a powder puff, then walked to the door. Together they went down into the entrance hall.

Stephen Berwind levelled an arm at Grace Richards, but spoke to McKee. "Jack, do you know who that woman is?"

"Yes, Stephen."

Before Berwind could gather his wits from the surprise, Jill, the now bedraggled and soaked serving girl, broke in with:

"She made me go out to the hothouse. She tied me there—because I knew her the minute I saw her!"

McKee glanced down at Grace, but said nothing.

Berwind said: "I figured she would be in the hot-house—"

"Right," agreed McKee. "I knew she was there, but didn't know that Grace had made her a prisoner. I thought it was because of Sam Shalk—"

"I like that!" snapped Berwind. "You knew she was there! And me tramping around in the rain—"

McKee raised his hand. "Just a moment. Let Jill tell how she recognized Grace Richards."

But Jill suddenly edged back out of the limelight.

McKee jerked his head to indicate the second floor. "I'll tell you, Jill. You were snooping around in Sam Shalk's room. Maids always snoop. You found Richards' picture, and the warning against Shalk's life. You were intrigued. The picture was stamped in your mind. Grace Richards does resemble her brother quite a bit . . . . Stephen, you missed out on that entirely."

All the while the others were talking, Doctor Rhoden had not moved from his chair. Neither had Nita Neale. Now she leaned forward, said bitingly:

"I hate snoopers!"

Jill whirled on her, snapped: "You have good reason to!"

"What does that mean?" butted in McKee.

The maid looked spitefully at Nita Neale, said: "She has spent many a night in Stephen Berwind's room."

Nita Neale sprang up yelling: "You dirty little snitching—"

"Quiet!" barked McKee.

Berwind got red in the face. "Jill is a liar, Jack."

"Sure," said McKee. "Especially when Nita uses the word 'snitching.' I don't care. None of my business. But it does explain several things. It explains Nita's jealousy in crushing the orchid you gave to Grace. And it explains her following Grace and me to the roof garden. Nita mistook me for you because I came out of your room."

"My room!"

Nita murmured: "That flash of lightning—"

Suddenly McKee smacked the knuckles of his right hand into the palm of his left. That flash of lightning had scared her—reminded her of the glare of the spotlight in the theatre.

Doctor Rhoden went over to Nita, patted her on the shoulder. "I'll get you a glass of water," he said quietly.

McKee shook his head. "We'll wait a while, doc. No water—now." To Jill he said: "Just one more thing. Did Sam Shalk annoy you?"

The little maid looked up at McKee. "He got fresh, very fresh until I warned him that I would tell you. He stopped then."

"All right," said McKee. "That clears up about everything."

He walked over to the phone, lifted the French instrument from its base. Then he put the phone down again. He glanced over to Stephen Berwind. A bitter, disillusioned tone was in his voice when he said:

"I now have every detail of the case, Stephen. You can make it easier for yourself by confessing."

BERWIND pursed his lips, lifted his eyebrows. "So I'm the murderer, eh?"

"Right. To begin with you're quite a ladies' man. That costs money. So you started a racket of defending accused murderers and admitting them to Chair Haven—for a regal fee. Sam Shalk was a rat. After you got him in here, he turned to blackmailing you. You figured you'd have to get rid of him—so you naturally turned to your hobby . . . . Botany." McKee's words were dull, listless, like a man condemning his own brother. He went on:

"You poisoned Sam Shalk's demitasse. Boxcar Walters was too dangerous to have around, so you poisoned his whiskey. Nita saw you do it. She didn't stop you. I don't know whether it was her hate for Walters or her love for you which prompted her to protect you. Anyway, you two had a row over

Grace Richards here—and you couldn't afford to rely on Nita's temper for your safety."

Berwind lifted his eyebrows still higher, flipped a hand toward Nita. "The young lady looks very much alive to me."

McKee frowned. He said savagely: "Don't joke, Stephen! I want to get this over with. I'm not enjoying it!" Then he quieted down. "The poison you meant for Nita was almost given to Grace Richards. I caught it in time."

Berwind smiled, a very patient smile. "Honestly, Jack, you know how much weight pretty theories have in court. Facts are demanded. You are a lawyer. At least I thought you were when I took you into partnership. Why, man, you'd be—"

McKee butted in. "When you told me that you threw the knife at Sam Shalk you made me think you were protecting Nita Neale. But when I found Julius W. Richards' picture I knew it was Lona. But you never suspected Lona's real identity. You just tried to muddle me up."

The same patient smile was on Berwind's face. He said, quietly: "You'd be the laughing stock of the Bar Association."

"A laugh," said McKee, "is just what I want to talk about. I found that your mud-stained volume of DuMolin—"

Berwind's face changed. It became set, determined. He took a paper packet from his vest pocket, unfolded it carefully, and looked over at McKee.

McKee could guess what was in that packet. And he could guess what Berwind was going to do with it. He started to talk fast. "DuMolin said some very interesting things about the 'sardonic' or Sardinian laugh. And Moris, too, gave quite a discourse on the plant which causes *risus sardonius*. I gathered that this plant mentioned in classical literature has commonly been believed to be a species of *Ranunculus*, either *Ranunculus sceleratus* or *Ranunculus Philonotis*."

Berwind just stood there, the packet in his hand. He said nothing. McKee rushed on, his brain working frantically.

"Anyway, Stephen, you are quite skillful in crossing plants—a genius, I might say. For you have cultivated a plant poisonous enough to cause the laughing death. There is evidence of transplanting in the hot-house and on the roof garden. Also the caked mud on DuMolin's book."

The paper in Berwind's hand moved closer to his mouth. He seemed fascinated by it. He was only half listening to McKee. Yet McKee pounded on.

"This fatal laughter was not caused by any hilarious feelings on the part of Sam Shalk or Boxcar Walters, but because their facial spasms looked like laughter to us. The symptom is characteristic of strychnine poisoning—"

McKee whipped his pipe from his pocket, yelled: "Hands up, Stephen!"

BERWIND'S eyes jerked to McKee's gunlike pipe. And the gun-menace instilled in mankind momentarily shut all else from his startled mind.

McKee yelled louder: "Riggs!"

Berwind flung a wild-eyed glance at the butler. McKee was already heaving across the hall. He struck Berwind, knocked him clear off his feet. The paper flew out of Berwind's hand. Berwind landed flat on his back, McKee on top of him.

Purple cords of veins bulged on Berwind's face and throat. He jerked, twisted, flung himself about like a maniac. McKee was heavier, stronger, but his wounded arm handicapped him. He gasped:

"Riggs—your belt! . . . . Strap his feet!"

Riggs threw himself bodily on Berwind's legs, wrapped them in his belt. Then McKee suddenly heaved upward, bringing Berwind with him. With a swift movement he jerked Berwind's slicker down off his shoulders to his elbows. Berwind's arms were pinioned to his sides.

Berwind suddenly relaxed, slumped back to the floor, lay there panting like an exhausted animal. Towering over him, grim, feet firmly planted, arms akimbo, stood McKee. He was not gloating. He shook his head slowly, said:

"No, Stephen, you're not taking the suicide way out. You are going to court—stand trial for these murders. You are going to face the same horror that fine Old Tully Laborden faced. You are going to realize the harm you have done to this haven for unjustly-accused men and women."

McKee abruptly turned away, dragged his feet over to a chair and sank wearily into it. He pulled out his handkerchief to wipe perspiration from his forehead. The handkerchief fell open in his hand. McKee's eyes fell to the lipstick marks. Then his eyes ranged over to Grace Richards. She was looking at the handkerchief, too. And she was smiling.

Suddenly the hallway blazed with bright electric lights, and the glare of them dwarfed the candle flames to mere pinpoints.

"The wires are up, sir," said Riggs.

McKee went over to the telephone. His hand on the instrument, he sent a bitter glance at his former partner trussed on the floor. Riggs was standing beside him holding the packet of poison tightly in his hand. Nita Neale had her arms crossed over her eyes to shield them from the brilliance of the suddenly turned-on lights. Jill was standing near Riggs, stunned by the horror of McKee's deductions. Doctor Rhoden sat staring into space, an unlighted and forgotten cigar in his mouth. Grace Richards had eyes only for McKee.

Then as McKee lifted the phone he looked up at the smiling portrait of Tully Laborden. And that kindly face seemed to murmur a word of gratitude.

McKee heard a click come over the wire, then the operator's voice. McKee cleared his throat, said: "State police barracks."

Wade Hammond stood transfixed in the doorway

Wade Hammond Knows the Lethal Sting of

Fangs of the Cobra

By PAUL CHADWICK

Author of
"Gun Trap," "Tentacles of Doom," etc.

Wade Hammond had planned a quiet evening at home. But a victim of the insidious Cobra changed those plans into a nightmare of stark terror. For Wade Hammond met a dying man with gay ideas—a living man with drab ideas—and a night club hot-cha dancer with mixed ideas.

THE strident ringing of the doorbell brought Wade Hammond around in his chair with a jerk. He thrust a lean finger into the book he was reading to mark the place and stared across the den of his snug bachelor apartment.

His eye wandered past cabinets filled with curios, primitive weapons and pieces of pottery—mementoes of his many travels. Stuffed heads of big game, shot in the far corners of the earth, stared back at him from the walls.

The doorbell sounded again. It was continuous this time, as though some one, out of patience, were holding an angry finger on it.

He shut his book with a snap, wrapped his silk-tasseled dressing gown around his tall figure and strode to the door with long, quick steps. His movements were as poised and precise as those of some fast-running, well-oiled machine.

He stopped beside the door, touched the button operating the electric lock in the vestibule below and waited. The button would spring the catch and afford his visitor admittance.

The ringing ceased abruptly, but seconds passed and no one came up the stairs. Wade's long, lean face with its thin mustache line grew alert.

As a special investigator of crime, acting *sub rosa* in homicide cases, the ringing of that doorbell had often presaged a visit from Inspector Thompson, or from some stranger asking his help. Who could it be now, he wondered.

He waited another half minute, and a hard look came into his eyes. He had enemies in the underworld, friends of criminals he had sent to the electric chair. A time might come when some assassin's hand would reach out for his own life.

He crossed quickly to a table, opened a drawer and drew from it an automatic in a worn leather holster. It was a weapon that had been with him on many adventures when, as a newspaper correspondent and soldier-of-fortune, he had prowled the out-trails of the world. He drew back the safety catch and slipped the gun into his pocket. A moment later he opened the corridor doorway and went down the apartment house stairs.

It was raining outside. He could see the glow of a street light on wet pavements, hear the moaning lash of the wind. Somewhere a taxi honked dismally.

The night switchboard operator wasn't in sight. No one was visible through the glass of the vestibule door. But he opened it cautiously and stared out, then drew in his breath in a hissing gasp.

On the floor of the vestibule a human figure lay sprawled. The starkly pale face of a young man stared up at him; eyes wide, bloodless lips moving incoherently. He bent closer and stared in amazement. On the young man's face, stamped there with some sort of dark ink, was a hideous design—the head of a snake with open jaws and sharp fangs.

The young man made a gurgling sound in his throat and lifted one trembling arm. He pointed back through the doorway toward the street—and Wade understood.

He leaped across the man's body to the front of the vestibule and looked into the night. Far down the block the red tail-light of a car was disappearing. As he watched, it was swallowed up by the rain-swept darkness.

He ran down the steps, crossed the pavement and stooped down. Tire tracks showed faintly where the water had been pressed back from the asphalt. The rain was obliterating them. There was no time for him to make a photo as an expert from the Bureau of Criminal Identification might have done. But he recorded the markings on the sensitive film of his brain. He would recognize them if he saw them again.

He turned back into the apartment building, running long fingers through rain-wet hair. The figure of the young man was still there, slumped flatter now. The staring eyes were closed, the bloodless lips still. Wade felt one of the stranger's hands, held it for a moment, and nodded to himself. There was no pulse beat. The young man was dead. Then he saw the bluish markings near one of the veins on the young man's wrists—and prickles of horror crept along his scalp. He bent closer and stared more intently. The markings had been made by the fangs of a snake!

IT was fifteen minutes later that a headquarters' car arrived in answer to his summons. In the meantime he had gone through the dead man's pockets and had established his identity. A wallet showed that his name was Thomas Bailey. A business letter indicated that he was employed by the Zeddler brothers, bankers who owned the controlling interest in the Central Savings Bank.

Wade straightened up as Detective Murphy of the radio car patrol came through the door with the tails of his wet slicker flapping around his legs. Outside, a cop named Sullivan sat at the wheel of the police cruiser chugging at the curb.

Murphy said: "What is it, Hammond, what's the trouble now? Have —"

He stopped speaking as his eye fell on the dead form of Bailey. His big face assumed the alert expression of a terrier watching a rat hole. "Who's the guy and who bumped him?"

"That's what I'd like to know," said Wade softly. "He was coming to see me. He must have had something to tell. But somebody got to him first. Look at his face, Murphy!"

Wade heard the big dick's sharply indrawn breath.

"It's a snake's head, Hammond—what the hell—" his voice trailed off.

Wade's voice was harsh. "There are marks on his wrist where a snake's teeth went in, Murphy. Telephone the medical examiner, and let Thompson know about it. I've found where he worked. I'm going up to get a coat and hat. You can leave Sullivan here—and when I come down we'll pay a visit to this man's bosses. They may know something about him."

All cars were the same to Wade Hammond. He sent the slim-bodied police cruiser roaring through the night streets till Murphy beside him gripped the top of the door for support.

"Take it easy, Hammond—the pavement's wet."

Wade's only answer was to send the car whizzing around the tail end of a lumbering milk truck. He spun the wheel, straightened out and went roaring down a long avenue. He was seeing the darkly despairing face of young Bailey as though it hung on a curtain before his eyes. He was seeing also that strange mark on his forehead and the disappearing tail-light of that mystery car.

The long avenue widened till handsome residences showed on either side. Elm trees dripped water from branches arching overhead. Wade slid the car in to the curb and leaped out.

"Here we are, Murphy. This is where the Zeddlers hang out."

The house that they entered was large and built of brick, and a sleek butler opened the door. Wade nudged Murphy.

"You do the honors," he said. "I'll watch—and get the lay of the land before I begin asking questions."

The big headquarters dick opened his slicker and let the butler see his badge.

"There's been a murder," he said. "We want to talk to your bosses."

The butler's eyelids flickered and it seemed that his face grew a shade paler.

"Mr. G. C. Zeddler is ill upstairs. Go into the drawing room. I'll speak to his brother, Mr. A. J."

Murphy snorted and muttered under his breath.

"Why do these rich guys use all the letters of the alphabet, Hammond?"

"That's another mystery, Murphy."

WADE lit a cigarette and smoked in silence till a step sounded in the doorway. A thick-set, broad-shouldered man entered. He had yellow eyes like a cat's and he stared at them sharply.

"What's this I hear about a murder?"

"I'm from headquarters," said Murphy showing his badge again. "Did a young man named Thomas Bailey work for you?"

A. J. Zeddler gave a visible start. He drew a nervous hand across his chin.

"Yes, we employed him as a secretary. Why, what's happened?"

"He was found dead. Somebody bumped him off."

"Good God!" The exclamation on Zeddler's lips seemed genuine. Wade stepped closer and spoke quietly.

"I found him in the vestibule of my apartment, Mr. Zeddler. There was a mark on his face—a snake's head. Do you know anything about it?"

It was almost as though some one had struck Zeddler in the face. His heavy features paled and he stepped back.

"The Cobra!" he said. "Yes—I know. I got a threatening letter yesterday. Here, I'll show it to you—wait a minute."

He left the drawing room with hurried steps. Wade turned. Murphy was standing silent, looking around. Rain beat a monotonous tattoo on the windows opening on the lawn. There were French doors between them with a balcony beyond.

Wade edged forward to look out, and as he did so he gave a sudden start. Murphy behind him cried out harshly—for at that instant the lights in the room had winked out.

It was surprising, spine-chilling. They stood in utter darkness except for the faint glow from the corridor outside—and Wade was suddenly conscious of a draft of cold air on his face. It was like the touch of dead fingers and, as he realized its significance, his blood seemed to freeze. Some one had opened the French doors to the balcony!

In the brief second that he listened there was the stealthy sound of movement in the room. He sensed that he was silhouetted against the light of the corridor doorway and he stepped aside with a sudden constricted feeling in his throat.

Some one made a grab for him then. Fingers of steel clutched his arm. He glimpsed dimly a ghostly, horrible shape moving down toward his wrist. Death seemed to be in the room with him. He twisted, struck out, and breath hissed through his teeth.

Murphy called out to him, hoarse with anxiety.

"Are you all right, Hammond? What's the matter—what's happened?" He heard the big dick's footsteps pounding toward him. He could not seem to speak; those steely fingers were reaching for him again.

A sense of nausea gripped him as though the danger that faced him was unspeakably loathsome. His balled fist struck a human body and he heard a grunt.

Then he heard Murphy leap upon the unseen attacker, a snarl in his throat.

"What the hell! Here—hands up—"

Murphy's words ended in a choking, terrible cry. It was a cry that seemed to freeze Wade Hammond's blood. He heard the sound of bodies struggling; heard breath whistling through clenched teeth and a man making smothered, ghastly noises in his throat.

HE reached for a match paper, tried to light one. But something knocked it from his fingers. He drew out his gun and fired blindly at the spot. The shots seemed to rip through the darkness of the room like the reports of a cannon and the walls beat the sound back deafeningly, into his ears.

"Murphy! Murphy!" he called.

He heard the French doors slam, heard some one go out.

Walking unsteadily, he crossed the room, groping for a wall switch. His feet bumped into something, something soft and yielding and the skin of his scalp tightened in horror.

He found the switch beside the door, pressed it and flooded the room with light. He saw then that there was another switch over by the French doors. But his eyes swung from it to the floor. Murphy lay there, his face contorted and his eyes fast glazing. He tried to speak, tried to move his lips, but no sound came from them. On his forehead was the hideous mark of the Cobra and he was clutching his left wrist tensely, clutching it where tiny bluish marks showed on the skin.

Wade ran to his side, stooped down. But Murphy's head fell back. The poison in his veins seemed almost as quick in its effect as a bullet fired from a gun. The death rattle sounded in his throat.

Wade rose and ran to the French doors, gripping his automatic in his hand. He flung them open, stepped out onto the balcony and felt the chill lash of rain in his face. A street light spread ghostly radiance across the wet grass of the lawn; but he could see nothing, no movement, and the water would destroy tracks. For seconds he stood there, trying to pierce the darkness while the rain beat against his face. Then he turned back into the room.

He saw A. J. Zeddler enter and give a gasp of horror at sight of Murphy's body.

"What is it? What's happened?" the banker said.

He held a card in his trembling fingers and on it Wade saw some words printed and the mark of the Cobra's head.

"He came here," said Wade harshly. "He got Murphy. Where's your telephone."

Zeddler jerked his thumb toward the outside hallway, and Wade ran across it, brushing by the butler who was standing white-faced near the door. He found the phone in the closet, called headquarters and turned in a report of the second murder. Zeddler was at his elbow when he came out. He spoke huskily.

"Doctor Vail, our family physician, will be here any minute to attend my brother who is ill upstairs. It's possible he can do something for that man in there."

Wade shook his head.

"Murphy's beyond help now. The Cobra struck quickly, but it was me he was after. Murphy died saving my life. He was as fine as they come."

As he stopped speaking, the doorbell rang and the butler, trembling still, opened it.

A TALL man with a pink face and a clipped blonde moustache stood in the threshold. He entered with a black case in his hand and looked from one to the other, seeming to sense their strained attitudes.

"Doctor Vail," said Zeddler huskily. "This is Hammond, of the police. There's been a murder here—a detective killed. And our secretary, Bailey, was killed tonight, too. The Cobra's been at work."

A shadow drifted across Vail's eyes.

"What about your brother? Was there any noise when all this happened?"

Zeddler started as if he remembered for the first time that there had been shots.

"Yes—good God! Go to George quickly."

The doctor turned and took the stairs three at a time.

"What's wrong with your brother?" said Wade.

"Heart trouble. He's been ill for days. Doctor Vail has been in constant attendance—just keeping him alive."

Wade nodded and left Zeddler. He prowled through the rooms on the lower floor until a siren outside told him that the police had arrived. An instant later steps sounded on the porch.

He went into the hallway to greet Inspector Thompson, owlish head of the homicide squad, who entered with three men and the assistant medical examiner. In brief words he told what had happened and saw the strained look that came over the old inspector's face at mention of Murphy's death. Behind a blunt exterior Thompson hid a soft heart.

He turned, giving crisp orders to his men, then entered the drawing room to view the dead man, with A. J. Zeddler at his heels. Wade, without asking permission, ascended the stairs and moved down a hallway toward a door that was slightly ajar and through the crack of which he saw a glow of light.

At sound of his steps Doctor Vail

suddenly appeared. His face was grave and he put a finger to his lips.

"Tonight's events may have serious consequences for my patient," he said, speaking in a hoarse whisper. "Mr. Zeddler is very low. I'm sending for a nurse."

Wade looked past the doctor toward a bed where a man lay. He heard stertorous breathing and saw bluish lips in a white face. But the man in the bed suddenly opened eyes which fixed themselves upon him and beckoned with one pale hand.

Wade entered the room, walking up to the bedside.

"Are you a detective?" asked the sick man.

"Unofficial," said Wade, "but I've helped the inspector more than once."

"Whoever you are," said Zeddler, "find this fiend who calls himself the Cobra. He sent my brother a threatening letter demanding money. And tonight I heard a man cry out downstairs followed by the sound of shots. What was it?"

Wade glanced at the doctor and Vail answered for him, lying adroitly.

"Nothing much, Mr. Zeddler. A detective your brother called in to investigate the extortion letter accidentally discharged a pistol."

The sick man lay back with a weary sigh and Wade turned toward the door. Then his eye was suddenly caught by something on Zeddler's bureau. It was a small thing, a paper of matches, but printed on it was the name of the Jungle Grove, a well-known night club. What member of the Zeddler household, he wondered, patronized that gay resort. Could it be that the sick man on the bed had been there? With a swift movement he pocketed the matches.

He went downstairs and spoke to Inspector Thompson, but the chief of the homicide squad shook his head in discouragement.

"We can't find anything, Hammond. No tracks—no clews. A man came through those French doors—but who was he and where did he go?"

"You've got me, chief." Wade's voice was low and his eyes were bright. He wasn't ready yet to formulate any theory. The whole thing was a mystery.

TWO interesting things occurred within the next twelve hours. The medical examiner turned in a report that snake venom of super strength had been found in the blood of both Bailey and Detective Murphy. And at four o'clock in the morning of the night that the murders had taken place Doctor Vail and the attending nurse announced the death of G. C. Zeddler.

His brother, A. J. Zeddler, was like a broken man when Wade arrived to make an exhaustive search of the grounds by daylight.

"George will be buried tomorrow," Zeddler said. "At his request he has not been embalmed and the services will be brief and simple." His voice suddenly took on a metallic harshness and he leaned toward Wade with blazing eyes.

"The Cobra is as responsible for George's death as though he had injected a dose of his foul poison into my brother's veins. Are the police imbeciles that they cannot find him?"

"We're doing what we can," Wade said.

He saw that the banker was close to the breaking point. The man's whole body was quivering; and yet he had the feeling that Zeddler might be holding something back—some secret information perhaps.

Wade saw the funeral notices the next day. The body of G. C. Zeddler was to be interred in the family mausoleum in Cypress Vale Cemetery.

Wade picked up the French type telephone in his apartment, and with a frown of concentration on his face he called police headquarters.

"Hammond speaking. It might be a good idea, chief, to have a man shadow A. J. Zeddler. He won't talk, but I think he's got ideas about the Cobra."

"Just what do you mean?"

"That's all, chief. Keep an eye on him—it can't do any harm."

Smiling grimly at the inspector's profane rejoinder he hung up. He spent three hours reading up on poisonous reptiles and their venom. At four that afternoon he called the Jungle Grove Night Club to see when it opened. At seven he presented himself at the door and drew the blonde hat-check girl aside. He pulled from his pocket the match paper he had taken from Zeddler's bureau and showed it to her. Her eyes were cold and she snapped her gum against pearly teeth, then parked it under the hat counter.

"Don't expect me to get excited over that, mister. They swipe lots of 'em here."

Wade grinned.

"Do you know the people who come in here?" he asked.

"Yeah, why?"

"I mean do you know them by name?"

"Some of 'em."

"Did you ever see one of the Zeddler brothers—the bankers?"

"Did I? Say—" The girl suddenly froze up on him and assumed a dead pan. "Who the hell are you, mister?"

Quietly Wade pulled out his wallet and displayed his special investigator's card signed by the police commissioner himself. As quietly he selected a crisp five-dollar bill and slipped it into the girl's fingers.

"Gee!" she said.

"Which Zeddler was it?" asked Wade.

"The younger one. 'George' she called him."

"Who?"

For an instant the girl hesitated, looking at the five-dollar bill.

"It's real money," she said. "What the hell! I mean Marlene Lunt—you know, the hot-cha girl who has an act here. That old bird was crazy about her. He used to come to see her often."

"When did he come last and what time does she go on?"

"About a week ago. Her act doesn't begin till ten. Anything else you'd like to know?"

"No, sister. You've earned that five dollars. Just keep quiet and look pretty."

She unparked her gum again, and Wade sauntered off. He got Marlene Lunt's address from the telephone book and sped to it in his roadster. It was a swanky apartment; but again Wade showed his special card and the superintendent admitted him. Miss Lunt didn't know she had a visitor till Wade buzzed her door.

She looked startled and not too pleased when he pushed past her into her apartment. She was a smoky-haired brunette with a voluptuous figure and eyes that could do things.

"Who are you?" she asked.

Wade stared around her apartment and saw a wardrobe trunk and three suitcases all packed up.

"Going away?" he asked.

"Yes, to the country."

Wade walked over to a table and picked up three steamship booklets setting forth the delights of European travel. He held them up.

"You were thinking of the water, weren't you?" he said.

"I changed my mind."

He moved up to the wardrobe trunk then and placed his finger on a big label that said: *S. S. Berengaria.* He looked at the clock. It was Saturday. The ship sailed at midnight.

The girl, Marlene Lunt, had suddenly turned pale. Her fingers shook as she lit a cigarette, and she started across the floor toward a desk. There was something feline and sinister about the swaying of her lithe hips and the sidelong glance she shot at Wade.

He stepped forward and caught her hand just as she drew a pearl-handled revolver from a drawer and tried to turn it on him. He twisted it from her fingers. She backed away panting, and breath hissed from between her teeth.

He caught her suddenly, thrust her into a closet and turned the key in the lock.

"Don't make any noise," he said. "Nobody will hear you anyway. I'll be back later."

FOG was creeping over the city as he went outside. It was almost as thick as the fog of mystery that surrounded the murder of Thomas Bailey and Detective Murphy.

Wade called up headquarters.

"Any news of A. J. Zeddler?" he asked.

"No. A man's still on the job shadowing him."

Wade hopped into his car and drove toward the banker's house. There might be some way to make Zeddler talk. If not, a fantastic idea was forming in Wade's mind, a murder theory —but there were pieces missing. Some one must know the answer.

He parked his car down the block, and a man moved out of the shadows and hissed at him. It was the headquarters dick assigned to the case.

"Keep out of sight, Mr. Hammond. Zeddler's just coming out now—getting into his car."

It was true. Ahead, in front of the house, the broad-shouldered figure of A. J. Zeddler was getting into a big limousine. But there was no chauffeur. Zeddler was taking the wheel himself.

Wade drew the detective, whose name was Van Brunt, back into the shadows.

"I'll handle this from now on."

He waited until the limousine rolled out of the drive and purred down the street. Then he caught Van Brunt's arm and pulled him forward. They sprinted for Wade's car.

Wade sent it forward with silently meshed gears, and for blocks he kept Zeddler's car in sight.

"Where the hell's he going?" whispered Van Brunt.

Wade didn't answer. His eyes were bright, staring ahead. They moved out of the city, out where houses were scarce and where there were lots of trees. Then Zeddler's car stopped in the shadows by a high wall. The lights flicked off.

"It's Cypress Vale Cemetery," Van Brunt said hoarsely, and Wade nodded.

He turned off his own lights and climbed out. Ahead a key grated in a lock and the massive iron gate of the cemetery swung open. Zeddler's broad-shouldered form disappeared through it.

With Van Brunt at his heels Wade followed. Their rubber-soled shoes made no noise. They kept in the shadows. Zeddler didn't know he was not alone. After a time Wade spoke softly.

"You stay here, Van Brunt. Come if you hear shots."

He glided off into the darkness and his face grew tense. A faint light had shown for an instant far ahead. On all sides of him the ghostly white shapes of gravestones rose. He picked his way among them toward the light that seemed to have no right to be there at this dark hour. It was ten o'clock and the cemetery had been closed since six.

Then he saw Zeddler again. The man was crouching now, creeping forward toward the light, his stocky form bent over like a great bear. There was something gleaming in his hand.

And Wade saw now where the light came from. It was from the partly open door of a huge mausoleum. Prickles of horror ran up his spine. He was not sure what ghoulish work was going on inside.

HE waited, fingering his own automatic; and he saw Zeddler close to the mausoleum's door. Then the door opened wider and Zeddler went inside.

Looking beyond Zeddler he saw a man with a dark handkerchief over his face prying open the lid of a coffin. The man was intent, bending over. But he rose as Zeddler spoke.

"Who are you and what are you doing?"

The banker's voice was hoarse, his whole body was trembling. The man with the handkerchief over his face stared with the cold ferocity of a killer. Then Zeddler cried out and swayed like a drunken man.

For the lid of the coffin moved aside and a figure rose from it to a sitting position. It was the figure of Zeddler's brother, G. C. Zeddler, whose death certificate had been made out twenty-four hours before. His face was pale now and contorted but he was alive.

A. J. Zeddler rushed forward furiously.

"What does this mean?"

He made a fierce clutch for the man in the handkerchief, but the man stepped back and drew something from behind him. Wade gasped in horror.

On the man's right hand was a glove in the form of a Cobra's head. The jaws worked with thumb and forefingers; sharp fangs showing, and before Wade could move he had plunged the fangs into the elder Zeddler's arm.

With a choking cry A. J. Zeddler staggered back. He tried to speak, failed and sank to the floor writhing. And at that moment the man sitting in the coffin spoke.

"You've killed him, Vail—you've killed my brother. I didn't intend that. You're a murderer!"

"Yes!" the single word hissed from behind the handkerchief, the snake's head on the man's right hand flashed out. But before it reached the figure in the coffin Wade's gun barked twice.

A cry of pain and fury came from the lips of the masked killer. The arm with the snake's head glove fell limply, crimson dripping from it. He backed into a corner, glaring at Wade. The handkerchief fell away and Wade saw the blond features of Doctor Vail. Then, with a movement so quick that Wade could hardly follow it, the doctor thrust his left hand between the snake's jaws and pressed them shut with his thumb.

A horrible, mirthless smile spread over his face. He looked at Wade, swaying slowly. Then his knees buckled under him.

The younger Zeddler was like a man stricken dumb. Then words came:

"I didn't plan for any killings. God help me, I didn't. It was Vail who did it. He would have killed me, too. I see it now. I'm a thief, but not a murderer. And see—here's the money. I can return it all."

Zeddler's voice rose wildly as he drew a satchel from between his legs in the coffin and held it up.

"The bank was failing—it would have crashed. I took the money from the vault—the last half million. I was going to leave America and go where no one would ever find me. Vail was paid for the part he played; the drugs that made it seem I was dead."

"What of Marlene Lunt?" said Wade sternly.

Zeddler moaning covered his face.

"You know about her then. She was beautiful—her beauty maddened me, drove me to crime. She was to meet me on the boat to-night. We were going away together."

"I know it," said Wade softly. "It's funny, Zeddler, what small things will sometimes trip up a criminal. That match paper on your bureau, for instance—I couldn't figure why a man with heart trouble would be going to the Jungle Grove. It made me investigate—started me on the right track.

"I hear Detective Van Brunt coming now. You'll stay in prison a long time, Zeddler. It's too bad you didn't put all that brainwork into building up your bank. But I'm glad the depositors aren't going to lose that half million anyway.

"And I'm glad, too, there won't be any more biting with that Cobra's head. Vail had distilled venom stuck in the fangs. He killed your secretary when the young man grew suspicious and came to me. It was Vail's car I saw disappearing that night. And when your brother began to figure things out and came here he killed him, too. He was a murderer at heart with a sense of the dramatic—and there's no telling how many more people he might have killed if he hadn't been stopped."

Satan's Hoof

Leaves a Trail of Mangled Murder

"Ken Carter" Novelet

By NORVELL PAGE

Author of "Gallows Ghost," "Statues of Horror," etc.

Sinister superstition held sway over that New Orleans race track. And the curse reached out and touched Detective Ken Carter while on a visit here. He was shunned, feared; couldn't even get a bellboy to handle his luggage. Then came the mighty tread of Satan's Hoof, with its wake of mangled murder. Ken Carter was still feared—but not shunned by the bloody finger of suspicion.

Carter felt fear feathers brush his spine

CHAPTER I

THE MAD COLONEL

THE lightning blazed blue white, glittered on rain that sheeted across the taxi windows. On its heels the thunder crashed like a cannon, a typical New Orleans downpour. Ken Carter saw with relief the hazy yellow lights of the Royale Hotel. The taxi swerved to the curb.

Carter swung his lithe, long body through the Niagara that poured down between the taxi and the marquee, looked around for a bellboy to take his bag. There was none. Frowning, Carter lugged his heavy suitcase toward the door. He caught a fleeting glimpse of a black face.

A boy ducked out and leaped for his bag. Once more lightning, like an unbelievably huge flashlight, poured electric glare into the street. The boy snatched back inside again.

Carter cursed and slapped open the door on the verge of harsh speech, then saw that fear trembled in every inch of the boy's coal black body, actual paralyzing fear. But fear of what? Carter frowned and strode long-legged, high wide shoulders squared beneath his tailored brown topcoat, across to the marble counter behind which a dapper, wax-mustached clerk smiled. The huge gilt and crimson lobby seemed dusty.

The Royale was not the finest hotel in New Orleans, but its cuisine was noted and Carter appreciated good food. He scrawled his name across the register and the clerk dinged a bell with a slapping hand.

Carter followed the black boy, lugging his bag now, toward the elevator. An upright old man with a clean-shaven flushed face and jet-black hair sweeping back from heavy brows smiled at him and moved into his path. Carter stopped, peering at him inquiringly. He heard a thump and looked about in time to see the boy, having dropped his bag, scuttle across the lobby and behind the elevator cages. His face, glancing back, was panic-stricken.

Carter was thoroughly angered now. He said, "If that rain would let up for ten minutes, be damned if I wouldn't go to another hotel. These bellboys are absolutely crazy."

The welcoming smile faded from the florid face of the upright old man. He frowned his heavy brows.

"It's the curse," he muttered and a worried fright crept into his face. Slowly he forced himself to smile again, though his eyes remained clouded. "Thank you, Mr. Carter," he said, "for coming so promptly. If you will come up to my room we can go into the thing in more detail."

Carter frowned, "I'm sorry. I don't understand."

"I'm Colonel Hartain," the man said, "Colonel Jove Hartain."

Carter still stared at him. The hotel must be full of mad people, he thought, these pesky bellhops who jumped at a whisper and dashed away, and now—

"I'm sorry," said Carter, "the name doesn't mean a thing to me."

"Then why are you here?" Colonel Hartain's voice sharpened.

Carter said calmly, "I came down for a vacation."

"When did you leave New York?"

"I really can't see that it's any concern of yours," Carter said, turned his shoulder on the man and snapped his fingers for a bellboy. He might have been alone in the Sahara Desert, a paralyzed deaf mute for all the attention he attracted from the bellhops.

Colonel Hartain's voice at his elbow was harsh. "You're very rude, young sir. If I didn't need your help so badly, I'd have nothing further to do with you. I can only assume that you did not get my telegram."

Carter said without turning his head, "I did not."

Hartain moved around in front of him. There was a pleading in the depths of his pale blue eyes that was not evident on his face.

"But you will help me?" the Colonel asked. "They've put the curse of the Devil's Hoof on me. They've frightened my stable boys so that almost all of them have quit. There isn't a negro in the hotel who doesn't run when I come near."

CARTER whirled suddenly toward him. "Then I suppose you're responsible," he said, "for my not being able to get a bag upstairs."

The man nodded his head ruefully. "I reckon so."

Carter said, "Look here, I don't mean to be rude, but I came down here for a vacation, to have a bit of a fling at the races, and I can't take any case right now. If you like I'll wire for some of my men to come down here. But I, myself, can have absolutely nothing to do with it."

The man put his veined puckered old hand on Carter's arm and Ken saw for the first time that he carried a cane in his left hand and leaned heavily upon it. He concealed it half behind his leg, as if ashamed of his infirmity.

"You don't understand," the man said. "I've told you I'm Colonel Hartain, Colonel Jove Hartain. I have a racing stable and some enemies of mine have put the curse of the Devil's Hoof upon me. They're trying to force me out of the big race."

Carter said firmly, "I'm sorry, but that's the best I can do."

He saw anger stir in the colonel's face, stepped back a pace, picked up his handbag and started for the elevator. The negro boy slammed the door in his face and although the car was empty it shot upward. Carter cursed and dropped his bag upon the floor. He heard a sharp footfall behind him. A rasping voice, hoarse with anger, grated in his ear.

"Traitor!" It was Hartain's old voice, vitalized by rage. "You've sold out to my enemies, have you?"

Carter whirled just in time. Hartain, his face crimsoned by anger, his pale blue eyes flashing, had raised his heavy cane and it was swinging in a swift arc toward Carter's head. Carter skipped lightly aside, seized the cane as it whistled down and wrenched it from the man's hand.

Hartain took another step toward Carter, then his left leg gave way under him and he collapsed on the floor. Still no one came near them. There wasn't a negro on the floor. A few men standing remotely on the far side of the room stared, but none offered to interfere.

Carter bent in commiseration over the feeble old man lying helpless on the floor, put his hands under the older man's arms and lifted him. Hartain struck out ferociously with his fist at Carter's face. Then someone small slipped between the two men and Carter looked down with surprise upon blue-black hair, upon a small head that did not come to his chin. A girl's low voice came in upon their anger.

"Father, father," it said. "You mustn't act this way. Stop now, father. It isn't good for your heart, you know."

Above the gleaming blue-black of the girl's head Hartain still glared at Carter, but as the girl continued to talk his anger faded and he dropped his pale blue eyes.

"Come, father, come upstairs with me. It's getting late. You must rest."

The man said, "All right, Frankie," and with a hand upon her shoulder began to limp slowly away.

Carter strode after them on positive feet and said, "Just a minute please."

THE girl stopped and anger darkened her black eyes as she turned upon him. Her mouth was red as ripe cherries and scornful. She said sharply, "I want nothing to do with you. Tussling with an old man."

Ken Carter bowed ironically. "I can appreciate your viewpoint, being a man of sentiment," he said. "But I do object to being hit over the head with a cane even by an old man. However—" he proffered the cane extended over his crooked arm like a sword—"I gladly surrender the spoils of war."

The girl took the cane with her left hand, but the scorn did not leave the smooth olive oval of her face. She turned away and Carter watched her march away, proud and erect, every line of her sweetly curved body radiating her scorn and anger, as she helped her old father across the lobby and up slow stairs.

Carter glanced rapidly about him. The bellboys still were not in evidence. Angrily he strode across and slapped the marble counter.

"Listen," he said, "either you get your bellboys in hand, get them to take my grip upstairs and operate the elevators, or something worse than a Devil's Hoof, or curse, or whatever it is, is going to descend on their benighted heads."

The clerk was pale behind the pointed ends of his waxed mustache. He said, "Yes, sir! Certainly, sir! Right away, sir!" and ducked out under the counter himself, skipped across the lobby to a small corridor and herded out a bellhop, talking at him vehemently as the two crossed back to Carter.

The bellhop rolled white-rimmed eyes, but took the bag. He kept a good ten feet ahead of him all the way to the elevator where he stood in a remote corner. Carter eyed him speculatively. His fright was genuine, but the cause of it was obscure to Carter. He was familiar with voodoo, but this Devil's Hoof was something new.

Carter spoke so abruptly the boy jumped.

"Do you know anything about the Devil's Hoof?"

The negro's agitation increased. He glanced sideways out of his big eyes, then jerked them hurriedly away. His teeth began to chatter. "'Deed I don't sir. 'Deed I don't. I don't know nothin' about nothin'."

The car stopped and the boy skipped out quickly, darted ahead. Half between anger and amusement, Carter followed.

"Are you sure, Rastus," he called after the boy, "that you don't know what the Devil's Hoof is?"

Carter heard a gentle chuckle and whirled to stare at a man who stood in the open door of a room.

"I suppose you have met Colonel Hartain," the man said.

Carter nodded. "I did. There isn't a boy in the hotel now who will come anywhere near me since I did."

He stared into the face of the man. It was quizzical. The hair was snowy and long, and he wore an imperial and a mustache, white, too. He chuckled again.

"I'm Colonel Whittier Jackson," he said and Carter proffered his card.

"I reckon I could tell you about the Devil's Hoof if you're interested," Colonel Jackson said.

"I wish you would."

"Well," said the colonel, "it's like this. The negroes long have had a superstition that when it thundered it was the devil riding his horse across the skies against a host of angels. Lately there's been a new twist to the thing. The door of Hartain's stable was found smashed with a hoof mark upon its center. A hoof mark larger than any horse known, even bigger than a percheron, and the story got around mysteriously that Hartain was cursed.

"He has the idea that it's some trick being worked by racing enemies of his, but the negroes take it much more seriously. The other night the door of his room was smashed, crushed in the middle by a huge hoof. The print was plain on the soft wood and naturally the negroes are somewhat worked up about it. I think the Colonel is worried too."

CARTER muttered, "The Devil's Hoof, eh? Well, I hope it stays 'way from my do'."

He laughed and the other man laughed, too. "That goes for me, too," he said. "I have a few horses myself."

Abruptly Carter felt that eyes were upon him, and glancing over the Colonel's shoulder, looked into the green eyes of a woman. She was standing where the bright overhead light shone down on red hair that was like fire in the dull sobriety of the hotel room. She had drawn about her a plainly cut negligee of heavy green satin that emphasized every inch of her superbly mature body.

She moved slowly forward as she met Carter's eyes, neither hurried nor slow, but with a luxurious lounging pace of sheer graceful animality.

"This is my wife," the Colonel said. "My dear, this is Mr. Ken Carter of New York. A detective, he tells me."

Carter bowed slowly, his face expressionless.

The woman dragged out words. "So this is Ken Carter. Boy! Have I heard of you!" Her voice was a drawl, but it was not a honeyed Southern accent. It was a drawl from farther north where Ken Carter was much more intimately known—and feared.

She lifted her arm with slow grace, offered a tapered white hand to Carter. The slashed long sleeve of her negligee parted over it with a startling sense of nakedness.

"You do not come from the South," Carter said.

The woman let her head sink forward slightly. Turning her green eyes upward to stare at Carter beneath the smooth black line of her brows.

"You seem to know everything, mister," she said, "and you're a regular devil with the ladies, I guess."

Carter smiled grimly. "Then you better beware of my hoof."

Out of the corner of his eye, Carter saw Jackson's face grow long, a startled glance flickering across his face.

The woman only laughed lazily, tilting back her head. Her throat line was exquisite.

"Look in on us sometime," she said, and the colonel also extended his invitation.

Carter bowed again and went on, found his boy had thrust the key into the lock of his door and fled. His bag rested by the entrance.

Carter stared down at it a moment, then shrugged and unlocked his door. It was too late now to hunt up another hotel, but in the morning he would certainly leave this place, find headquarters where superstition did not have quite so wide a sway.

Grumbling to himself, Carter pressed open the door and stepped inside. He reached out a hand fumbling for the switch and suddenly the lights went on. He blinked at the glare, and looked into the red-masked faces of two men who leveled revolvers.

CHAPTER II

HELD PRISONER

CARTER stared from one man to the other, from one gun muzzle to the other and said casually, "To what do I owe the honor of this visit?"

The men's eyes, glittering through the slits of masks he realized now were made with bandana handkerchiefs, told Carter nothing. He said cheerfully, "You won't mind if I remove my hat? I was brought up quite well and it makes me uncomfortable to wear my hat in the house."

He took his hat in his right hand and tossed it into the air. It whirled and, descending accurately—Carter's long years of juggling on the stage stood him in good stead now—it flopped squarely into the face of one gunman.

In the instant it settled, Carter dropped to the floor, plunging against the legs of the second man. The man did not fire, but hacked down savagely with his gun barrel. The blow caught Carter on the shoulder. Sharp pain shot through him. He jerked the gunman's legs and they went down in a huddle.

The lean detective sprang immediately to his feet, snatching for his armpit gun. But he got no chance to use it. The second gunman had flicked aside the hat which had blinded him and rushed with a down-slashing gun.

Carter dodged that with the swift split-second balance of movement that his juggling training long ago had given him. He drove his left fist into the pit of the man's stomach. He hurled him back a full two feet, strangling, gasping for breath. Once more Carter grabbed for his gun.

His feet were jerked out from under him. He threw his head forward to escape a blow on his back when he struck the floor. Almost before he landed, the still panting gunman he had punched leaped feet first toward him.

Carter twisted in the air, rolled, dodged the feet. The gun slashed down again, glancing off the back of Carter's head. He stumbled to his feet, half dazed, jerking up almost with a reflex action of his roll. He was reeling. The room was swaying before him. His gun was in his hands now and staggering through squinted eyes that refused to focus properly, he leveled it at the man who crouched before him.

"Hands up!" he ordered grimly. "You don't dare shoot, but I do."

Carter heard a soft movement behind him. He tried to whirl, but the daze of that terrific blow to his head was still upon him and his feet stumbled. Another blow fell hard and this one did not glance. Carter sank with a low moan, unconscious to the floor . . . .

When Ken Carter recovered consciousness, he was hunched down on the floor in the tonneau of an automobile that was bounding over a rough road to a continuous accompaniment of lightning flashes and rolling thunder as if the machine bumped tireless wheels over cobblestones.

Carter, opening his eyes slowly, peered about him in the darkness. Lightning rimmed the dark figure of one man on the back seat. Carter saw a gun in his hand. Cautiously Carter moved his hands. Bonds held them and they were powerful and tight. He could not make them give a fraction of an inch.

His feet were tied, too. Carter struggled quietly against the ropes for a while and finally, finding it did no good, demanded. "What's the meaning of this?"

Instantly his face was painted with white light from a hand torch.

"Come around, have you?" the man jeered.

"What is the meaning of this?" Carter demanded again.

The man chuckled behind the hand torch.

Carter's teeth set grimly. "Crooks don't get away with treating me like this."

The man laughed again in the darkness. It was a giggle, a high and crazy tittering, but there was nothing funny in it. It made chills creep up and down Carter's back.

"Mister," said the man, "just you rest easy about that. You're not going to have any chance at all to make us pay up."

Carter said grimly, "So it's murder, is it?"

The man giggled again and the sound of it got under Carter's skin and made it crawl.

Suddenly the auto lurched more violently than usual, skidded in a half circle and slid to a stop.

"Well, here we are," the driver called back and the man on the back seat threw open the door at Carter's feet, then piled out into the driving rain. Carter made out a faint yellow light. Then lightning danced across the sky and he saw vividly a decrepit cabin built of logs and slabs of wood, with a sagging roof that cringed beneath the lash of wind-tossed tree limbs.

The yellow oblong of a door opened and there was a vague huddle of shadows before it. Presently the men came trooping back again, a third person with them. A giant of a man bent over Carter, caught Carter beneath the arms and with no apparent effort lifted him out of the car, slung him across his shoulder like a sack of meal and splashed off again toward the cabin.

Carter was immediately wet to the skin from the flailing rain. Rage consumed him. He was furious at this ill treatment, angry at the absolute craziness, the inexplicability of all that had happened, but he did not take it out in futile threats. He had warned the men once.

SUDDENLY yellow light fell around him and the best of the rain stopped. He was inside the cabin. The man who carried him let him gently down upon the floor against the wall. Two other men tramped in and the door shut. Carter glanced quickly about. Obviously a negro cabin. A rickety table against the wall, boxes and a couple of feeble chairs completed the room's furnishings, except for the straw pile in the corner which was a bed. On the table a dirty-globed oil lamp burned smokily. The dampness drove odors out of the walls, out of the very floor. The cabin smelled like an animal den.

The two men who had brought Carter still clung to their red masks, but the third man, the negro whose cabin this apparently was, had not bothered to cover his face. It was savage in the extreme, beetling low brows, a flat nose, thick lips.

The giant who had carried Carter threw a clean blanket, got from heaven knew where, over Carter's body and peered down at him, for once without that insane giggle.

"You'll do lots better if you don't try to escape," he admonished. "Just you stay quiet and in an hour or two, maybe come morning, you'll be turned loose again."

The man strode over to the other two, talked in an undertone, then plunged out into the rain. Carter presently heard the motor, heard it fade away, then nothing but the beat of the rain. The two men left behind built a small fire of chips on a stone hearth and crouched over it, talking in mutters.

Carter gradually let his head sink forward, and assumed the deep regular breath of slumber and waited with slitted eyes. The bestial-faced negro glanced toward him presently and grunted words like animal sounds. The other man peered at him and the negro yawned prodigiously, and flopped on the pallet.

Carter could have laughed aloud with triumph. His eyes darted excitedly about the room, seeking something with which to sever his bonds. They lighted finally upon an old dull hatchet against the wall.

Softly, Carter began to snore, still keeping his watch upon the man who crouched by the fire. He was hunched down on his hams, head sagging, his hands clasped behind his neck in the forlorn posture of primordial man. Carter steeled himself to patience and waited an hour of slow seconds before he dared to stir.

Then, finally, he began to wriggle snakelike across the floor toward that hatchet. It took ten minutes of cautious effort to reach it, then Carter backed up against the wall and groped for the edge of the blade with bound hands. It was the work of a few instants then to saw through the rope.

CARTER had barely finished when the negro on the pallet reared up on an eblow, glaring across the room with his small animal eyes. Instantly he was up and charging across the cabin. Carter had no time to unbind his feet. His hand snaked behind him, seized the hatchet and, with a thrust, he was leaning against the wall on his tied feet, the hatchet poised.

With his feet free, Carter would have felt himself a match even for this powerful negro, but as he was and with his arms still half numb from their lashing, he would not stand a chance. Gripping the hatchet, he shouted peremptorily:

"Stop there or I'll bury this hatchet between your eyes!"

The negro hesitated in his rush. Carter leaned forward, the hatchet ready to hurl.

"The blade will strike the bone between those eyes of yours," he went on, "but it won't stop there. It will bite into your brain. And after that you won't know anything. You will be dead."

The negro was nonplussed by this form of attack and he wavered, trying to decide what to do, those small eyes of his shifting from side to side.

Carter suddenly leaped forward, jumping with both feet at once, and brought the head of the hatchet slamming behind the negro's ear. It was a blow to kill an ordinary man, but the negro did not even fall at once. He swayed, while his eyes glared, lost his balance and tumbled. The sound of his fall jerked the second negro to his feet with a loud cry. He snatched a gun from his pocket.

Carter was wavering, unbalanced on his feet. As his second captor leveled his gun he dropped to his knees. The bullet whined above his head and before the man could aim again Carter had hurled the hatchet with the deadly precision of his years of juggling. It circled once in the air and struck on its blade between the man's eyes.

His head was hurled back upon his shoulder, his back arched and he pitched backwards, striking the stone fireplace as he fell. The gun exploded again and fell from his nerveless hand.

Carter dragged himself on hands and knees across the room, snatched up the gun, and with it resting beside him, went rapidly to work upon his bonds. The huge negro he had struck with the blunt end of the hatchet was stirring again, legs twitching like those of a dog in a dream. The leg-rope knots were stubborn.

The negro got up dazedly, touched his head with his hands and began to stare about as Carter finally loosed the rope.

Carter's feet were numb. He managed with great difficulty to manipulate them into a walk until he could lean against the wall, clutching the pistol in his right hand. The negro reeled to his feet, crouching, his powerful shoulders hunched, fingers opening and closing menacingly and his small glittering eyes flicking about the room toward the body of his companion, the hatchet blade embedded in its skull.

A whimpering moan came from his throat, his huge teeth were bared by thick lips. He began to run back and forth like a dog and suddenly he was upon the body of his companion and had wrenched the bloody hatchet clear. He held it high and charged.

Carter fired squarely into the man's body. He grunted, checked, and charged on, jerked down his mighty arms with the hatchet aimed at Carter's head. The detective ducked sideways, firing again, but his numbed feet played him false and he swayed as he pulled the trigger.

THE bullet went wide and smashed the lamp on the far side of the room. There was an instant's darkness, then the odor of kerosene permeated the room and suddenly flame leaped up, enveloping half the wall of the cabin.

Outside wind and rain still whooped and the distant mutter of thunder continued. The wind moaned into the cabin and the flame danced and quivered in an ecstasy of light.

The negro's hatchet, missing Carter by inches, had imbedded itself in the wall and he struggled furiously, whimpering little moaning sounds from his mouth, as he fought to wrench it free.

Carter backed on stumbling feet toward the door, but he was still five feet from it when the negro wrenched the hatchet free again. Blood was bubbling from the wound in his body where Carter's bullet had pierced. He pressed the palm of his huge left hand against it and lunged once more toward Carter with the raised hatchet. This time Carter did not dodge. He took careful aim and sent three bullets crashing in quick succession through the man's head.

The terrific impact of the bullets thrust the man's head backward. His mouth opened in a strangled cry and his huge body thudded to the floor with a crash that made the cabin shake. The hatchet blade buried itself almost at Carter's foot. The lean detective drew back from the fearful corpse of the negro. The back of his head was almost blown away by the bullets.

Flames lit the cabin luridly now. The entire far wall was ablaze. Choking smoke whirled about him. Carter drew a handkerchief from his pocket, wiped clean the gun of fingerprints and flung it on the body of the man he had killed with the hatchet. He spun about and reeled from the cabin.

Circulation was rapidly returning to his feet now and the process of walking soon restored them to full efficiency. A glimmer of lightning lit the horizon fleetingly and the lurid red glare of the flames, spouting now through the flimsy roof of the cabin, sent their glare after him, guided his feet toward the road.

Suddenly Carter stopped, staring. Was an automobile parked there? Could it be that his captor had returned as he had promised? Suddenly the blinding light of a hand torch thrust into his eyes and the high giggling laugh of the giant smote his ears.

"Better stand right there," the voice said, "I got a gun in my hand and it might go off. That was a right nice piece of work you did back there in the cabin," and the giggling laughter rose again. "Saved me having to split up money with them."

Carter could see nothing of the man behind the broad gleam of the flashlight.

"Now 'spose you turn your back toward me," the man went on, behind the light. Carter had no choice but to obey. "Now lie down on your face."

Anger stirred in Carter. There was muck beneath his feet. His shoes sucked in it when he moved.

"You might as well do it," the high voice went on, "or I'll have to smack you down and do it anyway."

Fairly trembling with anger, Carter finally obeyed, flopping down upon his knees and then upon his chest in the oozy mud. Instantly a weight flung upon his back, driving his face into the wet slop, smothering him. He held his breath, struggling, but the weight of the man upon his back was overwhelming.

Face to face, Carter might have contended with him, but in the mud with this huge weight upon his shoulders, he could do little more than writhe. His arms were seized and bound, then his legs and, half strangled, he was carried like a sack of oats across the man's shoulder to the car and thrown upon the rear seat.

For good measure, then, his captor strung a rope about the rear of the car and about Carter's throat, holding him securely in the back seat.

The man climbed in front, flashed the light back on him and tittered again his high mad laughter.

"I reckon that rope around your throat might be rather uncomfortable going to town," the man said, "but I reckon it won't kill you and I don't want you rising up behind me like you rose up behind that black boy in the cabin."

Uncomfortable? Good Lord, the rope would strangle him!

CHAPTER III

Arrested for Murder

THE rope didn't choke him, but the ride back to town was a nightmare that Carter would remember all his life. Arms bound helplessly behind him, a rope tight about his throat, binding him to the cushion, and the light car bounding along the rutted road, bouncing him against the rope, jerking it tight about his throat, half strangling him, rubbing his throat raw until the mere touch of the rope was a torture.

A lesser man would have cried out in pain, but Carter grimly closed his mouth and resolved that the men behind this abduction should pay and pay heavily for what they had done to him. What was the reason behind it all, he could not discover. But two had paid already and the rest—

It was all utterly mad. First, Colonel Hartain stopping him in the lobby of the hotel, flying into a rage over his mere refusal to take the case; the negroes about the building terrified by a ridiculous superstition; then, entering his room and having guns shoved into his face; being kidnapped —and all for no apparent reason.

Carter clenched his jaws, set himself grimly to stand the torture of that rope about his throat and waited. At last they hit the comparatively smooth streets of the city and Carter was driven to a house in the black quarter into which his captor carried him. He dumped Carter on the floor, cut his bonds, and sprang back with a leveled gun.

The room was dimly lighted by an oil lamp. Carter rolled over. Wrists and legs were almost useless. A ring around his throat burned intolerably from the chafe of the rope.

He sat slowly erect, massaging his wrists. His clothing was thick with mud, his face smeared. His captor, eyes glittering, said, "You can wash up now, Mr. Carter, if you want to."

"Thanks so much," Carter said. His mouth was a thin line. He got up on numbed feet and threw a swift glance around. A bowl of water rested on the table against the wall. Carter inspected it and spotted a suitcase, his own, beside it. He frowned, whirled about. The giant was crouched by the door, the gun leveled.

"There ain't no windows in here," the man said softly. "There's only this here door and I'm going to be outside it. As long as you stay in here you can do anything you like. If you open the door, I'll shoot."

Carter glared at the man, saying nothing, and the giant whisked out the door. Ugly light glowed deep in Carter's eyes. His tall, broad-shouldered frame was taut with anger. But he decided to make the best of the situation for the present. At least he could clean up.

He turned gladly toward the bowl of water, washed and quickly donned fresh clothing from his suitcase. In its bottom he found his two guns. Carter frowned; his peaked brow shot a glance toward the closed door. Swift examination showed the guns were loaded and in working order. He made his throat comfortable with a vaseline-coated bandage, put out the light and, guns in hand, tensed to the door. He snatched it open. The street outside was empty.

Carter's swift keen eyes searched the houses near by. No, there was no one watching. This was the queerest part of the entire kidnapping. Frowning heavily, Carter grabbed up his suitcase and abandoning his dirty clothing, strode from the place, walked rapidly along the street until he spotted a taxicab, climbed in and ordered that he be taken to the Gibson House. He thought grimly to himself that he had had enough of the Royale to last him a long time. He was fond of good food, but there were limits to his endurance.

He deposited his grip at Gibson without even waiting to look at his room, returned to his taxi and ordered, "Police headquarters."

He walked in and strode, grim faced, up to the desk.

He said, "My name is Kenneth Carter."

The sergeant stared at him with widening eyes in a flat pasty face. He leaped to his feet and signaled two policemen lounging about the room and they crossed swiftly and closed in on either side of Carter. The sergeant's voice was shrill and excited.

"It's a lucky thing you decided to surrender, Carter," he said. "Fighting my men would be dangerous business."

Carter frowned. "Surrender? What do you mean?"

The sergeant said shrilly, "You'll find out what I mean," and came out from behind the counter, got on his uniform cap and called through a back doorway.

"Hi, Jeb, come on out and take charge here. Gotta take a guy somewhere," and with the sergeant ahead and the policeman on each side, Carter was marched out of the building.

"What's the meaning of all this?" Carter demanded. "I demand to know or I won't go another step."

THE sergeant turned toward him, his pasty face still excited and his voice shrill. He said, "I advise you, Mr. Carter, not to make any trouble. Maybe it's all a mistake. I don't know. But anyway you got to go over here to be identified by a woman. If she can't identify you, it's all right."

Carter said, "I won't go anywhere until I know what this is all about."

The sergeant looked him up and down. He said, "I don't want to do it, but if you force me to I'll put the handcuffs on you and there'll be a warrant, too."

Carter frowned, "What I'm trying to find out," he said, "is what the warrant would say."

"The warrant," said the sergeant, his shrill voice almost breaking, "will charge murder."

Carter sliced the air with the side of his hand. "You're completely mad," he said. "This is the damnedest, craziest town I was ever in in my life. I came here to report that I was kidnapped in my room, banged over the head with a gun and half strangled to death, and you say I've done murder. It's ridiculous."

"Ridiculous or not," said the sergeant, "you've got to go over and see this woman."

Carter slammed into the car. "Okay, okay, I'll go. But I warn you it's going to be a long time before New Orleans hears the end of this case."

He sat like a ramrod in the back of the car between the sergeant and one of the policemen, while the other cop climbed into the front seat of the flivver which bounced them over the streets.

The sergeant evinced interest in Carter's story of kidnapping, but the detective refused to say anything at all about the case.

"To hell with you," he said. "You've made the pinch, now see if you can make it stick. You're all going to look like fools before I get through with you."

The sergeant looked at Carter with eyes pale in a pasty face, but only leaned forward and spoke to the driver.

"The Royale, fast."

CARTER cursed strenuously. He was fed up on the Royale. He was fed up on New Orleans and the superstitious blacks. He said vehemently, "I suppose that damned Devil's Hoof has kicked somebody in the slats."

The sergeant said softly, "Oh, you *suppose* that, do you?"

"Oh, go to hell," Carter sighed wearily and settled his broad shoulders back into the corner of the seat to rest. He touched his throat with solicitous fingers.

The police car whined a soft siren down Market street, whirled into Fortescue, spun another corner and snubbed up short before the Royale.

Two police swung out and stood alertly, with their sharp eyes on Carter as he wearily stepped to the pavement. He went quietly toward the door with the sergeant at his elbow and the two guards trailing.

A negro peered out with startlingly white eyes, whirled with a muffled shout and ran inward. Carter's eyes went ugly. He had had enough of this business. They marched on across the lobby and people's heads went together in whispers like the sibilance of a rising storm on the grass plains.

The sergeant ushered Carter into an elevator that creaked upward and the operator cringed away with shrinking shoulders from the nearness of Carter. The lean detective smiled grimly, his long face sardonic, and stepped nearer the negro. Tremors raced over boy's body.

He stopped the car, slammed back the gate and his sigh of relief at Carter's exit would have been ludicrous except for the mounting irritation that gripped the detective.

"How much longer is that mummery going to continue?" he demanded.

He got no answer, but the sergeant

knocked at a door. A man's subdued voice called, "Come in."

The police stepped aside for Carter to go in first. He stared at each of them individually, then shrugged, put his hand to the knob and thrust open the door, took a long stride into the room, then another.

A girl started to her feet, jabbed a stiffened arm with a finger pointing at his face.

"That's the man!" she cried.

Her voice broke, but she stood white-faced and stared at him with black hating eyes, the daughter of the man Carter called in his mind "the mad colonel," Jove Hartain.

Carter frowned at her.

"So what?" he demanded between his teeth.

"Do you deny that you quarreled with her father?" the sergeant demanded.

Carter looked slowly around the room. Colonel Jackson with his pale face framed in white hair, his soft white mustaches and imperial, stood just behind the girl, looking at him with reproach. A diminutive youth with a wizened, freckled face and a rakish hat set on his head as if he never took it off, glared at him from the side of the room.

The frown on the detective's long face deepened. He ran his hand slowly up over the twin peaks of his forehead into his dull hair, as always when he was worried.

"Well, are you going to talk here or at police headquarters?" the sergeant demanded.

CARTER whirled toward him, his demeanor unchanged except for the anger deep in his gray cool eyes. The two police suddenly snatched out pistols. He Ignored them.

"Listen, Two-bits," he told the sergeant. "I've been pretty decent about this business so far. I came to you to report that I had been kidnapped and maltreated by three men, abducted from my room in this hotel. You immediately insisted that I come here and gave the lie to my story.

"Now you are making veiled threats. You can change your tone and act decently or I'll talk neither here nor at headquarters and you'll find yourself in the hottest water you've ever touched the tip of your finger to."

The sergeant bristled, thrust his well-fattened belly forward and glared at Carter, but there was nothing threatening in the detective's manner. He had spoken quietly with an air of being able to fulfil exactly what he prophesied, and the police officer hesitated. He blinked his pale eyes, screwed up his pasty face in worriment. Slowly the truculence went out of him.

"It's just that you don't know the seriousness of the thing," the sergeant said finally.

The deep voice of Colonel Jackson cut in. "Mr. Carter is right, Sergeant Knowles. You have no call to be so peremptory. Mr. Carter, though, I think you'd be wise to answer a few questions."

Carter bowed stiffly. "I'm not objecting to answering a few questions, but I do object to this—" he shrugged and let it go. "You were asking if I quarreled with Colonel Hartain. I most certainly did not. He stopped me in the lobby and assumed that I had come in answer to his telegram asking my help. I had come for a rest and told him so. I refused to take some case which seemed chiefly made up of negro superstitions, and he became angry and tried to strike me with his cane. I took it away from him. That's all there was to that."

"My father believed this man had sold out to his enemies. I think he was right," the girl's low vibrant voice put in.

Carter turned toward her. Her small, shapely body was held rigidly. Her eyes still blazed with hate.

"I think I was quite nice about the thing, as a matter of fact," he told her. "Being a man of sentiment I did not like to inflict my anger on an old man and especially—" he bowed with a grave face—"a man with so charming a daughter."

The girl took three swift steps forward and slapped Carter. Her face was livid with anger and Carter's matched it.

"Even though," he continued in an utterly calm voice, "I considered the man completely mad."

The girl slapped him again, clenched her fists and beat on his unyielding chest until Colonel Jackson, his kindly old face worried, took her by the arm gently and led her away. She burst into tears then, dropping her head against his shoulder.

"Frances is kind of worked up," the old man's deep voice intoned.

"So I gathered," said Carter drily. "I considered her father mad because he credited some silly superstition or another about the Devil's Hoof, the sort apparently possessed by a super-Percheron which smashed the door of his stable and afterwards split the door of his room here.

"The negroes apparently had become convinced of it, too, for from the moment that he spoke to me I could not get a boy to come within ten feet of me to carry my bags or for any other purpose."

He turned to Sergeant Knowles. "You must have noticed that yourself."

"I did," the police officer said grimly, "and I don't blame them."

Carter shrugged. "Apparently the whole town is mad."

The colonel shook his white head slowly. "No, my friend," he said. "You would not think anyone mad if you knew what has happened. The Devil's Hoof killed Colonel Hartain in his room a few hours ago."

Carter's face showed his incredulity. "A horse kicked Colonel Hartain to death?"

The colonel shook his head slowly. "No, the Devil's Hoof. The same one that smashed in doors, a huge thing too big for any horse that ever lived."

"Nonsense," said Carter sharply "There must have been some human agency in the thing, then."

"That's right," said the sergeant sharply. "And you're it. I arrest you, Kenneth Carter, for the murder of Colonel Jove Hartain."

CHAPTER IV

The Angel's Kiss

CARTER spun savagely toward the sergeant and the officer piped out, "Watch him, men!" in a voice gone suddenly thin. The two policemen sprang forward with drawn pistols, long barreled thirty-eights which they leveled at the detective's abdomen.

He glared at them, then laughed abruptly, throwing back his long head. It was not a mirthful sound.

"All right," said Carter, "if you're going to arrest me, I want a lawyer at once."

There was a telephone on a table near by and he crossed to it. The police started to interfere, but he looked at them, cold-eyed, above the mouth-piece of the phone and Colonel Jackson spoke in his gentle, deep voice.

"Surely, sergeant, you're not going to deny the man his just rights?"

"I want New York," Carter spoke rapidly into the mouthpiece. "Ellison Roberts, yes. His number is Wing-gate 9-8459. Yes. And put that through fast."

It went through fast and Carter swiftly outlined the situation to his lawyer. It took an hour for Roberts to arrange a writ of habeas corpus through a correspondent law firm in New Orleans and at the end of that time, Carter strode up to the sergeant's desk.

"I want to see Hartain's body," he said. "It is obvious that you intend to do nothing further about the case and if I'm to escape going through a ridiculous trial I must catch the murderer myself."

Sergeant Knowles glared at him belligerently with his pale eyes. "You won't find the trial ridiculous," he promised in his thin voice. "Not when the jury finds you guilty and the judge puts on his black cap."

"Yes, yes," said Carter, "I've seen men sentenced to death, sergeant. take me to the morgue, or give me an order."

The sergeant said grimly, "I'll go. I've been looking you up, Mr. Kenneth Carter, and I find many things about you I do not like. You have killed many men. You would not stop at killing one more if it meant money in your pocket."

Carter slapped the palm of his hand sharply on the top of the desk. "That will be enough of that talk, Sergeant Knowles. When I have killed, it has been to save my own life. And those I killed already had taken human life."

Sergeant Knowles was angry, but he controlled it well. He shrugged finally and stepped down from the dais on which his desk rested, picked up his uniform cap and growled, "Come on with me."

The police car moaned its siren again, the soft warm air of the Southern night fanned their faces and Carter suddenly realized that it was nearly daylight.

"Say, sergeant," Carter turned toward him, "how about a bite to eat before we go the morgue? I just remembered I haven't eaten since luncheon yesterday on the train. You must know some all-night place about here that serves decent food."

The sergeant eyed him suspiciously in the white rays of street lights that zipped past, but finally nodded a grudging head.

"And something to drink, sergeant," Carter insisted. "I'm slowing down and I've a hunch I won't get much sleep in the next twenty-four hours or so."

"Listen," growled the sergeant, "If you're trying to get me in trouble—"

"Nonsense," said Carter. "You don't have to drink if you don't want to. And you can close your eyes every time I lift the flowing bowl."

SERGEANT KNOWLES still peered at him and Carter had about given up when Knowles leaned forward and spoke to the driver. They pulled up before a dark doorway on a side street. The man threw wide the door when he recognized the sergeant and Carter followed him down a dim hall into a room of shaded lights where a half dozen men elbowed a bar and tables in nooks held shadowed couples whose figures had but a single head.

Carter slid into one of the few empty booths and pulled the table aside to make way for the sergeant's belly.

"I will have," Carter pronounced, "an Angel's Kiss."

The proprietor screwed up a mustachioed face, spread apologetic hands. "I am so sorry."

"Don't know the Angel's Kiss?" Carter's voice reflected his astonishment.

The man pantomimed again. His plump, rosy face was distraught. He was sorry again.

"Nothing but the Angel's Kiss will do," Carter said, turning to the sergeant. "Don't you think that would make an admirable antidote for the Devil's Hoof?"

The rosy face above them went blank. It remained bland, Carter saw, but a veil had been drawn across the eyes. So, here, too, the superstition of the Devil's Hoof was known.

Carter shoved the small table over so that it squeezed the sergeant red in the face.

"I must have an Angel's Kiss if I have to mix it myself," he declared. "I'll fix one for you, too, sergeant."

He shoved past the still gesturing proprietor, assuming a mildly tipsy air, and ducked under the bar, looked reflectively at the array of bottles behind it, picked up brandy and cointreau for a start. He measured assiduously, shifted bottles so that even the bartender was puzzled over the movements, and finally drew down two tall glasses and poured the frosted mixture into them. He tasted it.

"Ah!" he expressed his satisfaction, ducked under the bar and marched back to the booth where the sergeant gazed in perplexity at the tall drink set before him.

"Taste it," Carter insisted, "and if you don't find it the antidote for anything at all, Devil's Hoof or not, then I have no further respect for the drinking judgment of the South."

The sergeant tasted it gingerly, moved his lips with little sounds, took another sip.

"Not bad," he pronounced. "Though I don't care much for mixed drinks. What's in it?"

"Chiefly flavoring," said Carter. "It's no wonder they don't know how to mix it. Your discernment will already have told you that it has a bit of brandy."

"Yes," the sergeant admitted, and tasted again.

The angels were generous. They gave the sergeant four more kisses. Carter handed him the fifth and he slopped a bit over on his hand and giggled.

"Believe I'm a little shpiffed," he said with slow difficulty.

"You? Nonsense," Carter jeered. "But I'll say this, sergeant, the Angel's Kiss is—"

The sergeant giggled again. "Yeah, I know. A good antidote for the Devilsh Hoof." He leaned across the table, throwing out a haphazard arm. "You know, s'funny thing, but you're not bad fell—fellow 'tall."

Carter bowed across the table with laughter that was not all pleasant in the depths of his eyes.

"You honor me, sergeant."

"No, no, don't." The sergeant wagged his head. "You're good fell—fellow. But I shtill think you know more about this Dev—Devilish Hoof n' you're telling. Negro boy saw you go into Hartain's room, said. Saw you come out leading big black horse. Shilly, that." He giggled to emphasize its silliness. "But he was shure wash you going out. Then poleeshmen took him to shtation, he got away. How you 'splain that?"

Carter's eyes were sharp. "Maybe his name was Mose," he suggested in a melodramatic whisper.

"Moshe? Moshe? Whash that got to do with it?"

"Was it Mose?"

"No," said the sergeant, "Smatter of fact was George, George LaFitte."

CARTER shook his head. "Too bad," he said, "if it had been Mose, now, and he had lived on a street that began with Ch."

"C—Ch?"

"Yes."

The sergeant shook his head and giggled. "You're wrong again, lived on —on." He dug in his pocket and thrust a notebook, opened, toward Carter. The detective made a rapid mental note. "George LaFitte, 17 Romondo Street."

Carter returned the notebook gravely, his face expressing disappointment. "Then I can't give you any explanation at all for his escaping," he said.

The sergeant shook his head mournfully, raised his glass and emptied it. He started laughing suddenly, put his forehead down on the table and shook his shoulders with laughter. He straightened up and sang in a cracked voice. "Kish me again, kish me again."

Carter leaned across and clapped him on the shoulder. "That's good, sergeant. That's damned good," he told him energetically. "I'll fix you up right away."

He did, slid the tall, frosted glass in front of him and placed one for himself.

"Excuse me a moment," he said.

He walked across to the proprietor, spoke to him confidentially. "You'd better keep the sergeant here till he sobers up. He wouldn't thank you for letting him go out on the street like this."

The man nodded worriedly. "You are right, sir, and yet I dislike having him left here. Could not you, yourself—"

Carter waved a vague hand. The sergeant, he informed the man, had taken a sudden and violent dislike to him. He would understand how such matters were. He paid the bill and walked out. The sky was graying in the east and the police chauffeur behind the wheel was asleep. Carter did not disturb him. He walked swiftly toward a brighter street and succeeded in finding a nighthawk cab that took him to Romondo Street.

Silly, of course, to hope to find a negro who had escaped from the police at his home, but there was no harm in looking. There might be something in the house that might somehow point to the murderer. Yet he had small hopes as he penetrated the crooked, black and unpaved street that was little more than an alley. The first light of day could not penetrate its narrowness.

Whoever had murdered the colonel had been infernally clever, had planted a clever frame-up against Carter. It would be absolutely impossible for him to prove an alibi; and if this negro witness with his wild tale were found, it might help pile up incrimination.

Carter stumbled in the darkness and drew out a small flashlight which he flicked on the ground before him. The alley's floor was black mud, soaking wet from the rain earlier in the night. Carter's shoes sucked up and down in its stickiness, being nearly pulled from his feet.

He turned the white circle of his light on the house fronts and spotted almost immediately the nearly obliterated 17 that designated the home of George LaFitte. It was a dilapidated little one-story shack and its door hung agape.

Carter went up to it cautiously. Where, he wondered, were the police who undoubtedly must have been set to watch for the witness's return? He pushed the door and it swayed inward. Carter put his foot on two huddled objects on the floor and the chills ran cold up his back, raised his hair on end.

It was not that a policeman and a negro lay dead upon the filthy floor. It was the way they had been killed. Their heads had been crushed as if by an enormous hoof, and the prints were deep, too, upon their crushed chests.

CHAPTER V

A Jockey Rides Death

CARTER closed the door quietly behind him and stood over the bodies with the strong white glare of his light delineating every horrible detail of the men's deaths. The Devil's Hoof, for there was no doubt that this was what had killed the men, had struck the negro squarely in the face. The entire countenance was crushed in. Another had struck him on the chest and bits of rag were embedded in the wound.

In the case of the policeman the first blow had come from the rear and the back of his skull was demolished. Carter, feeling faintly sick at his stomach, hair still tingling along the back of his neck, suddenly whirled and flashed the light behind him. Nothing there.

He swept the minute circle of white over the entire room. No, nothing there, nothing to fear. Carter crossed back to the door and shot home a bolt that was woefully fragile. It could not stand a single blow of the Hoof. Then Carter began a minute inspection of the room. There were chewed up places in the floor such as might be made by the cleats of a horse.

The room was bare and scantily furnished, but Carter went over the place conscientiously, and in a drawer he found two small round sponges about the size of a silver dollar. He stared at them and his eyes narrowed. He put them slowly back in the drawer, took a final glimpse of the bodies and, unbolting the door, strode out into the early morning sunlight.

Within the lightless interior, he had not realized that the sun had risen, but the air was gloriously fresh with dawn, a mockery to the grisly death that lay within. Striding back up Romondo Street, Carter carefully obliterated every footprint he had made in the mud. He saw there were no hoof marks.

Carter walked five blocks before he found a cab. Grimly he ordered that he be taken speedily to the Royale. He grinned mockingly at himself. If the negroes knew now what he knew they would flee even more swiftly from his approach than they had on his two previous visits to the hotel.

He did not pause at the desk, but strode straight across and entered an elevator. He looked at the negro steadfastly and the man began to roll his eyes.

"Up, Rastus," Carter said softly.

The car jerked into motion and the door opened with alacrity, slammed almost on his heels and he strode down the hall and knocked at the room of Frances Hartain. He had to rap three times before he heard a soft footfall within and the girl's low voice, "Who is it?"

Carter muffled his mouth with his hand, "From the police."

"Just a minute," the girl's voice retreated and presently he heard a key fumble in the lock and it was thrown wide. Carter stepped in and shut the door behind him.

"You!"

Anger contended with fright in the girl's voice. Carter began to talk swiftly.

"Listen, Miss Hartain, I'm not here to do you any harm, but I had to practice the deception to get in. I think I have a clue to your father's murderer."

The girl had straightened from the first retreat of fear and stood angrily straight, her head thrown back proudly, her black eyes flashing, her young body stern beneath the shapely severity of a white silk negligee.

"Get out of here," she ordered sharply.

Carter fought down his rising impatience.

"Did you ever hear of a negro named George LaFitte?" he asked.

THE girl said bitingly. "You should know he's one of the stable boys you drove away with your Devil's Hoof. Colonel Jackson gave him a job."

"Did your father run a crooked stable?"

The girl's eyes darted about the room. She took two quick steps and picked up a bookend. "Will you get out of here or must I—force you to leave?"

Suddenly Carter smiled. He rarely did, but when he wished to, it made his face charming. Even his crinkling eye corners joined in it.

"Miss Hartain," he said, "I admire your courage tremendously, but—" he suddenly became serious—"you are being misguided now. I had no hand in your father's death, but I am going to find out who did. It is a necessity, since if I fail they will try me for his death. Won't you give me a little help in running down these murderers?"

The girl looked him over carefully, the heavy bookend still ready in her hand.

"Honestly now," Carter said again, "if I were the murderer, what earthly reason would I have for coming to see you like this? I would only be inviting trouble. I came because I thought you might give me information as to these enemies of your father with whom he apparently thought I was in league."

The girl still eyed him, but thoughtfully now and finally she put the bookend down and moved slowly back across the room toward the chair into which she sank.

"You are right, I suppose," she said. "I am behaving unreasonably, but I suspect everyone now. Evidence does point strongly to you, but I have looked over some letters my father received from friends in New York which spoke of you in the highest terms. What do you want to know?"

"Who are your father's enemies?" Carter asked swiftly.

The girl shook her head.

"His race track enemies?" Carter persisted. "I am convinced that this entire thing centers around the race track."

The girl shook her head heavily again. Her face was pale, drained of color, and her black hair was like a funeral veil.

"You are undoubtedly right about that," she said. "About the race track angle, but I can't help you. I know that father was threatened if he did not promise either to sell his horse or to agree to pull it up in the big race tomorrow so that it would lose. They promised good money if he would, death if he wouldn't. They knew father needed money, but we expected to get it from the race. We will get it from the race. Plurius can beat them easily." She stopped a moment, went on more slowly.

"Father," the girl choked on the word, "father got these letters anonymously. They told him if he agreed, to put a certain ad in the papers. Father flew into a rage. These people gave him to understand that every other horse in the race had been framed to lose, through its owner, trainer, or jockey.

"Father's helpers were incorruptible. He trained the horse himself. And our jockey was too loyal to be reached. It wouldn't do to kill the horse. Plurius must run to keep the odds on their own entry long, so they can clean up on bets."

"But which is their horse?"

"I don't know," the girl said, "I can't see—"

A hoarse shout that was almost a scream rang out in the hall. There was a terrific thump against the wall and Carter plunged across the room, yanked open the door and charged out. A huge black shape flitted down the hall silently and as Carter pursued, disappeared. He stared at the stone wall through which the thing, whatever it was, had apparently disappeared and the hackles of fear rose on his neck.

CARTER whirled back up the hall and saw the crumpled figure of the diminutive youth Carter had seen before, the night when he had been confronted by Frances Hartain and accused of murder. Over the boy the girl bent solicitously. Carter strode up to him. A hurried examination showed he had been merely knocked unconscious despite a raking scar on the side of his head from which blood oozed darkly.

Remembering that terrific thump against the wall, Carter glanced up and there was outlined, a hole in the plaster, the complete imprint of the Devil's Hoof!

Carter stared at the thing, remembered the huge dark shape flitting down the hall and frowned heavily. Some horrible plot was under way. That much was obvious, but the means of death, and that strangely disappearing shape . . . .

He stooped and lifted the light body of the boy and bore him swiftly into the girl's room, laid him on a couch. The hall was thronged with people now and Carter was forced to slam the door in their faces. It was the work of a few moments to revive the youth.

The girl leaned over him, pale-faced.

"How are you, Johnny?" she asked anxiously. "Oh, please be careful of yourself, Johnny."

The boy sat holding his head in his hands. "Don't you worry, none, ma'am," the boy said. "I'm going to take care of myself for that race tomorrow."

"What happened?" Carter threw in swiftly.

The boy glanced up and, seeing Carter for the first time, reared uncertainly to his feet.

"What the hell are you doing in here?" he demanded in his sharp, high boy's voice.

The girl answered him, assuring him that she was convinced that Carter was working for their good, and the boy finally subsided, growling.

"What happened?" Carter repeated.

The boy raised his thin shoulders in a shrug. "I don't know," he said. "I was walking along the hall on my way to see Miss Frances, and suddenly I got scared, not for any special reason, just scared. I turned around and saw a big black shape and then something hit me."

"You didn't see what it was?"

The jockey shook his head slowly.

"Didn't see nothing."

"What hit you," said Carter slowly, "was a glancing blow from the Devil's Hoof. If it hit you fairly, you'd be dead now."

The jockey stared up with his wizened, freckled face at Carter and said nothing for minutes. Finally he spoke up, "Well, that black shape I saw was big enough to be a horse, but this is the first time I ever heard of a horse on the fourth floor of a hotel."

Carter said softly, "And I, too."

Abruptly the boy whirled toward the girl. "Miss Frances, what I came to tell you is George LaFitte was killed by the Hoof this morning some time. And they're looking for this guy Carter here because a taxi driver took him there just before dawn."

Carter's mouth was a grim line. "That will be the sergeant getting his revenge. I got him drunk," he explained with a slight twitching of his lips that could not be called a smile, "and got LaFitte's address from him. He said the boy had reported seeing me leave the room of your father and then the negro had escaped from the police. I went to see him just before dawn to see if I could learn something from him of the persons that made him tell that lie and I found their bodies, those of LaFitte and a policeman."

"Yah, you ain't expectin' us to believe that, are you?" the boy jeered.

Carter looked down at him. "Johnny," he said gravely, "I have long ago given up caring whether people believe me or not. I don't care now if I am not hampered in my investigation. If you don't mind, Johnny, we won't tell the police where I am right away."

The girl turned toward him, and the boy as well, staring fixedly into his face. Frances said finally, "I don't see what's to be gained one way or another by telling."

The jockey got to his feet, "Well, I do," he said shrilly and ducked past Carter and bolted to the door, dodged out before the detective's long stride could take him, slammed the door.

Carter grabbed the knob and suddenly there was a scream of wild terror in the hall. He yanked the door, but it would not open. The slamming had locked it and Carter lost precious time fumbling with the lock. The door yielded suddenly, almost throwing him into the floor. He darted out into the hall.

Jockey Johnny lay crumpled on the floor, his skull horribly crushed by the Devil's Hoof!

CHAPTER VI

The Devil Dies

CARTER took one glance, then thrusting Frances back into the room, closed the door.

"What is it? Oh, what is it?" the girl demanded. She stood wringing her hands, staring at Carter with her eyes large in a white face.

"Nothing we can help," he told her. "Listen, Frances. I want you to keep tight hold of yourself for the next half hour for our capture of the man who killed your father depends upon it. Will you try?"

The girl continued to wring her hands. Her effort at control was almost physical in its intensity, but gradually her posture became natural, her hands dropped to her sides and her face became dead calm.

"It got Johnny, I suppose?" she asked listlessly.

"Yes," said Carter. "Now here's what I want you to do. I want you to go out in the hall and declare that you saw the murder, that you know how it was committed. Be a little hysterical about it, then rush back in here and dress and rush out again, very determined. You have a gun?" The girl shook her head and Carter took the small automatic from a side pocket and gave it to her. "I'll be near you. I don't care where you go. Go to Colonel Jackson's suite at the Gibson. That will do."

The girl's face now had become determined, her full sweet lips set. "In other words," she said, "you want me to serve as bait for a new attack in which we will capture the murderer?"

Carter nodded, "That's it precisely. Are you willing?"

The girl said very quietly, "More than willing."

"Okay," said Carter, "I'll duck out when you go into the hall, but I'll be near by. Remember, slightly hysterical, but get away before the police arrive."

The girl nodded again, opened the door and rushed out. The hall was filled with people and Carter had no trouble slipping out unobserved.

"I saw it! I saw it!" Frances cried, a shrill edge on her voice.

People whirled toward her, a white ripple of faces.

"I saw him killed," Frances cried again. "I know the murderer!"

Colonel Jackson was among those clustered about the crumpled body of the jockey. He pushed through the crowd toward Frances.

"Who was it, Frances?" he demanded, his voice vibrant. "Come, we'll tell the police, catch the murderer."

The girl, playing her hysterical rôle, stared up into his white-whiskered face as if she had not recognized him. Suddenly she whirled and ran to her room slammed the door. The colonel knocked on it. Carter shoved up to his side.

"Did she say she knew the murderer?" he asked swiftly.

Jackson nodded his white head. "She did and now she has locked herself in her room. I'm afraid she may harm herself in some way."

"But this is important," Carter declared vehemently. "Let's get to a phone and call the police. We can go in the next room here."

JACKSON looked at the door. "I don't like to leave for a moment," he said. "Something, anything might happen now. Why, she is in actual danger if word gets to the murderer."

"Right," said Carter, "but I'm armed. I'll stand guard here and won't let her out until you get back."

The colonel hesitated. "I reckon you're right," he said finally and actually ran toward the door of the next room, knocked and thrust at the door. It yielded and he went in. Carter heard him shout over the wire.

He knocked softly at the door. "Frances," he called. "It's Ken Carter. You'll have to leave this second."

The door opened instantly and the girl slipped out, fully dressed. Carter strode with her to the elevator, standing empty and sent it creaking down himself.

"Colonel Jackson was about to gum the works by holding you there until police came," he said. "You'll have to hurry. I think if I were you, I'd still go to Jackson's rooms. It's the last place he'll think of looking for you."

"You'll be with me?"

Carter said, "Yes, but not at once. I've got to go up and collect the colonel so he won't crab our game with the police."

The girl slid her hand into the pocket of her sports coat, Carter saw the outline of the gun. He smiled at her with tight lips, "Brave girl," he said, whirled on his heel and was gone. He strode swiftly across the lobby, met the colonel plunging from the elevator.

"Where is she?" he demanded.

"She came out of her room and short of holding her physically I couldn't stop her. She had a gun." Carter was speaking swiftly. "She wouldn't let me get in the elevator with her and when I got down here she was gone. I think she has ideas of avenging her father herself."

The colonel stood with his fists clenched at his sides. "That is what I would expect of Frances," he said softly.

He stood for a moment staring down at the floor. "Well, that being so, I reckon there's nothing else for me to do. I'll be getting back to my rooms. Sallie will be wondering what's happened to me."

He moved off slowly. Carter darted to a side door, and grabbed a taxi, sped swiftly toward the colonel's hotel. His forehead frowned in thought, his eyes narrowed. He took off his hat and ran a swift hand up over his dull hair. Then, abruptly, he leaned forward and tapped on the glass.

"Faster, faster!" he ordered.

The taxi did two-tire whirls about corners, slid to a halt before the Gibson. Carter was out instantly, tossing a bill to the driver. His stride across the lobby seemed unhurried, but it covered space rapidly. The elevator droned upward to the fifth floor. Carter ducked into the entrance of a stairway and waited tensely.

A few seconds later a giant negro stalked down the hall, his coat swinging loosely from enormous shoulders. Carter knew that giant, the man who had kidnapped him! The man walked up to the door of Jackson's suite of rooms and, as the door opened, Carter ran swiftly forward and jabbed his gun into the man's back, went in with him and shut the door.

Jackson's gorgeously red-headed wife stared from one to the other of them with green eyes that were startled. Her hands pulled the smooth green silk of her negligee more closely about her.

"What's the meaning of this?" she demanded coldly. "Why bring this negro here?"

Carter asked swiftly, "Is Frances Hartain here?"

The redhead nodded.

"Fine," said Carter. "This negro was here to kill her. He is the same one that kidnapped me from my room the other night just after I had talked to you and the colonel. I think he is the one who wields the Devil's Hoof."

THE woman shrank back, her tapered hands spread white against the green, pressed to her body. Her eyes went wide on the negro's face. Frances stepped out of the door leading to the next room. She was pale and the pressure of her lips dampened their curve.

Standing behind the negro, Carter nodded his head slightly toward the prisoner, then winked.

Frances let out a small cry, pointed her hand rigidly at the negro, then ran back into the other room. Mrs. Jackson saw her and her eyes went wide. Suddenly the door of the suite was flung wide and Colonel Jackson strode in.

"You here, Carter?" he asked puzzled.

"I managed to trail Frances' taxi and rushed over to protect her. I just got here in time. This negro was ready to murder her, too, and Frances has identified him."

Mrs. Jackson ducked her head in a swift nod. She no longer crouched, but stood to the full height of her mature loveliness.

"That's right, Whittier," she said slowly.

"The dog!" The colonel cried out and his hand snatched a gun from his pocket. Carter struck it up.

"No summary justice, colonel," he said coldly. "We'll turn the man over to police for proper action. This lynching business never did appeal to me."

Carter's gun was completely in charge of the situation.

He raised his voice. "Frances?"

The girl showed herself in the doorway.

"Go out the door of the other room, go downstairs and summon police. Bring them up with you when you come," he directed.

She whirled and was gone. The sound of a door closing floated back.

"I'll go with her," Mrs. Jackson said suddenly and moved toward the door.

"You'll stay where you are," the colonel's deep voice was abruptly harsh.

The woman stopped by the door. She was against the wall, a brown dark wall that outlined her exquisitely in her green silks. Her eyes narrowed.

"Watch yourself, Whittier," she said sharply.

"I reckon I can watch myself, and you, too," the man said in a slow, flat voice. "I should have started that long ago, long before you made me—"

"Shut up, you fool."

Carter stood quietly, gun in hand and let them talk, eyes flicking from one to the other. The negro stood impassive in the midst of this and the colonel moved on heavy feet to his side. He said something in a swift undertone and the negro started as if pricked with a needle.

Carter sprang forward with leveled gun.

"Hands up, Jackson," he ordered.

Behind the white-headed old man he saw the negro's giant form get into action. He saw his arm swing wide, gripping a huge hammer. Mrs. Jackson screamed clear and loud, a shrill cry of absolute terror and ducked for the door. Another scream started but was cut short. There was a sickening crunch as the hammer struck. Carter darted to one side, aiming at the negro.

The colonel fired first. The negro's crouched body straightened with a grotesque surprise and the colonel fired again slowly. Carter looked down at his own pistol with grim lips and did nothing. He held it ready.

The negro's body rose on tiptoes, his face twisted about with fear and hate and surprise mingled upon its gross features. "Colonel—master," he mouthed hoarsely and fell dead. Furniture quivered with the weight of his fall.

Carter said quietly, "Surrender your revolver, colonel, it's all over."

The old man turned heavily on his feet toward the detective and his shoulders were bowed.

"Yes," he said slowly, "it's all over."

THERE was a sudden commotion at the door and Sergeant Knowles thrust in with Frances and other police.

The sergeant's shrill, acrimonious voice rose sharply:

"Arrest Carter!"

"No," said Frances swiftly. "He didn't do it. It's a trap that he—"

Suddenly she saw the crumpled bodies on the floor and her voice stopped in her throat.

The sergeant said hoarsely, "Good Lord, the colonel's wife."

Jackson was staring at Carter with haggard eyes. "So it was all a trick, Carter?"

The detective said briefly, "Yes. How in the world, colonel, did you ever allow yourself to become entangled in a thing like that?"

The man's lips twisted beneath his white mustache. "Just an old fool, Carter. I loved her, God help me, and there was no money. She would have left without it. She planned the whole thing, gave the orders. I fought at first, but later it was easier just to drift.

"Well, she has paid now as she should, by her own device. You checkmated me, Carter, when you sent Frances from the room. I thought that she had identified the negro, that she knew the whole thing. Killing you would have done no good unless she could be put out of the way, too."

He gestured toward the negro where he lay crumpled with his hand still on the hammer. It was a huge thing with a mushroomed end shaped like a horse's hoof and with a horse shoe welded to it. The negro had carried it looped under his arm and the huge breadth of his shoulders had concealed it.

"Michael was my blacksmith," he said, "built the special shoes I use for my horses on the track. He made the hammer for Sallie after she read some legend about a knight a long time ago who used some such weapon for murders and spread superstition to cover it up."

The colonel turned his weary face, his weary body, toward the sergeant of police. The girl moved, stumbling, across to Carter and buried her face on his shoulder, her shoulders jerking with sobs.

"Sergeant," said the colonel, "I confess the murders, through this man, Michael, of Colonel Hartain, of his jockey, of a negro stable boy called George LaFitte—we were afraid he would weaken in his identification of Carter after we frightened him into it—and of a policeman who was guarding him."

"I understand all except that shadow in the hall," said Carter.

The colonel smiled tiredly. "A stereopticon focused through a slot in the hotel room door, throwing a big black shadow. We swung the thing to one side and the shadow appeared to flit down the hall. We cut it off and the shadow vanished."

He looked them all over slowly, shook his head sadly at Frances' crying.

"And now is there anything else?" he asked.

"Yes," clipped out the sergeant, "You're under arrest, Colonel Whitter Jack . . . . Stop! Stop!"

The old colonel had straightened as the words drummed on his ears. Abruptly, but unhurriedly he raised the pistol to his head. He squeezed the trigger even as the sergeant rushed forward to stop him.

"YOU see, sergeant," Carter explained an hour later, "when I checked over the persons who knew of my little altercation with Hartain, and who knew the cause, that they knew I might be framed for murder by the kidnapping, the only persons I could think of were Jackson and Miss Hartain. And Miss Hartain had neither the strength, nor the servant who could kill as these people were killed. The Devil's Hoof had frightened all her servants away."

The sergeant shifted in his chair on the other side of the table and raised a tall frosted glass to his lips, smacked his lips appreciatively. He took it down and looked pensively into the pale purple drink.

"Then when I went to LaFitte's cabin," Carter went on, "I found there two small sponges such as crooked stables sometimes thrust up a horse's nostrils to hamper its breathing so it can't win the race. And I found out LaFitte was at the time of his death a stable boy of Jackson's, which indicated he ran a crooked stable. Then, too, that wife of the colonel's was surely not his calibre. I've met too many of her kind in New York. That gave a hint of the motive.

"But there was no evidence against him, so I rigged the trap."

The sergeant set down his glass reluctantly. It was empty.

"A nice job," he said.

Carter shook his head. "I've done better."

The sergeant shook the glass, "Better than this? You're crazy. It's the best Angel's Kiss you ever mixed."

Carter threw back his head and laughed.

"So you're going to forgive me for that little affair."

The sergeant screwed up his pasty face, but his pale blue eyes were cheerful.

"On one condition."

"And that?"

"Show me," said Sergeant Knowles, "how to mix an Angel's Kiss."

Smashing "**Ken Carter**" Novel

The SINISTER EMBRACE

Next **By NORVELL PAGE** **Month**

The Wax Witness

With Hard-Boiled Murdock Crashing Royalty

By CARL McK. SAUNDERS
Author of
"The Key to Hell," "Trigger Traffic," etc.

The gun swished up—and then down.

With Captain John Murdock, a duchess was given no more consideration than a Tinpan Alley dame. Royalty and ragamuffins were one and the same to him. Murder was murder. And if a duchess got mixed up in a killing, it was just plain tough—on royalty.

THE hotel manager said: "They're in what we used to call the bridal suite. It's on the eighteenth floor. But you can't go up tonight."

"Huh? Can't go up?" John Murdock answered. "What the hell's the matter. Elevator busted down or somethin'?"

The hotel manager shook his head. "No, but these people aren't just ordinary guests. They are visiting this country at the invitation of the President. They're—well—they're entitled to different courtesies. They—"

"Someone murdered a girl up there, didn't they?" Murdock cut in.

"Yes—that is—it looks that way."

"She was one of your employees, wasn't she?

"Yes. A maid."

"Well, what the hell. Let's get down to cases. A murder's a murder whether it's pulled off by a queen or a newsboy. What do you know about it?"

John Murdock, chief of detectives, leaned back against the door in the manager's office and chewed on the end of his cigar. He looked quite out of place. He was clothed in a suit that hung on his huge body like a sack. His shirt wasn't overly clean and his shoes were scuffed and muddy. He needed a shave, and he probably needed sleep, for his eyes were bloodshot and circled with heavy lines.

The two men who had accompanied him from headquarters fitted into the luxurious quarters of the manager's office much better. Bert Andrews was tall and bony. He had slouched down in an upholstered chair until he was almost hidden by his own knees. Jimmie Spence, a younger man, was dressed in white flannels and a dark coat. He looked like what we imagine the rising young business man looks like.

The hotel manager said: "It happened about an hour ago. The switchboard girl got a call from 1810, insisting that I come up there at once. She called me at home although that's against the rules. You see—well—a duchess—"

Murdock nodded. "Go on, but cut it to the bone."

"Of course I came down at once. When I got upstairs Stewart met me. He's the duchess's secretary. He said that when the duchess and her party came in a few moments before they heard a noise in one of the side rooms. Then they heard a scream and the sound of breaking glass. Stewart says that he and Brundt hurried in to that room in time to see the vague figure of a man going out a door that opens on the corridor. He says that they chased after him, but that when they got to the door he was gone. They hurried down the corridor but didn't catch a glimpse of him.

"Then they came back and looked out the broken window. They could see the body of the girl on one of the little twelfth-floor balconies. We went down and brought her body in. Fortunately that balcony room is vacant, and her body's in there now. Room 1206. She—well, the house doctor says that she was stabbed before she was pushed through the window."

MURDOCK nodded. "Who's Brundt? You mentioned a man named Brundt."

"I don't know. Just one of the party."

"Who are the others in the party?"

"Well, there's the duchess and some cousin or niece named Sophia Weiner. There's Stewart, Brundt, a couple of valets and two maids. I don't have their names. I can get them for you."

"Don't bother." Murdock shook his head. "I'll get 'em myself when I talk to 'em."

"But—"

"Let's go." Murdock stepped away from the door and opened it. Andrews and Spence got up to follow him. The manager bustled forward and grabbed Murdock by the arm.

"You can't go up there now," he cried. "Don't you understand. You can't go now. Tomorrow—tomorrow morning will do just as well."

Murdock shook off the manager's arm and started down the hall toward the elevators. But the manager followed him.

Murdock said: "Beat it. I'm busy."

"But you don't understand," insisted the manager.

"Understand—hell," Murdock exploded. "A girl's been murdered, ain't she?"

"But the duchess," the manager cried. "You—you don't treat people like her that way. It isn't just that she's a duchess, but she's the nation's guest—the President's guest. This—this has got to be hushed up. I talked to the police commissioner. He's coming down. He said that he would do what he could. I—I—"

Murdock rang for the elevator. He said: "We don't hush up murder in Central City."

The manager stepped back. He grew angry. His face got red.

"We'll see just who's running things," he challenged. "I'll get the commissioner again. I'll call the mayor. I'll call—I'll call—"

Murdock grinned. "Go ahead. Call anybody. Call the President. You may know your job, mister, but I know mine, too. An' right now it's takin' me up to Room 1810."

The elevator stopped and the three detectives stepped inside.

Murdock said: "An' that's that."

Spence nodded. "But it's only a starter, chief. I'll bet you get jerked off this case so fast it makes you dizzy."

"Maybe—an' then maybe I won't," Murdock answered. "We'll look 'em over an' then we'll decide what to do."

MURDOCK knocked on the door numbered 1810. When there wasn't any answer he knocked harder. He was about to knock a third time when he heard a whisper on the other side of the door, and a moment later the door was opened a crack.

The detective pushed his way inside and his two companions followed. He said:

"My name's Murdock. I'm chief of detectives here in Central City. What happened?"

The man who had unlocked the door was small and slender. He was dark-skinned, he had little black eyes and a trick moustache. He stammered: "I—I—don't understand."

Murdock looked around the room. There wasn't any sign of the other person the man must have been whispering to before he had opened the door. The detective scowled and stepped over to Jimmie Spence.

"Step out in the hall," he whispered, "an' keep your eyes open. I don't want anybody walkin' out on me."

Then he turned back to face the man. "You Stewart?" he asked.

The man nodded. "John Francis Stewart."

"American?"

"No. English."

"English, huh? Slickest crook I ever knew was English. Funny. You don't look English."

Stewart shrugged. Murdock noted that he was biting at his lips and that his fingers were twitching nervously.

"Let's have the story," the detective suggested.

"About—about the girl who—who fell out of the window?"

Murdock nodded. "Sure. We'll start there anyhow."

"I really don't know much," Stewart began. "We just came in the room and heard a noise. Then there was a scream. Then—"

"Wait a minute," Murdock interrupted. "I think it might be a good idea for you to get all the rest of the folks in here. We might have a little session."

"What!" Stewart gasped. "You—you don't mean—"

"Sure. All of 'em. Brundt, the maids, the valets, the chauffeurs, the what-nots an' even the duchess. I ain't never seen a duchess."

"But—but the duchess has retired."

"Yeah? Well, she came over here to visit America an' to see how it was run. This is too good an opportunity for her to miss. Get her up."

"But—but you don't understand. The duchess—well—"

"Listen, Stewart. That's an order. Get her up or we'll move into her bedroom. Get everybody up an' get 'em in here."

"But—"

Murdock stepped forward. "Did you hear me," he snarled. "Get goin'."

Stewart backed away. His face was twisted into mean lines and his little black eyes were narrowed. He muttered a curse under his breath. Then he turned sharply and crossed the room. He opened a door and slammed it behind him.

Bert Andrews, who had been standing near Murdock throughout the interview, said: "What the hell, chief. Looks to me like you were piling up a lot of trouble for yourself."

Murdock grunted. He fished a cigar out of his pocket and stuck it in his mouth. "That man ain't any more English than I am," he growled. "There's something screwy about this layout an' I'm gonna get to the bottom of it."

"You're gonna get your ears knocked down."

"Yeah? Well, you get out in the hall

an' help Spence. I don't want anyone to leave here. If I need help I'll holler."

MURDOCK strolled around the room, scuffling the rug, for ten minutes before anyone appeared. Then, two men came in together. Both were of average size, of medium age, and both were neatly dressed. Murdock took down their names in his book and ordered them to sit down. He didn't question them.

Brundt came in next. He was a huge, overbearing individual with a ruddy countenance and bushy hair. He crossed over to Murdock and said: "What's the meaning of this?"

Murdock answered: "Sit down an' you'll learn."

"It's outrageous," Brundt declared.

Murdock nodded. "Lots of things are. The price of beer, for instance."

Brundt sat down. He scowled at the detective and began tapping on the rug with his feet.

A moment later two women entered. One was quite small and rather pleasing to look at. The other was larger. She was clothed in a red silk robe. What looked like a rubber cap was over her hair. Some type of patented wrinkle remover elastic was fastened over her chin and neck and another elastic bandage was tied across her forehead. The portion of her face that was visible was daubed with a greasy cream. She was peculiar looking to say the least.

Murdock repressed a smile and said: "The duchess, I presume?"

The woman nodded. She sat down and looked at the detective without speaking.

Stewart, who had followed the two women in, said: "We're all here but one of the maids. I've looked all over for her. She doesn't seem to be in. If you care to search, yourself—"

Murdock shook his head. "That's O. K."

Stewart then turned to the duchess: "I'm sorry," he apologized. "I tried to prevent this disgraceful thing from happening. I can assure you that it will be reported to the authorities."

The duchess inclined her head. She looked quite bored.

"I'm sorry, too," Murdock interposed. "That is, I'm sorry about the girl who was killed. Nice girl, I understand. We don't put up with things like that in Central City."

"Your ways of justice are so interesting," murmured the duchess. Her voice was flat and toneless.

Murdock grunted. He said: "I want to know just what happened here tonight."

"We know nothing about it," Brundt snapped. "This is farcical. I don't intend—"

He stopped short and looked at the door. Someone was knocking.

Murdock said: "Open it."

Stewart scurried forward and opened the door to admit a short, stocky man with iron gray hair. The man came two paces into the room and paused.

"Just what is the meaning of this, Murdock?" he asked.

Murdock shrugged. "Hello, Commissioner. Glad to see you."

THE Commissioner snorted. His roving eye caught the duchess and he continued across the room. Bowing before her he said:

"I can't tell you how much this disturbs me, ma—ma—your highness. I wouldn't have had it happen for the world. I only hope that you'll forgive us and remember, when you return to Savonia, the more pleasant incidents of your journey across our great nation."

The duchess bowed, but it was Stewart who answered.

"This is outrageous, Commissioner. I wish to prefer charges against this —this detective. He's been most rude. He's been insulting. He's been—"

The Commissioner turned to glare at Murdock. "You needn't worry," he said to Stewart. "I'll prefer those charges myself. It will be a pleasure."

Murdock moved over and leaned

against the wall near the door. He said, rather softly, "You seem to forget, Mr. Commissioner, that a girl was murdered in this room tonight. First she was stabbed—then thrown from the window. It's always been my impression that murder was a rather serious affair."

"That'll be enough, Murdock," the Commissioner snapped. "I'll take charge here. You may step outside and wait for me at the elevator."

Murdock shook his head. "Sorry, Mr. Commissioner, but just now I happen to be in charge of an investigation of murder. Tomorrow you can prefer charges against me, order me to stand on my head, or write a letter to the editor of the paper. But just now I happen to be running things."

"Why you—you—" the Commissioner sputtered, his face flaming, his breath coming short. "I—I'll—"

"Sure. I know," Murdock agreed. "But don't say it or do it. Just cool off. I'm sort of glad you came down. You're gonna get a first-class lesson in crime detection. Have a chair."

The Commissioner tried again. "Murdock, will you get out?"

The detective shook his head. "Sit down an' watch."

The Police Commissioner sat down. He sat on the edge of a chair. Murdock had never seen him more furious.

"Do you have a gun?" he asked.

The Commissioner shook his head.

Murdock frowned, reprovingly. "Ought to always carry a gun," he said. "They come in handy, sometimes. I usually carry a couple." He took one out of his pocket and exhibited it. "Know how to use it, too," he commented.

The Police Commissioner stared at Murdock, but said nothing.

"'Course, if you don't have a gun it's a good plan to duck when the shootin' starts. It's a good plan, anyhow."

Stewart cut in to say: "Let's get this over. Just what do you want?"

"I want the story of what happened here tonight," Murdock said. "An' I want it straight."

Stewart nodded. "I'll start off. We were at a reception tonight. It was, I believe, on the south edge of town. We left early, before eleven, and came straight to the hotel. Just after we entered the room we heard a noise in that room over there." He pointed toward a door and Murdock nodded.

"Almost at that same instant," Stewart continued, "we heard a scream, then the sound of breaking glass. Brundt and I hurried into that room.

"Who stayed here?" Murdock asked.

"Just the duchess and Miss Hoel." Stewart indicated the woman with the duchess.

"Where were the two valets?" Murdock wanted to know.

"In their own room across that way I guess. I really don't know. You'll have to ask them. Of course they weren't at the reception."

MURDOCK looked over at the two valets. They were both nodding. He shot a glance at Brundt. Brundt was still tapping nervously with his feet. Murdock said: "Go on."

"We saw what looked like a man when we got to that room," Stewart continued. "We couldn't see him plain. He was just going out the door into the hall. We chased after him but even though we ran down the corridor we didn't catch another glimpse of him."

"What did he look like?" the detective asked.

"He was—er—tall and heavy."

Murdock grunted. "That all you can say?"

"That's all. We didn't see him plain."

"What about it, Brundt?"

"Huh!" Brundt looked up, flushing. He said: "Er—er—yes. That's all there was to it."

Murdock laughed. He said: "Hooey!" He looked over at Stewart and suggested. "You'll have to do better than that."

Stewart seemed a little pale. He wet

his lips with his tongue and glanced nervously around the room.

The jangling of the telephone seemed to startle everyone. Stewart hurried forward to answer it, but Murdock beat him to the phone.

"I'll take it," he said. "You go sit down an' get your imagination to working."

The detective put the receiver to his ear and said, "Hello." He listened for a moment then said: "We got tied up." He listened a moment longer, said: "Yeah, half an hour." Then he hung up.

Turning to Stewart he asked; "Wanna change that story?"

Stewart shook his head.

Murdock looked at the half circle of faces confronting him. "Anybody else wanna speak up?" he inquired.

No one answered him. Brundt was tapping the carpet again with his feet. Murdock fastened his eyes on Brundt and the tapping stopped.

After a moment's silence, Murdock spoke:

"Then I've got a little three-part story to tell you. It won't take me very long. It starts out like this. The Duchess of Savonia decides to pay a visit to America. It's a rich little country, Savonia, an' the duchess is quite a popular person. She comes over here. She says the right things. She catches the popular imagination an' has a swell time. Eventually, during the course of her visit, she arrives in Central City. That's part one.

"Part two deals with a maid in this hotel. To be honest, I don't know very much about her, except that she was a curious sort of a maid. This suite of rooms happened to be a part of her responsibility. She did her work, today, probably about as usual, but maybe she was disappointed in not seein' the duchess.

"Maybe she was just plain curious. At any rate, she came back up tonight either on the pretext of fixin' things up or just to see what royalty looked like. She got in on a situation that wasn't any of her business. She learned too much. She had to be put out of the way. So she was stabbed an' shoved through a window. That's part two."

MURDOCK moved over a bit to the left. He shoved his hands in his pockets and leaned against the wall. He seemed entirely at ease.

"Part three," Murdock continued, "has to do with what the maid bumped into when she came up here tonight. You know, the underworld's been havin' a tough time payin' its bills lately. Legalized beer cut into their revenues quite a bit. They've had to develop more rackets. Perhaps the most successful and certainly the best payin' racket is kidnappin'. What that maid bumped into was a plot to kidnap the Duchess of Savonia. That's why she was killed."

"What!" gasped the Police Commissioner.

Murdock ignored the interruption. "To round out the third part, a gang of hoodlums planned to kidnap the duchess an' get a fancy price paid to them for her release. They planned the job to take place here in Central City, tonight."

The Police Commissioner stood up. "Who are they, Murdock?" he demanded. "We must take measures to protect the duchess. We've got to do something about this."

Murdock said: "Sit down, Commissioner." He wasn't looking at the Commissioner, but was watching Brundt. "I don't know just what we ought to do about it. Technically, the duchess has already been kidnapped."

"What!"

Murdock nodded. "That woman you bowed to—the beefy one, ain't no more duchess than you are. These people in this room ain't part of the duchess's party. They're the kidnappers."

A tense silence followed Murdock's announcement. The Police Commissioner shot a quick glance around the room. His face had paled. He was moistening his lips with his tongue and his hands were clenching and unclenching, nervously. Both Brundt and Stewart were watching Murdock with hawklike intentness. The two women and the two other men were sitting rigid in their chairs, their eyes fastened on the detective.

Stewart forced a shaky laugh. "This is pure nonsense," he said. "It's ridiculous."

Murdock shrugged. "For the last ten minutes," he said rather deliberately, "this man you said was named Brundt, has been tapping on the floor with his feet. But it wasn't just tapping. He used the Morse code an' the message he tapped out was: *'He's wise—Get ready.'* He tapped it over and over. He must have had a hard time gettin' attention.

"Then that telephone call was from an accomplice. He wanted to know what was holdin' things up. He says he'll be in Room 876, Rome Hotel, in half an hour an' that everythin's jake. We'll pick him up over there."

Brundt said: "You won't pick him up. You won't have any interest in such things in half an hour."

Murdock grinned. He was still leaning against the wall and his hands were still in his coat pocket. "Maybe I won't," he agreed. "Of course you know that you're all under arrest. I'd advise you to think a couple of times before tryin' anything rash. I got a gun in each hand an' I'm a little nervous."

Brundt leaned forward. "You're a wise guy, ain't you?" he snarled.

One of the women gasped. "Marty—don't!"

BRUNDT snapped: "Shut up." He looked around the room and then back to Murdock. "Let's get him, boys," he said. "No dirty—"

His right hand whipped up a gun. Across the room a woman screamed. That scream was punctuated by two shots, so close together that they were almost blended. Brundt twisted sideways as a bullet from Murdock's gun tore through his chest. His body sagged back.

The Police Commissioner sat as though paralyzed. He didn't see Murdock draw his gun and fire that first shot. It all happened too fast. At one moment the detective was leaning against the wall—a moment later he was away from that wall and his hands that had been in his pocket each held a gun.

It seemed to the Commissioner that everyone was shooting. He heard Stewart gasp and saw him slide to the floor—he saw one of the other two men charge forward, seem to stumble, and fall. He saw the second dart behind a heavy chair. There were more shots. The upholstery in the chair gave up little puffs of dust.

He didn't know when he got down on the floor, but when the door burst open and Andrews and Spence came running in, he was flat on his stomach. He felt a little undignified, but Murdock was sitting down, too, and when he noticed that he felt a little better about it. The two women were cowering together over in a corner. He wondered how they had managed to get over there, then Andrews was bending over him and asking whether or not he was hurt.

He shook his head and got up.

Spence asked: "What the hell's it all about, chief?"

"You look these cripples over, Jimmie," Murdock answered, "an' maybe I'll be able to tell you in a minute."

The chief of detectives headed across the room, opened a door and fumbled for the light. He switched it on, glanced around, and started for another door. Andrews and the Police Commissioner followed him.

IT was in the third room that Murdock found that for which he was searching. There, neatly laid out in a row, were eight bound figures. They were not only bound but with one exception they all seemed to be asleep. Murdock bent over the first, the figure of a man. He made a short examination and then said: "Doped. Bert, get a doctor."

While Andrews was telephoning, Murdock untied the only one of the eight who was conscious, and then with the Commissioner helping him, managed to get her to a chair.

"Unless I'm cockeyed," Murdock said to the Commissioner, "this is your duchess. In some way or other that gang in there managed to dope the whole bunch except her. Then just to be safe they tied 'em up. They were just about ready to walk out when we walked in. You see, the kidnappin' party was almost a duplicate of the real party. They didn't dope the duchess because she had to go along with them."

"But—but how did you know about it?"

"I didn't know—that is, not at first. I just got suspicious of Stewart. He said he was English an' I knew he wasn't. I thought I'd look 'em over. From what I've read about the duchess I didn't think she'd mind. Then when a woman came in the room all covered with bandages and cold cream I got more suspicious. When she just sat there an' didn't say a word, I was sure something was screwy. The duchess likes to talk. Brundt's tapping in the Morse code an' the telephone call finished it."

The Commissioner nodded. "I guess I was a little hasty," he said.

Murdock shrugged. "Forget it. You stay here an' entertain the duchess until the doctor comes. I've got several things to do."

From the next room Murdock called headquarters and asked them to send over to the Rome Hotel to pick up whoever was in Room 876. After that he went back to the room where Spence was waiting.

"How do they look?" he asked.

"A couple can use a doctor, a couple need an' undertaker."

Murdock nodded.

"The women are ready to talk, chief," Spence went on. "They say the maid busted in on the party when they were tying them up. She saw what was going on and raised a rumpus. In the scrap that followed one of the men got mad and stabbed her. It seems that she staggered back and crashed through the window herself. They had planned on leaving her here and doping her like the rest. A pretty kid, too. Looks like a wax doll."

"I guessed it was something like that," Murdock said.

The Police Commissioner came bustling in. His face was shining. He said:

"The duchess is a great woman. She wants to see the reporters. She's going to give them her version of the kidnapping attempt. She says that she is going to praise the police force of Central City—that it's more efficient than Scotland Yard. She's not mad at all. A great woman."

Murdock grinned. "At least a wise one."

"And she wants to see you, Murdock. She wants to thank you personally. She says that Savonia is going to send you a medal."

"A what?"

"A medal. You know. Something to wear on your chest."

"Like hell," Murdock scoffed. "You don't catch me in a deal like that."

"You're caught, Murdock," the Commissioner answered. "I've already accepted for you. It's too good a thing to turn down. It'll be a great thing for Central City—and—er—incidentally, for the police department."

A New Adventure of

"Hard-Boiled" John Murdock

Next Month

Lee Nace Bucks the Big Boss of

The Tank of Terror

The man was too quick

A Complete Detective Novelet

By LESTER DENT

Author of "The Diving Dead," "The Skeleton's Clutch," etc.

Grim and horrible were those warnings of the Big Boss. They were found in automobiles, office buildings and in homes. They were the mutilated corpses of men boiled in oil. And they told the Oklahoma police not to be too inquisitive. Into this hotbed of horror came Lee Nace to buck a triple-decked deal of the Big Boss—a reward-hungry newspaperman—and the two-gun Robin Hood of the oil country.

SHE was tall, blonde, streamlined. The roadster was long, cream-colored, and also streamlined.

She was making motions at powdering her nose, using a pancake compact with a mirror fully four inches across. She held it braced against the steering wheel.

Utter concentration tensed her beautiful face. The big, flat powder puff dabbed the compact with strangely erratic frequency. It slapped only the mirror—never the powder cake.

Oklahoma sunlight, white and hot, sprayed blonde and roadster. To the right, it cooked overgrown stucco buildings of the Tulsa Municipal Airport. To the left, it toasted flat classroom and barrack structures of a school of aeronautics.

In spasms, the sun leaped from the

blonde's compact mirror. Her powder puff, whipping systematically, was dividing the beam into dots and dashes.

On hands and knees beside the airport waiting room, Lee Nace crawled. He was very long, bony, blue-eyed. He was gathering together the wind-scattered sheets of a letter.

Standing and staring at Nace were six or seven people who had been his fellow passengers on the recently arrived New York plane.

They were fascinated by the scar on Nace's forehead. It was a perfect likeness of a small coiled snake—an adder. A Chinaman had once hit Nace on the forehead with a knife hilt which bore a serpent carving, and he was destined to forever carry the scar.

Ordinarily the scar was unnoticeable. But it flushed out redly when he was angry or worried. He was worried now.

Inside the ornate, modernistic waiting room, a male voice was shouting: "Telegram! Wire for Private Detective Lee Nace! Telegram!"

Nace continued picking up the sheets of his letter. He pretended to reach each. When he had spilled the sheets, he had taken pains to make it seem an accident.

Slyly, over the paper, he read the heliograph message being flashed by the blonde's compact mirror.

"A reception committee!" she sunflashed. "Three of them—man with the telegram is one. The other two are wearing coveralls—to hide bulletproof vests."

Nace captured two more sheets of his letter, pretended to read but kept his eyes on the mirror.

"The one with the telegram is 'Robin Hood' Lloyd," the girl continued. "He's Oklahoma's bad boy."

She ended her transmission.

Nace arose and barged in under a striped canopy which could be telescoped out to meet arriving planes. He entered the flashy waiting room.

"TELEGRAM for Lee Nace!" droned Robin Hood Lloyd.

The Robin Hood was a lean, young-old wolf. His chin bore scars, irregular, wavy lines—marks of an ancient beating with knuckles.

Two men sat side by side on a modernistic divan. They were chunky. Their faces might have been meaty blocks covered with a good grade of brown saddle leather.

Both wore khaki coveralls. Both had newspapers spread open in their laps.

Headlines on the papers read:

OIL SCANDAL GROWING!

There was a picture of a man with a flowing white beard. He looked like Santa Claus. Under that was another black-faced type line.

EDITOR APP LEADS STOLEN
OIL INVESTIGATION

Nace sidled, long-legged, for the seated pair. These men did not know him, or they would not be using the telegram ruse to spot him.

He was still moving when his long arms shot out. His hands, long-fingered, bony, swung hard against the right ear of one man and the left ear of the other. Their heads, driven together, made a hollow *bonk*.

Each man gave one convulsive quiver as he became unconscious. Then they lay back on the modernistic divan, mouths agape, eyes pinched. The newspapers slid off their laps, revealing frontier six-shooters.

Robin Hood Lloyd stood and stared, a yellow telegram envelope dangling from his right hand. Suddenly he dropped the envelope and began to shake his right hand madly.

A small revolver, dislodged from an armpit, dropped out of the sleeve and hung swinging on a string.

Before Robin Hood could seize his hideout weapon, Nace's fist lashed. It hit the handiest spot—the undershot jaw which gave the Robin Hood his wolf look.

Oklahoma's bad boy flippered his hands convulsively. He was not entirely knocked out, and feeling himself going down, wheeled in an effort to land on all fours. He failed and hit the floor all spread out.

The sound as he came down was a metallic clank, as of a pile of scrap iron dumped on the tile floor, rather than a man.

Nace had read about this Oklahoma cut-up in the New York papers. The fellow went around armored like a knight of old—not only with a bullet-proof vest, but with steel leg and arm shields.

The Robin Hood rolled on his back, made a tent over his face with his hands, and moaned loudly.

Nace rushed, bent low, long arms hanging down.

He never did know exactly what happened next. One of the men on the modernistic divan unlimbered with a gun. Or maybe it was both of them. A bullet slammed against Nace's right side. It spun him just enough so that the second slug got him in the stomach. The Robin Hood managed to draw back both feet and kick him in the head.

Nace's eyes became two gory bonfires of pain. His insides felt as if they were torn out. He started to cave.

It soaked through his dazed brain that he would die if he did. He hauled up, swayed around, and ran blindly for the white blur he knew was the sunlit door.

When he got outside, he knew it only because he seemed to be in a white-hot snowstorm. He pawed his kicked face, beat his body where the bullets had hit.

He wore a bullet-proof jacket which had saved his life, but the slugs had mauled him horribly.

Flaying his tortured brain, he managed to remember where they had stacked the baggage from the plane. He veered for the luggage heap. His canvas zipper bag was there. He wanted it. It was his war sack, his bag of tricks, his life preserver. He was too drunk with pain to realize he could not get to the bag before the trio in the waiting room could come after him.

Nace never carried a gun. He subscribed to a theory that toting a firearm tended to make a man helpless, if ever he was caught without it.

FINALLY he snapped out of the daze. He swiveled around drunkenly on a heel.

His hand, clawing inside his coat, fished out a little metal tear gas firing cylinder. He exploded it in the waiting room door.

On the opposite side of the building, the roadster engine was moaning anxiously. The blonde waited, tense at the wheel.

The Robin Hood and his two followers floundered out into the sunlight. Blinded by the tear gas, they were holding hands to keep track of each other. They acted like three small boys trying not to get lost.

"Come on, guys!" rapped the blonde. "Blow!"

The blinded Robin Hood tried to climb into the roadster hood, under the impression that he was getting in the back seat. He hauled out a single-action gun, jabbed it above his head and fanned out its five slugs. Then he found the car door and piled in. "O. K. That'll hold 'em! Blow!"

The roadster seemed to snug its oil-pan belly to the ground, then jump. Scooting away, it left a rain of gravel.

"Did you get the dirty so-and-so?" the blonde demanded.

"Hell no!" The Robin Hood held his jaw with a clench so tight that tendons on his hands whitened out like chalk rods. "Damn! Did he hand one on my kisser!"

"My heroes!" The girl's voice was dry. But her eyes were brightly glad.

As if it were clawing cats, the wind tore her blonde hair about. It was so very blonde, that hair, that it was plainly dyed.

Nace staggered around the airport waiting room, covering as much ground to right and left as he did ahead.

The field operation office was in the same building with the waiting room, but there were doors, probably closed, through which the tear gas had not penetrated.

Like a dude out of a bandbox, a man popped out from an office window. He wore striped trousers and a gray lap-over tea vest. The pearl grip of a derringer protruded, charmlike, from his watch pocket. He pulled his tiny gun, leveled it. The thing made a sound like a giant firecracker and kicked his fist back in his face. He looked foolish when the slug dug a geyser of dirt not a hundred feet from where he stood.

Nace leaned, white-faced, against a wall, said, "Better get a bow and arrow!"

The dapper man looked around and grinned. "When I do hit 'em, though, I make a big hole! Say, skipper, you look like hell!"

The pain had faded the adder scar off Nace's forehead. It was coming back slowly.

"And I was the cookie who was gonna show how it's done in the East!" he said wryly. "I done swell! Yes, I did!"

The nattily dressed man reloaded his derringer with a cartridge as thick as his little finger. "Y'know who that was?"

"Mr. Lloyd, I believe."

"You said it, skipper! Oklahoma's contribution to the wild and woolly West—the Robin Hood himself. The lad who can walk down Main Street in Tulsa, from the Louvre to Brown-Dunkin's, and not a cop can see him—because they're afraid to. 'Officers again escape Robin Hood,' is the streamer an Oklahoma City rag runs every time he had a gun fight with the law."

Nace grimaced. "You talk like a newspaper man. What sheet?"

The dressy man skidded the derringer back into his watch pocket. "The *Telegram!* Halt Jaxon's the name. Oil editor."

"Know Ebenezer App?"

"I ought to! He pays me!"

"Let's go hunt him up!" Nace suggested.

Dapper Halt Jaxon made a whistling mouth. "You must be Lee Nace, the private shamus the governor hired to come from New York to come here and work with the boss."

"The same!"

Nace walked behind the waiting room and came back with his canvas zipper bag. "Do we go?"

"We do!"

Jaxon led the way to a roadster. It was a speedster, low and yellow, remindful of an overgrown canary.

CHAPTER II

THE HOT OIL RING

THE canary car tweeted a horn when it pulled out of the airport parking. It tweedled a different one when it turned into Sheridan Drive, heading toward town. Not once during the trip in did it sound the same horn twice.

"I was sent out here to meet you." Halt Jaxon offered a cork-tipped fag from a silver case.

"I need something stronger!" Nace produced a stubby pipe and a silk pouch. "Whew-w-w! What a reception! Is that the usual thing out here?"

"If you're going up against the Robin Hood, it is. I guess you're out here on this hot oil trouble."

"What hot oil trouble?"

"For cryin' out loud! Don't you read the newspapers?"

"Where'd you get the idea your troubles mean anything to Broadway rags?"

"Oh! So it's like that. Well, for the last year or so, most of the Oklahoma oil fields have been shut down. They passed laws—"

"Proration!"

"Go to the head of the class! The governor had to stick the militia in some fields to close 'em. They're just discovering that, while the fields were shut down, somebody stole a lot of oil."

"What do you call a lot?"

"We ain't pikers! Thirty or forty millions."

"Barrels?"

"Dollars!"

Nace felt tenderly of his shoe-bruised face. "You wouldn't kid me?"

"I might, but I'm not. I tell you, they're just getting into the damn mess. The governor has investigators all over the state. Wherever they dig, they turn up a dead cat.

"Down at Bowlegs, they found a farm of 55,000-barrel crude tanks plumb empty. In the Oklahoma City field, a lot of leases are running salt water where they should be making oil. The oil has been pulled out by mysterious persons unknown—lifted, heisted, stolen!"

"Can't they put a finger on anybody?"

"Sure—small fry. But some great big bright brain is behind the whole thing. They can't learn who. I'm telling you, skipper, it's the most colossal robbery in history."

Nace wiped crimson off his fingers. "What'm I supposed to do? Make news for App's paper?"

"App owns a lot of production up in the Osage which ain't production any more. He'd like to know who pinched the oil! And any news fit to print, we print."

The canary car swung past MacIntyre airport. Off to the left, derricks in the Oil Exposition grounds stuck up, a horny, cactus-like cluster.

"THE hell of it is the way they get drowned in hot oil!" Halt Jaxon said.

Nace stuffed his pipe, then looked at the stem. It was cracked. He took a small metal case from his zipper bag, extracted a fresh stem from the assortment it held. He chewed an average of a stem a day out of the pipe. The total often reached three or four when the going got tough.

"What's this—drowned in oil?"

"Several state investigators have been found that way. Also oil men and roustabouts. They're simply drowned—and pretty badly scalded."

The tower of the Exchange National swelled up ahead. Immaculate Jaxon tooled his canary roadster toward it, trying out different horns on the traffic.

"They all got too close to the master mind," Nace mixed his question with a mouthful of smoke. "That it?"

"It's a guess. Yours is as good as anybody's."

"The bodies found in any particular oil tank?"

"Never in any tank." Jaxon touched a button; a horn gave a cow-like moo. "They find the bodies in the damnedest places. One was leaning against a lamp-post as stiff as a board. Some of them have been in hotels, houses—all over."

"That's a hell of a note!" Nace drew on his pipe.

The roadster paused for the traffic light on Main, then made a turn.

"App left this message in the office mailbox." Jaxon fished a finger daintily in the pocket of the tea vest, as if afraid of soiling it. He produced a strip of coarse white copy paper.

Nace took it, read the typewritten message:

JAXON:

Lee Nace, a private detective, will arrive on the three o'clock plane. Meet him and bring him to the hotel Crown Block, room 1820.

APP.

Nace stiffened his brake leg instinctively as the gaudy roadster shaved another car. "Don't they have any traffic laws down here?" A moment later he said. "I hope App doesn't think there's anything secret about this. I'm sunk if he does."

"Yeah, that's right," Jaxon agreed. Then he added, "Unless you sent some agents ahead?"

"Who do you think I am? The army?"

Jaxon grinned. "Well, I didn't know. The A. P. has carried stories about you. You're supposed to be good. I thought maybe you had help. You'll need it."

Nace nodded toward an up-and-down sign which said *Telegram*, and asked, "That's the plant, huh?"

"The sweat shop itself!" Jaxon maneuvered his roadster around a corner.

The wind was from the south, bringing a smell of distilling crude from West Tulsa refineries.

Jaxon asked unexpectedly, "What about the blonde in the Robin Hood's car?"

Nace looked interested. "Well, what about her?"

Jaxon laughed. "I see you didn't get a close look. What a form she had. Oh, man!"

THE Crown Block Hotel was not quite the largest in the Southwest, but it was generally conceded to be the most sumptuous.

When an oil man hit it rich, his first act was to take a suite in the Crown Block. It did not matter whether he made his strike in Seminole, Borger, Oil Hill, or East Texas. He took a suite in the Crown Block. It was sort of a ritual—a man's way of telling the cockeyed world he was on top.

Jaxon swerved his roadster in to the curb. They got out, Nace with his canvas zipper bag. There was a flurry, then hard looks, when bellboys tried unsuccessfully to capture Nace's bag.

They walked a gauntlet of doormen in Czaristic uniforms, and waded in a sea of rich, thick carpet. A silent elevator wafted them up, and they single-filed down the corridor, more rich carpets sponging underfoot.

The door of 1820 was massive, shiny, of mahogany, with a ponderous wrought-bronze lock.

Nace's eyes roved with habitual alertness. Suddenly he grunted, lifted one foot off the carpet and hopped to the wall. Propped against it, he began untying his shoe.

"Must've picked up a rock at the airport!"

His hand, apparently resting against the wall as a brace, made a slight rubbing motion.

There was a small, irregularly shaped chalk mark on the wall. This was almost unnoticeable to the casual eye.

When Nace took his hand away, the mark was gone.

Nace tore a bit of inner sole from the shoe, put it back on. Then he opened his canvas bag. He took several expensive looking cigars from a case and pocketed them. The adder scar, seeming to come from nowhere, was once more coiling redly on his forehead.

"Let's go!" His voice was dry, with a bit of a rattle.

Jaxon rippled knuckles on the door. A voice invited them in. Opening the door, Jaxon stepped back politely to let Nace in first.

Three men appeared suddenly, shoulder to shoulder, inside the room. The Robin Hood and his two followers.

Frontier six-guns bulked big in their fists.

The blonde, without uncoiling herself from a chair in which she sat, said, "Come right in, boys! Cut yourself a piece of cake!"

Nace ambled into the room, hands held far out from his sides. He was so very tall that he instinctively ducked a little as he entered.

Halt Jaxon rolled his eyes, made faces. "So the note was a come-on!"

"Can the guff! Come on in here!" The Robin Hood made a meaningful gesture with his thumb and a gun-hammer.

Gun snouts followed Nace and Jaxon, crowding them to the wall. The blonde uncoiled from her chair, closed the door, and stood with her back pressing the panel.

Her blonde hair was done in a flat patty on the back of her neck. She slid slender fingers under this, and brought out a tiny derringer, similar to Jaxon's, but of smaller calibre.

The Robin Hood eyed the small gun with wolfish concentration. "Where'd you get that, sister?"

"From Monkey Ward."

"Don't get sassy!"

NACE put in, "Where's this Western chivalry I've been hearing about?"

The Robin Hood switched the tall private detective from head to foot with eyes which were unafraid and predatory. He growled, "You behave and keep that mouth shut, and maybe nobody'll get hurt."

He came over and slapped Nace's armpits, lifted coat tails. Frowning, he searched more intensively. "I'm a son-of-a-gun! You ain't heeled!"

He fell to examining Nace's bulletproof vest. The thing seemed to fascinate him. He thumbed open his own vest and compared it with Nace's.

"Where'd you get that?" he asked. "I might buy one like it!"

"Made it myself," Nace advised. "Let's get down to business."

"Sure! Sure!" The Robin Hood turned to his two companions. "I want to talk to Nace alone. Take this over-dressed hombre away. Haul him off to that cabin north of Shell Creek. Hold him until you hear from me."

Jaxon was standing beside a floor lamp. As the two men approached him, he elbowed the lamp violently.

The fixture slammed one man in the face. The fellow ducked back, startled. Jaxon flung upon the other, grasping the gun wrist with both pudgy hands.

The Robin Hood made a growling noise. He slapped his coat violently—two big sixes appeared as if by magic. He hesitated, growled again, then jabbed the guns back out of sight. He leaped for Jaxon.

The blonde, running toward Jaxon, got in the Robin Hood's way and also in the way of the man the floor lamp had hit. She grabbed Jaxon by the throat and began choking.

Freeing one hand, Jaxon slapped her with the back of his fist. The blow reeled her away. She collided with a chair and went over, tangled with rungs and armrests.

"Beat it!" the Robin Hood rasped at her. "We'll handle this!"

The blonde, still mixed with the chair, fumbled at her nape for the gun under her hair.

Nace, leaping to her, harvested the gun with a single clutch. He pocketed it. Going on, he came up behind the Robin Hood. Both his hands went under the tail of the man's coat. They grabbed a belt, pulled. There was a snap. Nace's hands reappeared with the Robin Hood's gun belt and both big revolver holsters.

The man the lamp had hit drew a gun. Nace swung the captured belt, whip fashion. Both six shooters flew out, but the holsters popped loudly on the man's face. The fellow squawled, lost his weapon. Nace round-housed a fist to his middle. The man closed like a book.

The Robin Hood was whirling. Nace let knuckles fly at the scarred wolf jaw. They landed squarely. Arms fanning spasmodically, the Robin Hood reeled toward the window. Unable to help himself, he popped head and shoulders through the sash. He all but fell to his death, eighteen floors below.

The Oklahoma bad man wore cowboy boots. Clutching their narrow toes, Nace hauled their owner back in.

Jaxon and his opponent swore, swapped blows, on the floor.

The blonde untangled from the chair, ran to a table on which her purse lay and scooped it up. She unclipped it, spaded a hand inside, then shoved purse and hand at Nace and Jaxon.

"Hold it!" she snapped.

Nace promptly jutted his hands above his head. Jaxon tore free of his dazed foe, lurched up and dived at the girl.

Nace tripped him. Jaxon tumbled end over end like a soft ball.

One of the Robin Hood's men crawled for his fallen gun. Nace, his hands still raised, jumped sideways, and mashed the fellow against the wall.

Ducking, Nace scooped up the gun. Continuing the same movement, he fell behind the bed.

The Robin Hood and his two followers staggered out of the room. The girl followed, banging the door shut.

JAXON bounced up from the floor, screaming. "You tripped me! There's ten thousand reward for that guy! And you trip me—"

"I kept you from getting a lead pill!" Nace snapped. Rapidly he gathered the guns scattered around the room.

When they ran into the hall, an elevator door was sliding shut.

"Gimme one of them guns!" Jaxon yelled.

"To hell with you, hothead!"

Jaxon made faces, ran back into the room. Nace bore a staccato thumb on the elevator button. Time crawled. A minute. And still no cage came.

"Here they go!" Jaxon squawled from within the room. Nace ran to his side. Jaxon was hanging out of a window. On the sidewalk far below, the Robin Hood, his two men, and the blonde, were legging it for a corner.

Jaxon tore at one of the guns in Nace's hands. Nace held on tightly, would not give it up. The runners below disappeared.

Cursing, his round face purple, Jaxon squealed, "A fine cluck you are! I could have potted the Robin Hood from the window. Damn your hide! Ten thousand reward—"

Nace waved a fist under his nose. "Shut up, or I'll feed you a mess of knuckles!"

Jaxon squared off belligerently. "Any damn time you feel lucky—"

"Just a newspaper fathead!" The adder scar above Nace's eyes was red as ink. "You dope! You balled things up!"

"I did like hell!"

"The Robin Hood had something on his mind. He wanted to talk, and I wanted to hear him! But did you give us a chance? Yes, you did—not!"

Jaxon hardened his fists. "I don't give a damn about that! You wouldn't come across with the gun. That costs me ten thousand. It burns me up!"

He swung a fist at Nace's face. Nace rolled back from the blow; his right arm came up; his hard knuckles smacked against Jaxon's biceps. It was an agonizing blow.

Jaxon yodeled from the pain in his muscles. Nace collared him, hauled him to the door, and gave him the boot. He slammed the door after the stumbling, enraged oil editor. Nothing happened for a few seconds; then elevator doors clanged in the hall. Nace looked out. Jaxon was gone.

Going to his canvas zipper bag, Nace carefully replaced the cigars which he had taken out before entering the room. Two were broken. He disposed of these in the bath.

Carrying his bag, he descended in a tardy elevator and left the hotel. He took a cab to the new Union Station, changed to another, and went to a small hotel on Boston.

There was a derrick firm on one side of the hotel, a well-shooter supply house on the other. Walking up two flights, Nace found a room number. He knocked on the door. Silence answered.

Car horns honked in the street below. Over on Main, newsboys were yelling, "The *Telegram.*"

Nace knocked again, a peculiar signal—two taps, then two more, widely separated.

The blonde opened the door.

CHAPTER III

Drowned in Oil

NACE went in, closed the door. He lowered his bag, then opened it. From it he took a sensitive microphone, fitted with vacuum cups. He stuck this to the door. Wires led from the microphone to an amplifier in the bag, thence to headphones.

The device was a highly sensitive sound pick-up. It would amplify any noise from the corridor a thousand fold. Should anyone approach, the instrument would make the noise like that of an elephant stampeding.

"Any chance that they suspect you are my agent?" he asked the girl.

"Don't make me laugh." The blonde patted her hair. "With this layout I don't even know myself. Gosh, Nace! What if this platinum dye won't wash off?"

"I guess I could stand that." As he took out the pipe, and plugged it, Nace eyed her.

Her first name was Julia. Her last name was the same as his own—Nace. She was a cousin, very distant. She had not been an operative in his agency for long and she was already good, and getting better. She had what it took.

"You didn't lose any time getting lined up," he said, making the words both a compliment and a question.

She laughed. "It was easy. Half the people in town know the Robin Hood by sight. But you can save your blarney. I haven't learned anything."

Nace fired his pipe, then clamped one receiver of the sound pick-up to an ear. "What do they want with me?" he queried.

"A talky-talk!"

"What about?"

"Search me. The Robin Hood is all hot and bothered about nothing. When he learned you were coming to town, he said he'd go out and meet you. I didn't know until later that he only wanted to talk."

"Everybody in town knew I was coming, huh?"

"The Robin Hood has his ways of learning things. He must have a spy on the *Telegram*."

"Is he mixed up in this hot oil?"

"Sure! But there's a catch to that, Nace. I don't know how he stands—whether he's in the ring, or out of it."

Nace eyed a fly-specked telephone. "Do you think you're safe, kid?"

"Believe it or not, this Robin Hood is the McCoy. He packs two guns and he's killed his men. He'll fight anybody. But he doesn't shoot in the back, doesn't shoot unarmed men, and respects women."

"Chivalrous, huh?"

"That's straight, Nace. Not one of the gang has made a pass at me; I haven't heard any dirty stories, and they make their eyes behave. Different from our eastern mobs, eh?"

Nace took off the listener receiver. He went to the telephone, picked up a directory, and thumbed through it.

"Who did you tell 'em you were?"

"Just a little girl who got turned out of the California pen a few weeks ago. For fifty dollars a New York printer faked me a newspaper clipping with my picture and everything."

Nace found his number. He placed a finger on the dial nobs. When the selector had made his connection he requested, "Ebenezer App, please."

Probably twenty seconds later, he began, "This is Nace. I just got into town . . . . Oh, Jaxon told you, did he . . . . It was a fake note that led us to the hotel."

A metallic gobble of words poured from the receiver. Nace listened to them for some time, asked, "Who is it?" twice, and hung up.

"App says he found out who's behind the hot oil ring," he told the blonde. "He said he accused the fellow and made him admit it—and for me to come over and make the pinch."

"Who is it?"

"App said he'd spill that when I got there. He flatly refused to name the fellow over the phone."

TULSA was a town of a hundred and fifty thousand. Unlike large cities of the east, alleys ran behind the business houses.

Leaving the hotel with his zipper bag, Nace stepped from the rear door into an alley. He swung rapidly for the corner. Newsboys on the street were shouting, "Oil scandal grows! Last oil drowning victim still unidentified." Every paper bore App's Santa Claus picture. "Mr. App pushes investigation!"

Nace ignored them, striding toward the Telegram Building. His eyes roved alertly. He saw men in field boots, Osages in bright blankets, pasty-faced clerks with puckers between their eyes that meant eyestrain.

The *Telegram* was a tall narrow building of brick. Pretty girls ran the elevators.

Nace thought of Julia as he rode up. Ordinarily she was a redhead. The combination of her looks and her brains was hard to find. She had been under his instructions for a month now. Numerous methods of signaling had been part of the training. Sun flashes with the compact mirror was one.

The tiny chalk marks, which he had stopped in the corridor of the Crown Block Hotel to erase, was another. They had warned him of the ambush in the room.

Nace swore. He had gone into that room deliberately. The reckless Jaxon had defeated his chances of learning something—perhaps something valuable.

Nace found a door bearing the name, "Ebenezer App, Publisher."

He went in and found himself in a reception room—green carpeted, tan-walled, fitted with leather chairs and a reception desk.

A girl with stringy brown hair lay across one of the chairs. She wore square-toed shoes and a brown frock with a starched white collar. She had a very long nose. Blood was dripping from her nose to the carpet.

Nace opened a door marked, "Mr. App—Private." The office beyond reeked emptiness. The furniture was expensive and in good taste. App's picture hung on the wall. The Shavian beard bristled. His cheeks were ruddy. His eyes were fenced with little wrinkles. With the addition of a big white mustache, he would have made a perfect Santa Claus.

Coming back, Nace examined the girl with the long nose. The fifth paper cup of ice water from the cooler revived her.

Jaxon came in when she was rolling her eyes and gurgling. He had combed his hair, put on a fresh shirt. Once more he looked as if he were right out of a bandbox.

He demanded, "What the hell's going on here, Nace!"

At this, the girl leaped up. She dropped her cup, pointed both hands at Nace, screamed, "He's the man who hit me!"

Jaxon sneered, "I wouldn't put it past him."

Nace lunged at Jaxon, fists up and hard. The oil editor spun and fled from the office like a frightened peacock.

Nace turned back to the girl but did not approach her lest he frighten her. "You're mistaken, you know! What happened?"

"A man came in! He said Mr. Nace was waiting outside." The girl's voice was scared. "He went in to see Mr. App. And then someone must have hit me. I didn't see who it was."

That was all she knew. When he had finished his questioning, Nace ambled out into the hall. Jaxon stood there, undecided. He walked off hastily at sight of Nace.

Nace went down to the city room. There was a big picture of App's Santa Claus countenance on the wall. Nace asked for a late edition, got it, was stared at, and left the building. He hopped a cab at the corner, said, "The morgue the city uses."

SLOUCHED on the cushions, Nace studied the newspaper, centering his attention on the unidentified man, who had been drowned in oil. The fellow had been found near Reservoir Hill two days ago.

There was little else of interest—except that no one seemed to know who he was. The body was being held at the morgue.

On the front of the morgue, a sign said, "Funeral Home."

It was a plain building. Fifteen years ago, when Tulsa was a village it must have been a private mansion. The doors had been enlarged to permit coffins being carried through.

Nace found a bright-eyed little man in charge. They went into a room where there were long marble slabs and much noise—laughter, shouts.

The funeral home, it seemed, also conducted an ambulance service. Two ambulance drivers and an assistant undertaker were rolling craps on a marble slab. They had turned a stiff body on the slab and were using it as a backstop for the dice. They reminded Nace of small boys trying to show how calloused they were.

In the rear of the room, the undertaker uncovered a cadaver.

The dead man was tall, lean. His skin, where the oil had not been wiped off, was strangely white. Fingernails, hair, eyebrows—all were gone.

Nace studied the long, sharp features. Somehow, they struck him as vaguely familiar.

"Hot oil got this one!" he said. "And I don't mean stolen oil, either!"

"The oil must have been scalding hot," the undertaker agreed.

"Have the others been like this?"

"You mean scalded? Sure!"

Once more Nace squinted at the features of the dead man. He could not get rid of the idea he had seen the fellow before.

"O. K.," he told the undertaker.

He went back, and stopped in front of the crapshooters bouncing dice against the body. He scowled at them.

"Cut it out!"

The dicers glared at him. "Who the hell're you?"

"Cut it out!" Nace said, and beetled his brows.

The trio scowled, changed feet. The strange crimson scar on Nace's forehead seemed to disquiet them. Then they gathered up their dice and went out, trying to maintain a dignity.

Disgust rode heavy on Nace's long, bony face.

The undertaker began, "What was the idea—"

"When you're dead, do you want three guys bouncing dice off your ribs—"

From the direction the three dice-rollers had taken, came gasps, low cries of surprise.

"Stand still, you monkeys!" gritted an ugly voice.

Nace came to life like an electrical machine switched on. He dived for the door, whipping out his tear gas firing cylinder. Reaching the door he got a glimpse of a man—a man he had never seen before. The fellow had a bulky, shapeless body, a long neck, and a chicken-like head. He carried an automatic shotgun, the barrel sawed off at the magazine tip. He slapped the automatic shotgun against his hip. He pulled the trigger three times.

The gun was ear-splitting. Across the morgue room other explosions crashed like echoes. Holes the size of washtubs opened magically in the wall. Plaster, lath, and bits of brick rained. Marble slabs upset on their stands.

Nace had jumped clear of the door. Now he retreated farther, dragging the undertaker.

ROBIN HOOD LLOYD appeared from nowhere, threw up his six. It boomed. The shot-gunner sagged, leaking scarlet from a blue-rimmed pit which had suddenly appeared directly between his eyes.

Nace and the Robin Hood glared at each other.

"Before I'm through with this, I'm gonna beat hell out of you!" the Robin Hood snarled. "But not now! I hear old Ebenezer App has been kidnaped! Anything to it?"

Nace hesitated briefly. "Yeah. And just before it happened, App found out who is heading the hot oil ring!"

"Thanks!" Backing swiftly, the Robin Hood disappeared. A car volleyed off.

A few seconds later Nace got his cab again.

Excitement was noticeable in the Telegram Building when he entered. In the glass-enclosed circulation room off the lobby, groups of clerks stood under a Santa Claus picture of App and talked. The pretty elevator operators were flushed and perturbed.

In the city room, Jaxon was talking to four policemen. The dressy oil editcr glared at Nace. "There's the bum now!"

The policeman came over, jaws out, eyes wintry. One jingled handcuffs suggestively.

Nace got in first word. "I'm a private detective—"

"We know all about you, brother!" frowned one cop. "We don't like your kind! And we don't like the way you're getting around this man's town!"

The adder leered redly at them from Nace's forehead. "So what?"

"So it's the can for you."

Nace put his zipper bag on a reporter's desk, opened it, and extracted a yellow fold of paper.

"What's that?" questioned the officer.

"Telegraphic commission from the governor—appointing me a special investigator in this hot oil business."

The policeman scowled. "Let's see that!"

TEN minutes later, Nace was alone in the newspaper morgue. The policemen had gone their disgruntled way. They didn't like it, but Nace had a special permission from the governor.

Jaxon after making ugly grimaces, to express his personal opinion of Nace, had gone off somewhere—probably to the oil editor's sanctum.

The morgue was a dingy room, a fly-specked Santy picture of App on the wall. There were great steel filing cabinets. These held drawers, and the drawers were gorged with envelopes. There were pictures, mats, clippings, cuts.

The cabinet bore alphabetic file letters. Nace was looking under the "L" guide.

He found a quart of white mule, a pair of dice and two packs of cards, which some reporter must have hidden.

There were four fat envelopes on Robin Hood Lloyd. They traced his life from the cradle. His associates, his family, his boyhood chums—all were named.

The file was a potential fortune. It contained material enough to write a book on Oklahoma's bad boy who was probably destined to take a place alongside Jesse James.

Nace read the clippings, replaced them, then left the morgue. As he was passing the city room, a copy boy ran out.

"Somebody on the 'phone wantin' you, Mr. Nace!" he said.

"I'll take it in the booth," Nace told him, and entered a little glass enclosure, and picked up an instrument.

Julia's voice came to him.

CHAPTER IV

THE OIL-BOILED TRAIL

"WHAT'S eating you?" Nace asked quietly.

Julia said, "I followed them!"

"Where are you now?"

"In a bungalow at the foot of Reservoir Hill. I tagged the Robin Hood to a house at the top of the Hill."

"Describe the house."

"I'll do better than that. Here's the number." She gave him a street and numerals. "There's several houses on the hill and this is one of the biggest."

"O. K.," said Nace. "What do you make of this jamboree?"

"Search me, boss! I'm fairly certain the Robin Hood is somebody big in the oil ring. But just now he's sure going around like a chicken with its head off!"

"You know there's a body in the morgue now."

"Yes."

"I just identified the corpse by pictures and clippings at the *Telegram*. It's the Robin Hood's kid brother."

"Hm-m-m!" Julia made a thoughtful humming sound. "That may explain a lot, boss!"

"I wouldn't be surprised."

Julia said hastily, "Are you coming out here?"

"What's the address of this place you're telephoning from?" Nace demanded.

Again she gave him a street and a number. "I'm going to hang around on the front porch!" she advised. "The lady who owns it is an old dear. She'll let me stay."

Nace drew on his pipe and ran a smoke plume into the upper part of the booth. His forehead, wrinkling, bunched the crimson snake scar. He thought for a minute.

"Hold the wire," he said.

"What?"

"I've got to see a man about a dog."

He planted the instrument on the booth shelf, but did not hang up the receiver. Whipping out of the booth, he dived into a hallway and went up a flight of stairs four at a time.

He knew the newspaper phone P. B. X. operator was in an office on the same floor with the morgue. He had noticed the phone room door.

Rising on tiptoe, he gave a good imitation of floating as he went down the corridor. Nearing the frosted glass panel of the P. B. X. room, he ducked low, so his shadow would not show. He gave the knob a gentle try. It gave; the door swiveled in.

The phone girl looked around, gave him a forced, uneasy smile. Her lids shuttered up when she saw Nace's peculiar scar. The sight seemed to frighten her.

"Wh-what do you want?"

"A look at your board!" Nace told her.

The girl's jaw dropped. Her swivel chair squeaked as she spun. She reached both hands for the web of connecting cords on the P. B. X. board.

"None of that!" Lunging, Nace brushed her hands back.

The girl leaped up, mouth agape to scream. Nace plastered a hand over her mouth and forced her back in the chair.

Slotted brass holders under each jack on the phone board bore designation cards. Nace examined these; he followed cords with his fingers. His inspection lasted at least a minute.

He frowned at the P. B. X. operator. The serpent on his forehead seemed to coil and uncoil, as the wrinkles came and went.

"You've got my connection cut in on an outside line," he pointed out grimly. "What's the idea?"

The girl shrank down into her chair. "You're crazy."

NACE shoved his telegram from the governor under her nose. She seemed reluctant to look at it.

"Read that!" he said harshly.

The girl read. She began to shudder. Her hands opened and shut like the paws of a stretching cat.

"Do you know that a murder accomplice can draw a life sentence?" Nace asked fiercely.

The girl spread her hands over her face and began to sob.

"Cough up," he commanded. "You're in a tough spot, kid."

The girl blubbered, "I didn't know it was anything very wrong. If I had I w-wouldn't have done it for fifty dollars a week."

"Who hired you?"

"A man I met at a dance."

"His name?" Nace prompted.

"Chick Oliver."

Nace thought of the chicken-headed man who had taken the Robin Hood bullet between the eyes. "Was he a little, squatty guy with a long neck and a head like a chicken?"

"T-t-that's him!" stuttered the frightened operator.

"He was killed about twenty minutes ago," Nace said ominously, knowing it would do no harm to frighten her a bit more.

She began to rock from side to side and whimper.

"What conversations were you to connect outside?" he asked.

"Anything for Mr. App," she moaned. "Then, a little while ago, I got a call asking for anything you received."

"What number did you connect the calls to?"

She gave him a phone number, then quavered, "I h-h-hope I h-h-haven't done any harm—"

"Oh, no!" he jeered, "You haven't done anything but nearly get me killed and get App kidnaped and probably murdered."

The girl rolled over so she could mash her features against the arm of her chair.

Nace trailed downstairs, grim-faced. He found the city editor—a youngish man with too much belly—and asked, "Got a back number directory?"

The directory was produced. Nace looked up the number the girl had given him.

"Clarence Oliver," was the name which followed the number. The address was out on Eleventh. A high number! That meant it was far out.

Nace went back to the P. B. X. girl's cubby. He had remembered his interrupted conversation with Julia.

The phone operator still sobbed in her chair.

Nace put on her headset and snapped levers. He called, "Hello!" several times but received no reply. Julia had left the wire.

"Did you touch these connections?" he asked the operator.

She shook her head, and tears fell off her chin.

"Keep your trap shut about this!" Nace advised her. "Maybe it'll come out all right."

He now called the house from which Julia had talked. A pleasant-voiced old lady—she sounded like an old lady—answered him.

"The blonde girl?" the old lady echoed, seeming surprised. "Oh, two men came for her a minute ago, and she left with them."

Nace turned somewhat pale, the scar on his forehead got red. His eyes acquired a frightened look.

"Thank you," he told the old lady in a thick voice and hung up.

A TAXI carried Nace out Eleventh. The machine traveled between forty and fifty, with the horn open. Eleventh was a mixed street. Scattered along it were small stores, greenhouses, root beer stalls, pig stands. There was an ice cream factory and oil field, tool concerns. They passed the Tulsa U. stadium.

Clarence Oliver's house was a little brick, very neat. The walk was of red concrete. There was a garage to the side, and a tennis court behind.

Watching both windows, Nace ran up the walk. He tried the door. It was locked. He batted the glass out with his fist, turned the spring lock inside and walked in.

The room was loaded with cheap brown furniture, bridge lamps, card tables, a radio. The rug was flowery. All the stuff looked new.

A faint odor reeked in the air. Nace sniffed. He breathed one word, "Oil."

Nace crossed the room, almost running. The hallway beyond was square; four doors opening off it gave to bath, kitchen and two bedrooms. Nace tried the bath. Nothing there.

He knocked open the end door and found himself in a kitchen, ornate with white enamel. The oil smell was stronger here, mingling with cooking odors.

A man-sized bundle reposed on the floor, near one wall. It was swathed in canvas. Nace found as he worked over it that underneath the canvas were layers of oilcloth.

Four Winchester rifles had been tied into the bundle to give it stiffness. No doubt the men who had carried it here had wanted it to look rigid, as if it were a piece of furniture.

It was the body of a man. Nace looked at the face. It was almost unidentifiable. There was a wad of white hair, which might have been a beard which had slipped. A Santa Claus beard.

"App had that kind of a beard!" Nace muttered.

Then he fell to straining his ears. He could hear footsteps out in front, coming up the walk. He went silently to a window.

There were three of them, all strangers. They approached suspiciously.

Nace eased backward quietly and sidled into a bedroom. While the three newcomers tramped on the front porch, Nace worked at his sleeves. He wore cuff links which were oversize, long, and narrow. Under his prying fingernails, tiny secret lids opened in the links. He took out small darts.

The darts were but little larger than pins. The tapering rear ends bore tiny metal vanes to make them travel straight when thrown.

The three men entered the house with the noisy abandon of fellows who felt themselves at home.

"Things don't look natural around here without Chick," one remarked.

"I'd like to know exactly what happened to Chick," muttered another. "Did Nace get him? Or did the Robin Hood?"

"We'll find out from the evening papers!" grunted a third man. "What we've got to do now is get rid of old App's body."

They filed past the bedroom door.

NACE threw a pair of his darts in one-two succession. He flung them hard. The men jumped, clapped hands to their arms, swore. Then both reeled crazily and crashed full length on the floor.

Eyes popping, the third man stared at the first two.

"What the hell?" he began. "What ails—"

Nace lunged at him, hands outstretched, fingers splayed. A moment later they were entangled, and rolling on the floor. The man got a gun out of his clothing. Grasping the hand which held the weapon, Nace beat it against the floor. Squealing, the fellow lost the gun.

The next instant, the fellow had produced a knife. The suddenness with which he did this smacked of the supernatural. The blade *zinged* across the front of Nace's bullet-proof vest, opening his clothing.

Nace fell on the knife and hand with his chest. The other was strong, and Nace's weight was not sufficient to pin him down. The man jerked free, sprang up.

There was only one thing Nace could do. He picked open the secret lid in one of his cufflinks, shook out a dart, and flung it. The other ducked wildly. But Nace had calculated on that. The dart thorned into the fellow's face.

Almost at once, the man crashed down.

Nace scowled at the recumbent form. He had not wanted to use that third dart. He had hoped to question one of the men. But now all three would be unconscious at least two hours. The darts were daubed with a drug which produced a stupor lasting that long. Nothing, as far as Nace knew, could revive the men before the two-hour interval was up.

Nace began searching his victims. He turned up money, keys, soiled handkerchiefs. After the fashion of crooks, they were carrying nothing which would identify them.

A coat pocket disgorged an object

which caused Nace to spring erect and swear thickly. He turned the thing in his hand. It had an ugly significance. It could have come into the possession of these men in only one fashion—with the capture of its owner.

It was the girl's flat pancake compact.

CHAPTER V

THE HILLTOP PROWL

NACE ran to the telephone. The number he requested was the one from which the blonde had called —the house at the foot of Reservoir Hill. The wait which followed was so long that he began to think he was not going to get his party. But the pleasant-voiced, elderly lady finally answered.

Nace asked for a description of the two men with whom Julia had departed. In return, he received an accurate word picture of two of the trio who lay unconscious in the room in which he stood.

"Thank you," he said, and hung up.

He bent over the three, shook them angrily, knowing however, that it was useless. That they had seized the girl, there was not the slightest doubt. But it would be two hours before anything could be done toward making them tell where they had taken her.

Nace went to the tennis court in the back yard. With his pocket knife he stripped off the thin, strong cords which supported the net. Carrying these back into the house, he bound the three senseless men. He tied efficient gags between their jaws, then plastered these over with adhesive tape which he found in the bathroom. There was a small basement under part of the house. It held only a gas-burning furnace. He left his prisoners there.

His taxicab was still waiting where he had left it a short distance up the street. He got in, perched tensely on the edge of the cushion, and directed, "Reservoir Hill. And make it snappy!"

Reservoir Hill was a knob at the north of the Tulsa City limit. A zig-zagging drive climbed its abrupt slope. The top offered a bird's-eye view of Tulsa, and mansions clustered there.

Behind the hill was the Osage—a hilly wilderness of scrub oak, spotted with oil derricks and compression pumping stations and a small refinery or two.

Nace dismissed his cab at the top of the hill and went on afoot. There was the faint sound of oil wells pumping in the distance. The tang of crude hung faintly in the air. Nowhere in Tulsa did it seem possible to escape the odor of oil.

The mansions on top were even more magnificent than they had appeared from below. In architectural style they ranged from Spanish, Irish and old English, to American Colonial. The fact that they were expensive, and the grounds well maintained, kept them from seeming garish.

There were no sidewalks along the wide, smooth, concrete parkways. Nace walked in the road, keeping to the left. Street names were painted, in black on yellow panels, on the raised curbs. His eyes searched these.

When he found the one he wanted, he walked on as if it were of no consequence.

He still carried his canvas zipper bag. Indeed, the valise seemed to be out of his hands only when he was in action. He lugged it along instinctively, much as another man wears his hat.

Sheltered by an ornamental hedge, he lowered the bag, opened it, and took out a small but powerful telescope. He wielded this until he located the house to which Julia had trailed the Robin Hood.

Somewhere near, a voice purred, "So now you've turned peeping Tom!"

NACE'S first reaction was to jump for cover. He did that. Concealed on the other side of the hedge, he scuttled twenty feet, then stopped.

The voice made hateful laughter. "Scared of little old Jaxon, skipper?"

Nace angled south a few yards, then worked through the hedge. He found Jaxon hunkered down behind a squatty fir tree.

Jaxon returned Nace's black look with an unpleasant smile. "So now I'm in your hair again!"

Nace glared. "Hell, but you're funny."

"Oh, yeah?" Jaxon seemed to consider the insult. "I reckon I don't rate an explanation of why you're here."

Nace wrinkled the serpentine scar on his forehead. "I'm not yet sure what you rate."

Jaxon leered. "If you're wondering how I got the tip-off on this place, skipper, I'll tell you! It was the phone girl. She listened in when your platinum-haired dame called you. Mighty slick, your sending the blonde on ahead! I didn't give you the credit."

"Why are you out here?" Nace asked him levelly.

"Didn't I just tell you? For the Robin Hood and the ten thousand reward on his head."

"Blood money, eh?"

"Any money is good money, skipper—"

Nace flung out a hand and shoved. Sputtering angrily, Jaxon upset. Attempting to stop Jaxon, Nace clutched and got the little derringer from the oil editor's watch pocket.

Sitting up, Jaxon lashed out with two angry blows. Nace dodged the fists, vanishing from their path in a way that seemed uncanny.

"Gimme that owl head!" Jaxon said.

Ignoring the request, Nace told him, "You can either go back to town, or you can behave yourself and go with me."

Jaxon considered this, straightening his double-breasted gray vest with angry jerks. In getting the derringer, Nace had torn the watch pocket. Jaxon fingered the frayed edges.

"You couldn't get rid of me!" the oil editor said finally.

"Okay," Nace told him. "But you make one crack-brained move and I'll crown you!"

"I'll get that ten thousand before this is over," Jaxon said grimly.

Nace opened his zipper bag to return the telescope. While he had the bag open, he removed four of his cigars, and pocketed them.

"I thought you smoked a pipe," Jaxon grunted.

"What do you care what I smoke?"

They set off along the street, side by side.

The house to which Julia had trailed the Robin Hood was situated on a street a block to the right. They headed for it, cutting across yards and haunting the shelter of shrubbery.

The house was probably the most unattractive on the hill, but at the same time one of the largest. It was gray brick, squarish of line, rambling—not unlike a cluster of big gray boxes jammed together.

The body of the house had a height of two stories, Atop this sat a square room, the sides almost entirely of glass. These windows were not curtained, and Nace kept a close watch on them.

No one stirred. The absence of curtains lent the mansion a deserted aspect.

Jaxon whispered shrilly, "The Robin Hood may not be in there. He may have left."

"Shut up!" Nace advised.

They crept up to within threescore feet of the house. There, behind a low, vine-covered fence of steel pickets, they reconnoitered. Using the telescope, Nace not only surveyed the house but also the yard and dwellings around them and behind.

To the rear, Nace saw something which caused him to start violently.

However, he made an elaborate pretence and continued his survey of the surroundings.

Then he tapped Jaxon on the shoulder. "You're going back!"

"What the—"

"Don't argue! Beat it!"

Jaxon made an angry face. "If you think I'm gonna be left out in the cold on that ten thousand—"

Nace showed him a granite-hard fist. "You're going to be left cold on the ground if you don't do what I tell you."

Jaxon considered this; then, mumbling disgustedly, he crawled away.

He had covered no more than two dozen yards when the Robin Hood and his two followers popped out of bushes and seized him.

JAXON put up a violent struggle. He kicked, wielded his fists and tried to use his teeth. He sought to cry out, but a hand over his mouth stopped that.

Nace made no effort to go to his assistance, but merely looked on, as if it were all some drama he had staged. A swipe from a six-gun barrel finally reduced Jaxon to a limp pile.

The Robin Hood approached. His two followers came behind, dragging the oil editor.

Nace and the Robin Hood exchanged sour looks.

"You do the damnedest things!" growled the Oklahoma bandit.

"That's a matter of opinion," Nace told him.

Diving out a quick hand, the Robin Hood searched Nace. He found the derringer which the private detective had taken from Jaxon.

"Hell!" he snarled, and tried to give Nace back the weapon.

Nace scowled, knocked at his hand. The derringer flew off in the shrubbery somewhere.

The Robin Hood sat back with a pained expression on his wolfish features. "If I ever catch you with a gun in your hand, I'm going to kill you dead!" he promised.

Nace replied nothing. In the eastern newspapers he had read of this fellow—and wondered how one man could garner such a reputation. Now that he was in contact with the Robin Hood, the answer was clear. The man had a code of honor and adhered to it. He was a character from the old, two-gun West, transplanted to 1933.

The Robin Hood shoved his wolf jaw out. "We're going in! There ain't nobody in there, but we'll go anyway! I want to talk to you."

They entered the house through a rear door which was unlocked and gave into a kitchen. The furniture, Nace noted, was swathed in dust covers. The place showed few signs of recent occupancy.

Jaxon was deposited on a divan. One of the Robin Hood's men went into the kitchen, ran water into his hat, came back, and doused the fluid on the recumbent oil editor.

"That bird's a neckpain," Nace said, indicating Jaxon. "Let's get our talk over before he wakes up!"

"An idea!" The Robin Hood jutted his wolf face at Nace. "I want to make a deal with you, feller."

Nace shrugged. "If the deal is to give you the name of the man behind this hot oil business, when I find out who it is—nothing doing!"

The Robin Hood's long jaw lowered almost to his necktie. "How'd you know that was it?"

"What else could it be?" Nace spread his hands. "The man dead in the morgue is your brother. You're out to pay somebody for getting him."

"I'll be damned!" grunted the Robin Hood.

"That's what you came to the airport to see me about," Nace continued. "And you arranged the hotel trap in case you couldn't get to me at the airport. You did fix that hotel business, didn't you—leaving the note in the newspaper office for Jaxon?"

"Yeah," the Robin Hood admitted. "Say—you're pretty sharp."

Nace eyed him intently. "If you're

not afraid of incriminating yourself, you can tell me some things."

The Robin Hood laughed harshly. "Say, feller, I ain't afraid of admittin' anything! If the law ever puts the shuck on me they've already got plenty to hang me. A little bit more won't hurt."

Nace grinned. "You know, I'd kinda hate to see 'em get you, at that."

"To hell with what you think!" the Robin Hood scowled. "I'll blow your damned head off if I ever catch you with a gun! What do you want to know?"

"Have you been mixed up with this hot oil ring?"

"Sure, I've beeen doing most of the dirty work." The wolf face became fiercer. "And I got it in the neck! The big boss is trying to hog the proceeds. I don't know who he is. I never have known."

Nace waved his arm. "What about this house?"

"This is where the boss always met us. That is, he'd come and talk to us from one room, while he stayed in another."

CHAPTER VI

THE SMOKE TRAP

NACE squinted at the Oklahoma badman, absently fingering the cigars in his pocket.

"Well, don't you believe me?" the man scowled.

"What difference does it make?" It was just as well, Nace reflected, to feed the fellow a little sass and keep him guessing. The Robin Hood might have likeable qualities, but that did not mean he was a pleasant customer.

Should he get the idea Nace was no longer useful, he would be as likely as not to shove a gun in the private detective's hand and demand that they shoot it out, Wild-West style. He was that kind of a character.

"I'm going to look around," Nace said, and started for a door.

"I've already done that!" The Robin Hood scowled blackly. "You stick here!"

Nace pivoted. "You know that blonde girl?"

"Sure! And don't you go making cracks about her, shamus! She's a straight little number!"

"Don't I know it," Nace said earnestly. "You don't, by any chance, know where she is?"

The Robin Hood hesitated. "I ain't seen her since we split up, after leavin' the Crown Block!"

"I thought so," Nace's voice suddenly sounded old, weary. "She has disappeared. Two lice working for the big brain back of the hot oil ring grabbed her."

The Robin Hood swore softly. "How d'you know that?"

That, Nace reflected, was something else to keep the fellow guessing. No good could come of letting the Robin Hood know that Julia was Nace's assistant.

Saying nothing, Nace passed through a door. He was cursed at, ordered to come back. He ignored profanity and summons, and began to search.

None of the upstairs rooms yielded anything. The glass-walled box of a room which sat atop the house was entirely bare of furnishings. There was dust on the floor, a thin film. It was smudged and tracked where men, in the hours or the days past, had crouched to watch the surroundings.

He ended up in the basement. This was very large, divided into several rooms—washroom, gym, billiard room, and a larger enclosure which held a furnace.

The furnace was an oil burner, and there was a fuel tank almost as large as half a railway tank car.

It was very warm in the furnace room. Nace put a hand on the furnace. It was hot. He opened the doors. The fires were out. There was no room for anyone to have been concealed in the furnace.

He went over and started to climb upon the fuel tank, with the idea of peering in the manhole at the top. Instead of doing that, he sprang back, ran to the stairs.

"Come down here!" he called. "I've got something for you!"

There was no answer from above.

"Come here!" Nace repeated sharply.

No reply.

Nace climbed the stairs with long jumps, ran into the room where he had left Robin Hood Lloyd and his companions.

Jaxon glared at Nace over the twin blue snouts of a derringer.

"I'm gonna collect that ten thousand yet!" the oil editor gritted.

THE Robin Hood and his two fellows had their hands at shoulder level. Their faces held fierce hate, and also wariness. The derringer held only two bullets. But that was enough to kill two men.

Waving his weapon to cover everyone, Jaxon sidled over and disarmed his prisoners.

"Jaxon—you nut!" Nace started forward.

"Get back!" Jaxon snarled. "I'd like nothing better than to sink lead in you!"

In a loud, wolf-howl of a voice, the Robin Hood said, "He had the hideout up his pants leg!"

"That's your hard luck!" Nace grunted. "You searched 'im—not me!"

"Shut up and plop down on your faces!" Jaxon ordered.

The Robin Hood's clawlike hands opened and shut. He exhibited all the signs of a man about to make a break.

"Go ahead—if you want to croak!" Nace told him, and lay his full length on the floor. "This lunk ain't foolin'! That ten thousand has got him crazy."

Reluctantly, as if their joints were afflicted with a stiffness, Oklahoma's master outlaw and his two satellites followed Nace's example in flattening to the floor. They let Jaxon bind them.

When the job was done, Jaxon stepped back. His face was flushed, his eyes gleeful.

"Now to call a flock of cops!" he gloated.

He went to the telephone, picked up the receiver and listened. Making one of his faces, he flung away from the instrument. "Line's dead! Wires must be cut!"

He seized upon Nace's bag, stripped back the zipper, and peered inside.

"Regular bag of magic!" He leered at Nace. "I'll just take this along. I don't want you gettin' away and turnin' your buddies loose!"

He walked outdoors. The rear door slammed.

Nace sat up. Twisting, he managed to reach his left trouser leg with both hands. He grasped it at the cuff, one hand on either side of the seam, and made a tearing gesture. The seam pulled apart.

Six inches of a thin hacksaw blade came out.

Jaxon had used wire clothesline for binding them. The hacksaw blade quickly cut through the bonds on Nace's ankles. He ran to the Robin Hood.

"Hold the blade!" he commanded. "I'll saw my wrists free."

Eagerly, the bandit complied. It required perhaps a minute for Nace to loosen his hands. Twice, he gashed himself. Then he sprang erect.

"Now untie me!" growled the Robin Hood.

Nace laughed harshly. "Who said anything about untying you?"

The bandit snarled like a wolf in a trap. "Damn you! If I ever catch you with a gun, it'll be your finish!"

Ignoring the ominous promise, Nace glided to a window and looked out. There was no Jaxon. But the man had had time to depart.

"Have you been watching this house all afternoon?" Nace asked the Robin Hood.

"Go chase yourself!"

"Have you? This is important!"

"Yeah—all afternoon!" the bandit admitted grouchily. "Why?"

"The blonde followed you here, and then disappeared. That proves she's not here—she couldn't have been brought in without you noticing."

"How come you know so much about that blonde?" the Robin Hood pondered.

WITHOUT enlightening the puzzled outlaw, Nace dropped from a window and dived into shrubbery. He angled northeast. Reservoir Hill sloped down there with less abruptness.

Weeds grew profusely, and to the size of small trees. A single narrow drive, the concrete somewhat cracked, angled down the slope.

He soon found what he had hoped for—a car standing in the weeds a few yards from the seldom-used road. It was a limousine, large, the body custom made.

Nace went to it and looked in. It was empty.

"Julia!" he called.

An echo came back at him from the side of Reservoir Hill, but there was no other answer. Nace walked a circle around the car, close to it at first, then more distant.

He found crushed weeds, more weeds which had been broken down, then straightened. A trail! He followed it a few yards.

Julia was tied in a ring around a small scrub oak tree—hands and feet lashed together in a ball. She was gagged with a handkerchief and copious quantities of adhesive tape, also blindfolded.

Nace freed her, helped her erect.

"Who was it?" he demanded.

She began to describe the two men he had left unconscious in the little brick house out on Eleventh.

"Not that pair!" he said impatiently. "Or did they leave you here?"

"No," she said. "It was someone else—one man! But I was blindfolded. I can't tell you a thing about him."

He shrugged, then led the way back up the Hill. Julia bobbed along at his side. The wind stirred her blond hair, and in brushing it out of her eyes, she pulled a handful around where she could look at it. She grimaced. "If this stuff don't wash off—I'll be a sight!"

She was limping, stiffened as she was by being tied around the scrub oak.

"How'd you find me?" she demanded.

"By using the old bean. They had you, and they couldn't have taken you to their hangout, because the Robin Hood was watching. So they had to leave you somewhere. I took a chance on it being near by."

"Do you know who's behind this?"

"Sure," Nace told her. "But don't ask me who. So far, he's been too slick for me to prove anything."

THE Robin Hood and his two companions glared at them when they entered the rambling, blockish brick mansion.

The Robin Hood stuttered, "Who—what—for cryin' out loud!" Then he rolled over on his face and groaned loudly. It had dawned on him that the blonde was Nace's agent. He snarled, "If I ever catch you with a gun—"

Nace looked at the girl. "You heeled?"

She laughed. "Sure! They never found my hideout, and I had no chance to use it."

Reaching under the patty of blond hair on her nape—it still retained some of its shape—she produced her tiny gun.

"O. K. Watch these cookies." Nace gestured at the basement. "I'm going down and have a look. There's a furnace down there, and a fuel oil tank. The outfit is rigged so that the oil runs through the furnace and is heated, boiler fashion."

The girl shuddered. "You mean—"

"That this is the joint where the victims have been drowned in oil—

or boiled in oil, whichever way you want it."

She shuddered again. "What gets me is whatever suggested such a means of murder!"

"Simple! Hot oil! Get it? Anybody gets too close to the hot oil, and he gets cooked in the stuff! Every time one of those bodies was found, no one had any trouble understanding what was back of it."

Nace descended the stairs, entered the furnace room and clambered upon the tank. He was wondering if there might not be a body in it. Apparently there was not.

Concealed in a recess behind the tank where wires for lowering bodies into the boiling oil, and great bolts of oil cloth to bind the cadavers in afterward, and to spread upon the floor so that there would be no stains.

The cache was in a metal box which fitted in a niche that was disclosed when bricks were lifted out.

There was quite an armament with the other stuff—three army rifles, a half dozen automatics, sawed-off shotguns, and a machine gun. The latter was no diminutive Tommy, firing pistol cartridges, but a full-size weapon, chambering long .30-calibre rifle slugs. It was a regulation military gun, airplane type.

Nace was looking at it when the next development came.

"Nace!" the blonde called from above. "Watch out!"

NACE scrambled madly off the tank, carrying the machine gun.

There was scuffling above. Before he came in sight of the stairway, he heard feet clattering down it.

Driving a hand inside his coat, Nace brought out one of the cigars. He clamped it between his teeth. Raking a match on a partition, he lighted the weed. He was puffing strongly when he came within sight of the stairs.

Blonde Julia stood on the steps. She was struggling, kicking. But she was held quite helpless by the man who was behind her, using her as a shield.

The man wore a long raincoat. His trouser legs were pulled up, so that only his hairy shanks showed below the raincoat. His features were entirely masked by two bandanas, one tied so that it hung behind, and the other in front, perforated with eyeholes. His hands were cased in cotton gloves. One held an automatic.

He pointed the weapon at Nace.

"Drop it!" His voice was hoarse, unreal—a disguised tone.

Meekly, Nace dropped the machine gun. He drew on the cigar and ran a plume of smoke from his nostrils.

"C'mon up here!" he was directed. "And get them hands up!"

He followed the orders to the letter.

The Robin Hood and his two satellites still lay on the floor, wired tightly. They glared, cursed in low voices.

"This is the big shot!" snarled the Robin Hood. "The guy who murdered my kid brother!"

"You had no business sending your kid brother punking around to find out who I was!" the masked man growled. Then, to Nace, he snapped, "You get over against the wall!"

Nace backed until his shoulders were clamped to the wall. The cigar protruded stiffly from his teeth.

There was a loud crack. Sparks, tobacco, geysered from the end of Nace's cigar.

The masked man jabbed both hands convulsively in the air. He slanted stiffly backward, as if his heels were hinged to the floor. In his masked forehead, on the right side, but where it had penetrated the brain, was a circular hole somewhat more than an eighth of an inch across.

He crashed his length on the floor, hitting so hard that his heels flew up, then banged back.

Nace took the remains of the cigar out of his teeth, pinched out flaming shreds of tobacco, and pocketed it. The firing barrel inside the cigar, chambered for a .22-long-rifle cartridge, was expensive. Another cigar could be built around it. The thing was fired by a hard pressure of the teeth.

Stooping, Nace started to strip off the mask. Then he hesitated, eyed the girl, and asked, "Want to bet that I can't name him?"

She shuddered. "Don't be dramatic!"

He shucked off the mask.

The cherubic, Santa Claus features of Ebenezer App, white beard and all, were disclosed.

THE Robin Hood, rearing up from the floor, cried out, "For yellin' out loud! The last hombre on earth that I suspected!"

"Sly old duck—he was!" Nace said grimly. He looked at the Robin Hood. "He owes his downfall to you!"

The bandit glared. "You're nuts! I didn't even suspect—"

"Maybe not! But it was your phenagling around with me when I first got here that started App worrying. He thought I smelled a rat, because I hadn't reported to him. He decided to fake his own death and clear out, I guess.

"Probably that body on Eleventh Street is one of his own men who was about his build. He dumped the fellow in oil, then took him out and bundled some white whiskers in with the body."

Julia walked to the door and outside. She didn't like to look at dead men. She called back, "But you said you suspected who it was?"

"Sure!" Nace grunted. "When App told me over the phone that he knew who was behind the hot oil business, he wouldn't say who it was. That was queer. It occurred to me that the old goat just wanted me to hurry over and find out he was kidnapped!"

Swinging over, Nace began untying the Robin Hood and his two men.

"What're you gonna do?" snarled the bandit.

"Let you go bye-bye!"

"If I ever catch you with a gun, I'm gonna kill you!" the Oklahoma outlaw yelled.

Leaving the bandit and his two men to get to their feet and finish untying themselves, Nace went to the body of Ebenezer App. He searched briefly—found a twin to the automatic which the man had carried and dropped when he died. Nace picked up both guns.

He examined the weapons. Both were clipped full of cartridges.

He tossed one to the Robin Hood.

The bandit caught it. He stared, surprised. "What the—"

Nace rapped angrily, "You've been shooting off that mouth about what you'd do if you ever caught me with a gun! Well—"

"You're askin' for it!" the outlaw ripped. He jutted the gun at Nace.

There was a terrific roar—two shots, almost one, but with a slight stutter which marked a shade in timing. One man had beaten.

The Robin Hood squawled. He waved his gun hand madly over his head. It was mangled, and scattered scarlet drops over walls and ceiling.

His automatic skittered along the wall behind him.

Without a word, but with an expression of agonizing chagrin on his wolf face, the Robin Hood whirled and dived through a window. His two men followed him. Running rapidly, they were soon lost to sight.

Nace went to the door.

Blonde Julia gave him a frown.

"Dramatics!" she snapped. "Some day, that stuff is going to be your finish!"

Nace pretended he hadn't heard, and watched a police phaeton moan up the hill and careen into the drive. Dapper Jaxon sprang out, along with numerous policemen. The oil editor was like a peacock hen with a brood of blue chicks.

"Hot after his ten thousand!" Nace said dryly. "Speaking of dramatics—you're gonna hear 'em when he finds his bird has flown!"

A Man Must Sell His Soul Because He Bears the

Mark of the Moon Man

The notorious Moon Man was dead—officially. He had faked his death to save his father—the police chief—and the father of his girl from the disgrace of dishonorable discharge. But now the Moon Man had to come back. Some tremendous power was forcing him to forget the chief, forget Lieutenant McEwen, and forget the girl he loved. Some power was compelling him to play the role of the lowest of two-legged rats. And the first step of that path was marked by a dying man whose jaws were locked on a horrible secret.

Great "Moon Man" Novel

By

FREDERICK C. DAVIS

Author of "Silver Death," "Murder Moon," etc.

The Moon Man's signal threw the dancers into a panic.

CHAPTER I

THE SILENT HORROR

THE taxi came streaking down the black street with reckless speed. The snarl of its engine echoed between dark buildings. The beams of its headlights swung from curb to curb. With a squeaking of tires it swerved past a corner and bucked to a stop in front of police headquarters.

The pop-eyed driver scrambled out and reached for the door-handle with trembling hand. His face was sheety-white, his jaw agape. Before his numb fingers could twist, the door clacked open, and his passenger lurched out

—a passenger who was an amazing apparition of a man.

The face of the man was tightened in a fixed, sardonic grin. His lips were drawn backward and downward as if in wry mirth. But there was no merriment in the man's terrorized eyes, no humor in his quick, frantic movements. He seemed to be a man possessed, driven by a desperate anxiety to get inside headquarters.

He stumbled across the sidewalk. Beneath his flapping topcoat his legs were bare, his feet encased in loose bed-slippers. There was no hat on his grayed head. His left hand was bound huge with many layers of bandages. His breath hissed through the teeth of his clenched jaws as he tottered toward the door of headquarters.

The driver of the taxi hastened to assist his fare, but with a frantic wrench the man tore himself free. His shoulder hit the door, and it swung inward with him. He staggered again, and fell into the corridor. He rolled onto his back, pawing helplessly to raise himself, staring upward with that grisly, sardonic grin still tightening his lips.

While the strangely garbed man lay panting through closed teeth, the cab-driver stood transfixed, peering chilled at that horrible grin.

Inside headquarters, two men had been coming downstairs. Now they came to a quick stop on the steps.

One of them was Detective Sergeant Stephen Thatcher, son of Police Chief Peter Thatcher, young, trim, collegiate-looking. The other, whose grim face looked as hard as old leather, was the ace sleuth of the force, Gilbert McEwen.

"Good Lord!" Steve Thatcher gasped, peering down at the writhing form on the corridor floor. "Who's that?"

Gil McEwen went down the steps three at a time. He paused over the figure on the floor—over the man who stared up at him with that fixed, fiendish grin.

"By damn!" he said. "It's Amos Colchester!"

It was Gil McEwen's business to know the face of every prominent person in the city; but almost any one would have recognized the features of Amos Colchester. Colchester was President of the City National Bank; he was a social leader of the old school; his picture had been printed in the newspapers scores of times. He was wealthy, conservative, dignified. And now he lay here on the floor in headquarters, clad only in night clothes under a topcoat, grinning—grinning in that blood-chilling manner which made his features a grotesque mask.

His bandaged left hand was beating the floor in a desperate effort to get up. His right hand was clenched about something metallic which McEwen could not plainly see.

McEWEN stooped and pulled the man into his arms. Colchester's body was stiff and tense. Steve Thatcher spun and jerked open the door of the first-aid room, a few steps away. Carrying Colchester, McEwen strode inside. He put the man on the cot and straightened, breathing hard.

"Get the doc!" he exclaimed to Steve Thatcher, and shouldered out the door again.

Quick steps took him to the entrance of headquarters. There he stopped short, peering at a black figure standing on the sidewalk—the taxi-driver who had rushed Amos Colchester to the station. McEwen bounded at the man. He grabbed the driver's lapel in one tight hand and demanded:

"What happened to him?"

"I don't know!"

"You brought him here!"

"Yes, sure—but I don't know what's the matter with him. He—here."

The cab-driver pushed a hand toward McEwen, a hand holding a crumpled slip of paper. McEwen unfolded the sweaty ball. He read the scrawled words:

Take me to police headquarters quickly.

"He gave it to me!" the cab-driver exclaimed. "I was cruisin', lookin' for a fare. All at once I saw him in front of the cab—and dressed like he was. He pushed that piece of paper at me, and a five-dollar bill. I did what he told me to—got him here quick. I don't know—"

"Where'd you pick him up?" McEwen demanded.

"Clinton street, near Swope. He never said a word—just handed me that paper and the money. I figured maybe he couldn't talk. He kept grinning—grinning all the time and—"

McEwen gave a tug at the driver's lapel which jerked him toward the door.

"Get inside there!" he snapped. And as the driver shuffled through the entrance, he bawled, "Murphy! Murphy! Keep an eye on this bird!"

From the door down the hallway issued an answer. A patrolman came on a trot. McEwen left the driver in Murphy's charge, and shouldered back into the first-aid room. Steve Thatcher was just turning from the telephone.

"Doc's coming, Gil."

McEwen was peering down at the quivering, panting man on the bed.

"By damn!" he exclaimed. "Does he *have* to keep grinning like that?" He bent over the bed. "Damn' funny when one of the city's most respected citizens turns up in the middle of the night, dressed like this in the street, and—"

McEwen had seen that the muscles of Colchester's body were hard. He broke off when his investigating fingers reached the closed right hand of the man on the bed. The hand was clenching something. McEwen pried the fingers loose, one by one. It was not an easy job. He managed to take the thing from Colchester; and he peered at it puzzledly.

It was a small, brass head—a man's. The brass eyes were wide and protruding, the brass lips drawn into a horrible grin—like that of the man on the cot.

Colchester's free hand was gesturing wildly. He was trying to straighten up, and that grin was still on his face—that grin, which exposed tightly clenched teeth. The hand fluttered again, desperately.

"What's the matter?" McEwen asked quickly. "Can you hear me, Mr. Colchester? What're you trying to say? Can you tell me—"

Colchester's partly bald, partly gray head shook stiffly. Again he made motions with his right hand—and McEwen got it. Colchester was asking for something to write with. McEwen fished a pencil from his pocket, and a used envelope.

He thrust the pencil into Colchester's numb fingers. The man clenched it desperately. He began to scribble on the envelope—large sprawling letters. McEwen read them as they formed:

Red Six—protect me—

There the wandering pencil-point slipped off the paper. McEwen, frowning, turned the envelope over. Again the pencil scrawled:

Poisoned me—because—

A rigid convulsion seized the body of Amos Colchester. He stiffened back in the bed. McEwen cursed and peered.

In the corner of the first-aid room a telephone suddenly jangled.

McEwen ignored it. Colchester was panting; and the stiff, sardonic grin was still on his face. McEwen muttered:

"Red Six—what does he mean by that? Poisoned him. What the devil—"

The telephone clattered again. And down the corridor came a bawling call: "McEwen! Answer that phone! There's a man named Weeks on the wire asking for you—a matter of life and death!"

McEwen straightened and turned

strange eyes on Steve Thatcher. "Weeks?" he asked. "Weeks? Say, isn't there a man named Weeks associated with Colchester in business?" He grabbed the phone. "Hello!"

"This—this is Andrew Weeks talking," came a strained voice over the wire. "Is that you, Mr. McEwen? I—I want you to come out to my place at once. My life has been threatened. I don't dare tell you more than that over the phone. Come to my place as quickly as you can. If you don't hurry you may be—too late!"

McEwen swallowed. "Certainly, Mr. Weeks," he said. "Certainly. I'll be right out." He peered at the figure on the bed. "Mr. Weeks, are you aware that your friend—"

McEwen broke off. The receiver at the other end of the line clicked back to the hook. The connection was broken.

McEwen's eyes were glittering when he put the phone down. Steve Thatcher was bending over the man on the cot.

"He can hardly breathe, Gil," Thatcher said quietly. "He's making a terrific fight for air. If—"

The door knob rattled; the door opened. Dr. Standish, headquarters physician, shouldered in. He stepped close, saying nothing, and studied the man on the bed. He probed into his black case. He unlooped a stethoscope. He listened through it and gazed at the grinning face of Amos Colchester.

For a long moment he did not move. Then he rose, wagging his head, and stowed the stethoscope back in the case.

"Impossible to do anything for him," he said. "It's a case of lockjaw."

"Lockjaw?" echoed McEwen.

"Acute traumatic tetanus," answered the doctor. "How'd he get here? It's a miracle he was able to move at all. It's passed over his entire body now—paralyzed the muscles of the chest and diaphragm. He's dead."

"Dead!" blurted McEwen.

"Quite dead," said Dr. Standish.

McEwen blurted, "And murdered!"

"Murdered?" echoed the doctor. "Don't make a mistake, McEwen. Tetani bacilli are very common. They thrive in ordinary dirt. It's possible for any small abrasion to become infected. Any slight accident—a skinned knuckle—I see that his hand is bandaged—"

McEwen was peering at the scrawl of the man who had died. *Poisoned me.*

He raised his eyes to Steve Thatch-its tortured grin.

"Murdered!" said McEwen again.

He raised his eyes to Steve Thatcher's and spoke in clipped syllables, "We'll beat it out to Andrew Weeks's house."

CHAPTER II

TETANUS!

THEY left their car at the curb in front of a magnificent white house. Windows were ablaze, upstairs and down. They walked slowly along the path to the front door and rang. It was a long moment before any sound answered the bell.

Then a soft step sounded within the door. A hushed voice asked through the panels:

"Who is it?"

"Detective Lieutenant McEwen."

A safety chain rattled. The door inched open. Steve, standing at Gil's side, could see a section of a man's face, pale and strained. It was the face of Andrew Weeks. Weeks was one of the prominent attorneys of the city, portly and dignified; but now his face was a mask of fear.

"You must pardon my anxiety," Weeks said in a short breath. "I explained over the phone that it is a matter of life and death. I have been threatened. I—step inside, please. Step inside."

Steve Thatcher and Gil McEwen followed Weeks's gesture into a large library. Heavy drapes hung across the windows. Overhead lights were blazing. In a corner, niched into the bookshelves, a huge radio was playing softly, the music of a string quartet.

Weeks followed into the room with quick choppy steps. They all sat down. Weeks faced them across a desk.

"Who," asked McEwen, "has threatened you, Mr. Weeks?"

Weeks blurted, "I don't know!"

"You mean you have been threatened by an unknown person?"

"Yes."

"In what way? By letter?"

"No—not by letter. I have nothing to show you. But I know—I know my life is in danger. I am taking the gravest risk by calling the police here. I am appalled now when I think of what I have done. I am afraid that I—I had better keep quiet."

"So?" McEwen pulled his chair closer and peered across the desk. "Perhaps you'll change your mind, Mr. Weeks." He leaned forward stiffly. "Amos Colchester was a client of yours, wasn't he?"

Weeks's eyes jerked. "Yes."

"He was taken ill recently—"

Abruptly the soft music of the radio ceased playing. As the two men faced each other across the desk the voice of an announcer boomed into the library.

"Special news despatch! Ladies and gentlemen, we bring you through the courtesy of the *Clarion* the following news flash:

" 'Amos Colchester, well-known banker of this city, died tonight of lockjaw. Mysterious circumstances surround his passing. Yesterday Mr. Colchester was taken to the Governor Hospital for treatment of an infected left hand. Lockjaw swiftly followed. In an effort to prevent the spread of the infection, an operation was performed early last night and the focus of infection removed. Mr. Colchester, following the operation, was in serious condition and apparently delirious.

" 'Late tonight Mr. Colchester vanished from his hospital room. It was later discovered that, garbed only in slippers and topcoat over the customary hospital bed garment, he slipped down the fire escape to the street. In a desperate attempt to reach police headquarters before the infection took his life, being unable to communicate with the police in any other way, Mr. Colchester—' "

Andrew Weeks was sitting erect in his chair, his face white as death. His moan broke into the flow of the announcer's words:

"Oh, God!"

"You didn't know of that, Mr. Weeks," McEwen said quietly. "Colchester was at headquarters, dying, when you phoned me. He had made an effort to get his doctor to bring the police to him, but the doctor considered him delirious. Within a few minutes he was dead—dead of lockjaw, but before he died he managed to write me the information that he had been deliberately infected—murdered—"

"Oh, God!"

"Now, Mr. Weeks! What do you know about Amos Colchester's death?"

"Nothing—nothing!"

"Did he receive a threat on his life?"

"I don't know!"

"Look here!" McEwen's voice snapped. "Your friend, your business associate, has been murdered. I believe you know what's behind it. Under those circumstances, Mr. Weeks, you've got to talk!"

Weeks's throat worked. "I know nothing about it, gentlemen! Nothing!"

"But you know something about the threat on your own life!" McEwen declared.

"No!" Weeks sank again into his chair. "I—I shouldn't have called you, gentlemen. I have not been threatened. I have nothing to tell you."

"What?" McEwen's fist slammed again. "You told me over the phone that your life is in danger. Now you tell me that—"

"I was in error."

And as the two men sat facing each other across the desk—McEwen coldly furious, Weeks paralyzed with an unknown dread—a sudden crash filled the room.

GLASS splintered. The heavy drapes covering one of the windows puffed out, as a force hit it from outside. Something hard struck the carpet with a thump and rolled.

Steve Thatcher whirled toward the falling splinters of glass.

Gil McEwen sprang up, snatching at his gun.

Andrew Weeks leaped up with a cry and peered at the object which lay on the floor at his feet.

"Outside!" McEwen cried.

He glanced swiftly, darted to the wall, and snapped a switch. The library lights blinked out. Thick blackness filled the room. McEwen sprang toward a pair of draped French doors in the corner. He whipped aside the curtain, twisted the key, and pushed outward with his gun glittering in the moonlight that flickered in.

At the same instant Steve Thatcher whirled into the vestibule. He strode to the front entrance and snapped the door open. His gun was in his hand, and he was legging across the steps when the black force hit him.

Instantly, before he was aware of it, dark figures closed in on him. Unseen hands gripped his gun arm. Fingers clutched at his throat. His legs were grabbed and jerked from beneath him. In the space of a second, Steve Thatcher was pinioned in tightening arms, falling to the gravel.

He kicked frantically, but the grip on his legs was too powerful to break. He tried to strike out, but he could not move either arm an inch. He felt the gun torn from his fingers by hands covered with gloves. Then a blow took him on the head—a punch that made his brain spin and his senses flag.

Dimly Steve Thatcher sensed, as he writhed on the ground, swift footfalls in the grit of the path. He struggled to get up as he heard a motor start not far away. By the time he was on his knees, wavering to his feet, the cars were racing away. Steve Thatcher could not see them, but from the snorting of the exhausts he knew they were speeding like mad.

He tottered to his feet as a hoarse call came from behind the house.

"Steve! Steve!"

He stumbled along the dark wall. Near the edge of the garden at the rear he came to a stop, gazing uncertainly at a figure of black on the ground. Gil McEwen's furious voice came up, "Steve! Get these damned things off me!"

STEVE THATCHER struck a match. In the flare he saw that McEwen's right wrist and left ankle were fastened together with handcuffs—McEwen's own! His gun was not in sight. Steve Thatcher dropped the match and stooped.

"Key's in my vest pocket!" McEwen panted. "By damn! There must've been at least four of 'em that jumped me! I didn't have a chance!"

The bracelets clicked loose.

"Get back to Weeks!"

Steve Thatcher trotted off as McEwen scrambled to his feet. They pushed in through the curtained French door. McEwen groped for the electric switch and snapped it. A relieved burst of breath came out of him as the light flooded the room.

Andrew Weeks was sitting in the chair beside the desk, blinking, staring at the floor.

"Anyway," McEwen said grimly, "you're still alive! Steve grab that phone and signal the squad cars. It won't do a bit of good, by damn, but try it!"

As Steve Thatcher took up the phone, spun the dial, and began to talk, Gil McEwen crossed and peered at the object on the floor. It was scarcely more than two inches across, something covered with wrinkled paper. McEwen's hand went down.

"Don't touch it!" Weeks blurted. "Don't!"

McEwen snorted and picked it up.

He rolled the paper off the thing and let it rest in his palm.

It was a little brass head, its mouth twisted into a grisly sardonic grin.

And McEwen saw a word scrawled in heavy black on the paper which had enwrapped it—

Tetanus!

Slowly McEwen placed the things on the desk in front of Andrew Weeks. Weeks's eyes popped at them. There was silence now. Steve Thatcher had completed the squad call and replaced the telephone. Side by side with McEwen, he watched Weeks.

"Now you can scarcely deny, Mr. Weeks," said McEwen bluntly, "that you have been threatened—threatened as Colchester was. What are you afraid of now? We're the police. We'll help you—keep you safe. Who's behind this? Who killed Colchester by inoculating him with the germs of tetanus? Who's threatened to kill you the same way?"

Weeks blurted, "Before God, I dare not speak! I dare not!"

McEwen shouted, "You'll talk!"

Pale, trembling, Weeks shook his head. "No," he said. "I won't talk. You can do with me what you will. You can arrest me, give me the third degree—anything. But I won't speak. I won't speak one word about—about the meaning of this metal image. I'll never die the horrible death that Amos Colchester died, I promise you—never!"

There was silence. Gil McEwen stared long and hard; but at last he drew back. He said in scarcely a whisper, and with a nod, "It's no use —no use. I know when I'm licked."

THE library was quiet now. The words the three men had spoken could not have been heard beyond the closed doors of the room, not even McEwen's angry shout.

But there was one, far away, that heard.

In the center of the city, in the shadow of the Apex Building, the city's highest sky-scraper, sat the magnificent Royale Apartment House. Its ground-floor front glittered with the windows of exclusive shops. High above the street other windows shone with light. Higher than any of the others was a row of casements dimly glowing.

The rooms behind these windows, on the topmost floor, were all quietly, luxuriously furnished. In one of them a man was sitting at a magnificent carved desk. Fitted to his ears was a pair of phones. Before him was a small switchboard on which a red light was gleaming. Through the mechanism electrical impulses were throbbing, forming into a voice in the ear-phones—the voice of Andrew Weeks.

"I dare not speak! I dare not speak!"

So, a mile away, the voice of the attorney was heard. Andrew Weeks did not know that a secret microphone was concealed behind a painting in his library. He did not dream that his words were being overheard. And as he listened, the man at the desk in the Royale Apartment smiled mildly.

A buzzer sounded softly in the room. The man rose from the desk, lowered the phones, switched the red light out. He walked toward a curtained door opposite. Just beyond the drapes he paused, and affixed a mask on his face.

When he stepped into the adjoining room his face was covered by the mask of scarlet—and on that portion of it which covered his forehead was a black Roman numeral I.

He pressed one of an array of buttons on a table in the center of the room. An electric lock clicked, and a door opened. The man who strode in was also masked, but his mask was black.

"Number Fifty-two reporting," he said.

"Yes, Fifty-two?" asked the man in the red mask.

"The warning was delivered to Weeks at eleven-fifty o'clock. Detectives McEwen and Thatcher were in the house at the time. It was necessary to disable them before we could make our escape."

"There was no trouble? They saw none of you?" the man in the red mask asked.

"We took them completely by surprise. Of course, they were outnumbered. We were obliged to take their guns. Here are the weapons."

The black-masked man placed a paper-wrapped parcel on the table.

"I think," said Red Mask, "we may term the night's work a success. Weeks will hold his silence, fortunately for him. All of you, I suppose—" and the voice became low and purring—"have heard of the unfortunate demise of Mr. Colchester tonight?"

The black-masked man answered in a whisper, "Yes."

"That is all. You may go."

The man in the black mask turned, left the room, and closed the door behind him. The red-masked one lifted the paper-wrapped parcel, pushed through the heavily curtained doors, and returned to his desk. Removing his red mask, he unwrapped the parcel and peered at the two guns. Both were regulation police revolvers.

The man at the desk examined them more closely. On the butt of one he saw engraved initials—S.T. And on the polished metal of the gun he saw oily marks.

His eyes lighted as he studied the marks. He brought a bottle of gray powder from a drawer—mercury and chalk. As he dusted some of the stuff onto the gun, the marks became clearer. Through a magnifying glass he studied them again. And suddenly he sat straight, amazed.

From another drawer he quickly removed a bundle of newspaper clippings. Singling one out, he peered at a reproduced photograph. It was a close-up of a door knob, and on the door knob was a clearly defined thumbprint. Above the photograph was a caption:

THUMBPRINT OF
THE MOON MAN

Below was a list of the crimes perpetrated by the most notorious criminal the city had ever known. Innumerable robberies. Two kidnapings. A murder. Scores of crimes were listed, and the final line read:

Yesterday the Moon Man met Death at Suicide Leap

The man at the desk compared the reproduced photograph with the impression on the gun. Intent, scarcely breathing, he peered. When he straightened, his green eyes glittered. A throaty laugh came through his thin lips.

"So," he said aloud. *You* are the Moon Man, Steve Thatcher!"

CHAPTER III

THE RED SIX

TWENTY-FOUR hours had passed since the amazing death of Amos Colchester.

Steve Thatcher walked across a street which flanked the Royale Apartments just as the clock in the Apex Building spire boomed eleven. He was on his way home from a grueling day at headquarters. He paused and purchased a late newspaper from a stand which was just closing for the night. As he strolled on he glimpsed the headlines:

POLICE STALEMATED IN
COLCHESTER DEATH PROBE

Though Detective Lieutenant McEwen, who is in charge of the investigation of the Colchester case, spent the entire day attempting to elicit usable information from friends and associates of the dead man, he confessed late tonight that he had made little progress.

One man in particular, whose name was not divulged by the police, a man closely connected with Colchester's business affairs, was grilled all day, without success.

That man, Steve Thatcher well knew, was Andrew Weeks. Weeks had maintained a terrified silence. No means had been found to make him talk. "Stalemated" described the situation accurately. Steve Thatcher had left Gil McEwen exhausted and disgusted at headquarters.

Absorbed in his thoughts, Steve Thatcher scarcely noticed the taxi which creaked to a stop in front of the Royale entrance as he passed it. He was only dimly aware that a girl was stepping out of the cab and paying the driver. The taxi was starting up again, and Steve Thatcher was already past the entrance, when he heard a quick gasp and moan behind him.

He turned to see the girl sprawled on the sidewalk. She had dropped her purse; she was struggling to rise. Hurrying to her, Thatcher saw that she was young and theatrically pretty. Her mouth was pinched with pain as he helped her up. She raised one shapely foot from the pavement and clung to Thatcher's arm.

"How—how awkward of me!" she exclaimed. "I've turned my ankle. It hurts dreadfully!"

Steve Thatcher held her as she took a little hop, and said: "May I help you? Perhaps you'd better have a doctor look at your ankle to make sure it's not a sprain. I'll take you home."

She smiled confusedly at him. "You're very kind," she said with a little whimper. "It's really not that bad. And, anyway, I am home. I live in the Royale. If you will help me to my apartment—I'll be so grateful."

"Certainly. Shall I carry you? If—"

"I'm sure I can make it," she gasped.

He led her into the lobby, a spacious brown-and-gold lobby into one side of which elevators opened. One car was waiting. Steve Thatcher helped the girl into it, and she leaned against the wall, smiling.

And Steve Thatcher noticed the operator of the elevator as the car shot up. A more tremendous man he had never seen. The uniformed operator was broad as an ox, with great thick arms and a trunk that looked solid as oak. He turned a brutal, square face at Thatcher, and his sharp eyes gleamed.

Thatcher was just reflecting that the apelike operator seemed singularly out of place in the exclusive Royale, when the car slid to a stop.

"It's just across the hall," the girl said.

She hobbled to a door as Steve Thatcher helped her. Turning the knob she limped into an exquisite room, and he followed. As he hastened to assist her to a chair, he heard the door click behind him. And, when he was halfway across the room, he was amazed to see the young lady cease limping and laugh.

"Well," she said brightly, "you're a gallant young man, anyway."

"I beg your pardon?" Steve Thatcher asked.

"This is as far as you go with me," she answered him cryptically. "Thanks for biting so beautifully. Or am I really that good?"

"I don't—"

Understand, Steve Thatcher was about to say. But he began to understand immediately that something queer was afoot. Turning, he saw a man standing just inside the closed door. The man was garbed in tuxedo and masked. And he was leveling an automatic toward Steve Thatcher.

Thatcher frowned. "What," he asked, "is this, anyway?"

A DOOR at the corner of the room opened, and another tuxedoed man appeared. He, too, was holding an automatic. He briskly came to Steve Thatcher and spoke in a crisp voice.

"Don't be alarmed, sir," he said. "We will detain you only a moment. Allow me—"

His hand slipped inside Steve Thatcher's coat like lightning and slipped out again with a gun. Thatcher made a quick move to retrieve it—but it disappeared.

"We will shortly return it to you. Now, if you please," said the masked man, "this way."

Steve Thatcher simply stared. The

masked men were so suave and polite he was dumbfounded. He had no notion of what was happening to him. He knew that he had been duped—that the girl had deliberately tricked him into coming to this apartment—but the meaning of it all was beyond him.

"This way, sir, please."

The two masked men took Steve Thatcher's arms. He could make no resistance as he marched across the room. A door was opened before him, and he saw blackness ahead. Prodded with a gun, he stepped through, and the door closed behind him, muffling darkness all around him.

"Would you mind," he asked, "telling me what this is all about?"

"You will learn in a moment."

Steve Thatcher felt himself being conducted along a corridor. He saw a door open before him, and a glow of light appeared beyond. As he was led forward, surprise mounted in him.

At one end of the room was a large silver screen similar to those used in motion-picture houses. In front of it was raised a platform on which stood a desk. Behind the desk a man was sitting. His face was covered by a red mask, on the forehead of which was the black Roman numeral I. He was alone.

In the room there was silence.

The two black-masked men escorted Steve Thatcher to the raised platform. He stood upon it frowning, as the two men withdrew, peering down at the red-masked man.

"I still would like to know," he said, "what the hell this is!"

Through the slits of the mask eyes glittered—green eyes. There was a wry smile on the thin, cruel lips.

"I will explain. You are, of course, Detective Stephen Thatcher. I am—Primus."

He rose, and left the desk. In his gloved hands he carried a gun. Pausing before Steve Thatcher, he extended the gun, butt first.

"This," he asked, "is yours?"

Steve Thatcher peered at it. Curiously—now with a cold tingle coursing up his spine—he took it into his hands. His eyes snapped up, cold.

"It's mine," he answered. "This gun was taken from me last night. Outside the Weeks' home I was—"

"Of course," came the soft voice of Primus.

Steve Thatcher felt the gun taken from his hands. Primus returned to the desk, and placed the gun inside a metallic box which looked like a small projection machine, and snapped a switch.

Instantly an image appeared on the silver screen which covered one end of the room. It was a likeness of Steve Thatcher's gun. Only a part of it was shown—the butt and the smooth nickel near the cylinder. And there, on the metal, was an impression—a thumbprint.

Steve Thatcher's thumbprint!

STEVE grew cold. His throat tightened as the voice of Primus came smoothly.

"Observe, Mr. Thatcher, the projection of your gun. The print you now see on the metal was made by you a second ago. Notice—"

Cold and rigid Steve Thatcher stood as Primus picked up a pointer and stepped toward the screen.

"That your thumbprint is of the whorl type, characterized by a delta—a double-cored whorl. It is also marked by a small, lateral scar. Have you the impression clearly in mind?"

Steve Thatcher kept staring—staring at the print on the screen, enlarged a hundred diameters. He swallowed hard as Primus returned to the desk.

The image on the screen shifted off as the red-masked man removed the gun from the projection machine. Quickly another image appeared. Steve Thatcher recognized it. It was that of a newspaper clipping, a clipping headed: Thumbprint of the Moon Man!

The breath locked in Steve Thatcher's lungs.

"Observe, now," said Primus, briskly, stepping again toward the screen with the pointer, "the Moon Man's thumbprint is also a double whorl characterized by a delta and a small lateral scar. Observe, in other words, that your thumbprint, Mr. Thatcher, is exactly the same as that of the Moon Man.

"It is clearly demonstrated then, that the Moon Man, the notorious thief whom the police have tried in vain to apprehend, is not really dead. He is, obviously, very much alive. The Moon Man is none other than you—Stephen Thatcher, son of Chief of Police Peter Thatcher."

Through Steve Thatcher's numb lips broke a moan, "Oh, God!"

Primus fixed green eyes on him. He spoke one clipped, clear sentence:

"We give silence for silence!"

Stephen Thatcher was dazed. He was scarcely aware that the two black-masked men had reappeared beside him and taken his arms. As he was led away he was too dismayed to resist. Vaguely he was aware that he was being led to the door.

"Good night, sir," one of the black masks said. "Your gun."

And Steve Thatcher found himself alone in the corridor, the door shut in his face, the gun in his hands.

Suddenly he raised a fist and pounded at the door. No response came from inside. He rapped again; and silence answered. He twisted the knob; and it was firm. He pushed at the door; it did not budge. He drew back, breathless, appalled. A voice spoke behind him.

"Going down, sir?"

Steve Thatcher whirled to peer at the open elevator cage across the hall. The huge operator was looking out at him—the tremendous man with the square, apelike face. His eyes were shining like points of gimlets in the light.

"Going down, sir?" he asked again.

Steve Thatcher's mind was awhirl. Automatically he stepped into the elevator, pocketing his gun. When the car stopped he stepped out. In the lobby of the Royale he paused, still dazed—chilled to the marrow—wondering if the thing that had happened to him was not a dream—nightmare of a tragedy he had prayed would never occur.

Discovery that he, Detective Sergeant Stephen Thatcher, son of the Chief of Police, was the notorious Moon Man!

Discovery that the Moon Man was not dead, but alive!

"He knows!"

The thought numbed Steve Thatcher as he stood in the empty lobby. Who was the man whose face was hidden by the red mask? What purpose lay behind the strange incident in the apartment above? The secret that Steve Thatcher was the Moon Man had been disclosed—and he had been allowed to depart. What did it mean?

Conjectures fogged Thatcher's mind. And yet there was one certainty—a certainty that left him chilled with dread.

"He knows!"

And the words of the red-masked man rang in his ears:

"Silence for silence!"

CHAPTER IV

Enter the Angel

TEN miles from the city, and across the stream known as Murder River, and across the state line, sat the village of Claremore. Its only hotel was a ramshackle old building. The occupant of Room 20 was entered upon the musty ledger as Sam Daniels of Chicago.

Sam Daniels' real name was Ned Dargan.

A knock sounded on the door of Room 20. Ned Dargan snapped up from the bed. He had been lying there morosely most of the afternoon, remembering and trying to forget the past months of his life. During those months Dargan had been ambassador extraordinary of the Moon Man. It was Dargan who had worked hand in glove with that amazing criminal,

Dargan who had distributed to the poor and needy the money which the Moon Man stole from the undeserving rich.

Remembering and trying to forget. Remembering the black-cloaked figure with the silver, globular head who, to Dargan, was the finest man who had ever lived. Remembering true friendship, unselfishness, staunch loyalty. Trying to forget because now—

Dargan could see the black headlines that had struck him like a body blow:

MOON MAN KILLED AT SUICIDE LEAP!

Snatched from painful reveries by the knock at the door, Dargan whirled up. He was stocky, thick-trunked, with no neck and a cauliflower ear. His face went pale as he faced the closed door—because he was wanted. Wanted by the police as an accomplice of the Moon Man, wanted for innumerable robberies, for two kidnapings, for a murder which the Moon Man had not committed.

The hand on the door might be the hand of the law.

Dargan's hand stole toward his pocket—and paused as a voice called, "Mr. Daniels—you in? Special delivery for you."

Dargan sighed and relaxed. He opened the door, and an envelope was pushed through the crack. Dargan studied it with a frown. Who but the Moon Man could know where he was, under what name he was hiding—and wasn't the Moon Man dead?

Suddenly Dargan ripped the envelope open. A narrow strip of cardboard, colored green, fell out. Curiously he picked it up.

It was a theater ticket. It would admit one person to the Regent Theatter, Row F, Seat 16, on September 20.

This was September 20.

Dargan probed into the envelope, and found it otherwise empty. He studied the writing, but it looked utterly unfamiliar. He looked at his watch, and found it to be seven-thirty. In an hour the performance at the Regent Theater would begin; and here was a ticket for it.

Why?

Dargan paced the room. Was it a trap? Had the police discovered his whereabouts, and was this a trick to get him across the state line, so that he could be arrested without the formality of extradition? Beyond Murder River lay the city and the theater—and danger for Dargan. Danger of the chair . . . .

Seven-fifteen.

Dargan clenched his jaw and stuffed the ticket into his pocket.

"Hell!" he said.

He was taking the chance. He was going.

EIGHT-THIRTY, and lights blazed on the marquee of the Regent Theater. Limousines and taxis were whirling to the entrance. Men and women in evening clothes were drifting in. The lobby was crowded. Within a few minutes the performance would begin.

Across the street, from a shadow, Dargan studied the scene. He was alert, tense. He waited until the crowd was thicker, then hurried across the street and into the lobby. He passed through the door. An usher took his stub and led him down an aisle. Dargan settled into a seat as the orchestra crashed out the closing chords of the overture, as the bustle of the crowd quieted and the lights dimmed.

The curtain rose on a dancing, barelegged chorus. Dargan had no eyes for it. He found himself with one empty seat on the left of him, and two on the right. He waited. One dance number was followed by another. Laughter rocked the theater as comedians rattled wisecracks; but Dargan did not laugh.

He was waiting—wondering.

The stage went dark with a new dance number. Dim blue spotlights played as a misty dream waltz began. And in the darkness Dargan felt a movement. Some one was coming into the row of seats. Some one was quietly settling into the chair beside him.

Dargan's hand stole to the gun in his pocket. His shifting eyes could not see the man beside him, so baffling was the blue gloom. His hand tightened on the butt of his gun and—

A whisper came:

"Angel!"

Dargan jerked. He held his breath and tried to see the face of the man beside him. His throat was too tight; he could not speak.

"Take it easy, Angel. We're safe."

Dargan stuttered, "B-Boss!"

"Yes, Angel."

The spotlights shifted. A gleam struck the face of the man beside Dargan. Then he saw—saw what he could not believe was true. That the man was Steve Thatcher—the Moon Man. Alive.

"Boss!" Dargan whispered. "Boss! It's you!"

Steve Thatcher leaned close. "Listen fast, Angel. We can't talk much. Sorry I couldn't let you know. I had to fake the death of the Moon Man to protect my father—understand. But now you're not the only one who knows the secret. Listening?"

"Yes, Boss! Oh, I'm glad—"

"Bless you, Angel, but you've got to listen. Take this letter—got it? Read it carefully. There are instructions in it—full instructions. Beginning tomorrow you're going to take a job as a bootblack in the barber shop of the Royale. You'll be able to change your appearance so you won't be spotted. The letter explains everything."

"I'll do anything you say, Boss—anything!"

"You're the only one I can turn to for help, Angel. I'm in the tightest spot of my life. But no matter what happens, Angel, we've got to keep my dad from learning the truth about me—and keep Gil McEwen from learning it, and Sue."

"I'll kill anybody that tries to tell 'em!" whispered Dargan hoarsely.

"Angel, it's not going to be as simple as that. Not nearly so simple. There's some big criminal organization operating in this town, and they've got their claws into me. It's linked up with the Colchester death—just how, I don't know. It's dangerous, Angel. I don't know what we're up against, but I know what might happen if we made a misstep. Not only discovery but—"

The lights were going up; the ballet scene was ending.

"Follow orders, Angel! I'm leaving. God bless you!"

Steve Thatcher slipped out of the seat, to the aisle. When the lights went up, Ned Dargan again found himself flanked by empty chairs. Steve Thatcher was gone. Dargan sat with a letter in his hand—a letter he clenched tightly—a letter from the grandest guy in the world.

STEVE THATCHER pushed through the door of headquarters. He climbed the stairs and entered the office of the chief of police. Behind the desk in the corner Chief Thatcher was sitting—a white-haired, kindly-faced veteran. Gil McEwen was in the room, pacing the carpet. And in a chair sat a young, pretty girl—Sue McEwen, Gil's daughter, the girl Steve Thatcher was engaged to marry.

She rose and came quickly to Steve. She raised her face and he kissed her lips. She said happily:

"Steve, darling, I've been waiting for you. I've turned my wiles upon the head men here—" she gestured toward the chief and McEwen—"and they say you can be off duty tomorrow night. Which means, dear, that you're going to take me to the Embassy Ball."

"Delighted!" Steve said, and he kissed her again. "Got a costume? I'll find something to wear. We'll have a great time."

"I've an idea for a costume for you, Steve," Sue said with a laugh. "Why not go as the Moon Man?"

Steve jerked. "What? With Gil on duty there? He'd shoot me on sight!"

He managed a shaky laugh—but

his heart was cold. "Go as the Moon Man," Sue had said—to the man who was the Moon Man. Steve's eyes probed into Sue's, and were solemn. She could not suspect. And if she ever learned—if ever she learned the secret that the masked Red Six had learned—

He left the blood-chilling thought unfinished.

"I must run now, darling," Sue said quickly. "Come for me tomorrow night at nine. Good-night."

Steve kissed her full, red lips again; and she was gone. He peered at the closed door, still cold, still inwardly trembling. And he turned as McEwen's heels kept beating the carpet, and McEwen said:

"'Go as the Moon Man.' That's a funny one. It'd be hell if the Moon Man actually popped up at the Embassy Ball tomorrow night, wouldn't it? There'll be a dozen fortunes in jewels there—just his meat. Yeah, it would be plenty funny if the Moon Man showed up and—"

"The Moon Man is dead, Gil," Steve Thatcher said quietly.

"The Moon Man," McEwen answered, "is *supposed* to be dead. I saw his car go off the cliff at Suicide Leap. I saw the wreck sink into the quicksand. I saw his black robe disappear in the slime. But by damn! I can't get rid of a funny feeling in my bones that maybe the Moon Man didn't die—maybe the Moon Man is still alive, after all!"

Colder, appalled, Steve Thatcher could not speak.

"But—" McEwen's heels kept beating—"there's a bigger crook than the Moon Man operating now—a crook with so much power that he can turn respected citizens into accomplices. What do I mean? Just this—

"Colchester was murdered—shut up—inoculated with lockjaw. Weeks knows it. Weeks was threatened the same way Colchester was, with the grinning brass head. But will he talk? Not a word! Why? Because he's afraid of suffering the death that got Colchester. And what does that make him? Technically an accomplice after the crime—one of the biggest lawyers in the city!"

The telephone on the chief's desk rang. Peter Thatcher picked it up, listened, and gestured toward his son.

"Somebody asking for you," he said.

A cold premonition gripped Steve Thatcher as he took the phone. He took a deep breath as he put the receiver to his ear. He said quietly, "Stephen Thatcher talking."

"This is Primus speaking, Thatcher."

Steve swallowed. He said, numbed, "Who?"

"Primus. I think you understand perfectly. You no doubt remember the matter of the Moon Man's thumbprint."

Inwardly Steve Thatcher quailed. The words on the line mocked him, chilled him. What if some one were listening in—the sergeant at the headquarters switchboard? He could only answer, stiffly, "I remember."

"Good. I am giving you instructions. You are to appear at the apartment in the Royale at precisely eleven-fifty-six tonight. Eleven-fifty-six."

Amazement gripped Steve Thatcher—amazement that the red-masked man was talking so openly, calling him in the chief's office at headquarters. And he heard the ringing voice add, "Remember, Thatcher—*we give silence for silence!*"

The line clicked and went dead.

CHAPTER V

THE SINISTER POWER

ELEVEN FORTY-FIVE. Steve Thatcher walked quickly past the Royale Apartments on the opposite side of the street. He was feverish, nervous. Peering up, he saw windows glowing on the top story of the building—the windows behind which the red-masked menace was waiting? He did not know.

But he knew that he must obey the order that had been given him—obey until, at least, he learned the sinister purpose behind the call. For still, within his mind, Steve Thatcher heard the mocking words:

"Silence for silence!"

He turned quickly, and entered the lobby of the Apex Building, which sat opposite the Royale. He slipped into a telephone booth and called a number. Anxiously he waited until a familiar voice answered.

"Angel!"

"Boss!"

"I must talk fast, Angel. You've followed instructions?"

"To the letter, Boss. The room in this hotel was all waiting for me. I spent two hours in the other place this morning, using the stuff you told me to get. Gosh, Boss, you'd never know me now—my hair's blond, and my skin's a different color, and these glasses—"

"Good! What about the rest, Angel?"

"You had the job all set for me, too, Boss. I'm working in the barber shop in the Royale, shining shoes. I'll pass you notes as you said. I looked for the guy with the green eyes, but I didn't spot him. Gosh, Boss—what is he doing to you? If he ever tells anybody you were the—you know who I mean—I'll slaughter him!"

"Bless you, Angel, but you couldn't touch him. I don't know what his game is, but he's powerful—deadly powerful. You've got to keep covered, Angel, and watch yourself."

"And you, Boss—"

"I'm trapped, Angel— but I'm trying to work my way out. Hang on. Stick at the boot-blacking job and keep your eyes open. I'll see you soon. So long."

"So long, Boss!"

Steve Thatcher slipped out of his booth and peered at his watch. Eleven-fifty-five. One minute, and he was due in the rooms of the red-masked man. Nervously he crossed the street, and entered the rich lobby of the Royale.

An elevator car was waiting—the car manned by the gorilla-like operator. The immense man's eyes bored into Steve Thatcher as the car shot up. Once in the lobby on the top floor, Thatcher crossed to the nearest door. He hesitated, wondering, bewildered—and knocked.

The door opened silently.

Steve Thatcher stepped through and the door clicked shut behind him. In the dim light a tuxedoed, black-masked man was standing. This time he had no gun. His lips curved in a faint smile as he said, "Follow me please, sir."

The black-masked man walked through a door. Steve Thatcher hesitated, but followed. He felt the reassuring weight of his gun strapped beneath his armpit as he strode along a corridor. At another door his escort paused.

"Step inside."

Grimly Steve Thatcher opened the door. He stepped into a dimly lighted room. Its windows were heavily curtained, its floor richly carpeted. At the desk sat a red-masked man, a black Roman numeral I on his forehead. And through the slits of his mask his eyes shone at Steve Thatcher. He rose and said politely, "Be seated, Mr. Thatcher."

STEVE THATCHER'S lips twisted into a wry smile as he advanced to the desk and took an empty chair. He asked coldly, "Just what do you think you're getting away with, anyway?"

"I called you here," said Primus quietly, "to explain. I am very busy tonight, and I will not waste time. Of course, it is true, Mr. Thatcher, that none of your friends know you are the criminal known as the Moon Man?"

Steve Thatcher answered tightly, "It's true."

"Your father, the chief of police, does not know. Your friend, Gil McEwen does not know. Your fiancée, Sue McEwen, does not know. And if they did know, Mr. Thatcher—"

Steve Thatcher winced.

"It would mean disaster for you, would it not?" Primus asked suavely. "It would break your father's heart. It would separate you from the girl you love. Should they learn that you are the Moon Man—"

Steve Thatcher was sitting tensely forward in his chair. His eyes were gleaming; his jaws were clenched. Suddenly his right hand flashed. The gun from his armpit holster whisked into it. Steve Thatcher jerked the weapon level. He said tensely, "You won't tell what you know! I'll kill you on the spot before—"

Primus did not move. A faint smile curved his lips.

"Would you care to try it, Mr. Thatcher?"

A long moment Steve Thatcher stared at the glittering green eyes that probed his. He felt a power closing around him—an inexorable, terrible power he could not combat.... Slowly he lowered his gun.

"To continue," Primus said briskly. "I am going to explain this matter to you fully. As a detective, you will be most interested. I, and the five masked gentlemen you will soon see, are the leaders of what you would term a criminal organization. Our identities must remain unknown to you. Your identity will remain unknown to the others in the organization.

"If you saw the faces of the six of us you might be able to identify us in various rogues galleries in the world—Paris, Berlin, London, New York, San Francisco. We are, in a word, professional criminals — but very high-class criminals, Mr. Thatcher. Very."

Steve Thatcher listened in amazement.

"We are specialists, shall I say, in a perfected form of blackmail. We have means of learning unpleasant things about people—unpleasant to them—as we have learned a secret about you. Instead of demanding money from our, would you say, victims, we demand allegiance to our organization. We are given absolute fidelity by those who work for us, in return for our silence.

"Which, Mr. Thatcher, is why we say, 'We give silence for silence!' "

Intent, amazed, Steve Thatcher kept staring at the hard green eyes that were peering into his.

"If you could know the names of some of those who are our workers, you would be amazed. Some of them are prominent lawyers in this city. One of the lawyers joined our ranks because we learned of an instance of his committing subordination of testimony—a fact which would ruin his career if it became known. We have also among us doctors, business men in all fields, engineers, electricians, mechanics, bankers, brokers, teachers, —and now, I may add, a detective."

Steve Thatcher forced a laugh. "If you think you're going to force me—"

"Force you?" Primus asked. "Scarcely that. The decision is up to you, Mr. Thatcher. You become one of us, one of our workers, you follow our orders, you pledge us unswerving allegiance. Unless, of course, you prefer that your secret become known to Chief Thatcher and Gil McEwen and Sue McEwen—the secret that you are the Moon Man."

STEVE THATCHER asked through dry lips, "If I refuse to work for you—a gang of crooks—you'll inform my father—"

"Exactly. And if, after you've begun to work with us, you attempt any treachery, try in any way to disrupt this organization, attempt in any way to molest us—in that case, also, your secret will become known.

"Think your situation over a moment, Mr. Thatcher, and you will decide to give us your staunch support."

Steve Thatcher leaned forward tensely. "You don't know what you're doing! I was the Moon Man—yes. I broke the law—yes. But I never kept a cent of any of the money I stole. I stole for others—men and women who were starving and sick. I helped them with stolen money because there was no other way of saving them. I—"

"Very commendable, I'm sure," broke in Primus, "but the fact remains you are a criminal. The fact remains that if your secret becomes known, the results will be tragic."

"I know! But—"

"In our organization, Mr. Thatcher," Primus interrupted, "you will function in a unique way. You will inform us of any moves the police may make against us. You will keep us in close touch, for instance, with McEwen's investigation of Colchester's death. As our plans demand it, you will aid us in avoiding trouble from the police."

"You—you're saying that I'm to turn informer!" Steve Thatcher blurted.

"Exactly that. You, as a detective, will protect us from the police. And in one other way you will function. As, Mr. Thatcher, the Moon Man."

"What!"

"Yes. Upon occasion you will garb yourself in your black robe and mask of Argus glass. You will return the Moon Man to life. As the Moon Man, you will aid us. And, I fancy, once you have reappeared, the police may believe that you, Mr. Moon Man, are the leader of the crime ring. That will be very amusing to us—very."

Steve Thatcher's fists clenched. "You're going too far!" he exclaimed. "Don't you realize that a month ago the Board of Police Commissioners gave Chief Thatcher twenty-four hours to get the Moon Man—or there would be a complete housecleaning at headquarters? Every man, from the chief on down, was going to get kicked out. That's why I faked the death of the Moon Man.

"Now, if the Moon Man returns, the commissioners will carry out their ultimatum. The chief, McEwen, and everybody else on the force including myself, will get kicked out. Then how will I be able to function as an informer for you? I tell you you're defeating your own purpose by—"

"Mr. Thatcher," Primus interrupted smoothly, "have no concern on that point. Even police commissioners can be—let us say—influenced. After the Moon Man appears there will be no shake-up."

Unbelieving, Steve Thatcher stared. Was this man, this masked criminal power, suggesting that he controlled even the police commissioners? Was his organization so close-knit and far-reaching that even—

"Now step this way, Mr. Thatcher. But first adjust this mask over your face. You see—I, alone, know the identity of the Moon Man."

CONFUSED and dismayed, Thatcher was conducted to a curtained door. Once more he found himself in the huge, semi-dark room at one end of which hung the silver screen.

A man was standing on the platform, black-masked. He was holding a pointer in his hand. Steve Thatcher, eying him through a mask, was led to a chair in front of the screen. The voice of Primus spoke quietly, "It is our custom to deliver a short scientific lecture to new members of our organization."

The screen flashed. A bright circle appeared, and inside it were black lines like short rods to which tentacles were affixed. The black-masked man on the platform began to speak. His manner was composed and brisk. Steve Thatcher's immediate impression was that he was either a professor or a physician.

"You see on the screen an enlarged microscopic section of the tetani bacilli, the germ of lockjaw. These germs live and flourish in common dirt; they are present everywhere. They may be taken into the body through any small cut or abrasion. Once the infection sets in, the course of the disease is swift and terrible.

"There is no known means of checking or guiding traumatic tetanus. Not even the removal of the focus of infection always stops the spread of the disease. The power of the infection is almost incredible. For instance, one two-hundred-fifty-thousandth part of a drop of the broth in which the germs are cultivated, if introduced into the muscular tissue of a mouse, brings death within twenty-four hours.

"A culture of the germ, so small as to be invisible, produces the same effect in a man—horrible death within twenty-four hours. The first effect of the disease is a tightening of the muscles of the jaws, producing the *risor sardonicus*."

The image on the screen changed. A huge face appeared, the eyes staring, the lips drawn back and down in a horrible, sardonic grin—like the grin on the face of the dying Amos Colchester.

"The jaw becomes immovable. The victim cannot speak or take nourishment except through a tube inserted behind the wisdom teeth. Even then the muscles used in swallowing quickly cease to function. The infection spreads to the abdomen, producing cramps. Very soon the respiratory muscles are affected—and breathing ceases."

The grinning face still shone out of the screen as Steve Thatcher stared in horror.

"There is no known way of stopping the infection once it has begun. The tetano-antitoxin which has been developed is of no benefit whatever if used *after* infection has taken place. Once inoculation occurs, death is a certainty—a horrible death.

"The first effect is, as I have said, locked jaws. And locked jaws mean—silence."

THE screen went black. The masked lecturer turned and left the platform. Steve Thatcher jerked up, and stared at the red-masked six seated behind him.

"You see," said Primus to Steve, "any member of our organization who shows a tendency to talk out of turn is likely to die as Amos Colchester died."

Steve Thatcher blurted, "You killed Colchester! You trapped him, and he talked, and—you killed him!"

"Of course," said Primus casually, "we killed him."

"You dare—!"

"We give silence for silence. There is no reason why I should not be completely frank with you. The lecture you have just heard has convinced you, I'm sure, of the wisdom of discretion. It would be most unfortunate, indeed, if you took the risk of making any attempt to—interfere with us.

"In fact, you see, the entire responsibility of protecting us from the police rests upon you. In case of interference from the police in any way—but I need not warn you again."

Steve Thatcher stood silent, rigid, stunned by the irony of the grim predicament.

"Tonight," went on Primus, "we are launching important plans—plans in which you will take part. A meeting of our workers is about to take place in this room. I suggest you step aside and listen carefully to instructions."

Somewhere, a buzzer sounded.

A door opened. One after another, the five red-masked men passed into the room. Their masks were numbered in succession, with Roman numerals, from II through VI. They stepped upon the platform and took chairs facing the dark auditorium.

The Red Six!

Primus had melted away into the gloom; the five on the platform waited a moment. Secundus, Tertius, Quartus, Quintus, Sextus! Black man power masked in red.

Again the door opened, and others began entering the room. All of them were masked in black. They filed silently to seats arranged before the screen—tall men, short men, men who were built like athletes, men with round fronts; and women—women mingled in the masked audience. Through their masks their eyes shone.

And Steve Thatcher stared at them as the seats filled.

Presently the door closed. Secundus stepped to the front of the platform. He began calling a roll:

"Number Ten."

"Here!"

"Number Eleven."

"Here!"

Amazement gripped Steve Thatcher as the roll call mounted beyond the fifties. When it was completed, Tertius took the place of Secundus at the fore of the platform. He signaled, and an image flashed on the screen.

It was the plan of a large room.

"This," came the voice of Secundus, "is a plan of the ballroom in which the Embassy Ball will be held tomorrow night. You are to study it and fix in your minds clearly all the exits —doors and windows. A copy of it will be handed you with your orders."

Steve Thatcher studied the portly figure of a man seated near him. The lower part of that man's face was familiar. Was it Amos Weeks? Steve Thatcher believed so. Weeks, the prominent lawyer—and, Thatcher suddenly remembered, Chairman of the Committee on Invitations of the Embassy Ball.

The image on the screen changed to another map in smaller scale.

"This shows the location of the hotel and the streets around it. Pay close attention. At this point cars will be waiting. The written instructions which you will be handed in a moment will tell you exactly what car to go to, and when. All cars will proceed directly along Prince Street when the signal is given. Once beyond Main, they will scatter. The loot you will carry will be disposed of according to your individual instructions. Orders will now be handed out."

Secundus again began checking the roll. As each number was called, a masked person advanced to the platform and received a sealed envelope. As Steve Thatcher watched in amazement—realizing that the plans for a gigantic robbery were being laid—a voice spoke beside him, "Your instructions."

It was Primus proffering Thatcher a sealed envelope. Automatically he took it. Primus said softly: "You will, of course, follow these orders to the exact letter. You may go now. You will be escorted out. You will be interested to see that your number is Thirteen. Number Thirteen was recently that of our ex-member, Amos Colchester . . . . Goodnight, Thirteen."

Steve Thatcher was led away. He found the upper corridor empty. He was taken to the ground level in the elevator by the silent, apelike operator. He strode swiftly out of the lobby. Stepping into a doorway he ripped open the envelope and read.

The typewritten words chilled him. When he finished the closely printed sheet he was scarcely breathing. Agony filled him as one line of type burned into his eyes:

"You will appear as the Moon Man."

Steve thought of Chief Thatcher—that kindly old veteran whose heart would break if ever his son's secret became known. He thought of Gil McEwen who loved him. He thought of Sue.

And the Red Six had sternly commanded:

"You will appear as the Moon Man!"

CHAPTER VI

Counter Strategy

NIGHT again. The night of the great Embassy Ball. Even now the crowd must be gathering in the tremendous ballroom of the International Hotel. Steve Thatcher realized that as he strode swiftly past the front of the giant Apex Building.

He was cold, alert. Crossing the street quickly, he entered the gleaming barber shop which occupied one of the sections of the ground floor of the Royale Apartments. He went at once to the shoe-shining stand and climbed upon a chair.

"Shine, sir?"

Steve Thatcher looked down at a tow-headed man with sun-burned face. There was little about that fact that looked familiar. Yet the man had a cauliflower ear; he had no neck . . . . Ned Dargan.

"Shine," said Steve Thatcher casually.

Dargan, behaving as though he had never seen this customer before, plied brush and rag on Steve Thatcher's shoes. The shining-cloth flapped. Steve Thatcher pretended to read a newspaper, but he kept peering beneath its lower edge. He watched Dargan's blackened hands.

Suddenly Dargan did the expected—slipped a tiny, folded square of paper down past Steve Thatcher's right ankle, into the shoe.

Thatcher rose. He took a dollar bill from his pocket and handed it to Dargan. Receiving change, he walked from the shop.

Both men acted quickly.

Dargan hurried back to the barber shop lavatory. He entered, latched the door. He felt of the dollar bill in his hand then, carefully, with his thumb nail, cut at its edge. The bill separated—it was two bank notes, pasted together at the edges. And between them was a sheet of tissue paper covered with close, small writing.

Dargan read it swiftly. Instructions. Orders from the man he worshipped—Steve Thatcher, the Moon Man.

Steve Thatcher crossed the street to the lobby of the Apex Building. He sidled into a telephone booth and slipped the folded paper out of his shoe. In this manner he had arranged that Dargan and he would communicate. He read Dargan's scrawl:

Followed instructions given over phone. All set. Been watching for green-eyed man, but no luck. Has not yet come into shop. Be careful, Boss. And God bless you.

"No luck." The identity of Number One was still a mystery to Steve Thatcher. With a moan he tore the bit of paper to flakes and dropped them in his pocket. He lifted the receiver of the phone and called a number.

"Sue, dear, this is Steve," he said when the number answered. "I—I'm sorry, but I have bad news."

"But, Steve, I'm waiting for you now, all ready to go to the ball," Sue said. "Where are you? Do hurry!"

"Sue—I can't come for you," Steve blurted. "Please don't ask me to explain. I know it's a disappointment to you—it is to me, too, but—I can't come."

"Why, Steve! What's the matter? It was a date, and—"

"Please, Sue!" Steve Thatcher pleaded. "Believe me, I'm sorry. I'll see you soon, dear—but not tonight. I—I can't see you tonight . . . . Good-by."

He hung up quickly, and edged from the booth. Grim-faced, he trod away. His own words mocked him. *I can't see you tonight.* Steve Thatcher's heels hammered. *Not tonight.*

Because tonight the Moon Man, driven by a power greater than he could control, was returning to life.

THE Great International Hotel was ablaze with lights. Town cars, limousines and taxis were streaming to the light-flooded marquee. Men and women in weird and quaint and enchanting costumes were hurrying toward the grand ballroom. Tonight was the height of the social season—and the Embassy Ball was under way.

Under a glittering glass chandelier, countless couples were dancing across a polished floor. The strains of an orchestra were throbbing through the perfumed air. Flowers festooned the walls; the place was a riot of color. Costumes in a variety beyond any single imagination were in evidence.

And jewels flashed. Diamond tiaras on the heads of dowagers. Glittering pendants on the necks of débutantes. Pearls and rubies, brooches and rings. Wealth beyond measure flashed in the brilliant light of the ballroom as the orchestra played.

Uniformed police guarded the entrance and the doors of the ballroom. Others were at the windows. The force was out and on watch. And inside, at one end of the ballroom, his gray eyes glinting in the light, stood the alert and grim McEwen.

Suddenly he jerked. His gaze sharpened across the ballroom floor. He peered aghast at a figure he saw. A figure in a black robe, with hands black gloved. A figure who had a head which was a ball of silver. A figure with a listening, globular ball on its shoulders, was there in the ballroom —dancing with a little Dutch maid.

"By damn!" McEwen gulped. "I'm seeing things!"

His hand tapped the gun at his hip. Narrow-eyed, he glided across the floor. The black-robed figure was dancing close now, the silver, ball-shaped head shining. McEwen stared in amazement.

Suddenly his hand shot out and gripped the black shoulder. And his other hand reached for his gun.

"Reach!" he commanded.

The black-robed figure stopped dancing, and turned. The little Dutch girl gave a cry. The man whose head was a silver ball turned squarely at McEwen.

"I beg your pardon?" came from the glass mask.

"You're got!" McEwen snapped. "Take that mask off!"

"But really," came from the silver globe. "It isn't yet time to unmask."

"Take it off!"

The black-robed figure shrugged. Slowly the black hands raised to the silver globe. A twist, a lift—and the mask came off.

"Satisfied?"

McEwen peered into the face he knew. A long, narrow face, aristocratically chiseled. He stared and breathed hard.

"Are you a detective?" the man asked. "My word! you don't think I am really the Moon Man, do you?"

McEwen snapped, "Your name's Van Orton, isn't it—Arthur Van Orton? I know you. Let's see your right hand!"

McEwen grabbed at the young man's right hand. He studied the thumb. He knew the Moon Man's thumbprint, every ridge of it. It was impressed in his mind for all time. But the thumb he was peering at now could never have made the Moon Man's print. It was entirely different.

"What the hell?" McEwen blurted.

"Why, this is only my costume," young Van Orton said. "I thought it was a bully idea. You see, this is merely my baccalaureate robe, and as for this mask—it's nothing like the real Moon Man's. It's merely a fish-bowl painted silver, with eyeholes left clear. And anyway, I say—the real Moon Man is dead, isn't he?"

"The Moon Man is *supposed* to be dead," McEwen snapped. "You've got a hell of a sense of humor, rigging yourself out like that. You'd better change your costume or you might get plugged by one of the cops."

He turned, and strode back to the wall, muttering angrily. One of the city's younger socialites masquerading as the Moon Man. It griped McEwen. And it filled him with a queer dread—a heavy, uncanny feeling that perhaps, after all, the real Moon Man was not dead.

STEVE THATCHER, garbed in business suit, and carrying a suitcase, left a taxi at the side entrance of the hotel. He strode inside to the desk. He signed for a room, and a bell boy escorted him to the elevator and up seven flights.

Once alone, Steve Thatcher moved swiftly.

He opened the suitcase. Inside it lay a black robe, a pair of black gloves, and a globe of silver glass—the precious mask of Argus glass of which only one existed in the world. The mask of the real Moon Man.

A month ago the newspapers had shouted the death of the notorious criminal. MOON MAN KILLED AT SUI-

CIDE LEAP! Gil McEwen, chasing the roadster in which the Moon Man was fleeing, had seen the car lurch over the brink of the precipice that flanked Murder River. He had seen the wreck of the car submerge in the quicksand at the water's edge. He had seen the black robe of the Moon Man disappear in the ooze. And above, hidden in bushes behind which he had leaped when leaving the lurching car, Steve Thatcher had huddled, clasping under his arm the precious mask of Argus glass. He had not been able to bring himself to part with it. He had kept it safely hidden—safely hidden until tonight.

Beside the Moon Man's regalia lay another costume. Steve Thatcher got into it swiftly. It consisted of long, black trousers, a black frock coat and a stock instead of a collar—the garb of a cleric. Over his face Steve Thatcher affixed a domino mask. Then, quickly, carrying the suitcase, he left the room.

After walking down one flight of stairs, he took an elevator. Quickly he crossed to a small conservatory in one corner of the lobby, opposite the grand ballroom. He stepped inside, and found it empty. Carefully, out of sight behind a heavy chair, he hid the suitcase.

Then, sauntering, he went to the door of the ballroom and presented his invitation—an engraved card which had accompanied his instructions from the Red Six. He walked inside. Almost instantly he came to a standstill.

A man garbed as Mephistopheles was eying him through a mask. The mask was red. On its forehead was a black numeral I. Through the slits green eyes gleamed.

The green gaze turned Steve Thatcher's heart to ice. He walked past, striving to avoid any sign of recognition. He felt the green eyes following him, and wondered. Wondered if Primus knew him—had recognized him—suspected the plan that lay in Steve Thatcher's mind. Wondering if, before many minutes, he would feel the point of a needle prick him, driven by some unseen hand in the crowd—a needle tipped with ghastly poison .... The germs of tetanus!

Chilled, Steve Thatcher went on. His heart beating hard, he stopped again. He was eying a black-robed figure with a silver globe on its head. A figure which looked like the Moon Man. His eyes gleamed behind his domino as he studied that figure.

He had expected to see it. It had been mentioned in his orders. It was part of the cunning plan of the Red Six.

And then Steve Thatcher saw Gil McEwen, standing against the wall, chewing on a cigar. McEwen was eying the counterfeit Moon-Man grimly. Again Steve Thatcher felt an icy grip on his heart.

His plan for the night was a daring one. A thousand dangers threatened it. And one of them was that Gil McEwen might see, that Gil McEwen might learn the dread secret.

Steve Thatcher went on. Pausing again, he gazed at another masked figure—another man masked in red. And this mask was numbered IV—Quartus. Next Steve Thatcher saw Tertius—then Quintus. Within a few minutes he spotted them all—the leaders of the criminal combine—dancing with society matrons and debs.

Could they recognize him, Steve Thatcher, in the garb of a cleric? He dreaded the possibility. He could not be sure. For his costume was not part of the orders of the Red Six. It was part of Steve Thatcher's own daring plan.

He glanced at his wristwatch. Eleven-thirty. At midnight would come the call to unmask. And in fifteen minutes, at eleven forty-five, the zero hour of the Red Six would be at hand.

The minute when the organization of the Red Six would strike.

ELEVEN FORTY. Steve Thatcher, garbed as a cleric, crossed the ballroom quickly. He strode across the lobby, into the deserted conservatory. He closed the door and latched it.

Quickly he lifted the suitcase from its hiding-spot. He pulled upon him the black robe of the Moon Man, the black gloves. Lastly he placed upon his head the mask of Argus glass, the silver globe which seemed to be a mirror, but through which its wearer could see as plainly as though it did not exist.

One moment transformed Steve Thatcher from a cleric to the Moon Man. And he waited.

Eleven forty-two.

On the door sounded a knock. Steve Thatcher drew the latch. A figure slipped into the conservatory. A figure garbed in black, with black hands, and a silver ball on its head. The counterfeit Moon Man.

For a moment they peered at each other—the man who was masquerading as the Moon Man by orders of the Red Six—and the man who *was* the Moon Man.

"Quick!"

The second figure swiftly drew off his robe and gloves. Beneath he was was wearing the costume of a cavalier. He lifted the painted fish-bowl from his head; and his face appeared, masked. Swiftly the Moon Man stowed the regalia of the masquerader in the suitcase.

"Hurry!"

The cavalier slipped out of the door. Just inside the Moon Man stood alert, waiting, listening. Again he glanced at his watch. Eleven forty-three. Two minutes to the zero hour of the Red Six.

The Moon Man opened the door. He walked across the lobby. Other masqueraded figures smiled at him. He entered the ballroom and paused. He saw two men gazing straight at the silver globe which was his head.

One was the Mephistopheles wearing the red mask numbered I. The other was Gil McEwen. Mephistopheles danced away, his green eyes glittering. Gil McEwen chewed on his cigar and made a disgusted noise.

"Damn funny sense of humor," the Moon Man heard him say.

The silver head bent as the Moon Man again glanced at his watch. Thirty seconds to go. Thirty seconds until the red zero hour.

Swiftly the Moon Man strode across the glassy floor toward a raised dais at one end. His black robe flapped as he mounted it. His glistening head was bent, and his hidden eyes peering at his watch.

Eleven forty-five to the second.

Swiftly the Moon Man drew an automatic through a slit of his cape. He raised it to the ceiling. He pulled the trigger.

The blasting shot echoed startlingly through the ballroom.

CHAPTER VII

TRICK FOR TRICK

SWIFT action! Two score of dancers swiftly left their partners on the dance floor. Quickly they moved to the edge of the ballroom. From the folds of their costumes they drew guns.

Four advanced on the orchestra, brandishing weapons. With a discordant clash the music ended.

Two confronted Gil McEwen and leveled automatics at his middle while he stood in rigid amazement.

Pairs darted to each of the doors and quickly closed them. Others covered policemen with their automatics. Others stood on guard, leveling guns at the startled dancers.

And silence fell inside the room.

"Ladies and gentlemen!"

The muffled voice of the Moon Man echoed through the quiet.

"Ladies and gentlemen! No harm will come to you if you obey orders. Give up your jewels, money, and other valuables promptly. Stand where you are and don't move."

Hands above his head, backed to the wall by two automatics, Gil Mc-

Ewen peered at the silver-headed figure on the dais and snarled.

"That's him! That's the real Moon Man!"

Quick movement filled the ballroom. The organization of the Red Six began to function smoothly. There were a few outcries, a few screams. Weapons glittered everywhere. Eyes gazed at the commanding black figure on the platform. And a word passed quickly from mouth to mouth:

"Robbery!"

Armed men and women moved from dancer to dancer, carrying small canvas bags. Into the bags went the tiaras from the dowagers' heads, the pendants from the débutantes' throats, the rings from the fingers of the matrons. Swiftly, moving surely, according to the orders of the Red Six, the daring robbery proceeded.

Suddenly a shot cracked. A man howled. Startled silence fell. From the Moon Man's silver head issued his hollow voice:

"I urge you to behave, ladies and gentlemen! One of your number, I see, made an attempt to hold out. The next who attempts interference will no doubt be killed. I warn you!"

Silence again. Costumed figures moving from person to person. Jewels dropping into the fattening bags. All the while McEwen stood powerless against the wall, pinned to it by the automatics in the hands of the masked figures. All the while the Moon Man's glittering head turned in the light as his automatic waved.

Suddenly, glancing at his watch, he raised the gun again. Another blasting shot rocked through the air. The Moon Man called:

"Time's up!"

Swiftly the armed, masked figures who composed the Red Six's organization moved toward the doors. The Moon Man dropped off the dais and ran to the main entrance. His gun was still in his hand as he sped into the conservatory. He clicked the door shut and listened.

CLEARING the way with their guns, the masked bandits marched toward the entrance of the hotel, holding their bags of loot. On the sidewalk stood ten policemen, their hands raised, confronted by other masked figures with guns. In the street a row of heavy sedans were waiting, their motors purring, their wheels held by men who were also masked.

A commanding voice uttered "Hurry!"

The costumed figures crowded into the sedans. One car and another dashed off. The way ahead was clear. The plan of the Red Six had lured traffic officers from their posts. Ahead loomed a black, empty street—the start of the carefully planned getaway.

The parade dashed past an intersection and beyond. Each driver had particularized orders. Each person inside the car knew exactly where to take his bag of loot and dispose of it. Each had an escape provided for. And the way lay ahead—black street. Empty—save for one vehicle.

The driver of the foremost gang car saw it swerving from side to side of the street ahead and blared his horn wrathfully.

The vehicle was a wagon, a milk delivery truck. It was drawn by a single horse, and the horse was rearing, pawing the air, springing from curb to curb. The driver on the seat had lost the reins. The wagon swung crazily as he shouted wildly in an ineffective attempt to stop the animal.

Runaway!

The lurching of the milk wagon spilled the piles of crates in the rear of the truck. One of them fell. Glass crashed to the pavement as bottles splintered. Milk splashed and ran toward the gutters. Following the first crate, a second fell—a third—a fourth. Smashing fragments and flowing white! Jagged, glittering glass was strewn across the street.

The driver of the foremost gang car yelled.

"Stop 'em behind! It'll cut every tire!"

Too late. Every sedan was past the intersection. They were crowding close, bumper to bumper. The way was blocked by the milk wagon, still twisting from side to side, and by the glittering glass on the pavement. The cars nudged each other. The fragments ground under the tires.

Explosions! Tires bursting out air! Brakes squealing! And the criminal cavalcade came to a quick stop.

A driver leaped from the foremost car.

"Scatter! Abandon the bags! Keep under cover!" And again, in a scream: *"Scatter!"*

Tires burst again as the doors of the sedans clacked open. The costumed men and women leaped out. From the intersection policemen were running, guns out.

"Scatter!"

They ran—ran like mad. Colorful costumes mingled with black shadows. Now every car was empty. Now the masked gang was running, scurrying to any cover afforded by the street. They darted into unknown doors, ran to the next corner, scrambled into parked cars—and in an instant confusing blackness blotted them out.

In the sedans, as the police closed in on them, lay the bags of loot—untold wealth—abandoned.

INSIDE the door of the conservatory the Moon Man huddled. As a knock sounded he straightened. His fingers slid the latch. Quickly a man sidled in—a man garbed as a cavalier.

"The black robe—quick!" urged Van Orton.

The Moon Man faced the cavalier, arms outstretched. His silver head was bent with menace. The cavalier poised, startled, as the black-robed figure inched toward him.

"Get out of the window!" the muffled voice inside the silver shell of a head ordered. "Skip town and don't come back! That's orders!"

The cavalier recoiled as the black figure advanced. "I have no such orders. My orders say I'm to get back into the Moon Man costume. I daren't—"

"You're through taking orders from the Red Six now! You're taking orders from me!"

And the voice rang grimly inside the shell of Argus glass.

The Moon Man leaped. His black-gloved hands clutched at the cavalier's throat. The pleated collar crackled as the black fingers pressed hard. The cavalier gasped, and dragged to his knees, clutching at the black wrists, gasping for air.

"Will you go?" echoed within the glass mask. "Will you go?"

"If I disobey orders! You know—"

"Will you go?"

The gloved fingers were biting deeper. The cavalier's face, behind his mask, was red and changing to purple. He blurted through fluttering lips, in abject terror:

"I'll go! I'll go!"

The Moon Man's clutch loosened. The cavalier brought himself dizzily to his feet, still gasping. The Moon Man crossed quickly to the window, unlatched it, and peered into the street. This section of the sidewalk was dark; the turmoil at the entrance of the hotel was distracting attention from this spot. The Moon Man whipped back and gestured outward.

"I'll go!"

The cavalier scrambled onto the broad sill. He glanced once up and down the street. His terrified eyes clung to the globular head of the Moon Man as he lowered himself. The Moon Man waited at the sill only long enough to see the cavalier skirting off into the darkness.

He turned back, quickly. From its hiding place behind the chair, he swung his grip into the open. Quickly he whipped off robe and gloves, and rolled them. Carefully he lifted the precious glass mask from his head. His regalia he stuffed into the case, and the case he slipped again behind the chair.

Once more the Moon Man was Steve Thatcher in the masquerading garb of a cleric.

He eased to the door and opened it. Bedlam reigned outside. Dancers were crowding through the entrances of the grand ballroom, milling in the lobby. Over the hubbub Steve Thatcher heard the shouting of Gil McEwen. He sidled out, eyes shifting.

Shouldering through the crowd, he managed to reach the nearest doorway of the ballroom. In the shifting crowd he saw red masks. Steve Thatcher wriggled his way on until, suddenly, he saw the figure of Mephistopheles.

Thatcher squirmed back. The rows of palms along the wall offered him a moment's shelter. In the shadow of a clump of them he paused. Quickly he whipped the black mask from his face. As quickly he placed across his eyes another mask—a red one. On its forehead was a Roman numeral IV.

Thatcher slid out of the shadow, and worked his way again through the crowd, toward the Mephistopheles. The crowd was thick. Thatcher carefully kept himself covered as much as possible as he reached out and gripped the arm of the masquerading Primus.

The green eyes shifted like lightning, and glittered into Steve Thatcher's.

"In the conservatory, quick!" Thatcher whispered. "There's trouble!"

HE let the pressing crowd push him away. Hunching, to keep out of sight in the mêlée, he hurried back to the door. Quick glances told him that Mephistopheles—Primus—was searching for the mask numbered IV in the crowd. Steve Thatcher sidled through the door and into the lobby as the Mephistophelian figure followed.

He darted to the entrance of the conservatory. The door was still closed, the room empty, as he slipped in. Moving with desperate quickness, he dashed to the hidden suitcase, jerked it up, and flung it open.

In a second he had the black robe of the Moon Man over his frame, the glittering, globular mask in place on his shoulders. He whipped back, and paused near the door.

Turbulent noises came through the panels, and still the shouting of Gil McEwen was audible.

"Find that guy! Find the Moon Man! He's in here somewhere!"

On the door sounded a quick knock. Thatcher loosened the bolt and inched the door open. The red-garbed figure of Mephistopheles shouldered in. The Moon Man bolted the door again and stepped back, his breath hissing inside his shell of a mask.

Through the red mask the eyes of Primus shone malevolently.

"Well?" he demanded. "What's the trouble?"

The Moon Man's answer was swift. It was a black, clubbed fist that shot like lightning and clicked to the point of the masked man's chin. Primus' head drove back, and he staggered. The Moon Man paced after him as he brought up, shoulders hunched, eyes an icy green.

"Treachery!"

The Moon Man's hands were black claws. The tight-fitting costume of the Mephistopheles told him that Primus could have no gun concealed on his person. As Primus's right hand flicked toward his belt, the Moon Man stepped closer.

"You know the penalty for treachery!"

The right hand of Primus darted upward. His fingers made a quick, twisting motion. The Moon Man's glistening head lowered as he peered. He saw a tiny, cylindrical object in the hands of Primus. He saw part of it drop away, and part remain in the long, tapering fingers.

That part was a tiny, glittering needle tipped with something that clouded the bright, pointed metal.

"Tetanus!"

Primus leaped.

A hoarse cry came from the Moon

Man's globular head as he saw the needle flash, driving toward him. The needle tipped with the deadly tetani bacilli! The merest prick would mean horrible, torturous death! The tiny lightning of it flashed toward the folds of the Moon Man's robe!

The Moon Man's black hand darted down. As Primus' body thudded against his he groped for the hand that held the deadly needle. His fingers clasped the wrist. The thrust of Primus's hand was stopped as the point pricked through the black fabric of the robe.

With his left hand the Moon Man clutched at Primus's throat as his glittering head bent, as his unseen eyes peered at the flickering point of the needle. The man in the Mephistopheles costume was possessed of maniacal strength. The Moon Man was forced back—back against the wall. The pressure behind the needle bore in more powerfully—moving it again toward the black-robed body.

THE Moon Man twisted, hooking a leg out. His heel caught behind the tight-sheathed legs of Primus and levered. He thrust again at the pulsing neck as he wrenched from the wall. A quick lurch threw him forward, then a black-covered fist clicked again to the red-masked face. A moan broke through the thin, cruel lips, and Primus sprawled.

With breath beating in and out of the glass mask, the Moon Man towered above, arms groping. Primus lay flat, stunned, scarcely moving. He rolled slightly, and peered down at himself—peered at the silk-clad thigh of his right leg. A spot of bright metal was glittering there—clinging.

The needle had driven deep into Primus's flesh.

Frantically Primus snatched it out. He leaped to his feet, hoarsely crying out. The Moon Man sprang again as the glittering green eyes flashed at him. All the power of his black-covered frame drove behind his clubbed fist as he struck. The blow smashed full into the red-masked face.

Primus dropped, half-rolled, and lay still.

The Moon Man straightened, panting. Against the panels of the conservatory door the hubbub of the crowd was beating like surf. Still Gil McEwen's voice was audible.

"I tell you he's still in here! Find him! Find the Moon Man!"

The Moon Man whirled again to the suitcase. Quickly he pulled from it the robe that had been worn by the cavalier. He lifted also the silver-painted fish-bowl. Working quickly, he dragged the robe over the lax body of Primus. He fitted the bowl over Primus's head. As he rose, Primus stirred, making feeble attempts to rise.

Gil McEwen howling again, "No man leaves this place without having his fingerprints taken!"

The Moon Man crossed quickly to the conservatory door. Gil McEwen's voice had sounded near. Drawing the bolt, the Moon Man poised—and then he jerked the door open.

Gil McEwen was standing a few yards away. The click of the bolt, the sudden movement of the door, jerked his eyes. He turned, and stared—stared through the open door at the figure of black, at the figure with the silver head, which was looking out at him.

"Get him!"

McEwen shrieked the word as he snatched up his service revolver. The Moon Man stepped back quickly, and aside, slamming the conservatory door. As the bolt clicked into its socket, a gun blasted in the lobby, and a bullet drilled through the panels.

"Break that door in!"

The Moon Man darted across the room. Swift movements divested himself of his robe and mask. He shoved them into the grip—and became again Steve Thatcher in the garb of a cleric. Thatcher exchanged the red, numbered mask on his face for the black domino as he sprang toward the window.

The way seemed clear. He glanced back, to see Primus, in the black robe, trying to drag himself up. Steve Thatcher dropped over the sill.

Instantly a shout sounded beside him. "Hey, there! Wait a minute! Where do you think you're goin'?"

A HEFTY patrolman had seen Steve Thatcher crawling out. He was trotting from the crowd at the entrance. Thatcher backed away, in turmoil. He knew that the shout would bring a crowd around him in a moment. The officer was lumbering down on him like a vindictive elephant.

Thatcher whirled, began to run. The patrolman shouted again, "Hey! Stop him! Stop—"

The yell ended in a sharp grunt. As he darted toward the entrance of the hotel grill, which stood beyond, Steve Thatcher glanced back. He saw that a white figure had dashed from across the street, to the sidewalk near the open window. The white figure had collided violently with the patrolman. The impact had thrown them both to the sidewalk, and they were sprawling.

The second's grace was all that Steve Thatcher needed. He dashed into the grill entrance as he heard the white-clad figure gasp, "Sorry! Didn't mean to run into you!"

The patrolman was still on the sidewalk, groping, stunned, as the white-clad man brought himself up. He sped into the grill entrance after Steve Thatcher. Thatcher was passing through the inner door, reëntering the lobby, when the white-coated man panted up beside him.

"Make it snappy, Boss!"

Thatcher jerked, peered down. "Angel!"

Beneath the white cap, Ned Dargan peered up and grinned. His was a spotless costume. Across the pocket of the coat was a red-sewn name: *Sanitary Dairy System.*

"Boss! You all right?"

"Good as gold, Angel! You shouldn't have come here—but thanks! Did it work?"

"I had to come, Boss! And did it work! Say, I had a time making that horse run away, but I managed it. I sure spilled glass all over the street. It stopped the gang cars, all right. The gang's all scattered, but the cops grabbed the loot. Soon as I saw they had it, I beat it over here. I hand it to you—you certainly had a plan that wrecked that get-away."

Side by side they hurried across the lobby to the check-stand.

"The big robbery is a fiasco, Angel—thanks to your help. But stay out of sight. The Red Six may suspect. If they ever dream that I managed that 'runaway,' and that you helped me—You've heard of lockjaw. We may be covered now, and we may not. But watch yourself!"

"Don't worry about me, Boss, so long as you're okay. If there's any way I can help you—"

"No, Angel! Slip out of here, quick. Get out of sight. I'll call you later. And watch yourself!"

Dargan, grinning, shouldered into the crowd that filled the lobby with pandemonium. Steve Thatcher paused just long enough to check his suitcase at the stand before he thrust himself into the mob. Pounding in the air was a crashing sound. Patrolmen were crowded about the door of the conservatory, and two of them were heaving their shoulders against it.

McEwen was shouting: "Windows covered? Is he closed in?"

"Tight as a drum!"

"Smash that door!"

Even as McEwen howled the orders, the panel of the big door splintered. A patrolman reached through the crack and snatched back the bolt. McEwen thrust the door open and leaped in with service gat leveled.

He stopped short, peering.

In the center of the conservatory stood a black-robed figure. On his head was a ball of silver. Its black hands were fluttering; it was swaying dizzily. One instant McEwen paused, peering at it—and suddenly the black figure stumbled toward the open window.

"Wait!"

The rush did not stop.

McEwen's gun blasted. Bullets ripped into the black robe. The ebon figure twisted, stumbled. Against the wall it lurched. The silver head clicked to the bricks, and the room echoed with the smashing of glass.

McEwen peered down at the figure which lay on the floor. The face was bared of the glass mask, but still covered with the red domino. McEwen saw blood dripping; the mouth of tho black-masked man was hanging open, tightening into a grinning grimace. With a snatch McEwen tore the red mask off.

The face was strange.

"Never saw him before!" McEwen exclaimed. He reached down, snatched up the dead man's right hand, and peered at the thumb. "Aw hell!" he bawled. "This ain't him!"

A hush fell into the conservatory.

"I see it now! That's not the Moon Man's mask—it's only that painted fish-bowl. This bird's not the Moon Man! The real one's got away!"

Steve Thatcher, peering through the open door of the conservatory, smiled grimly. He turned, and sidled out of the crowd. In the churning maelstrom of humans in the lobby he lost himself.

BRIGHT sunshine streamed across the entrance of police headquarters as Steve Thatcher strode through it next morning. He climbed to the chief's office. He entered it to find his father there, and Gil McEwen, and Sue. Steve's eyes lighted when he saw her. Steve felt better than he had in days. For Primus—the man who would have enslaved him—was dead.

Gil McEwen was beating the air with a fist. "Most daring gang of crooks ever heard of! This bird that got killed—Max Reiss, international blackmail expert—he's one of 'em. And the Moon Man again—the real one. That bird Van Orton wasn't in on it, but the real Moon Man was! He's not dead—he's back again—heading the biggest criminal syndicate in history!"

Sue was coming toward Steve. McEwen went on, "I'll get that guy! I swore I'd get him, and I will. The time's coming when he's going to the chair, and I'm going to send him there!"

Sue said quietly: "Steve, dear, it's quite all right. If you had a reason for breaking our date why, of course, I understand. Missing the Ball doesn't matter—but I'm worried about you, Steve."

Steve took her hand. "Worried, Sue?"

"Yes. You've been acting so strange lately—as though something were wrong. Is there, Steve? Something wrong?"

"Not between us, darling," he said.

"Of course not," she smiled. "But if there is anything worrying you Steve—please tell me."

Steve Thatcher smiled as he gazed into the eyes of the girl he loved.

"There's nothing troubling me, Sue, dear," he said. "Nothing—nothing whatever!"

Hideous Death Visits

The House of Kaa

By
RICHARD B. SALE
Author of "Terror Towers."

The python mauled the corpse

Scotland Yard thought it strange that the firm of Gorgan & Wilkins imported only regal pythons. But no law was being broken. And they thought it very strange when the Cobra, a lone avenger from India, suddenly appeared in London. But the Cobra had once helped them, so there was no investigation. And the greatest surprise of all was the appearance of Deen Bradley of the British Intelligence—who had an amazing plan to offer.

JACK KIRK, whose profession had never been anything but sordid murder, paused before the dreary brownstone house on Rokor Street. He glanced all about him in a wary and frightened sort of way.

He could have sworn that some one was following him. If not some one—*something!* A black, misshapen, baroque giant. A flitting spectre.

Kirk had seen a shadow—only for an instant.

Then the shadow had disintegrated like the whispering dissipation of a gliding ghost.

Kirk shook his shoulders and blamed it on his imagination. He went slowly up the short flight of stairs in the front of the house and glanced at the sign over the door. It read:

GORGAN & WILKINS—REPTILE IMPORTERS

Quickly, Kirk pulled a key from his pocket, inserted it in the lock, and opened the door. He entered with alacrity, slamming it after him.

The main hall was dark as pitch. But Kirk knew where he was going. He ascended the long, creaking staircase to the second floor of the dreary place. A solitary light on the second floor led him to a door marked "Office."

He rapped sharply four times and entered.

Three men were in the room. He recognized them as Maxie Gorgan, John Wilkins, and the man from India, Wentworth Lane. They had been talking but now they looked up at him.

"Sit down, Jack," Gorgan smirked. "Lane here is reporting on our—ah—Indian importations." He grinned knowingly.

Kirk smiled and sat down. Lane bit his lip angrily.

"You can be as sarcastic as you like, Maxie," he snapped, "But I tell you it's so. I don't know about this end, but I do know that the police are close to catching us in Bombay. There was an American operative on my trail for several days before I left for London. You know, the one we checked on."

"What do they suspect you of?" Gorgan leered. "Maybe they think you're maltreating snakes!" He laughed harshly. "Listen, Lane, you're an agent for a company. You're an importer of reptiles from India."

"But the trouble is—the only reptiles I ever import to you are regal pythons. It's damned suspicious."

"If you're afraid—" Gorgan began coldly.

Lane leaped to his feet, his eyes blazing.

"You want me to deny I am. Well, I'm not lying for any one. And you can't make me! I *am* afraid! And I'm going to get out!"

GORGAN eyed Wilkins surreptitiously and nodded. Kirk, watching the proceedings, was mildly amused. He failed to see what had gotten Lane's wind up so. Lane had been a good reliable man on the Bombay end.

"Just a second, Lane," Wilkins purred softly. "Maybe you're right. Maybe we've misjudged you. We don't want you to quit."

"No," Gorgan added with a trace of acerbity, "you can't quit."

"Well, I'm going to nevertheless," Lane declared stridently. His voice lowered as he leaned forward. "Did you ever hear of the Cobra?" he whispered.

Gorgan and Wilkins looked dumb. They shook their heads.

"Did you, Kirk?"

Jack Kirk smiled amusedly.

"Yeah," he replied. "Sure, I've heard of him. Some sort of a guy who thinks he's a public avenger. Goes around alone."

Lane nodded. "That's he — the Cobra."

"But he's supposed to be in India." Kirk was enjoying this baiting Lane. "You know how those yarns get around the underworld. The last thing they had on that guy was when he put down the Persian uprising in Bombay. Last month, I think."

Lane said, "Yes, last month. And we started this business last month. It was all right when we got away with those emeralds and that Mahar diamond. I thought the whole layout was foolproof. But I haven't felt right since I shipped the Kubij opal to you.

That's a damned unlucky stone. It belonged to Sarankh, a rajah of the Hindustan country. I hired three dacoits to steal it, paid them well, and sent the stone through the customs with our regular snake freight.

"Right after that, this American detective came around and asked a lot of queer questions. But we have a good front with this reptile-importing set-up and I got around him.

"Then the Cobra stepped in—and I was so upset over the affair that I took the first and fastest boat here to see you. I tell you, a child could guess the answer from the fact that the only snakes we ship are pythons!"

Wilkins laughed. "Don't be an ass!"

Jack Kirk leaned forward. "What's this about the Cobra, Lane?" he asked frowning. "What happened?"

"The three dacoits I hired," Lane explained soberly, "were found dead the day before I left for London—*dead from cobra venom!* And there were tiny darts in their throats!"

"Darts?" Kirk echoed, feeling his own throat in dread.

Lane smiled mirthlessly. "Yes, darts. The mark of the Cobra. A dart in the throat covered with noxious cobra venom. That's how the devil gets his name."

"Listen," Gorgan snarled, "don't let him hypnotize you, Jack. This Cobra stuff is crazy! I've had enough of this cock-and-bull yarn, Lane. You're welching and you're taking the easiest way out. There's nothing wrong. The Kubij opal will arrive tomorrow with our python shipment."

"I tell you, I'm afraid!" Lane cried. "I'm quitting, Maxie. I'm getting out. I don't want any money from the jewels. I want my life. You can split my share among the three of you."

Maxie Gorgan rose steadily to his feet. His voice was icy and sinister. His hand stole stealthily inside of his coat.

"You can't quit this game, Lane," he warned.

Lane looked at him coolly, evenly. "You heard me, Maxie," he replied fearlessly. "When the Cobra steps in—I step out. And that's final."

The three shots from Gorgan's pistol sounded like one. Three hot slugs buried themselves in Lane's chest like lightning. Lane stared at Gorgan's tense face in stupefaction. His lips moved soundlessly. He struggled bravely to speak. Blood poured from his mouth. His legs sagged, and he fell forward on his face, crashing to the floor with an ominous thump. He did not move after he hit.

Kirk wet his lips and put out the cigarette he had been smoking.

"God, Max!" Wilkins exclaimed in horror. "You shouldn't have done it!"

Gorgan shrugged and put his gun back.

"It's his own funeral. I told him. We can't afford to have a welcher, Wilky. There's too much money involved. Besides, there's only a split of three now, and dead men tell no tales. Kirk—get rid of this stiff. Use the car outside. Dump him out at Yorkshire."

Kirk sighed.

"Okay, chief," he said.

JACK KIRK did not notice the black sedan which followed him and his macabre burden through Surrey. Kirk was intent upon the operation of his vehicle, since even the slightest accident would incur the intervention of police. And with a dead man to be explained, Kirk was taking no chances.

The black car trailed him tenaciously out past Surrey into the suburbs of London.

Nor could Kirk see the figure at the wheel of the mystery car—a dark incongruous figure, covered by a black cloak, its face concealed by the dark shadows of the turbid night.

To a prowling cat, whose green eyes might have pierced the darkness, the hawklike features of Deen Bradley would have been discernible. Deen was an operative of the Bombay Department of Justice. High-foreheaded, dark-skinned, he had black eyes which glittered coldly like ebony diamonds, hard, unemotional. He had no mustache. His face was thin and sharp. His lips, narrow and straight-lined.

He handled the car with natural dexterity, never shifting his cobra eyes from the red tail-light of the cadaver-car before him.

At Yorkshire, Kirk left the main highway and swerved to the right. Deen followed quickly, stepping down on the gas.

The American suddenly saw the brake-light of the other machine flare into being. Kirk slowed momentarily and, as he did so, a limp bundle tumbled lifelessly from the rolling car.

Then, Kirk sped away with amazing alacrity, his engine roaring sonorously into the night.

The fog drifting across the open countryside swallowed the lights of his car.

Deen slammed his brakes to the floor of the sedan, and the automobile skidded perilously to a halt. Beside it, in a ditch, lay the bundle which had been thrown from Kirk's car.

Deen leaped from the sedan and ran forward. He found a man, bleeding profusely and unconscious. He bent down and lifted up the fellow on his right arm.

The face of Wentworth Lane stared at him, eyes sightless and horrible.

"Zah!" Deen muttered in repugnance. "So it is murder, too!"

He grasped the wrist of the unconscious Lane and felt for a possible flicker of life.

Instantly he jumped to his feet and dashed for the sedan, carrying Lane in his arms. His strength was astonishing. He carried Lane, who was heavy-set, as though the latter was a child. Carefully he laid the wounded man on the cushions. Then he hopped agilely into the front seat and pressed the accelerator to the floor.

Twenty minutes later, Lane was on a white-enameled operating table in the Yorkshire hospital while two doctors bent over him, working furiously to save his life. Deen stood by, anxiously waiting.

Presently one of the doctors looked up and shook his head.

"He's dying."

Deen frowned. He asked, "There is no chance?"

"None. I don't see how he keeps alive. Two bullets through his right lung. A third against his spine. It's miraculous!"

The dying man gasped paroxysmally.

"Can he be made to talk?" asked Deen.

The doctor shrugged dubiously. He turned to a nurse.

"Adrenalin," he snapped.

He leaned over the naked chest of Lane and drove a hypodermic syringe into the flesh directly over the heart. Then he emptied the contents.

Momentarily, there was no visible result.

Then Lane's staring eyes gained the power of sight and recognition. They glanced around furtively. Finally they rested on Deen's dark face.

"You—"

"Yes. It is I. From India. I followed you. Quick, you must speak. You are dying."

Lane coughed rackingly.

"Gorgan," he muttered whisperingly. "Pythons—code word is—House of Kaa—"

His lips had hardly stopped moving when he sighed. His body relaxed.

The doctors made preparations to transfer the corpse into the mortuary for identification and signing of the death certificate. With the American to establish identity—

But when they glanced around for him, Deen was gone.

That night, the police found the cadaver of Jack Kirk in Rokor Street, London. Kirk was sprawled crazily in the gutter—dead. Protruding from his throat was a small dart, about a half an inch long.

The chief medical examiner found that Kirk had died as the result of the violent neurotoxic destruction of cobra venom.

And throughout the underworld of London, a dire, foreboding wail echoed—a wail that spelled the nemesis of criminals.

The Cobra had come to England!

"WELL, what are we going to do?" Commissioner Marshall asked sharply.

Inspector Ryder shrugged. The two men were sitting in the commissioner's office at the C. I. D. headquarters in Scotland Yard. In Marshall's hand was the coroner's report on the Jack Kirk murder the night preceding.

"I'd suggest nothing," the inspector said with a flip of his hand. "The department has been after Kirk for two years. He was a killer. One of the few English bandits who carried and used a gun. He was working for that Gorgan-Wilkins reptile firm over on Rokor Street. There's something damned queer going on over there, too. As far as I'm concerned, chief, I'd let it go."

"You mean—drop the case entirely?"

"Yes, sir." Ryder leaned forward. "We've had excellent reports about this Cobra from Bombay headquarters. It was he who brought those Persian renegades to justice after they murdered Kilgore, one of the C. I. D.'s best men."

"I remember that," Marshall nodded.

Ryder grimaced. "We owe him a good turn. Commissioner—I don't know who or what the Cobra is. But I *do* know that he gets results because he goes outside of the law. He saved me a lot of trouble getting Kirk. And there must be a reason. I wager that important business has brought the Cobra to London."

"Very well," the commissioner sighed. "Drop investigation."

At that moment, there was a knock on the door. An attendant looked in. "Mr. Bradley to see you, sir."

"Send him in."

The door opened, and the dark-skinned, hawk-faced Deen Bradley walked in.

"Happy to know you, Bradley," Marshall exclaimed, rising and shaking hands with sincere enthusiasm. "Meet Inspector Ryder. Bradley is one of the best in Bombay, Ryder."

"I know," the inspector said. "Thanks for helping us out on that Kilgore case down there."

"I did very little," Deen replied softly. "In reality, you should thank him who calls himself the Cobra."

"That's a coincidence!" Marshall cried. "Your Bombayan avenger happens to be in London. Did you read it? The Kirk affair."

"The commissioner's called off an investigation," Ryder remarked, eyeing the American keenly.

Deen nodded without a trace of emotion, said: "Very wise."

"But what brings you here?" Marshall queried. "Bombay cabled me to watch for you and give you any aid you asked."

Deen sat down and pulled a peculiar greenish cigarette holder from his pocket. Slowly, he inserted a cigarette in it and lighted it.

"For the last month," he began, "there have been strange robberies in India along the eastern coast. Emeralds and diamonds of priceless value have been purloined by hired dacoits. Most notorious was the recent theft of the Kubij opal of the Rajah Sarankh."

"We heard of that," put in Ryder.

"All these jewels are being exported from India," Deen continued. "Somehow they are being smuggled out—past the customs officials. More paradoxical—they are being smuggled *into* England past the watchful scrutiny of your revenue officers here.

"I resolved to investigate. It was no general sneak-thief job, I knew. It appeared to be an international imbroglio, carefully planned and executed. A jewel ring. I tracked a Wentworth Lane to London to lead me to the lost jewels. Last night, he too was murdered—by his own cohorts."

"But how can these jewels get into England past the customs?" the inspector demanded. "They are very rigid, you know."

"True, they are rigid," Deen murmured. "But do the customs men cut open the bellies of regal pythons to look for stolen jewels?"

Ryder stared at the American, dumbfounded.

"Good Gad!" he cried sharply. "Smuggling by snakes! You mean, then, that Gorgan-Wilkins reptile outfit is the center of the ring! They import nothing but pythons. And they hardly ever sell any of the snakes. The reptiles just disappear. I checked that when I first became suspicious of that company."

"You see," Deen explained, "it is very simple. The jewels are stolen in India by hired dacoits. Then, securely wrapped, they are placed in food which is swallowed by the pythons immediately prior to shipment. Since a big snake takes ten to eighteen days to assimilate and digest its food before throwing off waste, the seven-day sea trip to London is completed within that time. When the snakes arrive, they are killed and the jewels recovered from the stomach!"

"Amazing!" breathed the commissioner. "We'll arrest them at once!"

"No." Deen's voice was clear and firm. "You must not arrest them yet. You must help me. We will need evidence—the Kubij opal, perhaps. And I have a simple plan."

MAXIE GORGAN eyed John Wilkins thoughtfully as the latter paced the floor of the House of Kaa in Rokor Street. Wilkins was highly excited and nervous. He had been smoking incessantly.

"You're acting like a kid," Gorgan muttered.

"I can't help it, Maxie," Wilkins said. "This thing's getting my goat. First you knock off Lane—"

"Keep your mouth shut!"

"Aw, no one can hear us. Anyway, Lane dies first. Then Kirk, after dumping him, is found dead right outside with one of those damned poisoned darts in his throat. I wouldn't give a hang, Maxie, if it weren't for that Cobra story that Lane told us before you rubbed him out."

"You're getting scared over nothing," Gorgan said. "Suppose this guy who calls himself the Cobra *is* on to us. What of it? He's outside the law, isn't he? And he's a lone wolf, isn't he? And above all, remember, he's a man—a single man. And he'll have to come to us. He can't go to the police. One man. I can handle him, Wilky."

Wilkins shook his head.

"I'm leery. Suppose they're on to the shipment we got today. The pythons. They're here, aren't they?"

"Yeah," Gorgan growled. "And when you lose those jitters, we'll go down and get the Kubij opal."

"I don't like it, Maxie," Wilkins protested. "The whole organization is shot. With Kirk gone, who's going to fence the jewels after we melt them down? With Lane gone—who's going to take over the Bombay end of the business?"

The doorbell at the front of the house jingled stridently.

A deep pall of silence covered the office. Gorgan's hand crept inside his coat and brought out an ugly automatic. He waved Wilkins away and went to the window.

A solitary man was standing before them. A tall, gaunt man with piercing black eyes. No one else was in sight.

"Let him in," Gorgan said curtly. "Keep him covered all the time. Lock the door after you. Hurry!"

Wilkins complied nervously and went downstairs.

He presently reappeared behind Dean Bradley who entered the office smoking a cigarette, that same peculiar green holder held tightly between his teeth. He bowed to Gorgan.

"Sit down," Maxie said, nodding to a chair.

DEEN seated himself and smiled mirthlessly. "You may remove that finger from the trigger of your gun," he purred. "I am unarmed."

Gorgan flushed guiltily and his eyes narrowed. He lifted the pistol from his pocket and laid it on the desk in front of him, his right hand still curled around it.

"Frisk him, Wilky," he said.

"I did before," Wilkins replied. "No gun, Maxie."

Gorgan nodded. He said, "Okay, then. What do you want?"

Deen shifted the cigarette holder to the corner of his mouth. "I know you killed Lane," he said quietly.

Instantly Maxie Gorgan hurled himself to his feet and glowered at the American, the heavy Luger held tensely in his hand and aimed point-blank at Deen's skull.

"No need to fire," Deen said jocosely. "I could never prove it."

Gorgan hesitated, eyeing Deen warily. He sat down and fingered the trigger of the gun longingly.

"Who in hell are you?" he spat, "and what do you want? You'd better get down to business, mister. You're due for a slug."

"My name is Sam Trent," Deen replied. "I want to cut in."

"Cut in?"

"I know that Lane and Kirk were cogs in your jewel-smuggling organization," Deen said. "Since they are defunct, the necessity of engaging a capable man to assume charge of the Bombay headquarters is imminent. I learned all this from Lane. I saw, in India, that his courage was dissipating, that he would attempt to withdraw, so I followed him to London. Zah! There you have it. You need a man. I am he."

"You know a helluva lot for a stranger," Gorgan exclaimed belligerently, both disturbed and interested. "Maybe—since you're so smart—you also know the code word?"

Gorgan expected to catch Deen there. He paused triumphantly and his gun rose to a level with Deen's chest.

"But, of course," Deen said mildly. *"House of Kaa."*

Wilkins leaped to his feet like a shot. He cried, *"Kaa!* He knows it, Maxie. He must be straight. Lane would never have trusted him. How else could he have gotten hold of that? Kirk didn't even know. It was between Lane and you and me. For telegraphic correspondence to assure indentification."

"So Lane told you, eh?" Gorgan mused.

"Yes."

"You know about the—business, too?"

"You refer to the shipping of the jewels in the pythons—"

"Okay." Maxie held up his hand. "You know all right." He turned to Wilkins. "This may be a cross. I don't see how, but it may be. Better check him."

Deen smiled. "And how do you 'check' me?"

GORGAN regarded him coldly. "Lane told us more than once about a Yankee dick at the Bombay office who was always asking questions. We anticipated the guy might try something. His name is Deen Bradley. Maybe you're on the level. Maybe you're not. Wilkins—check those fingerprints he just left on the chair."

Deen frowned as Wilkins hurried forward and sprinkled a quantity of grayish powder on the spot where his hand had rested.

"You see," Gorgan said, grinning evilly, "Lane sent me a copy of that Yank dick's prints from India. We were taking no chances."

Deen's lips were a thin, bloodless line. The green cigarette holder stiffened between his teeth. Wilkins opened a file drawer and brought out two photographs. Carefully he compared them with the marks on the arm of the chair.

"The same, Maxie!"

Gorgan sighed, relieved. "I thought so. I thought if I prattled on a little, he'd leave his prints somewhere. So you're Deen Bradley, the famous Bombay operative, eh?" His voice snapped into a vicious snarl. "Well, you're on your last case! You're through. What do you think we are—pulling a raw stunt like this?"

Wilkins was trembling with excitement.

"What are we going to do, Maxie?" he demanded.

Gorgan smiled without humor.

"We'll take him down into the snake room. We'll put him in the pit and let him make friends with the big boy. The thirty-foot constrictor. The one we haven't fed for three weeks. Let's see how a rat can fight a python. And then we'll get the Kubij opal from the new shipment and take it on the lam. This business is all washed up, Wilky. We've made enough out of it."

Gorgan rose, his pistol ominously steady in his hand. "Okay, Deen," he growled. "Keep ahead of me. If you make any funny moves, this lead bites you instead of the snake."

Deen rose silently, his immobile face void of expression. He left the office, Gorgan's automatic prodding painfully into his back. They descended the stairs.

The descent took them into the cellar of the house, which Deen noted, was not damp at all, the floors being amazingly desiccated. Before a huge metal door, the two men stopped him. Wilkins accepted the proffered pistol while Maxie unlocked the door. It swung open. Gorgan snapped on the lights. They entered, leaving the metal door unlocked behind them.

Deen stared in astonishment at the room. It was enormous, the entire breadth of the house above. In the center of the room was a pit, about twenty feet deep. It was lined with opaque glass and was empty. An iron railing surrounded it. Near the railing, on the far side, was a large packing case.

"A pretty showroom, isn't it?" Gorgan leered. "Watch!"

Deen gazed into the bottom of the pit, fascinated. Gorgan went to the wall and pulled down a short lever. The glass partition on one side began to rise. Instantly there was a sickening slithery scrape. The macabre head of a huge serpent slid out of the compartment in the wall to wind a path across the bottom of the pit, shaking the kinks and curls out of its great length. It was orange-brown and repugnantly thick. It raised its terrible snout, hungrily searching.

"He wants living food," Gorgan growled alarmingly.

He moved threateningly on Deen while Wilkins still held the pistol in Deen's back.

With a lightning blow, Deen twisted around and cracked Wilkins on the side of the jaw with fearful strength. The punch clipped the man cleanly, eliciting a resounding crack. Wilkins fell like an ox. The pistol dropped from his nerveless hand as a red welt flamed on his chin.

DEEN dived for the gun, conscious of Gorgan behind him.

He felt a ringing blow on his head, as Gorgan slashed down his clenched fists like a lunatic. It stunned him momentarily. He fell dazedly on his side and struggled courageously for the pistol.

Maxie Gorgan reached it first. He lifted it and fired.

The slug ripped through Deen's coat and buried itself in the opaque glass of the snake pit behind the detective.

Painfully, Deen strove to raise himself, hanging precariously to the iron railing at his back.

Gorgan raised the gun quickly for a second shot.

"Wait!" Deen called breathlessly.

Gorgan hesitated, then relaxed his trigger finger still holding the heavy automatic at Deen's head. "What do you want? Talk fast!"

Deen nodded dejectedly.

"I admit defeat," he said in a low voice. "I have failed and therefore deserve to die. But before you kill me, I have one last request to make."

"What is it?" Gorgan snapped.

"I would like to smoke a last cigarette," Deen replied. "Surely you can not deny a doomed man that courtesy?"

A crafty look narrowed Gorgan's eyes as he threw a surreptitious glance at the glass pit and the huge python. He lowered the gun and nodded.

"Okay," he said. "Go ahead."

Deen rapidly felt in his pockets for his odd greenish cigarette holder. He found it and placed it between his teeth. Then he found a cigarette and started to make a pretense of lighting it.

Simultaneously, Gorgan sprang forward when Deen's head was slightly turned, and with almost preternatural strength, shoved the detective through the railing, hurling him cruelly into the glass pit.

Deen turned a complete somersault and landed thuddingly on his feet at the bottom. He turned. The regal serpent was not three feet away from him, its elliptical eyes regarding him with sinister austerity.

Meanwhile, Gorgan, certain that the detective was safely in the python pit, turned savagely to John Wilkins who had recovered from Deen's furious blow and was struggling to regain his feet.

"You're ace is in!" Gorgan snarled at him. "You're through, Wilky. This is just the chance I've wanted. Lane dead. Kirk dead. The dick with the python. And now—*you!* There'll be no split on the jewels. They're all mine, mine!"

Crackling like a madman, he aimed the deadly Luger.

Wilkins gaped at him in horror and shrilly screamed.

Crack! Crack!

Jagged blue holes appeared in Wilkins' forehead as red blood poured copiously down his neck where the two bullets ripped his skull to pieces on the way out.

His legs collapsed suddenly, even while his eyes rolled sightlessly at Gorgan's smoking gun. He fell—right into the glass pit and on top of the python's back!

The great reptile reared up in pain and shock. Its terrible head slashed around in a razorlike strike and knocked Wilkins' dead body clear across the bottom of the pit from the force of the blow. The curved rows of fangs bit into Wilkins' clothes. They were not venomous but chewed into the cadaver viciously.

The two crushing loops of the serpentine phantasmagoria fell over the dead man, encircled him, and began to contract, the muscles rippling comberlike beneath the scaly skin.

It was a horrid spectacle—a python crushing a dead man.

Deen stood by, unhurt, watching the gruesome scene in lethargic fascination.

Suddenly, above him, he heard a harsh, bitter cry. Gorgan had watched his plans go awry. Wilkins' corpse had diverted the snake from the detective. The snake would try and swallow the cadaver but would get no further than the head, since it is impossible for any living constrictor to gulp down a man because of the width of the shoulders. He would have to kill Deen himself.

Bestially, Gorgan flung up the pistol.

Deen was taken almost unawares. He saw the ugly black nozzle of the automatic draw a bead on his eyes. With the alacrity of a bullet, he hurled himself to the floor of the pit. Simultaneously, the gun spat flame and death.

The slug tore Deen's coat and crashed against the glass of the pit, crumbling the glass and leaving irregular footing against the side of the wall.

DEEN had lifted himself on his hands, half-kneeling. The peculiar green cigarette holder was between his teeth again. It was held taut, stiff against his gleaming white teeth.

Gorgan was pulling the trigger of the pistol frantically but the lead was going wild, breaking down the glass of the pit.

There was a piercing, whistling *hiss* like that of an angry, hooded hamadryad.

Gorgan was suddenly transfixed. His eyes bulged maniacally. A purplish cyanotic color pervaded his flesh. His lips moved jabberingly but uttered no sound. A thin trickle of blood coursed slowly down from his throat, from a minute hole directly above his jugular vein. A tiny black hole—a dart-hole.

Gruesomely, Maxie Gorgan fought against the powerful nerve-destroying cobra venom which was seeping through his blood stream and tearing the vortex of his vasomotor system and lungs to shreds. His breath came in agonizing, sobbing gulps and each one was filled with inhuman pain. His face slowly grew black as the toxin destruction grew greater.

For a second, his voice gained audibility.

"You—" he rasped, a death rattle sounding in his throat—"the Cobra . . . ."

He fell forward into the pit, smashing down on his face and rolling over on his back, dead.

Deen climbed out of the pit where the python had swallowed the head of Wilkins and was fighting to engulf the man's shoulders, an impossibility. He stepped on the scant indentations of broken glass which the bullets had created.

The sound of axes tearing wood floated down to the cellar. He glanced at his watch. True to the hour, the police—as he had outlined in his plan with Ryder and Marshall—were raiding the gloomy House of Kaa.

Inspector Ryder burst into the pit-room, almost at the same instant, service revolver in hand. He surveyed the wreckage of the pit and whistled in horror. Quickly he put a hot bullet through the skull of the regal python. He gazed down and saw the noxious dart imbedded in the upturned throat of Maxie Gorgan.

"The Cobra!" Ryder exclaimed.

"Yes," Deen said. "The Cobra saved my life. Quick, may I have your revolver?"

Ryder regarded Deen keenly. The green cigarette holder in Deen's hand caught his eye. For the time being, he said nothing. He handed his gun over.

Deen went around the pit to the packing case which stood next to the railing. He found a hammer and ripped the top unceremoniously off the base. There were three more pythons within, all small specimens, from six to ten feet in length.

One had a small white piece of adhesive tape on the back of its head.

Fearlessly, Deen reached in and yanked the snake out with both his hands. Holding one hand behind the neck, he laid the snake on the floor, placed the gun against its brain and pulled the trigger. The snake thrashed slightly and was still.

Then, opening a knife, the detective slit open the belly, cut away the fatty tissues and lacerated the stomach.

When Deen stood up, a gleaming, dazzling flash of red fire struck Inspector Ryder in the eyes.

"The Kubij Opal!" he cried.

"Exactly," Deen murmured. "The case is over."

Ryder eyed the green cigarette holder in the detective's other hand.

"But what of the Cobra?" he asked.

Deen hastily pocketed the holder. His eyes twinkled.

"The Cobra disappeared just before you came in."

The Whisperer Prowls

And Killers Crawl Into Their Holes

The man with the hypo rushed in

Smashing Detective Novelette

By ALEXIS ROSSOFF

FINGERING a week's growth of stubble on his chin, the Whisperer—nemesis of all lawbreakers—seated himself in the chair of Tony the Barber. A shudder coursed over his gaunt frame as he glanced at his own dissipated countenance reflected in the mirror. Dark shadows under the eyes; face unnaturally flushed. The Whisperer blinked and

The Whisperer—nemesis of all lawbreakers—took a shave and bay rum. Tony the Barber knew that the bay rum was a sign that the Whisperer was coming out of his haunts to tackle the city's latest horror murder. The underworld knew that sign, too. It meant that the Whisperer was on the prowl. That killers would run to their holes and cringe until the Juggernaut of justice had passed. But this time the Whisperer's manhunt was a bitter cup of gall.

looked away. Last evening's bacchanalian revel had taken more than its toll of him this time.

Tony the Barber, clucking like a worried mother hen, was hovering over him in an instant. "You drink too much, Mister Brady," the ancient Italian chided. "One of these days you die, and your friends no have to bury you. They just pour you back in the bottle."

The Whisperer smiled ruefully at the grim prophecy but did not argue. After all he and the barber were old friends. "Okay, Tony," he accepted and adroitly changed the subject. "How's that boy of yours—Mike—making out since he moved uptown with the money crowd and went to work for a lawyer?"

The razor flashed in Tony's gesturing hand. "Wonderful, Mister Brady," the Italian enthused. "It's too bad his mamma no live to see him. Mike's a good boy. Every week he send his old papa twenty-five dollars." Tony, his eyes misty, bent lower to confide. "All the time he wants me to quit the barber shop and stay home with Angelina and Dominick." A warmer note crept into Tony's voice at mention of his daughter. "Angelina is young lady now, Mister Brady," he chattered on. "Beautiful as the Madonna. And always she pray for you because she no forget that you got her the first job in City Hall." Tony paused before concluding. "Angelina, she's now confidential secretary to the police commissioner."

The Whisperer, wary of the razor gliding over his face, winked only an eye in agreement and fell to reminiscing. Had he too heeded the voice of ambition he might now be facing the beautiful Angelina across the police commissioner's desk. Brady gave vent to a sigh and dismissed the annoying picture from his mind's eye.

He bitterly tried to convince himself that he had no regrets. Wasn't he a good cop? Even the hard-boiled newspaper boys had to admit that much. What if he did drink to excess when off duty? People had no way of knowing that liquor gave him relief from the constant pain in his throat and helped him to forget the cheap gunman's bullet that had smashed his larynx and left him a croaking whisperer. Brady, the Whisperer, who would never wear a commissioner's shield because he could not make political and after-dinner speeches or give orders in a commanding voice.

With a guilty start he realized that the patient Tony was asking for a second time. "Bay rum, Mister Brady?"

The Whisperer thought for a moment then nodded his head. "Yes, Tony," he whispered, "and plenty of it."

The old barber chuckled. He had not been shaving Brady all these years without learning a few of the detective's pet eccentricities. When the Whisperer took bay rum it could mean only one thing to Tony. The commissioner had sent for the detective.

"I hope you're in no trouble, Mister Brady?' he asked sincerely.

The Whisperer shook his head. "Not this time, Tony," he allayed the old Italian's fears. "That is, at least not the way you suspect."

Tony beamed his relief, and Brady went on to explain in his jerky, whispering way. "The chief had me on the wire. Called me in to take over the city's latest horror murder."

TONY'S teeth chattered audibly. "I know," he volunteered. "I read all about it in the morning paper. Last night somebody strangle Mister Goldfarb, the jeweler, to death."

"Yep," the Whisperer quietly confirmed the Italian's story. "A strangler finally did for Goldfarb what the law should have done years ago."

Puzzled, the barber shook his head. "I don't understand. You mean that Mister Goldfarb was—"

"A bad man, Tony," the Whisperer finished for him. "A very bad man. He posed as a good citizen but actually he was a jewel fence, a double-crosser, a money-lender for crooked deals, and a police-informer."

He was about to quote more of the shady Goldfarb's black record but he thought better of it and didn't. Besides, another customer had entered the barber shop.

Noting the time and thinking of his appointment with the commissioner, the Whisperer stirred himself. "Nice job, Tony," he gave his approval of the barber's skill and got up from the chair. Turning, he met Tony's next customer face to face. The Whisperer nodded. "Behaving yourself, Frankie?" he asked pleasantly.

Frankie scowled darkly. "You'd be the first to know it if I wasn't, Brady," he growled.

The Whisperer's teeth flashed in an unruffled smile. "Thanks for the compliment, Frankie," he acknowledged. "Just remember that always and you will never have to say good morning to a judge again."

A moment later Brady quit the shop, followed by Frankie's hissing curses. "Lousy copper," he snarled, "I'd like to dance on your grave."

Facing away from Tony's waiting chair, he sped across the floor and into the telephone booth to call a number. When a voice finally answered him, Frankie spoke hurriedly.

"You'd better pass the word along, chief. Warn every one to lay low. The Whisperer is on the prowl again. How do I know?" Frankie laughed harshly. "I read the signs, chief," he explained. "Brady was cold sober, clean shaven, and stunk to heaven of bay rum. I just left him. So long."

In good humor, Frankie snapped the receiver back on its hook and jerked open the door of the booth to once more find himself face to face with Brady, the Whisperer, who had been standing just outside. Frankie's mouth flew open, and the detective smiled. "I figured you would be doing just that, so I came back," he spoke quietly. "No hard feelings, Frankie, but I would appreciate it if you would call that rat who you addressed as 'chief' again and tell him that the Whisperer intends to stay cold sober, clean shaven, and stinking to heaven of bay rum, as you explained, until he places the finger on the strangler who did for Goldfarb."

Of a sudden, Brady's whispering voice seemed charged with electricity. "Let me see your hands," he commanded.

Frankie's swarthy face grayed but his hands raised obediently. Carefully the Whisperer studied the long slender fingers and manicured nails, then sniffed in scorn. "Nope," he admitted reluctantly. "You're not the strangler, Frankie. Beating women and lifting pay envelopes from shopgirls' purses is your racket."

Fixing Frankie with a last pitying stare, he turned his back deliberately and started for the door. As he passed Tony, he jokingly advised. "Cut his throat when you shave him and you'll do the world a favor, old-timer."

The barber made no answer. After all Frankie, too, was a good, paying customer.

Visibly shaken by the ordeal he had just undergone, Frankie flopped down in Tony's chair. "You should have tipped me off when that mug came back," he complained.

It was the barber's turn to flare up. "Listen to me, Frankie," he commanded. "You have your business. Mister Brady has his. Barbering is mine. If you have trouble with the police, that's too bad, and I'm sorry for you but I take no side."

Still in an ugly mood, Frankie growled threateningly. "Better feel sorry for Brady instead of me. It's his number that's up, not mine."

Tony shrugged. "Shave?" he asked.

Muttering to himself, Frankie lay back in the chair.

IN police headquarters just around the corner from Tony's shop, the Whisperer was closeted with the commissioner. "You know something and you are keeping it to yourself, Brady," he accused heatedly.

The Whisperer smiled and carelessly crossed his long legs. "You got me wrong, chief," he answered evenly. "I don't know a thing. Just suspect, that's all."

The commissioner tensed. "Suspect what?" he snapped.

Brady yawned. "I suspect a lot of things," he admitted. "Number one: Goldfarb wasn't strangled."

The commissioner's breath whistled between his teeth. "Rats!" he snorted. "I saw the body with the marks of the fiend's fingers showing plain as day on the throat."

The Whisperer sighed. "I saw those marks, too, chief," he answered and went on to explain. "Being of the old school, I make it a practice to look in on every murder case, even when I'm not invited," he added pointedly. "There's always the chance that these new-fangled scientifically trained detectives who are bossing the job nowadays might overlook something."

The commissioner reddened slightly. The new, modern, much-publicized detective bureau was his own idea and pet. He resented the Whisperer poking fun at it but he concealed his feel: well.

"And did they overlook anything?" he questioned sharply.

Brady was enjoying himself. "Why, they must have, chief. Otherwise you would not have called me in," he answered innocently.

The commissioner waved his hands in a gesture of resignation. "You win, Brady," he announced flatly. "I'm out on the limb of public opinion. Break this case for me and I'll publicly take back everything detrimental I ever said about you old-timers."

The Whisperer stood up and stretched lazily. "That will be reward enough for me, chief," he accepted. "I'll either break this case or break my neck. It's a deal."

The commissioner grunted. "You're a good man, Brady," he grudgingly complimented.

The Whisperer laughed and clapped on his battered hat. "I take exception to your remark," he stated evenly. "But I forgive you the error. I am not a good man. Just a detective of the good old school."

He was halfway to the door when the commissioner called after him. "Mind telling me your plans now?"

"Why not in the least, chief," he readily answered. "First I intend to check up on the recent releases from the Big House. Among them there may be one who nursed a grudge against Goldfarb."

"You think then that revenge was the motive?" the commissioner guardedly injected.

"Just that, chief," the Whisperer assured him. "If it had been robbery or a shakedown, Goldfarb would have paid the price and been alive today."

Now that Brady was talking, the commissioner sought to further satisfy his own gnawing curiosity. "What is behind your belief that the victim was not strangled?" he asked suddenly.

The Whisperer smiled contemptuously at his superior's methods, but he elected to answer. "I base my contention on a single thumbprint."

The commissioner half raised from his seat behind the desk. "Preposterous!" he snapped. "The best fingerprint men on the staff searched every inch of Goldfarb's office and the only prints they found were those made by the dead man and his secretary."

Calmly the Whisperer ignored the

interruption and continued. "A solitary thumbprint on the unbroken lense of Goldfarb's eyeglasses. I picked those glasses up from the stone floor of the cellar that Goldfarb used as an office. They were removed from the dead man's nose and placed there by the killer in an attempt to set the scene."

The commissioner slumped down heavily in his chair. "I follow your trend of reasoning now, Brady," he admitted. "Had there been a struggle while Goldfarb was being strangled—and naturally there would have been—his glasses would have fallen to the stone floor and shattered."

The Whisperer smiled and reached for the door knob. "And that is as far as I am permitting you to follow me, chief," he flung over his shoulder. "From now on Brady, the Whisperer, travels fast and alone."

With effortless ease he glided from the office into the hall and closed the door behind him. A few swift strides and he entered the Bertillon room to converse with the sergeant in charge there.

"Locate the owner of that thumbprint I handed in to you last night, Pete?" he inquired.

Gravely the sergeant shook his head. "Not yet, old-timer," he admitted, "but if he is on record I'll find him for you."

BRADY thanked him and quickly wended his way out into busy State Street. A group of idlers lounging outside a pool room lapsed into a strained and noticeable silence as he drew abreast of them. Brady eyed the group, correctly identified each individual, and smiled coldly. A petty racketeer and his lieutenant, two rum-peddlers, and a puller for the local dice game.

"Lousy stuff you're putting out lately, Nick," he addressed one of the bootleggers. "Had a pint last night and it nearly burned the insides out of me."

The bootlegger grinned. "If I was sure that my stuff would do that to you, I'd send you over a case, Brady," he offered sardonically.

The Whisperer chuckled. "Don't like me, do you, Nick?" he asked.

"Nope," the bootlegger frankly admitted. "But then I don't hate you like I do most of those shakedown artists on the job with you. You're a tough mug, Brady, but you're a square cop."

Still chuckling to himself, the Whisperer turned the corner and stepped into the first taxi on the waiting cab rank.

"Uptown," he instructed the driver. "Anywhere on the main stem."

The driver, a veteran of the district, caught the odor of bay rum that suddenly filled the interior of the cab, and grinned knowingly. "The best of luck to you on your case, Mister Brady," he offered and stepped on the starter button.

The Whisperer nodded his thanks and relaxed against the cushions. A perplexed frown furrowed his brow. His pride was piqued. For years now the mystery of how the underworld knew of his goings and comings had baffled him. Frankie, the petty crook in Tony's barber shop, had warned some one that he, Brady, was on the prowl. And now the taxi driver had just wished him luck.

When the cab stopped at the next traffic light he leaned forward to engage the driver in conversation. "Any strangers show up in the old neighborhood lately?" he casually inquired.

"None that I know of," the driver answered, "but Fingers Davis is back from his four-year bit up the river."

Brady's mind clicked. Fingers Davis was a Peterman, a safe-cracker who had been caught and convicted on a tip furnished the police by Goldfarb, the murdered fence. There might be a connecting link there.

"Davis look like he was in the money?" he asked next.

"Nah!" came the emphatic answer. "Fingers is drinking a lot but it's cheap stuff he's buying. That last jail stretch must've killed his nerve. All he does is sit in Dinty's place and hint that he's going to even the score with the rat who double-crossed him."

THE Whisperer lapsed into silence. He'd have a talk with Fingers Davis at the first opportunity. There were two others—more important—whom he had to question first. Silk Gaston, former jewel thief and more recent gigolo. Goldfarb and Gaston had fallen out—so the rumor went—over the split of the proceeds from the sale of the clever Gaston's last and greatest haul.

And it was common gossip in the underworld that Silk, in his excitable Gaelic way had openly vowed to fix the murdered Goldfarb. A stool pigeon had given the information to Brady. The Whisperer's sketchy plan was set. Should Silk Gaston, in his opinion, fail to measure up as Goldfarb's murderer, he would next drop in at the swanky Inferno Club for a chat with Tito Moriani, the proprietor and self-admitted Prince of Darkness.

Tito's keen but crooked brain dominated a dozen rackets. He knew everything and every one.

The taxi rolled to a stop in front of the imposing Plaza-Cumberland, and the Whisperer smiled inwardly. The driver must have read his thoughts for the Plaza-Cumberland was both the residence and hunting ground of Silk Gaston.

Dismissing the cab, he waited until it was out of sight before entering the hotel. A pompous doorman caught the scent of bay rum as he passed and sniffed disdainfully. A commoner. The Whisperer was left to furnish his own momentum for the revolving door that admitted him to the ornate lobby.

Idly he strolled toward the information desk, his eyes busy. A swift smile suddenly toyed with the corners of his lips. He was in luck. The immaculately groomed figure hurrying toward him with extended hand was the man he sought. Pierre Gaston, sometimes known as Silk.

Plainly nervous and ill at ease, Silk Gaston spoke guardedly. "I have been expecting you, Brady."

The Whisperer frowned his annoyance. It was always like this. Wrongdoers anticipated every move of his. Standing there he made a resolve that once and for all time he'd find out and stop that annoying leak in his plans. "Why were you expecting me, Gaston?" he asked sharply.

The polished crook shrugged. "The underworld looks out for its own, Brady," he evaded. "It is enough when I say that I was tipped off that you were on the prowl."

Licking his dry lips, Silk Gaston steered the detective over to a beautifully brocaded divan in a quiet corner of the lobby. When they were seated, he resumed. "Brady, I am no fool. When Goldfarb was written off the books, I knew that you coppers would be looking for me. I admit that I threatened to kill that rat." An ugly light glittered in Gaston's eyes. "And eventually I would have done it," he stated savagely, "but luckily some one else beat me to him."

The Whisperer did not move. "Go on," he invited coldly.

Gaston fumbled with a cigarette. "That is all," he concluded. "Goldfarb, as you know, was a big, powerful man. I couldn't have whipped him with my hands, much less strangled him to death."

When Gaston finally placed the cigarette between his lips, the Whisperer stood up. "So long, Silk," he announced lightly. "Hope I won't be seeing you too soon."

Gaston's outer calm fell from him like a cloak, a half-fearful note crept into his voice. "You mean that you are not going to take me along down to headquarters and sweat me?" he asked unbelievingly.

The Whisperer smiled thinly. It bore out his old contention that all crooks are craven at heart. "Have no further time to waste on you, Silk," he answered contemptuously. "The fact that you are right-handed saves you. I've been watching you light and handle that cigarette of yours."

Long after the detective had quit the hotel, Silk Gaston continued to stand staring blankly at his own right hand. What had Brady meant when he said, "The fact that you are right-handed saves you."

WITH an hour or so to waste before Tito Moriani's Inferno Club opened for business, the Whisperer occasionally turned from the main stem into the side streets to visit certain speakeasies. Quick to notice that each of the illicit drinking places was strangely deserted, he elected to engage the bartender of the third place visited in conversation.

"What's happened to business?" he asked.

The bartender scowled and treated him to a hostile glance. "You!" he bluntly answered Brady. "All the shady lads got the office today that you are hunting for some one, so naturally they've all taken a run-out powder. You cops make it tough on a guy like me who's only trying to make an honest living."

The Whisperer chuckled as he toyed with his glass of mineral water. "It is tough on honest people," he agreed. "Especially when the crooks are lying low."

Still laughing he sauntered out to the street. He was nearing the corner when he recognized the pedestrian walking in front of him as being Galloway, a new detective of the main stem beat. A long stride or two and he was plucking at the sleeve of Galloway's carefully pressed dinner jacket.

"Busy?" he asked.

Galloway nodded. "Yeah," he answered. "I'm tailing that gigolo, Silk Gaston, around. Got a hunch he knows something about the Goldfarb murder and I have to pinch somebody. The commissioner ordered it so that the newspapers will stop headlining the inefficiency of the police department."

The Whisperer considered a moment. "Didn't think that the newspapers were that much interested," he admitted.

"The hell they're not," Galloway emphatically declared. "Fogle, who was Goldfarb's lawyer, is making an issue of the murder in the press to further his own political ambitions. That shyster is nursing a secret yen for the district attorney's job."

Brady lapsed into one of his customary silences, he was thinking of Fogle, the lawyer. Frail, actually a physical weakling, Fogle had come far as a criminal lawyer despite that handicap. But what he lacked in size he made up in shrewdness and a surprising knowledge of the loopholes in the law. Without Fogle, the murdered Goldfarb might have known the inside of many a prison. The alliance of the two had no doubt been profitable to both. Therefore Fogle, realizing that his goose who had laid the golden eggs would lay no more, was now squawking his head off to the reporters.

Stopping in the shadow of a towering building, the Whisperer addressed Galloway. "Lay off Silk Gaston," he advised. "That bird is out of it. I quizzed him and I know."

"Can't," Galloway protested. "I got my orders to bring somebody in."

THE Whisperer did not lose patience. "If you take Gaston in," he argued, "a smart mouthpiece will have him out on bail inside twenty minutes. What the commissioner wants is some dumb cluck whom he can hold onto, to stall the newshounds off with." Brady smiled. "Just a friendly tip, Galloway," he offered. "You're a nice lad, even though you did learn the sleuthing business out of books. Get rid of your party clothes and go down to Dinty's speak on Front Street. You'll find Fingers Davis there. Put the cuffs on him. He's made more than one threat against Goldfarb."

Galloway was too good a detective to ask questions. "Okay," he accepted. "And thanks. I'd like to team up with you sometime."

The Whisperer prodded him with a playful thumb. "Now, now," he chided. "You know that I am the horrible example of the police department. I drink, swear, and squander my money."

"Nuts," Galloway flung back scornfully, and melted into the theatre crowd. Brady smiled and walked in the opposite direction. He liked being by himself for it was always his belief that "he travels fastest who travels alone."

Catching sight at last of the brilliantly lighted Inferno Club, he quickened his pace. A party of merry-makers were ahead of him, and Brady bided his time before approaching the sleek, alert-eyed individual who guarded the portals of the swanky, exclusive night club.

"Boss in?" he asked.

The doorman looked him over, but failed to recognize him and therefore was not impressed. "Yeah!" he sneered. "He's in, but not to your kind. This is the Inferno. The four-bits-a-drink speaks are around the corner, buddy."

The Whisperer remained unruffled, but the dangerous hissing was in his voice when he spoke again. "That's your story," he snapped. "Now here's mine. You are going to drag your Francis inside there and tell Moriani that Brady is coming in to see him. Get going, mug."

Their eyes clashed for an instant and the doorman went. A few minutes passed and he was back again to announce, "The boss will see you."

The Whisperer grinned and shoved the guard to one side. "You're telling me," he jeered.

STRIDING on into the luxurious and crowded club, he paused behind a gilded pillar to orient himself. Moriani, surrounded by lieutenants and bodyguards, was holding his usual nightly court at a table just off the dance floor. As the Whisperer continued to watch, he caught a glimpse of Silk Gaston's immaculately groomed figure making a hasty exit through a door that led out into the kitchen. He let the gigolo go.

Brady knew where to find Gaston when he needed him. Hat in hand, he picked his way around and by the diners to Moriani's table, to be greeted by a flashing smile from the suave, thoroughly-at-ease, self-styled Prince of Darkness.

"Gentlemen," Moriani demanded attention of his followers. "Meet the eighth wonder of the world. An honest detective. Note that he does not even own a tuxedo."

Brady smiled. "I own one," he contradicted, "but I am saving it for the day the state executes you, Moriani."

Moriani laughed at his own expense. He could stand kidding as well as give it. "I am afraid that the moths will have the suit before that day rolls around, Brady," he warned.

The Whisperer's smile widened. "Don't bet on that," he advised. "You have been hovering on the starting line of the last mile for a long time now. Too long, in fact."

A hunted look flickered in Moriani's eyes for an instant and passed. "Sit down, Brady," he invited. "I can't say that I am glad to see you, but you are here now, so have a drink.

A torpedo arose at a signal from the boss and the Whisperer sat down on the vacant chair. "I'm not drinking," he informed Moriani.

The racket prince nodded. "So I was told, Brady," he explained, "but it slipped my mind for the moment."

A frown creased the Whisperer's brow. It was damnably annoying the way the underworld checked up on him. "Then you also know that I am working on a case, Moriani," he flatly stated.

"Every one knows it. You are looking for the strangler of Goldfarb, but you won't find him here in my club."

Brady's fingers drummed on the table. "Why so sure?" he asked quietly. Moriani's smile faded along with the bantering tone from his voice.

"I'll tell you why," he growled. "Because Goldfarb happened to have a hundred thousand dollars in cash of mine on his person when the killer rubbed him out. The money was gone when they found the body and now I am fine-combing the city for a trace of the yegg who lifted my dough." Moriani paused for breath, and the Whisperer spoke.

"Is that on the level?"

The veins in the racket prince's neck swelled alarmingly. "You ask me is that on the level," he hissed. "Take a look at my bank balance. Ask Fogle the lawyer. He was engineering the deal between Goldfarb and me. We were going to establish a chain of instalment jewelry stores clean across the country. There was a fortune in it."

"I don't doubt it," the Whisperer agreed. "Goldfarb would buy up swag and hot stones for a third of their value, have them reset and recut, and sell them to the public at enormous profit right under the noses of the police."

MORIANI scowled. "That was Goldfarb's end of the business," he defended himself. "I was only the bank-roll man and now my money is gone, but I'll get it back," he vowed. "Twenty grand of it was hundred-dollar bills. I'll find it."

The Whisperer did some rapid thinking. He was ready to admit that in seeking the revenge motive he had been working in a circle. Moriani's missing hundred thousand dollars changed the whole aspect of the case. "Did you notify the police?" he asked, just to make conversation.

"The police!" Moriani scoffed. "What can they do that my mob can't do? I am my own law. Besides when the boys bring in that heel who lifted my hundred grand, I want to deal with him my own way."

The Whisperer frowned. "Bad business, Moriani," he warned. "One of these days your luck will desert you and you will walk that last mile I've been telling you about."

The racket prince's teeth flashed. "Don't make me laugh, Brady," he jeered. "I don't depend on luck. I'm smart. Fourteen times now you cops took me in on suspicion of everything and I have yet to spend a night in jail or leave a copy of my measurements for your Bertillon files."

Brady's smile was a challenge. "It wasn't you who was smart," he mildly contradicted. "It was your lawyer. By way of example: a smart guy wouldn't hand a hundred thousand dollars over as you did to a trickster like Goldfarb without so much as a receipt to show for it."

Moriani scowled. It hurt his vanity to have Brady show him up in front of his own mob. "Don't be a wise guy," he grated. "When the hundred grand changed hands, Fogle, who, confidentially, is also my mouthpiece, was there in Goldfarb's office to see that there were no hooks in the contract papers. He's got the receipt."

The Whisperer ceased his idle drumming on the table. "A hundred grand is a lot of money and a big temptation even to an ambitious lawyer like Fogle," he reflected aloud. Deliberately he had planted the seeds of suspicion, and Moriani fell for the ruse.

"Fogle wouldn't dare double-cross me," he flared up. "I've got too much on him."

Suddenly the racket prince relaxed and laughed. "Use your head, Brady," he sarcastically advised. "A skinny little runt like Fogle couldn't crush a fly, much less strangle a brute of Goldfarb's size."

The Whisperer grinned sheepishly. "I guess you are right about Fogle, Moriani," he admitted. "My old brain doesn't click like it used to."

A mirthless laugh trickled from the racket prince's mocking lips. "I wouldn't say that, Brady," he purred. "Your brain works the same as always. Like a cop's. The trouble with you and the rest of your kind is that you won't admit that the shady boys are smarter today. They've been educated and they're organized."

The Whisperer heaved a sigh and pushed back from the table. "Right again, big shot," he agreed. "The bad boys must be educated when they can make a sucker, for a hundred grand, out of a wise guy like Tito Moriani."

The shot went home, and the racket prince scowled. Brady was grinning now. He extended his hand and Moriani clasped it mechanically and shook it. "No hard feelings, big shot," he offered. "And just to prove that I mean it. Here's a friendly tip for you. Never underestimate a cop, any cop. You made a crack a moment ago that while you had been arrested fourteen times the police never succeeded in either mugging or fingerprinting you."

THE Whisperer paused and straightened up. Then for the benefit of all the hard-eyed, tight-lipped individuals seated at the table, he carefully removed a dish of soft, colorless wax from the palm of his right hand, and held it up for them to see. "Your thumbprint, Moriani," he explained in a whisper. "You gave it to me when you shook my hand just now."

The racket prince's face blanched. His frightened eyes swept over his equally startled lieutenants in silent command. It was a moment fraught with danger for the detective. A gunman's hand stole obediently toward a concealed shoulder holster. Brady saw the movement and laughed.

"You haven't the guts to draw that gun, louse," he taunted, "and only because I am looking at you. Maybe I'd better turn my back."

Moriani recovered a semblance of his former composure. "Let's talk this over, Brady," he suggested. "I'm not going to insult you by offering a bribe, but I must have my print back."

The Whisperer smiled, amused. "And if I don't choose to return it?" he questioned.

Moriani's expressive hand described a swift gesture, and the detective nodded in understanding. "Threatening me with a ride, hey," he interpreted correctly. A sudden wicked gleam sprung into his deep-set eyes. "You're a bigger heel than I first suspected," he coldly insulted Moriani. "A second ago I had no intention of keeping your dirty fingerprint, but I've changed my mind now. I'm going to place it in my private file along with the tracks of other rats who have interested me." Defiantly Brady leaned on the table. "Those rats died horrible deaths, Moriani," he whispered mockingly. "Just like you are going to die as soon as I find the time to set a trap for you."

Moriani retreated as far as the back of the chair would permit him to go. "I am not looking for trouble with you, Brady," he attempted to make amends. "You started it."

The Whisperer straightened up, disgust written on his lean face. "Yep," he agreed coldly. "I started it and it will be well for you to remember that I always finish what I start. This city won't be large enough to hold you and me, Moriani, from now on. If I were you, I'd blow this town. Otherwise you are slated to ride behind a lot of flowers, and the sad part will be that you won't be able to smell them."

Clapping on his badly worn hat, Brady turned his back and sauntered off to a near-by table to shake hands with a distinguished-looking gentleman who was one of a party seated there. "Mister Saunders," he spoke as loud as his broken voice would permit. "You are the district attorney of this city. Now if I should die or disappear mysteriously any time within the next week, Tito Moriani will be responsible. He just threatened me with a long, one-way ride."

Two guests who were about to depart from Moriani's table abruptly sat down again at a look from their frightened boss who had been straining his ears to catch the Whisperer's conversation.

"Don't you want us to bump him, chief?" one of the two guardedly addressed the trembling racket prince.

Moriani's hands fluttered like frightened birds. "No, no," he hastily countermanded a previous order. "That lousy dick has just placed me on a spot with the D. A. Watch him. Protect him. Don't let anything happen to him until I get back. I am going away at once, tonight, for a long vacation."

AGAIN strolling along in comparative safety on the city's brightly lighted main stem, the Whisperer's reaction was not in accord with that of the pleasure-seeking throng of which he was an unwilling part. The Goldfarb strangler was still at large. Free and unsuspected, with a hundred thousand dollars of Moriani's money in his possession. A newsboy, shrilly hawking his wares, caught the detective's attention.

"Extra! Police capture suspect in Goldfarb murder case."

The Whisperer purchased a paper and glanced at the headlines, still damp from the press. Fingers Davis, notorious safe-cracker and ex-convict had been picked up on suspicion and was now safe behind bars. Brady smiled. It was evident that Galloway —the young detective to whom he had given the tip on Davis—had worked fast. The press would stop pounding the police department for a few hours at least, much to the harried commissioner's relief.

Thought of the commissioner gave the Whisperer an idea. He turned into the next cigar store and entered the telephone booth. The number he asked for was that of police headquarters. The commissioner was still there. They were sweating Fingers Davis.

"Brady calling," he identified himself. "Nothing to report on the Goldfarb case, chief. I'm going home to sleep." Quickly he hung up and shrugged. The commissioner would certainly be furious. For the time being the Whisperer was ready to admit that Lady Luck had frowned on him. The fickle jade had led him up a blind alley. Well, tomorrow was another day, and probably she would smile again. Not wishing to be disturbed, he checked into a quiet, side-street hotel and went to bed.

THE following morning found his gaunt frame stretched out as usual in Tony the Barber's comfortable chair. And for once Tony was strangely uncommunicative. Watching out of half-shut eyes, the Whisperer was quick to perceive his old friend's agitation.

"Something on your mind, Tony?" he broke the silence.

The barber straightened up and laid down his razor. "Maybe yes, maybe no, Mister Brady," he answered. "It's about my boy, Mike. Last night he came to see me for the first time in six months."

The Whisperer smiled. "What's wrong with that?" he asked.

Tony's lips trembled. "My Mike is not the same boy," he confessed sadly. "He didn't laugh and his eyes had a funny look. Over and over he kept telling his sister and me that he is going away for a long time."

The Whisperer laid a sympathetic hand on the worried Italian's arm. "Forget it," he advised. "Mike has probably been working too hard and needs a rest. He's a good boy."

Tony smiled his gratitude. "Thank you, Mister Brady," he acknowledged, then hesitated. "Maybe you do me a favor," he asked apologetically. "Maybe you go have a talk with my Mike. He always love you ever since he was little kid and he listen to you."

Brady stirred uncomfortably. "Sure," he promptly agreed, "but what's behind all this."

The old barber tensed, reached into a pocket and quickly produced five new one-hundred-dollar bills. "These," he answered. "My Mike gave them to me. Called it a bonus or something like that from his boss."

The Whisperer closed his eyes and relaxed. Only his brain and his lips moved. "Mike works for a lawyer, doesn't he?" he asked softly.

"Yes, sir," the worried Tony supplied the information. "For Mister Fogle, a very big lawyer."

The Whisperer sat bolt upright in the chair. An eager gleam lighted his deep-set eyes but the trained caution of his calling prevailed. "You're in luck, Tony," he announced tonelessly. "I was going to call on Fogle, anyway. So I'll have a chat with Mike while I am in the lawyer's office. Kill two birds with one stone, if you understand what I mean."

Tony's agitation increased. "I understand," he admitted. "But I no like to hear you say, 'kill two birds with one stone.' It sounds bad."

The Whisperer forced a laugh. "Forget it," he advised for the second time. "Mike's a good boy."

Out of long habit Tony picked up the bay rum bottle and Brady nodded. "It doesn't smell as good as it used to," he jokingly complained. "The racketeers must be cutting it, like they do whiskey."

It was nearing lunch time when a taxi finally deposited the Whisperer on the sidewalk in front of the pretentious building that housed the offices of Fogle the lawyer. Since leaving Tony's shop he had spent a busy and somewhat hectic morning. The commissioner had bawled him out. He'd been in and out of the Bertillon room a half dozen times and finally he had engaged the coroner and his staff in a heated argument.

The Whisperer smiled now. He had won the argument with the learned coroner. Together they had journeyed to the morgue to view Goldfarb's body, and there Brady had convincingly proven his point—the real cause of the murdered man's death.

ENTERING the building he was swiftly transported to the fifteenth floor. Outside of Fogle's office, he carefully placed something in the palm of each hand. All set now, he opened the door and stopped to grin at the startled young man who had bounded to his feet at his entrance.

Slowly, the Whisperer advanced. His hand extended. "How are you, Mike?" he greeted the lone occupant of the front office. "You don't look well, lad. I was talking to your dad this morning and he's worried about you."

Mike winced beneath the unexpected strength of the handshake, and the Whisperer chuckled. "Not as strong as you used to be, Mike," he kidded good-naturedly. "Inside work is making a softie out of you."

The color slowly crept back into the young man's face. "I never was very good with my right hand, Mister Brady," he explained.

The Whisperer grunted. "That's right," he agreed. "I should have remembered that you were the best left-handed pitcher that ever flipped a baseball down in the old neighborhood. Let's try that left of yours."

Their left hands clasped and this time it was Brady who winced. "You're still there with the old grip, lad," he complimented.

Mike smiled. His strange uneasiness was passing. "You here on business, Mister Brady?" he politely asked.

The Whisperer's large bony hands went into his coat pockets and came out again. "So I am," he confessed. "Meeting you made me forget. Is Fogle in? My business is with him."

Mike disappeared into an adjoining office, and Brady chose the time to again place something in the palm of each hand. Mike returned in a moment to announce, "Mister Fogle is very busy, but he will see you."

The Whisperer thanked him and walked into the next office to face the underworld's greatest mouthpiece.

Brilliant and alert, conscious of his own exaggerated importance, the little lawyer remained seated behind a massive desk. Perfunctorily he shook hands and immediately launched into a scathing tirade. "Haven't any time to waste on you cops," he snapped waspishly. "Forty-eight hours ago, my friend and client, Goldfarb, was ruthlessly strangled to death and the police department has not located a single clue."

Sheepishly toying with his battered hat, Brady did not deny the charge. "I admit that we have gotten nowhere," he apologetically agreed, "but this is an exceptionally hard case to break. The murderer is clever."

"Bah!" Fogle cut him short. "A clever killer would not resort to strangling his victim. The fiend who murdered Goldfarb was a lustful brute. If I were to hunt the dives and the slums, I'll wager I could find him within an hour or two."

The Whisperer shifted his weight. "The police are doing that now, Mister Fogle," he explained.

Swiftly Fogle's mood changed to one of annoyance. "Then what are you doing in my office, Brady?" he demanded irritably.

THE Whisperer nervously mopped his perspiring brow. "I came to ask you, Mister Fogle, if you wouldn't have a heart and stop rapping us old-time coppers in the newspapers. You'll cost some of us our jobs if you don't lay off. The commissioner called me in and gave me merry hell this morning," he ruefully confessed.

Fogle puffed up like a pouter pigeon. His vanity was pleased. "I don't want to take the bread and butter out of any man's mouth," he magnanimously admitted. "But I have to do my duty as a citizen. Crime must be suppressed. And the police have to do their part." Suddenly he stood up. What passed for a smile creased his birdlike face. "I will muzzle the press for a few days," he agreed. "But show results."

The Whisperer sighed gratefully. "Thanks," he accepted, then asked. "Perhaps you won't mind helping us, Mister Fogle?"

The lawyer smirked. "Not in the least," he readily acquiesced.

Brady cleared his throat. "As Goldfarb's lawyer I'm wondering if you would give me the names of those your murdered client transacted business with. Say those within the last week or so."

Fogle carefully weighed the question before condescending to reply. "There was Dillman, the jeweler; Marsden, the gold assayer; Frankel, the real estate broker—" he checked off rapidly.

Brady picked up a pad from the desk, sought hastily for a pencil, and failed to locate one. Fogle, his eyes half-closed, was still recalling names from memory, and the Whisperer did the only thing left him. He reached across the desk and picked a silver one from the two or three showing in the lawyer's upper vest pocket. His eyes had been studying the pencil for the best part of five minutes.

A smothered cry escaped Fogle, and he clutched at Brady's hand but the detective was too fast. Deftly he unscrewed the metal cap and stared. "Well, I'll be damned," he exclaimed. "I thought it was a fountain pen and it turns out to be a hypodermic syringe." Curious, he pressed down on the plunger and a thin stream of colorless liquid deposited itself on the sheet of paper beneath his hand.

Gravely he handed the syringe back to the trembling lawyer. "Sorry, Fogle," he apologized. "I didn't know you were a drug addict. I mistook your hypo for a pen."

The syringe once more in his possession, the lawyer licked dry lips and forced a ghastly smile. "Don't get me wrong, Brady," he pleaded. "I am not a morphine addict as you suspect. Lately I have been cursed with an acute case of nerves. Go all to pieces over trivial things. I have been working too hard. This hypo contains a powerful sedative prescribed for me by my physician."

The Whisperer laughed. "Well," he chuckled. "That's a horse in a different garage. For a moment you'd fallen away to here in my estimation. I don't like addicts."

"I don't either," Fogle nervously agreed.

"Better take a shot of that stuff,

you're all unstrung, man," the Whisperer advised him.

The lawyer shook his head. "I'm all right now," he announced. "Let's get done with our business." This time he was careful to hand Brady a pencil, and Brady laboriously jotted down the names as Fogle repeated them. Then carefully folding the piece of paper and placing it in a pocket, the detective thanked the lawyer and made his departure.

REACHING the sidewalk, he hailed the first taxi that came along and fairly flung himself into it. "Police headquarters," he tersely instructed the driver, "and break every speed law getting me there."

"What and get myself pinched?" the taximan argued.

The Whisperer leaned forward. "Listen, buddy," he insisted. "You're going to get a pinch if you don't step on it. Get a load of this."

The driver looked, caught the flash of Brady's shield, and grinned. "Okay, flatfoot," he accepted the ultimatum. "Me and Barney Oldfield now rides neck and neck."

In and out of elevated pillars, past frantically waving traffic officers and through red lights, the cab hurtled on a record run to headquarters.

"Wait for me," the Whisperer commanded and was out on the sidewalk before the cab's protesting brakes had stopped screeching. He mounted the steps two at a time and barged in on the astounded sergeant in charge of the Bertillon room.

"Three more thumbprints for you, old-timer," he hurriedly explained. "Got them in a lawyer's office from two smart fellows who didn't know any better than to shake hands with Brady, the Whisperer. Match them up with the thumbprint found on the lens of Goldfarb's eyeglasses."

Carefully he marked and handed over three wax discs. Two bore the thumbprints of Mike the Barber's son. The third print was that of the unsuspecting, egotistical Fogle.

"Back in five minutes," he called, and went out of the Bertillon room like a shot. Down the corridor he fled and into a smaller room that had recently been converted into an up-to-the-minute chemical laboratory by the enterprising police commissioner.

Excited, his thoughts far in advance of his speech, he waved a sheet of ordinary pad paper before the startled eyes of a bewildered chemist. "Analyze this," he insisted.

"But this is not the handwriting department, Brady," the chemist protested.

"Handwriting, my big brown eye," the Whisperer snapped. "The writing on this paper don't mean a damned thing. I wrote it myself."

THE chemist threw up his hands in a gesture of despair, and the Whisperer realized that they were getting nowhere. Restraining himself as best he could, he painstakingly explained how he had deliberately ejected the liquid contents of a hypodermic syringe on the sheet of pad paper. What was the nature of the liquid contained in the hypo? That was what he wanted to know. Was it chemical, drug, or what? Was it harmless or deadly?

Fingering the sheet of paper gingerly, the chemist carried it over to a table. And while the impatient Whisperer watched and fumed, calmly went to work on it. Twice he had to push Brady away from his elbow and finally was compelled to request that the detective leave the laboratory altogether. "Come back in ten minutes," he crisply ordered the detective, "and I may have an answer for you."

With only that small grain of comfort to buck him up, Brady returned down the hall to the Bertillon room. The sergeant in charge looked up as he entered, and grinned. "Got your man for you, old-timer," he triumphantly announced. "The thumbprint on the lens of the murdered Goldfarb's eyeglasses and that on this wax disc which you gave me to compare, are identical."

The Whisperer picked up the wax disc, glanced at the identifying mark which he himself had placed on it, and nodded his satisfaction. His case was beginning to shape up.

The sergeant, who had been watching him, hazarded an opinion. "You'll be bringing in the Goldfarb strangler now, Brady."

The Whisperer stirred. "No!" he answered slowly, "I'll be bringing in no strangler for the very good reason that Goldfarb was not strangled."

The sergeant sniffed. "Cut out the kidding," he advised. "I read the coroner's report, and I also had a look at the corpse."

Brady shrugged. He was in no mood for argument. "A bird is never wrong until he is proven so," he answered evasively, and walked out of the room. Besides, the ten minutes had elapsed.

Concealing his anxiety, he once more entered the laboratory. "Any luck?" he asked.

The chemist blinked owlishly. "Chemistry is not a matter of luck; it is science," he lectured coldly. "And I am a technical man." Deliberately he paused, then concluded with a single word. "Hyacine."

The Whisperer grinned sheepishly. As was his habit when confused, he toyed with his battered felt hat. "But what is hyacine?" he managed to ejaculate.

A man of few words, the chemist handed him a scrap of note paper. "I figured a detective wouldn't know," he caustically explained, "so to save time and my voice I wrote it all out for you in schoolboy English."

Grateful, the Whisperer began to read. His eyes narrowed and the muscles of his lean jaws tightened. "Thanks," he whispered when he finished reading, and went out the door like a runaway horse.

Parked in front of headquarters, the taxi driver saw him coming and instinctively stepped on the starter button.

"Where do we go from here, flatfoot?" he asked as Brady bounded into the cab.

Jerkily the Whisperer gave him directions and the cab lurched ahead under a full burst of power. So absorbed was he with his own thoughts, the taxi-driver had to tell him twice that they had arrived at his destination.

Mechanically he paid and tipped the man and strode into the building. For the second time that morning the elevator deposited him on the fifteenth floor. This time the Whisperer did not bother to knock. A turn of the knob, and he walked into Lawyer Fogle's office.

Young Mike was still there and again he nervously stood up. "Forget something, Mister Brady?" he inquired.

For a full, silent moment the detective regarded the lad. This would be a sad memory for Brady. He'd always been fond of Tony the Barber's son.

Some sixth sense warned Mike that all was not well and he paled noticeably.

The Whisperer stirred. "Sit down, Mike," he commanded wearily. "I've something to say to you."

THE barber's son slumped obediently into a chair and Brady drew up a second one to sit facing him.

"Mike," he began gravely. "You choked Goldfarb! Why?"

The barber's son half rose from the chair, his eyes staring wildly, and the Whisperer gently pushed him down again. A dry, tortured sob shook the lad. "I did it," he confessed before he could check himself. Then fear gripped him. "No, I didn't," he contradicted. "I didn't know what I was saying. Fogle warned me not to talk. He said that the police could not make a case against me, and that he'd keep me out of the electric chair."

Only the Whisperer's eyes moved. "Mike," he persisted. "You're lying now. A left-handed man choked Goldfarb. The heavier bruises on the right side of the murdered man's throat told me that. And you are left-handed. Also, you gave your father five new one-hundred-dollar bills. It was part of Tito Moriani's hundred grand that Fogle, your boss, turned over to the murdered Goldfarb."

The Whisperer paused. "Mike," he spoke sadly, "much as I hate doing it, I have to place you under arrest for—"

Too late Brady saw the look in young Mike's eyes. Instinctively he jerked his head to one side, but not quickly enough. A metal paper weight, held in the hand of Fogle, who unobserved had stolen into the front office, descended with terrific force on the detective's unguarded head. The Whisperer caught a glimpse of the little lawyer a split second before the lights went out for him in a final burst of exploding Roman candles and St. Catherine wheels.

Painfully he groped his way back to the land of the living to discover that he was a prisoner. His own handcuffs were on his wrists; a belt held his feet securely. A groan escaped him, for his head throbbed cruelly, and a figure arose from a chair over by the door. The Whisperer bit a second groan off short and smiled a twisted smile instead as he recognized Mike.

"Going to finish me now, Mike?" he asked coolly.

Mike's big hands opened and closed convulsively. Sullen defiance born of fear made him answer. "It's your life or mine."

Tactfully Brady changed the subject. "Where's Fogle?" he asked.

Mike hesitated. "Gone out to get some dope," he enlightened. "We're going to drug you, then take you out of this office—"

"And strangle me," the Whisperer finished for him.

Mike's lips trembled. "I can't help myself," he dismally defended himself. "I'm not afraid of the electric chair. But the disgrace would kill my father and sister."

But for the ache, Brady's head was surprisingly clear. He realized that his life hung in the balance. He had to talk and talk fast before the lawyer returned.

"Mike," he said quietly, "you didn't kill Goldfarb."

A HAUNTED look crept into the lad's eyes. "You're trying to trick me," he mumbled. "Fogle warned me that you might." A violent shudder shook him. "God," he moaned, "I wish it were true. But I saw Goldfarb die before my eyes with my own hands about his throat."

"Yes," the Whisperer agreed. "We'll let that go for the time being. Now why did you choke Goldfarb?"

On the verge of going completely haywire, Mike talked incoherently, but the Whisperer managed to piece out the story.

Goldfarb and the lawyer had been arguing over the division of Moriani's hundred thousand dollars in Goldfarb's office, and Goldfarb had gotten mad.

"He knocked my boss down with a blow and started to kick him," Mike explained. "I couldn't stand for that and be a man, so I pitched into the fight. Goldfarb and I tussled. He tried to gouge my eyes out and I grabbed him by the throat. We fell to the floor alongside my boss and suddenly Goldfarb went limp in my hands.

"It was all over in an instant. He was dead and I was his murderer." Mike took a deep breath. "Mr. Fogle was good to me," he defended his employer. "He tore the dead man's clothes and removed his glasses and upset the furniture to make it look as though a terrific struggle had taken place." Mike's voice took on a hysterical note. "Mr. Fogle gave me a thousand dollars and advised me to run away until the excitement over the killing died down. He was going to bring me back then and defend me."

The Whisperer's patient smile widened a trifle. "I listened to your story, now you listen to mine, lad. Fogle murdered Goldfarb for Moriani's hundred thousand dollars, and he diabolically pinned the crime on you. He gave you a thousand dollars of Moriani's money and advised you to leave town. Had you done so, he would have tipped off the police to your whereabouts and they would have picked you up. Those hundred dollar bills in your pocket would have convicted you of the crime because there isn't a doubt in my mind that Fogle made a list of the serial numbers on those bills along with the others of the remaining ninety-nine thousand dollars. That list produced in court would have hung you."

"But he wouldn't have done that," the bewildered Mike interrupted.

"You don't know that cold-blooded killer like I do, son," the Whisperer pressed. "In my pocket here you will find a written statement telling all about a deadly poison named hyacine. Six drops of it injected into the human blood stream cause instantaneous death. And that's exactly what Fogle did when you and Goldfarb fell on the floor alongside of him. He stabbed Goldfarb in the back with a hypodermic syringe containing hyacine that he carried in his pocket."

Dazed, Mike rocked on his feet. "I've seen that syringe in the boss's pocket," he muttered. "He told me once that it contained a harmless nerve sedative."

THE Whisperer nodded. "Fogle told me that, too," he readily admitted. "But being a detective I didn't believe him. I took a sample of the contents of his syringe and had it analyzed by the police department chemist." Brady's eyes went to a phone on the desk. "Call up the chemist, lad," he suggested. "He'll verify the truth of my statement, and then call up the coroner. Only this morning, he re-examined Goldfarb's remains upon my insistence, and found traces of hyacine in the body."

Like a drowning man grasping at the proverbial straw, Mike caught a glimpse of new hope, and wavered. "If I could only be sure," he whispered.

"You can," the Whisperer assured him. "Goldfarb was a powerful man who could have stood all the choking you gave him and still lived. That was what made me suspicious in the first place. His windpipe wasn't even crushed."

Nauseated and weak, Mike suddenly braced. Hot tears streamed down his cheeks. "You're my father's friend and I believe you, Mr. Brady," he sobbed. "I've been a bad boy." Determinedly his hand went into a pocket and came out again holding the key to the handcuffs that imprisoned Brady's wrists.

He had just turned the key in the lock when a maddened scream behind him arrested him and caused Mike to turn. Fogle was crouched in the doorway, a maniacal gleam in his eyes.

"You fool," he snarled. "Get out of the way. I'm going to kill him."

A step at a time he advanced, the deadly hypodermic syringe he always carried clutched in his fingers. Mike stood as though hypnotized, and the Whisperer groaned as he struggled to clear his hands of the unlocked cuffs. Fogle was moving faster now. He was doomed. A prick of the deadly needle, the pressure of the half-mad Fogle's eager thumb on the plunger, and he would join the murdered Goldfarb in death.

Brady closed his eyes and steeled himself, then to his ears came the thud and scuffle of struggling bodies. Mike and the insane lawyer were locked in a fierce embrace. Tony's son had a desperate death grip on Fogle's skinny throat. Steadily he forced the would-be killer back out of reach of his intended victim. The madman was gasping for air. His face had turned a sickly blue.

The Whisperer shouted encouragement; flung away the handcuffs and tore at the belt that held his feet, but even as he fought to free his feet, the needle of the syringe buried itself in young Mike's back. Both men went to the carpet in a tangled twisting mix-up—then lay still. Mike's hands were still locked around Fogle's throat.

The Whisperer kicked free of the restraining belt at last and crossed the floor in a leap. It took all of his strength to loosen Mike's fingers from around the lawyer's neck. A glance was enough. Fogle was dead.

The Whisperer sat down on the floor and gently lifted Tony the Barber's son onto his lap. For the first time in his hard-boiled career, tears clouded Brady's eyes.

"Mike," he whispered in a broken voice. "You were a good boy."

The lad's eyes fluttered open. A peaceful smile softened his waxen lips. "Thanks, Mr. Brady," he acknowledged faintly. "You are my father's friend. He always believes you. Please tell that to him."

A tired sigh, and young Mike passed on to join his dead mother who had loved him well.

The Goldfarb case was closed. A magnificent funeral had wended its way through the big city's Little Italy. A great funeral headed by a cordon of police and the saddened police commissioner himself.

A week passed and the bedraggled, dissipated Brady, the Whisperer, seated himself in Tony the Barber's chair. Somewhat hesitantly he held out a neatly wrapped package and explained.

"An anonymous admirer of your son sent this to you, Tony. Ninety-nine thousand dollars."

The Whisperer dropped his eyes. Tony need never know that the money was Tito Moriani's and that Brady had found it on Fogle the lawyer's person.

Tony, his old eyes moist with gratitude, shaved him in silence. "Bay rum, Mr. Brady?" he asked when the job was finished.

The Whisperer shook his head. "No," he refused. "It's the smell of a different rum that I'm craving tonight."

Solemnly he shook hands with the grieving old Italian. "Mike was a good boy, Tony," his voice cracked. "A very good boy."

Brady, the Whisperer, shambled away to the nearest speakeasy. The small-fry denizens of the underworld could come out of their holes. A new ache in his bullet-torn throat was bothering him. He was going to drown his secret sorrow.

Another "Whisperer" Story Coming Soon

Men Blubbered and Wailed Before—

The Death Master

A strange, sinister figure, cowled and robed like a monk, bent to an unholy task in the marrow-chilling rain. A grave was defiled, a casket borne away from the burial ground by slinking shadows. Jerry Thacker's senses reeled, but he knew he was on the trail of a Satanic scourge. That trail led to the den of the Death Master, into the terror tentacles of the hooded man-devil.

Yellow-robe jerked out a revolver.

By

G. T. FLEMING-ROBERTS

Author of "One Big Slip," "An Elephant Remembers," etc.

MARROW-chilling rain, fine as Scotch mist and driven by a cutting northwest wind, tried its myriad of needle points against Jerry Thacker's hard, lean face. Ordinarily he liked rain; but when the western sky was like a piece of gray flannel so thick that it made you wonder if really a bright sun was setting on the other side—well, that was carrying gloom a little too far.

Beyond, where the highway turned abruptly to the left, was a grass-topped knoll, the brow of which was enclosed by a rusty iron fence of the pattern common to old-country burial grounds. Scattered throughout the enclosure, like sheep enchanted by the snaky-locked Gorgons, were gravestones, yet unyielding in their unequal struggle against time.

As he approached the graveyard, Thacker saw the dog. A mongrel of several hound breeds it was. It sat on lean haunches, a somber silhouette against the leaden sky—and it howled. Wind out of the west brought the doleful note, and the shudder that went with it, to Jerry Thacker. A mound of new-turned red clay explained the hound and its lament. But for the second figure that appeared on the brow of the hill, Jerry could find no obvious explanation.

A man—or perhaps a woman—clad in a long, flowing and hooded garment of a color that appeared brilliant yellow in spite of evening's impending gloom, hurried across the burial lot. Swinging from the hooded creature's hand was a many-thonged lash. The whip whirled back, lashes whistled out and bit into the lean flank of the black hound.

Jerry found himself trying to quench the rage that fired within him. And he succeeded. On the delicate mission he had undertaken, he could afford no slip-ups due to lack of control. He crept into a roadside thicket lest he be seen by the monkish person.

At the touch of the lash, the dog sprang back, crouched low, and bared his fangs. "Good dog!" Jerry muttered. Again the whip lashed out, and this time pain broke the animal's courage. With tail between its legs, it crawled on its belly away from the new grave. The yellow-hooded person turned towards the road and for moments stared down upon the clump of brush in which Jerry was hidden. And when Jerry saw what was beneath the hood, cold sweat bathed his body. For under that yellow hood there was no face—only a veil of sombre black!

Perhaps it was fancy, but Thacker *felt* hidden eyes upon him, felt the sinister contact with his own eyes. The yellow monk turned, and stalked to the other end of the ridge. There, the strange figure stood, a sinister yellow blot against the dark horizon.

And while the gray of evening deepened, while the horizon purpled, Jerry waited. The strange figure stood motionless, while dusking light robbed its garment of color. Ten more minutes, and night would complete its dismal conquest.

Jerry Thacker scuttled from his hiding place. He was amazed at how quietly he moved. His very soundlessness startled him. Hurrying wind slanted the rain sharply and made miniature tidal waves in every puddle. He made the left turning, crawled beneath bramble-grown wire fence into a field at the south of the graveyard. He could see a blue-white light bobbing its way across the knoll. A gasoline lantern, he judged. Even at a distance, he could make out two shadowy figures moving with the lantern.

Crouching low, lest his silhouette be seen against whatever light might be reflected from the town behind, he hurried towards the Southern boundary of the graveyard. The fence surrounding the burial lot was thickly hedged on this side with small-grown shrubs, and he was thankful for the shield thus offered him. On hands and knees across the rain-soaked soil he crawled until, parting the branches, he could see what went on.

The man who carried the lantern was a huge negro. Following closely, was the yellow-clad figure already so indelibly etched on Jerry's mind. The negro stood the lantern at one end of the newly turned grave, unslung a spade from his back and attacked the mound of clay. The robed person stood looking on—so Jerry supposed—for the black veil completely covered the man's visage.

TO what hideous end this ghoulish task? Jerry wondered. There could be no doubt but that something lay hidden beneath that mound that was badly wanted!

"Hurry," the yellow-hooded person urged. "This rain may have already packed the earth too solidly."

It was a shallow grave. Soon Thacker

could hear the spade thump hollowly on the coffin. But why did they disturb the dead! Like a hyena, this thick-lipped black; like a scavenger, this hooded, monkish person. What could be done with a body? Why exhume the corpse? The skeleton, of course! A well-mounted skeleton brought around five hundred dollars. Sell the cadaver to a medical school. But it was madness. No man would take such a risk for a few hundred dollars. But this hooded creature—was he man, or—or what? And by the time he had found the answer in the darkest pit of his memory, his face and hands were covered with icy sweat.

The negro was down in the grave now. His spade made dull, clumping sounds as it cleared the casket of retaining clay. Then, Jerry could hear grunts of exertion as they hauled the coffin from the grave. "Yellow-robe" pulled back the lid of the casket, while the negro stood at one side, hands folded. Prayers or imprecations tumbled over his bulbous lips.

"Mr. Lester Grove," came the hollow voice from behind the veil, and there was a sneer of contempt in the words. The hooded man straightened up, clapped his hands, and pointed to one end of the casket. Then he walked to the other end. With the negro bearing most of the burden, they started with slow, funereal pace across the burial ground.

Jerry Thacker stood up. The men had disappeared on the other side of the knoll. Another shadow crept its way among the headstones to the open grave. Mounting the pile of clay thrown up by the grave robbers, the shadow took the form of a hound. Again, shuddering through the black air, came the dismal howl as the dog mourned beside the yawning grave.

Jerry turned his back on the cemetery. He ran the mile back to Brentington.

Wet, dripping, and mud splattered, Jerry Thacker rushed into the lobby of the Palatial Hotel and Boarding House. He had registered for a frowzy room immediately upon his arrival in Brentington. Thacker crossed to the phone booth, entered, and put in a long-distance call for the Cosmo Life Insurance Company of Indianapolis. When his connection rang through, he said: "Hello, Flossie; will you get me the governor?"

In another moment, J. P. Thacker, boss of the Cosmo, was booming his voice over the telephone.

"This is me, Dad," spoke Jerry. "Got into this nickle-plated metropolis all safe and sound. And, Dad, there's something funny in the air down here, and I don't mean rain!"

"Good!" J. P. barked. "Let's have it."

"But I'm not sure it's quite along my line. Maybe a private detective would have been better. I don't know just yet what it is."

J. P. interrupted his son to tell him that that was just too bad. "And don't call me again until you get your hands on something definite!" The Cosmo's boss severed the connection.

Jerry stood as if stunned, the receiver still in his hand. Then another sound came from the supposedly "dead" phone. It was a very faint click as if some one near at hand had stealthily replaced the phone receiver. What if some one had heard his conversation with his father? It was possible that there was a phone extension. He meant to find out.

JERRY turned in the booth. Suddenly he saw the door of the hotel lobby swing open slowly. A white-faced old man walked with wooden stride through the tiny lobby and straight towards the phone booth. His right arm was flexed, and his fist held a long pistol. His eyes did not swerve from Jerry's startled face. Not the faintest sign of life stirred beneath his pallid skin. A fraction of a second before the man's forefinger constricted upon the trigger of the gun, Jerry collapsed like a broken jumping jack on the floor of the booth. The sound of the shot roared in his ears. Broken glass rained around his face and tinkled to the floor.

Yet Jerry was unharmed physically. Had he been another man, he might have thrown open the door and charged after the old man with the gun. But Jerry had one remarkable trait—he remembered names, and not only faces, but the separate features of those faces. And the man who had attempted to kill him had the features of a former acquaintance of his, one Calvin Smith. Had Smith left the grave alive and forty years older than when he had been interred six months ago?

Jerry's senses reeled. He pushed open the door of the phone booth and peered around the corner. The tiny lobby was empty. He hauled to his feet and ran to the open door. The rain-swollen night was filled with the roar of a powerful car. As the car rolled by, Jerry saw the man who resembled Calvin Smith in the back seat. And the hands that gripped the steering wheel were half enveloped in voluminous yellow sleeves!

The jig was up! Somebody knew why Jerry Thacker had come to the country town of Brentington. Somebody was anxious that he should leave—preferably, that he should leave in a coffin.

Across the street, above Jake's Barber Shop, rain made scintillating topaz of the lighted window marked:

COSMO LIFE INS. CO.
Martin Torenga
Agent

Jerry Thacker looked up and down the puddled, dismal street. Then he sprang from the hotel door, splashed through the mud until he came to the darkened stairway leading to the rooms above the barber shop. He mounted squawking steps and knocked on the door of the Cosmo Agency.

"Martin," he called. "It's Jerry Thacker. Open up."

"Jerry!" a pleasant voice called back. "Just a minute." The sound of hurrying feet and Martin Torenga opened the door.

Jerry Thacker had never got used to Torenga's face—or rather the waxen thing that served Torenga for a face. They had been buddies during the war, Thacker and Torenga. Then, just before the armistice, a shell had burst close upon the two pals.

The shock had put Jerry out, but it had done more than that to Torenga. That shell had blasted Torenga's features, and when at last he had been released from the hospital, he had worn the wax mask that to some extent reconstructed Torenga's face. But at best it was a poor, lifeless thing, void of all human expression. It was out of sheer pity that Thacker had obtained the agency appointment for Torenga.

Jerry scarcely repressed a shudder as he stared into Torenga's deep-set eyes—all that seemed alive in the waxen visage.

"I don't know," said Jerry as he shook Torenga's hand, "but what you'd look better without that damned mask, no matter how badly scarred your face may be."

Torenga's hollow laugh checked him. "Some day, Jerry, I'll let you see my real face. Then, you won't wonder. But say, what time did you get in?"

"This afternoon," said Thacker. "And I've been looking around a little. Say, what's the matter with this town? Everybody acts as if they were scared to death."

TORENGA nodded his head. "They are. Ten strange, sleeping deaths in the past year. Six of those victims were insured with our company. That's why I thought somebody better look into the matter."

Torenga pulled up a chair for his friend. When they had settled themselves, he said: "Jerry, you and I have seen death; but if Lester Grove was dead when they buried him, I'll eat my hat! And his wife—that's what got me wondering—his wife suddenly appeared out of nowhere to cash in on that fifty-thousand-dollar policy. I didn't even know he had a wife until he took out his insurance. Even so, she didn't show up until after his death."

Jerry nodded. "That's what you said in your letter. But what about this yellow-robed person who seems to be haunting me?"

"You've seen *that*, too!" Torenga exclaimed. "You know, I've been under the impression *he* was purely a legendary figure."

"Who?"

"The Yellow Hermit, so the story goes around here. He built himself an old stone house north of the cemetery. That was about a hundred years ago. He lived alone, supposedly. But legend has it that every evening the hermit's house was the scene of carousings in which many strange, cowled creatures like himself took part." Torenga paused and drummed on the arm of his chair. "Jerry, have you read Blackwood on secret worship? If you have, you've a pretty good idea as to what the Yellow Hermit was supposed to be up to."

"You mean he was a devil worshiper?" Jerry's mouth gaped with incredulity.

Torenga nodded. "Then, according to the tale, the Yellow Hermit disappeared. The devil came for his own, of course! But you're not the first to report the Hermit's return. There's not a lad hereabouts who will go near the deserted stone house after dusk."

Jerry laughed a bit uneasily and launched into the story of the unholy grave robbing he had witnessed. "Does that in any way coincide with your idea of devil worship?" he asked when he had finished.

A shudder rippled along Torenga's shoulders. "Perhaps," he said. "Nothing is too ghastly to be undertaken by the evil powers"—

"But," Jerry interrupted, "even the devil wouldn't countenance insurance frauds. Getting down to reality, I see only one explanation."

At that moment came a rap at the door. Torenga answered the summons. A tall, ruddy-faced man entered the room. He stared rudely at Thacker and said: "May I see you alone, Mart. It's about that business we were discussing."

"No," replied Torenga, "not alone. It so happens that Mr. Thacker is visiting this town for the same purpose—to investigate this Yellow Hermit scare, though he's tackling it from a different angle. Jerry, this is Mr. Dartner, the mayor of our town."

Thacker and Dartner shook hands. Said the mayor, as soon as this formality was over: "If you're anything like a detective, you may be able to help me, Thacker. I'm in a spot. I'm being threatened, for something I didn't do, by a man who ought to have been dead three-quarters of a century ago. Read this." He pulled a piece of paper from his pocket and handed it to Jerry. Then he walked to the window and stood looking down on the street.

Jerry opened the paper and read:

One hundred years ago, your family drove me away. I have returned and my vengeance shall be visited upon the son of my persecutor. I may bury you dead, or yet I may bury you alive! Mine is the choice.

The Yellow Hermit.

Ping! The muffled sound of a shot. Glass in the front window was suddenly shattered. Dartner pivoted woodenly, staggered to the center of the room, and toppled to the floor. The front of his coat was stained with crimson. West wind frolicked through the broken window, drenching the sill with rain.

TORENGA'S cry rang hollowly beneath his waxen mask. "Go downstairs. Get the marshal. This is murder!"

Jerry flung through the door, raced down the steps. In the street, cold rain splashed his fever-burning face. The town marshal—where could he find him? He jerked to the left in front of Jake's Barker Shop. His shoes crunched something against the sidewalk. He stopped, looked down. Glass from Torenga's window. Glass on the outside? The shot that had struck Dartner must have come from within the room itself! Jerry pivoted and raced back to the staircase. He bounded up, seized the doorknob of Torenga's room and gave it a wrench. The door did not yield. He hammered with hard, anger-driven fists. Insane, melodic laughter rang out. Jerry backed away, hunched his shoulder, and charged the panel. It creaked. He tried again. The panel slivered and split wide open. He thrust in his hand, turned the key, and swung open the door.

The room was dark and silent save for the pattering of rain on the window sill. He reached in his pocket and brought out his snub-nosed automatic. He groped for the light switch and snapped it on. The room was empty, and on the carpet where Dartner had fallen, only a crimson stain remained to mark the tragedy. Bewildered, Jerry turned around.

A door at the rear of the room was open. He raced through the kitchenette and found a back door leading down an open stair into the alley. It was clear to him that somebody had fired at Dartner from the rear of the apartment with a silenced gun. But at such a range wouldn't the bullet have drilled the window, rather than smash it? Perhaps not, passing through Dartner's body. But the killer—Torenga? It seemed impossible!

He clattered down the steps into the alleyway. At the other end, a car with twin red tail lamps rounded the corner. Jerry ran around the building into Main Street. He crossed to the hotel and went to the parking lot behind. He got into his car, spun the motor, and drove into Main Street. North of town, they had said, he could find the deserted house thought to be the headquarters of the Yellow Hermit. It was worth trying.

Out past the town limits, he sighted the car with twin tail lamps. He dragged down on the brakes and watched the car swing past the burial ground. He switched off his lights and let his own car coast to the corner. The car he pursued had apparently turned into what had once been a well-kept drive, but was now choked with weeds. Jerry wheeled his car onto the shoulder of the road and sprinted down the weed-grown drive. In the distance he could see the shadowy bulk of a house—a two-story affair, flat-topped like a prison.

Jerry reached the edge of the lawn and crouched low behind a bed of shrubbery. He saw the car parked in front of the doorway. Apparently whoever had been in the car had entered the house. He skirted the bushes and ran breathlessly to the car. Again he crouched low, waiting and wondering how he might enter the building.

"Put up your hands!" a toneless voice breathed.

Jerry caught his breath, straightened up, and turned around. His hands crawled up. A man wearing a black slicker and hooded rain hat menaced him with a rifle. The man pulled up a flashlight and sprayed its white beam on Jerry's face.

"Have you the word?" asked the man. "I have orders to shoot anyone who does not have it."

Reflected light forced shadow from beneath the guard's hood. It was the man who looked like Calvin Smith!

Jerry steeled himself. "No," he said through clenched teeth. "I do not need the word, Calvin Smith!"

THE effect of the name was amazing. The guard's jaw dropped; his face paled. Jerry saw the rifle shake. "No, no," he yammered. "You—you have made s-some mistake. I—I—how could I be Calvin Smith? He is dead. I am living."

Jerry's right fist launched itself in a fast, pistonlike blow that packed all the power in his lean, hard frame. His big, bony knuckles crashed against the point of the guard's chin. At the same time the man toppled backwards, Jerry seized the gun and wrenched it from the man's grasp. The guard who looked like Calvin Smith crumpled to the earth, his arms and legs twisting grotesquely beneath his crisp black slicker. Jerry tossed the cumbersome rifle aside and drew his automatic. He stooped over the fallen man and rasped: "One smart move and Calvin Smith dies for all time!"

But the man was unconscious. Jerry appropriated the man's rain coat and hood together with a bunch of keys that he found in one pocket for his own use. While dressing himself in the borrowed garments, he noticed that while Smith's face looked like that of a man of seventy, his bare arms were as well knit as his own. Jerry caught a glimmering of what kind of a plot he was up against.

Having trussed up Smith with strips torn from his clothes, Jerry dragged him to a corner of the house and hid him in the shadows.

Then he hurried along the wall until he came to a small door. He selected keys that seemed likely to fit the lock, tried them, and in another moment he stepped into a small, ill-lighted hall. At one end was a narrow flight of stone steps. He mounted swiftly and found himself in a narrow gallery. Light emanated from a small, barred opening in the inner wall. By jumping up, he managed to catch hold of the grating and pull himself up. He could then look down into a small room lighted by long white candles mounted in wall sconces. Along one side of the room was a bench littered with odd-shaped bottles. In the center of the room, across a pair of trestles, was an earth-stained coffin—probably the one removed from the cemetery. A door opened at one end of the room and two persons entered. One was the yellow-robed creature and the other a woman with chalky face and haggard eyes. The yellow fiend strode across the room to the casket. The woman followed, her death-white hands clutching at the creature's yellow robe. The hooded man turned angrily and struck the woman across the mouth with the back of his hand. She recoiled. For a moment, rage burned in her eyes until tears came to quench it.

"You're a big shot, aren't you!" she sneered.

Yellow-robe seemed to increase in height. "I may be the most powerful man in the world, in time. Today, Calvin Smith, a man who was once called respectable, tried to commit murder at my bidding. He is utterly my slave, just as you are, Tonia. How many men would you kill for one drop of my vital fluid?"

The woman's appeal became frantic. "A dozen! Try me and see. Smith didn't get that guy from the insurance company. Let *me* at him! Listen, boss, I'm too young to croak! Haven't I done everything you asked? Haven't I impersonated the wives and mothers of all your living corpses in order that you could collect the insurance?"

Her attitude became threatening. "Listen, if you don't give me a drink of that stuff right now, I'll go out of here and straight to the state police. You got this town scared, but the state will soon crimp your schemes!"

SHOULDERS beneath the yellow robe shrugged. "Go ahead. I'm nearly through with the insurance business. I have taken half of the money my clients collected. The rest, according to my agreement, I have turned over to them. And they will pay it all back—all back into these two hands." And he extended his grasping fingers in front of him. "All of three hundred thousand dollars they will give me for little sips of my vital essence! And when they have spent all their money, they will pay me with services—theft, murder, anything I desire. All this for the fluid that keeps them alive! Keeps them alive!" he echoed and burst into a laugh of mad merriment. "Keeps them in a life that is worse than death!"

He whirled on the woman. "Get out! Go to the police. Do I care? I have schemed to bring that Paul Pry of the Cosmo Company here tonight. I will let him see *beneath my veil*. Then, I will put him out of the way for a few days. When he comes to, everything within this building will be gone. He will remember only my face. And when he tells the police who I am! Ah, but I am clever!" He seized the woman by the shoulders and shoved her roughly through the door.

Yellow-robe crossed the room to the casket and threw back the lid. From his position at the barred window, Jerry could see the corpse, white faced, thin featured, peaceful. The yellow fiend took the corpse by the wrist and lifted the arm. Jerry noticed that though buried three days, the body showed no sign of rigor. Yellow-robe took a hypodermic syringe from his work bench and plunged it into the arm of the corpse. The pale skin flushed; the nostrils dilated slightly.

Suddenly, the door of the room was thrown open and a short, fiery-haired man wearing a surgeon's smock came into the room.

"Oh," he said to Yellow-robe, "you have injected the adrenalin. Wouldn't it have been more kind to let him sleep on into eternity? I'm about fed up with this. Better that he should have remained buried alive, than that he should return to what you have prepared for him!

Yellow-robe turned his veiled face towards the other man. "Going soft, Dr. Hunt? Well, we'll soon be through. Then we can reap the harvest we have sown. Think, ten pairs of hands to do our slightest bidding. Whatever enterprises we decide upon, we have only to plan. The dangerous work will be done by our ten slaves!"

Dr. Hunt shrugged. "It's your own business, of course, but if you'll take my advice, you'll retire on the money we've made out of the insurance hoax. You'll have ten slaves who can rob banks for you, kill your enemies, protect you. But you know as well as I do that they cannot live long at the rate you are pouring *that stuff* into them. Vital essence, you call it. Tincture of hell is the better term!"

At that moment, Jerry's shaking hands would no longer support him; for the eyelids of the man in the coffin fluttered open and his white hands grasped at empty air in a feeble effort to sit upright. Lester Grove, three days buried, had *come to life!*

Jerry dropped noisily to the gallery floor and stumbled along the dark passageway. It was not until he ran into a heavy steel door that he collected his scattered senses. His ear against the door panel, he could hear Dr. Hunt and Yellow-robe talking.

Jerry was about to enter the room and risk cornering the two criminals with his automatic, when the sound of many feet hurrying down the gallery drove all thoughts from his head. Men were coming down the hall—quite a number of men. Jerry pulled the hood of his rain hat close about his face, flattened himself against the wall and waited.

THE men coming towards him moved in single file. Some walked with lazy, stumbling steps, and others pushed their companions and laughed drunkenly. There must have been eight or ten of them. The leader of the band saw Jerry and called out: "Hi, Smith! You're a jump ahead of us, aren't you?"

So they took him for Calvin Smith. That was just as well. Jerry mumbled something back at them.

The group lined itself up in front of the door, and Jerry fell in with them. Dr. Hunt opened the door, and they filed into the room. All hilarity ceased in the presence of the yellow fiend. The men crowded against the wall and stared as Yellow-robe and Hunt assisted the weakened Lester Grove from the casket to a couch that had been prepared for him at one side of the room.

Then yellow-robe went to his workbench and took up a bottle of dark-colored liquid. Jerry looked at the faces of his companions. Some were pale, dry-sinned; others were moist and red. All eyes were eagerly turned toward Yellow-robe and his bottle. Dr. Hunt approached Yellow-robe with a tray full of small, glass cups.

"Have all of them paid?" the veiled creature asked.

Hunt nodded, plunged his hands into his trouser pocket and brought out a fat roll of bills. This money he deposited in a steel chest that rested on the bench. Yellow-robe was in the act of filling the glass cups, when a door opened at the other end of the room. The gigantic negro stumbled into the room, his fat lips blubbering. "Mastah," he shouted, "it's done escaped!"

"What!"

"That man-thing you brought from the city done escaped. He's runnin' around this house somewhere. He got my gun."

Yellow-robe's fist pounded into the black man's face. "Damned imbecile! Went to sleep on the job, did you! Well, you'll suffer for this!" He reached into the sleeve of his robe and brought out his many-thonged lash. He would, no doubt, have beaten the negro senseless had not Dr. Hunt stopped him.

"After a while," the doctor whispered. "Get rid of these." He nodded toward the line of waiting men.

Yellow-robe nodded and proceeded with his pouring, while Hunt passed the tiny glass cups that had been filled.

Dr. Hunt approached Jerry. "Smith!"

he snapped. "I thought you were ordered to guard the entrance. You've had your share of the vital fluid. That detective from the insurance company may come."

Jerry's automatic suddenly sprouted from beneath his black rain coat. "He has come, Hunt. Put up your hands!"

Hunt stepped backwards. His tray of cups clattered to the floor. His hands shot upward. Beyond the doctor's white shoulder, Jerry could see Yellow-robe turn slowly around while his hand crept inside his clothes.

"Hold it, faker!" Jerry snapped.

But the fiend jerked a revolver from beneath the folds of his robe. Jerry's automatic whipped sideways and spat fire around Hunt. Yellow-robe staggered, clawed at his shoulder, and fell forward on his face. Hunt's two hands stabbed down, seizing Jerry's gun wrist before the latter could bring his automatic around again. Jerry's left fist drove hard to the point of Hunt's chin. The doctor released his hold, staggered back, grasping at empty air. Jerry stepped to the center of the room and wheeled upon the group of men. "Don't try anything funny, any of you!"

But the men, Yellow-robe's slaves, were a pitiful group of wailing, blubbering creatures. "You have killed him—killed the master," one sobbed. "Now, we will all have to die. Only the master knows how to prepare the vital fluid!"

"So he told you that, did he!" Jerry exclaimed. "Vital fluid, eh? Well, just ask Dr. Hunt. Unless I'm pretty dumb, you've been made slaves of opium! That's how he was going to get you to rob and murder for him. You've been paying for your own ruination. You've been taking laudanum!"

JERRY turned his gun on Hunt. "Get over there with the poor fools you've been doping. I'm watching you while I take a look at this master of yours! I'm afraid I haven't killed him!" Jerry backed away until his heels touched the form of the yellow fiend. Then, he stepped over the man, stooped, and jerked off the black veil. Martin Torenga's waxen face leered up at him!

"Good Lord!" Jerry straightened up. The shock of the revelation sickened him so that he paid no attention to the door that creaked open behind him.

"You in the black rain coat!" a voice snapped. "Drop that gun!"

Numbly Jerry obeyed. He turned around. The creature that held a steady automatic on him had the most hideous face he had ever seen. The nose was a mere button of blackened flesh; the lips formed a ragged, black scar; cheeks were purpled, pitted like a sponge.

"Whose side are you playing on?" asked the monster. "Take off that rain hood."

Jerry obeyed.

"Good heavens! Jerry Thacker, and I nearly potted you!" A laugh broke from the scarred lips. The creature came toward Jerry.

"What—who are you?" Jerry stuttered.

The man passed over his burn-scarred face. "Of course you wouldn't know me. Probably wouldn't even recognize my voice without my mask."

"Torenga—you—" Jerry turned his eyes on the yellow-robed figure at his feet. "But—"

"He just borrowed my mask," Torenga laughed. "They held me prisoner here tonight until I got the best of that black fathead. But just what is this? Know yet?"

"You're damned right!" Jerry exclaimed. "I thought it was artificial catalepsy from the beginning."

"What?" Torenga interrupted.

"Don't you see," Jerry explained, "this Yellow-robe and his pal, Hunt, bargained with certain ignorant men of this town to have their lives insured for large sums. Hunt and his boss paid the premiums, I suppose. Then came the sleeping death, as you called it. In other words, the insured submitted to Hunt's cataleptic trances—trances that can be brought on by drugs, hypnosis, or a combination of both. Pulse becomes almost imperceptible; respiration is very slight. Apparently the insured men were dead—and, of course, it was Hunt who wrote the death certificates. The burials were carried out as usual in order that the people in town might not be suspicious. Later, the corpses were dug up and brought back to life. The resurrected men were then disguised so that they could reënter life—though in the case of Calvin Smith, the disguise was pretty thin."

"BUT," Torenga asked, "who stood to gain by such an unholy process? How did they collect the insurance money?"

"Oh," Jerry went on, "Yellow-robe used a woman—another dope fiend in his power—to impersonate the beneficiaries of each policy. You'll find that the insured were men who were pretty much alone in life, so that no trouble from relatives was anticipated. The policies were made out to anyone of the assumed names of this woman impersonator long before the men 'died.' From what I overheard tonight, I gather that it was a fifty-fifty proposition. Hunt and Yellow-robe got half of the insurance money and their cataleptic subjects got the other half.

"But that isn't the worst of it! Yellow-robe wasn't content with the monetary returns. I think he was subject to grandiose illusions or some other insane complex. He *enslaved* those poor devils after they had been resurrected from the grave. He told them some wild tale about having to drink a certain vital essence in order not to return to the cataleptic state. That essence was tincture of opium. And that was clever of him. He deliberately imposed the opium habit on them, and sold them the stuff at exorbitant prices.

"In that way, he stood to gain *all* of the insurance money; and because they were dependent upon him for the dope, they wouldn't dare squeal on him. They were utterly within his power. He planned to make them rob banks for him, commit murder and other similar services. He got Calvin Smith to shoot at me tonight, and doubtless one of his slaves shot Mayor Dartner in your apartment."

"Dartner!" Torenga gasped. "Why, Dartner's wound consisted of a broken mercurochrome bottle. He had a gun in his hand all the time he was looking out of that window. He shot through the window, spilled the mercurochrome on himself, and fell to the floor. We were both taken in by this trick. When you went downstairs, he stopped playing possum and pointed his gun at me. That's how I was taken prisoner."

Jerry didn't hear any more just then. He turned around, bent over Yellow-robe, and unfastened the waxen mask. Beneath, he saw the face of Dartner, mayor of Brentington!

He straightened up. "I begin to get the drift. I wish I'd got him through the heart instead of through the shoulder!"

"What was his idea of borrowing my mask?" Torenga asked.

"Why, he was going to wear it, bring me here as a witness that *you* were the yellow-robed devil. He would have probably silenced you forever, and nobody would have been the wiser. Superstition concerning the Yellow Hermit who was supposed to worship the devil was enough to frighten folks around here into keeping hands off. But when you and I got on his trail, he schemed to throw the whole blame onto you!"

Torenga recovered his mask and placed it over his pitifully scarred face. "What can we do with these dope fiends? It doesn't seem right to turn them over to the police—victims of ignorance."

"I think," said Jerry, "that you and I are going to cover up their little part in this unlisted crime of playing dead. I think part of the recovered insurance money is going to pay for their medical treatment. They'll submit to it quick enough when they learn how terrible death is when it comes by the opium-poisoning route!"

Sinister person after person fed Marty Quade, private dick, thousand-dollar bills, each giving the password of the unknown Croesus whose gold had led the sleuth to meet him aboard that fateful Florida rattler. And when Quade was content to let the bank notes pour in, those mystery bills drew him and a beautiful senorita into a shocking murder trap in a ruthless . . . .

Killers' Club Car

"I intend that you shall all jump from the train."

"Marty Quade" Novelet

By

Emile C. Tepperman

Author of "Murder Wheels," etc.

MARTY QUADE had finished his grapefruit, and was going to work on a generous plate of bacon and scrambled eggs when the hotel page boy came into the dining room calling: "*Mister* Quade! *Mister* Quade! Mist—Oh, there you are, Mister Quade."

Marty had a mouthful of bacon and egg. He managed to say sourly: "How many times do I have to tell you not to yell my name around the place, Sammy? What you got there?"

Sammy stuck out his tray, on which there lay a bulky white envelope addressed in typewriting to "Mr. M. Quade, Hotel Baltic, New York." In the lower left-hand corner was also typewritten, and underlined: *Of vital importance—please deliver at once!*

Marty grunted, took the envelope, glanced exasperatedly at the tray, which Sammy continued to hold under his nose. Marty said, "All right, I give up," and put a quarter on the tray. Sammy grinned. "Thanks, Mr. Quade. That letter was left by a Western Union messenger just now. He said there was no answer."

"Okay, Sammy, scram. My eggs'll get cold." Marty continued phlegmatically to finish his breakfast, leaving the envelope at his elbow. Sammy goggled. "Gee, Mr. Quade, ain't you curious?"

Marty scowled. "I said, scram!" He reached out for the quarter on the tray, and Sammy backed hastily away, shrugged, and left the dining room. When the eggs and bacon were finished, Marty stirred his coffee, then slit open the envelope, drew out the contents, laid them on the table, and stared at them. They consisted of the following:

Item: A long Pullman ticket of the Florida East Coast Railway, good for one continuous passage from New York to Miami.

Item: A small white ticket calling for lower berth No. 3, car No. B17, on the Florida Special, leaving Pennsylvania station that same morning, at ten-thirty.

Item: A single United States Treasury note in the denomination of one thousand dollars.

Item: A neatly folded sheet of writing paper upon which was typed the following amazing communication:

Dear Mr. Quade:

I have good reason to believe that my life is in danger.

Your name was given to me by my bank as a reputable private detective who is expert with a gun, and who has never been known to fail in any commission which he has undertaken. I must, without fail, be in Miami tomorrow afternoon where I am to board the Carribean Clipper of the Pan-American Airways. There are those who will attempt to stop me on the journey, and even to *kill me.*

I wish to hire you to deliver me safely on board the Caribbean Clipper. When you have seen me off, you will have earned the thousand dollars herewith enclosed, together with another thousand which I will pay you then. The fee is high, but the risk is great—so great that I dare not disclose my name to you until I meet you on the train. Use the enclosed ticket. When the train leaves Philadelphia, the real danger will begin. I will then disclose myself to you by approaching you and asking: *"Do we stop at Conshohocken?"* I will then tell you further details.

Please Mr. Quade, accept this commission. It means my life and future happiness. If you do accept, please go up to your room, and raise your window, and look out for a moment. I will be watching and will then expect you on the train at ten-thirty."

There was no signature. Marty crinkled the thousand-dollar bill, inspected it closely to see if it was counterfeit. As nearly as he could judge, it was genuine. He finished his coffee, put away the various items in the envelope, signed his check, left a tip, and went out into the lobby.

SAMMY, the page boy, was standing near the desk. Marty took him by the arm, led him to one side. "Want to make yourself a five-spot, kid?"

Sammy grinned. "Give me the gun, and point out the guy."

"Never mind the wise-cracks, kid. Here's what I want you to do. Take off that snappy uniform coat, and that nifty little cap. Roll up your shirt sleeves, and go out in the street. Cross over, and look around for anybody who may be watching my window. I'm going upstairs to look out. Try to notice who's watching, and follow him. Find out where he goes, and if possible, who he is. Get it?"

Sammy's eyes were glowing with excitement. "Geez, Mr. Quade, it's real detective work, ain't it?"

"Uh-huh. Here's five bucks for expenses, in case you have to take a cab. And you better bring me the right change. I'll pay you your fiver when you report. Now git!"

Marty watched the boy go into the coat room to leave his uniform coat, then Quade went over to the telephone booths, entered the one with the dial phone, and called a number. "This the Bank of Pan-America?" he asked. "Is Mr. Poindexter in yet? Lemme talk to him. This is Quade."

In a moment he had his man. "Poindexter? Marty Quade talking . . . . No, it's not about my bill. I want to ask you a question. Did you recommend me to anyone in the last twenty-four hours?"

Poindexter, who was the head of the bank's extensive investigation department, had used Marty frequently, and swore by him to others, and at him to his face. "Hell, of course I did. I've sent you enough business so you can afford to do the bank's work gratis. I gave out your name four or five times yesterday, but I don't know what you'll get out of it. They were just casual inquiries."

"Listen, Poindy, I don't want the casual ones. Did you recommend me to anyone who seemed to be in a special sort of jam?"

"Why, not exactly—except that Austin Hackerman called me up at home at six o'clock this morning and asked me for a reliable man who could use a gun. I told him that automatic of yours has been the death of a small army of crooks."

Marty frowned. "Never heard of him. Am I supposed to know him?"

"He's a depositor. Handles a lot of trust funds. He's going to Paraguay this morning. Did he call you? I hope to hell he takes you along with him, and I never see you again."

Marty gripped the receiver tightly. "Did you say Paraguay? Would there be any danger to him that you know of?"

"I couldn't say, Marty. What little I know about him doesn't amount to much. He was down in South America for a number of years as a scout for an investment syndicate, and he made close friends with Rodriguez Delcastro, the then President of San Félice, on the border of Paraguay. He's the guardian of Delcastro's daughter now, and the executor of the late president's will. I understand he's going down there now in connection with some big deal that should net him millions. I shouldn't be surprised if there's danger in it."

"Thanks, Poindy," Marty said shortly. "Austin Hackerman, eh? I'll remember the name. I'll be dropping you a line, pal—from Miami!"

He hung up on Poindexter's puzzled queries, and hurried upstairs to his room on the fourth floor. His window faced on Forty-sixth Street. He peered out from behind the curtains, saw Sammy in his shirt sleeves, busy at the business of being a detective, and as inconspicuous as a garlic peddler on Fifth Avenue. Broadway was just around the corner, and there was a steady stream of people moving down the street. There were many loiterers, and it was impossible to tell just where the prospective client would be stationed.

Marty shrugged, pushed up the window, and leaned over the sill. Just as he got his head out, the window started to slip down, because the frame was well-oiled and Marty had forgotten to hold the window up. Marty ducked, and it was that which saved his life. There was no sound of any explosion from anywhere, but suddenly the window pane, where his head had been, was shattered. There was a *ping*, and a bullet embedded itself in the woodwork of the wall at the opposite side of the room.

Marty pulled his head in so fast that he grazed his neck on the window frame. The crashing glass made a jangling racket. Marty pressed back against the wall alongside the window, looking across at the bullet hole in the wall. It was down near the baseboard, which indicated that it had come in at an angle from above, probably from the roof of one of the brownstone tenements opposite.

There were no more shots. Some one pounded on the door, and Marty heard the floor maid's worried voice: "Anything wrong in there, Mr. Quade? I heard glass smash."

Marty called out: "No, I guess it was a mistake."

He looked at his watch. Nine-thirty. Just an hour to make the Florida Special. And they were taking pot-shots at him already. He moved around the room, putting his toothbrush, shaving paraphernalia, some extra shirts and a suit of pajamas into a week-end bag, but taking care not to get in line with the window. There was no use calling the police. Whoever had fired at him was probably gone by this time. The police would only mess around, questioning him and wasting time, probably make him miss the Florida Special. And after that pot-shot, nothing in the world could make Marty miss the train.

IN about twenty minutes Sammy appeared. Marty answered his knock, let him in. He looked at the broken glass scattered on the rug. "Geez, Mr. Quade, that was funny—how your window busted when you opened it. What happened? Did you bang it or something?"

"Yeah. Something. Come on, make it snappy. Did you spot anyone?"

"I did, Mr. Quade. There was a little Japanese guy that was standing in the doorway of the United Cigar store on the corner, and looking up at your window. He was dressed like a chauffeur. I watched him, and the minute you looked out, he started to go away. I saw the window bust. The Jap turned around for a second, but then kept on going. He walked over to the Eighth Avenue Subway station, and I followed him down to the platform on the uptown side. When the train came in, I boarded it with him."

Sammy stopped, gulped, lowered his eyes.

"Well," Marty snapped impatiently. "Where did he go?"

"I don't know, Mr. Quade." Sammy put out a hand, apologetically. "I thought I was doing fine, but I guess he was wise to me. As soon as I was in the car, he ducked out, went back on the platform. I started out after him, but he reached in and shoved me back in the car. The doors closed and the train started to move, and there I was in the train, and him grinning at me from the platform!"

Marty groaned.

"Geez, Mr. Quade, I'm awful sorry."

"It's all right, kid. It can't be helped. Here's your five. You tried hard, anyway. Now take my bag down, and get me a cab."

Before stepping out into the street, Marty felt to see if his automatic was loose and handy in the shoulder holster. Then he ducked quickly across the sidewalk, and into the cab, saying: "Pennsylvania Station."

No one took a shot at him . . .

There was quite a crowd on the Florida Special, considering that it was the end of April. Marty allowed the redcap to carry his small bag down into car B17, and deposit it under the seat of Lower Three. His seat, being a lower, faced forward. The seat belonging to the upper, facing his, was already occupied by a small, wiry, eyeglassed Japanese in the trim whipcord uniform of a chauffeur!

Marty's face showed nothing as he nodded to his traveling companion. The Japanese bobbed his head, spread his lips in a wide smile. "How you do, sar? You have a pleasant journey, I hope. No? Thank you."

He said it all in one breath, as if he would stumble over the words if he hesitated. Marty grunted and said, "Same to you," and turned to inspect the other occupants of the car. Lower One, just ahead of him, was occupied by a girl. She was hardly more than twenty, with heavy black hair. Marty couldn't see her eyes, because she was sitting with her back to him. He could only see her profile, which showed a skin that was freshly pink-and-white. He had to look past the Jap's shoulder to see her, and he was conscious of the Jap's eyes, behind their glasses, studying him. Marty suddenly tautened as he noted that the girl had taken a small compact from her handbag, and was holding it at such an angle as to afford her a view of himself and the Jap. He quickly glanced away, so as not to meet her gaze in the glass.

Across the aisle, a stout man sat in Lower Seven, with his feet resting on the seat opposite. He was thumbing through a magazine, and as Marty glanced over, he saw that the stout man hadn't been reading the magazine, but had been watching him. The stout man hastily looked back to his magazine when Marty turned toward him.

The car was filling up. The porter came down the aisle carrying three bags, and ushered two men into the private compartment at the head of the car. Both the newcomers were thin, with hard faces and sharp, nervous eyes. As the porter was opening the door of their compartment, they turned in the corridor and looked back toward where Marty was sitting. One of them whispered to the other, then they both nodded. Marty could easily distinguish the bulges under their left armpits, and he saw that the taller of the two had a cast in his right eye.

The two men entered their compartment, and Marty swung his eyes back, to find that the Jap was still looking at him, and still smiling that soapy smile. Marty glared at him, got up, stretched, and went forward to the washroom.

He found the porter there, took out a five-dollar bill, and held it between his thumb and forefinger. "Look, George," he said. "How do you like this?"

George's eyes opened wide. He showed two rows of white teeth, and quickly put the bill in his pocket.

Marty showed him his private detective's badge. "Just so you'll know I'm on the up-and-up, George. There may be some doings on the train before we hit Miami. That five was so you'd know whose side you're on, in case anything starts. There'll be ten more in Miami, if you play ball with me."

George rolled his eyes. "Ah'll play ball wiv you-all, suh. Ah sho' will!"

"All right. Now tell me—where's that Jap going?"

"Miami, suh."

"And the girl in Number One?"

"She's gwine to Miami, too, suh."

"The man in Seven—you know, the fat one?"

"Miami, suh. He's got the upper, but he's sittin' in the lower seat. The upper's empty till Philly. At Philly, he'll have to move ovah, 'cause the passenger foh the lower gets on there."

At that point they were interrupted by the entrance of the tall man with the cast in his eye, who was occupying the compartment with a companion. The tall man frowned when he saw the porter and Marty. He was very thin, and his face looked even longer than it naturally was because of the size of his ears. His gaze flicked from Marty to the porter. He took out a dollar bill, gave it to the colored man, and said in a nasal voice: "Go and get me a highball—with plenty of Scotch in it. Bring it to Compartment A."

George took the money, went out. Marty had turned to the sink, and was just squirting some soap out of the automatic ejector on to his hands, when the tall man stepped up close to him and jabbed something in his back. "It's a gun, pal, in case you don't know, pal," he said nasally.

MARTY stiffened. "What am I supposed to do—with soap on my hands, I mean?" he asked.

"Never mind the soap," the other snarled. "Just turn around slow, and raise your paws. Act nice, now."

Marty spoke very mildly. "Sure, sure. I always act nice." He turned around slowly, raised his hands, until they were on a level with the other's eyes. The fingers of his right hand were splayed out, but the thumb and middle finger of his soapy left hand were touching at the tips. He suddenly snapped the middle finger away from his thumb, and a gob of soap flew directly into the tall man's eyes. The other jerked backward involuntarily, and in that instant Marty's bunched right hand came over in a thudding blow to the gunman's chin. There was a sharp *snap*. The other groaned, buckled, and collapsed to the floor. The gun clattered down beside him.

Marty stooped quickly, pocketed the gun, then poked his head out through the curtains leading to the vestibule. Nobody was outside.

Marty swiftly came back, opened the door of the men's room which was just off the wash room, and dragged the tall man into it, shot the latch home. The quarters here were cramped, but Marty deposited his burden on the floor against the wall, and straddled him. The tall man's eyes flickered, opened, and he looked up at Marty sullenly, feeling of his chin.

Marty was swinging the man's gun in his hand, and he asked pleasantly: "What's it all about, my friend? Why the gunplay?"

The other retained his sullen look. "Go to hell!"

Marty kept on smiling. "I hate being held up," he said. "The least I'm entitled to is an explanation. You're going to give it to me now, or I'm going to slug you around a little. Were you ever slugged around with the barrel of your own gun?"

"Nuts! You can't get away with it. I'll yell."

Marty shook his head. "You wouldn't. It's a crime to hold a man up with a gun—even on a train."

"You couldn't prove a thing."

"All right, I'll slug you anyway. Do you explain?"

"Go to hell!"

Marty raised the gun, and the man shouted: "Help! Help!"

The man's voice was like a whisper against the rumbling of the mighty train. Marty brought the gun barrel down in a gentle slash along the man's cheek, and little drips of blood began to appear from his cheekbone to his jawline.

He raised a hand to protect his face, groaned, then sighed. "All right, you win. I'll talk."

"Fine!" Marty glowed. "Let's begin with your name."

"John Smith."

"Nice name," Marty commented, and raked the other's cheek again.

"A-r-rh—that hurts! Wait, I'll come clean. The name is Larkin—Nick Larkin."

"That's better," Marty grunted. "Now let's have the rest of it."

"So help me, mister, there ain't no rest of it. My friend in the compartment, and me, we got on the train to contact you. I was supposed to talk to you here on the train—ask you a question. But I heard you was a quick guy with a gun, so I figured I better have the drop on you when I asked it."

"What was the question?" Marty demanded.

"I was supposed to ask you: *Do we stop at Conshohocken?*"

Marty leaned against the door of the men's room, and looked down at Larkin. "Well—why poke a gun in me when you ask me that?"

"Well, my friend in the compartment told me I might have some trouble with you. He said he sent you a letter, which was why you was on the train, but now he don't want you no more. So I was supposed to give you a thousand dollar bill, and tell you to get off at Philly." Larkin grinned wryly. I figured I could make you get off an' not give you the grand. But I guess I was wrong."

Gingerly he felt in his fob pocket, extracted a folded bill, and gave it to Marty. "There's the dough. You was too fast for me."

Marty took the bill, unfolded it, with a puzzled look in his eyes. It was a thousand dollar note. "What's your friend's name?"

"I ain't supposed to say. It's supposed to be very confidential. He said you wasn't to ask no questions, but to get off at Philly and go home. He said you could consider your services at an end."

"I see," Marty said drily. "Would your friend's name be Hackerman, by any chance?"

Larkin's eyelids flickered, but his face showed nothing. "You ain't supposed to asked. My friend said that if I told you the password, that would be enough."

Marty shrugged. "It's okay by me. I'll get off at Philly. And thank your friend for the two grand." He unlocked the door of the men's room, stepped out through the washroom into the vestibule, leaving Mr. Larkin to get out as best he could.

The dark-haired girl was still sitting in Lower One, the Jap in Upper Three, and the fat man in Lower Seven. The door of Compartment A was closed.

Marty went through the car, and made his way toward the club car at the rear of the train. It was a job to plough through five Pullman cars and a diner, swaying along at swiftly increasing speed, but Marty finally made it. He was still trying to figure the thing out. The Jap, the dark-haired girl, and the fat man, were all obviously interested in him more than casually. If Larkin's story were true, then who had shot at him back at the Hotel Baltic with a silenced rifle? The fact that Larkin had asked the question about Conshohocken didn't mean anything. He and his mysterious friend in Compartment A might have seen the letter in some way.

STILL frowning, Marty picked up a magazine in the club car, ordered a highball from the Filipino in charge of the bar, and sipped it while he sat looking out at the long ribbons of rail unwinding behind the speeding train. He didn't read the magazine. His forehead was corrugated in thought, and even a second highball didn't make the thing any clearer to him. Why should a man hire a private detective by letter, pay him a thousand dollars, then take such a queer means of firing that same detective—paying him an additional thousand? At the third highball, the conductor came through and picked up his ticket.

Marty was working on the fourth, still looking out of the observation window, when a shape loomed up beside him and plopped into the swivel chair next to his own. It was the fat man from Lower Seven—the one who had been inspecting him furtively. The fat man smiled uncomfortably, ran a pudgy finger around his already wilted collar, and said conversationally:

"Hot day to travel, isn't it?"

Marty said, "Yeah," and kept on looking at the receding tracks. He waved toward the two, long black converging lines that seemed to slip out from under the speeding train. "If you look at them long enough, somebody told me, and drink enough highballs in the meantime, you can get nice and dizzy. I'm testing the theory."

The fat man laughed nervously. He was fidgetting in his chair. "That's all right if you can take it. I can't take it."

He rang for the Filipino, ordered beer. When the white-coated steward brought the beer, the fat man paid him, waited until he had gone back to the bar, then looked around the club car almost furtively, ascertained that they two were alone. Then he leaned over toward Marty and said: "Excuse me. *Do you know if we stop at Conshohocken?*"

Marty was in the middle of a long gulp from the tall glass. He finished the gulp, put the glass down on the combination ash tray and end-table alongside his chair, and said: "Well, well. So we meet at last. Do you by any chance own a thirty-thirty rifle with a silencer attached to it?"

The other wrinkled up his forehead, pursed his lips. "A rifle? With a silencer? Why no. But why—"

"All right, skip it. The name is what?"

"Er—Truswell, Mr. Quade. Carl Truswell is the name. It was I who sent you that note. It was fine of you to come. But about the rifle. I don't understand."

Marty was thinking swiftly. A man in Compartment A claimed to have sent him the note—had given him a thousand dollars additional, with the request to get off at Philadelphia. Now this man appeared. He said absently: "Oh, about the rifle? That was just an idea. Some one took a pot shot at me with a silenced rifle just after I got the letter."

"Well, Mr. Quade, I assure you it wasn't I. After paying you a thousand dollars, I'd hardly want to kill you. But that proves that my fears were not ungrounded at the time."

"What do you mean—at the time?"

"Well you see, Mr. Quade, I've—er—made satisfactory arrangements with the people from whom I feared—ah—violence, and there is no more danger. I shall be permitted to proceed unhindered to my destination. You, of course, Mr. Quade, may keep the thousand dollar fee. It's no more than right. In fact—" he produced a fat wallet, fingered out a crisp bill and handed it over—"I'm going to give you the other thousand which I promised you, just as if you had come all the way with me. You can get out at Philadelphia, and catch the train back to New York. Concern yourself no more with this whole thing, Mr. Quade!"

Marty veiled his eyes, and took the bill. "You're very generous, Mr. Truswell. You sure you don't need me?"

"Quite, Mr. Quade. Well, I was very glad to know you. I trust you will have a pleasant trip back to New York. I am sorry that I inconvenienced you."

"Not at all, Mr. Truswell. I'd make the trip ever day for three thousands dollars."

"*Three* thousand?"

"Excuse me. I should have said two thousand." Marty got up, shook hands with Truswell, and watched him lurch through the club car, back toward the Pullman. Then he sat down again, motioned to the Filipino to get him another drink, and entered into silent contemplation of the miracle which had brought him three crisp, genuine thousand dollar bills in one morning. To assist him in this pleasantly silent contemplation, he had gone on to his fifth highball, when a woman entered the club car.

Marty recognized her at once as the dark-eyed girl who had been sitting in Lower One. She cast a quick glance around, looked suspiciously at the Filipino, and hurried over to Marty.

"Excuse me," she said, with a slight hint of Latin-American accent. "Do we stop at—" she struggled with the next word, as if it were difficult for her to pronounce, then got it out in syllables—"*Con-sho-hocken?*"

MARTY almost dropped his glass. He covered his confusion by arising and bowing. His roving eyes took in her soft, rounded figure which was thinly covered by a silky dress of bright-green, spring-season material. Her mouth was soft, her lips red. Her skin was creamy white, the sort that promises to be smooth to the touch. There was in her eyes a lively sort of interest, mingled with a hint of urgent apprehension.

Marty said: "Conshohocken, eh? Nice place, Conshohocken. Quite popular. What can I do for you, miss?" Outwardly, he was calm. Inwardly, he was all tied up in a knot. Manifestly, it was impossible that all these people should have written him that letter. It had been urgently secret, yet one would have thought that it's contents had been published on the first page of every newspaper in New York.

The girl had one hand at her breast, the other tightly gripping a small, white-leather purse. "I am Beatriz Delcastro," she said breathlessly, looking back fearfully toward the entrance of the club car, as if she feared pursuit. "I am the one who wrote you that letter." As she hurried on, her Spanish accent became more pronounced. "Eet was so vairy nice of you to come. But now, I have—what-you-call—arrange' my troubles. I no longer need your so able asseestance. I can go on to South America without danger. But I thank you, Mr. Quade."

"That's all right, Miss Delcastro," Marty murmured. "I understand just how you feel. So many people feel that way. By the way—" as she looked at him blankly—"do you happen to own a thirty-thirty rifle with a silencer?"

"But—I do not understand."

Marty grinned. "Don't pay any attention to me. That was just an American joke. I suppose you want me to get off at Philadelphia, then take the train back to New York?"

"But yes. How did you guess?"

Marty sighed. "I begin to suspect I'm really not wanted on the Florida Special. Okay, lady. Philadelphia it shall be."

She brightened. "Your fee—I promised you another thousand dollars when we shall have arrive' at Miami—you shall have it now." She opened her purse, extracted a single bill, and handed it over. Marty took it gravely, turned it over in his fingers. It was a thousand dollars.

"I am so sorry that I have inconvenience you," she was saying.

"Not at all, Miss Delcastro. I'd make this trip every day for four thousand dollars."

"*Four* thousand?"

"I should have said two, shouldn't I? I trust your journey will be successful, Miss Delcastro."

She covered her eyes with long lashes, murmured: "Thank you—good-by," and swayed toward the door of the club car. Marty was following her with his eyes, when suddenly there appeared in the doorway the diminutive figure of the Japanese chauffeur. He held a small gun at his hip, and his beady eyes flicked from

Marty and the girl, to the Filipino bar-boy, who was staring at the gun, goggle-eyed.

The Jap hissed: "Do not move, pliss, yes?" The girl uttered a tight little scream that was drowned by the noise of the train. Marty stood taut, the fingers of his right hand crooked, ready to streak for the automatic in his shoulder holster.

The Filipino boy, near the door, close to the Jap, started to tremble, and to back away. His face had turned a mottled gray. The Jap reached out, seized him by the shoulder, spun him around, held him as a shield, and advanced toward Marty and the girl.

"Pliss," he ordered Marty, poking his gun out past the trembling Filipino, "you will open the back door and step out on the platform."

Marty asked bleakly: "What do you intend to do?"

The Jap smiled, showing sharp teeth. "I intend, sar, that you shall all jump from the train. If you like it bettar, I can shoot you and the lady very dead with this gun. Maybe you would like to jump from the train instead. The Filipino must jump with you, because I want no witness."

Marty said dully: "You can't make the lady jump!"

"No? But I can shoot her. Pliss to do what I ask very quickly. I have so very little time." He smiled almost apologetically, but he held the gun steadily beaded on Marty.

Marty stood still. He was stalling for time. The muzzle of the Jap's gun looked very businesslike. "But why do you want to kill Miss Delcastro and myself?"

The Jap's eyes flickered. "The young lady knows. Unfortunate for you that she sent you that lettar—and for this Filipino, too." He sighed, as if regretfully. "Now you must all jump."

The Filipino had been trembling in the Jap's grip. Now he uttered a startled yelp, and tried to twist away. The Jap snarled, raised the gun and hit him hard on the side of the head. The Filipino slumped, unconscious. But the Jap had made a fatal mistake. In the second that the muzzle of the gun was turned away from him, Marty stepped in swiftly, brought a hard right whizzing past the slumping Filipino's ear to connect with the Jap's mouth.

The Jap squeaked, dropped the gun, and raised both hands to his lips. Marty bored in, brought up a right and a left, and a second right. The yellow man doubled over, flopped, lying astride one of the swivel chairs, with his hands brushing the floor. The Filipino lay in the aisle, also unconscious.

Marty turned to the girl. "Well, Miss Delcastro, I guess we don't have to go through with the jumping act."

She was looking at him with frank admiration. "Meestair Quade, you are marvelous! You moved so fast that I did not know what was happening until it was fineesh!"

Marty said sourly: "Thanks. It looks like I'll earn part of those fees. I guess you won't want me to leave you now?"

"But yes! You must get off here. My guardian is to meet me at Philadelphia, and he has arrange' for me to be very safe for the rest of the trip. Eet was he who tol' me to send you back."

"Your guardian is Austin Hackerman?"

"But yes! You are so clevair, Meestair Quade! How did you know?"

Marty frowned, cast a quick glance at the still unconscious Jap and Filipino, and stepped closer to her. "Look here, Miss Delcastro, would it be too much for me to ask what this is all about? What is this dangerous mission that you're going on?"

She smiled. "I trust you, Meestaire Quade. I can tell you this. I go to my native country of San Félice, which is near to the border of Paraguay. It is that my father—" she crossed herself devoutly—"who rests in heaven, owned much gold mines in San Félice before the revolution. My family fled here after the revolution, and the gold mines have not been worked for fifteen years. Now the government has declare' an amnesty to political refugees, and it has announce' that it will sell all sequestered property for back taxes, but that the rightful owners may claim them upon payment of those taxes. So I go to San Félice to pay the taxes and claim the mines."

"I see," said Marty. "And how much are those taxes?"

"Feefty thousand dollar. Mr. Hackerman has withdraw the money from the Bank of Pan-America. He joins me here at Philadelphia—weeth the cash. There were those who would like to possess those ancestral mines of the Delcastro's, and I feared that I might be stopped on th-e-e way. Eef I do not appear in San Felice by the day after tomorrow, the mines weel be sold at auction, for a small fraction of their value—they are worth many millions. I have been threatened, and one attempt has already been made upon my life. That was why I engage' you."

"I get it," Marty said tersely. So this Jap, and those others in B17 were all trying to stop you. They tried to buy me off, all posing as the original sender of the letter. Funny—how they all knew what was in it."

THE train had already pulled out of the Philadelphia station, and was gathering speed. Marty had not heard the approaching footsteps in the club-car vestibule. Now he stopped, staring at the group of men who had pushed into it. In the lead was a stocky man with a high forehead that was bald in the middle, with fringes of grayish hair along the edges. His face was soft with good living, and his hands were white and smooth.

At sight of him, Beatriz Delcastro uttered a glad little cry. "Meestair Hackerman!"

Behind Hackerman were Nick Larkin, whose lips were twisted in a vicious smile, Larkin's friend from Compartment A, and Carl Truswell. Larkin, Truswell, and the other man, all had guns with which they covered Marty and the girl.

Hackerman walked a little in advance of the other three, but well to one side, so as not to obstruct their line of fire.

Larkin called out: "You, Quade! I'm just waitin' for you to make a move. I got to square up with you for that smack on the jaw!"

Marty grinned thinly, said nothing. He was studying Hackerman.

The girl stepped forward impulsively. "Oh, Mr. Hackerman! I am so glad that you have come! You have the mon-ey!"

Hackerman pushed her gruffly away from him. "Out of the way! This is business!"

She staggered a little under his shove, and Marty took half a step forward, stopped short as Larkin pushed past Hackerman and the girl, poked his gun into Marty's chest. "Hold it, punk," he growled.

Marty's eyes blazed, but he held himself taut. The girl gazed at Hackerman with wide, unbelieving eyes. "B-but—Meestair Hackerman! You are my guardian, ees it not?"

Hackerman barked at her: "Forget that guardian stuff!"

Carl Truswell, from behind, snickered, and his fat jowls shook as he laughed. "Yes, my dear, forget that guardian business. The good Mr. Hackerman has now shed his sheep's clothing. Ha, ha!"

Hackerman growled over his shoulder: "Shut up, Truswell! We're going to kill her and this detective. It'll be murder. You don't joke when you do murder!"

Truswell chuckled. "Now don't get sore at your partner, Austin. It's my money that's backing this. You should let me have my little joke for my good money."

Beatriz Delcastro was breathing hard. "You—you will—*murder* us? You, my father's friend? B-but why?"

Marty, whose eyes had locked with Hackerman's, said gently: "For your gold mines, Miss Delcastro. Don't you see it yet? He's going down to San Félice and buy in your gold mines for himself. He lost his own money in the market. He's going to recoup now—at your expense."

Larkin jabbed Marty with the gun. "Sure, you're a wise guy. Only save it. Open your pan again, and I'll chop it up a little—the way you chopped me. In fact, I think I'll do it anyway."

Carl Truswell said impatiently: "Here, here—don't fool around, Larkin. He's a dangerous man. Keep him covered. No personal spites at this time."

The fourth man, who had not said anything yet, now spoke. "Yeah," he said through thin lips. "Is this a tea party? Let's get down to cases."

Hackerman was bending over the Jap. "H'm," he said. "Hoya wasn't much good against you, was he, Quade. I guess you'll take more handling than he could give you."

Marty said: "Will you kindly tell me who was the bird that took the pot-shot at me with the silenced rifle back at New York?"

Larkin guffawed. "That was my friend here—" he motioned toward the fourth man, his companion from Compartment A—"Jake Krevel. I told him he was a lousy shot with a rifle, but he wanted the job."

Krevel nodded brightly. "Sorry I missed you, Quade. But it was just a fluke, your bending your head at that minute."

"Yeah," said Marty, "just a fluke. You know, Krevel I hate being shot at. I'm going to pay you off for that."

"Ha, ha," said Krevel. "You ain't gonna do much payin' off after today."

Trueswell snapped: "Well, let's get it over with. What are we gabbing for? Come on, make them jump off the train, or throw them off. It'll look like an accident."

BEATRIZ DELCASTRO broke in, still uncomprehending: "You—you are going to kill us? But I do not understand. Who is this man—" she pointed at Truswell—"and these other wicked men?"

Marty laughed shortly. "It's not hard to understand, Miss Delcastro. Hackerman wants those mines of yours. He's probably got Truswell to put up the money to buy and operate them. With the cash he drew in your name, plus Truswell's capital, they'll be able to pull millions out of your mines. These two birds, Larkin and Krevel, are just a couple of heels earning a little pin money. Of course, you showed Hackerman the letter you sent me, so he knew just what it contained. He tried to have Larkin, and then Truswell, buy me off with thousand dollar bills, and when they saw I wasn't getting off at Philadelphia, they got rough. Now they're out in the open. They're going to commit murder, Miss Delcastro, and put themselves in line for a nice little walk to the death house."

Hackerman shook his head. "No, Quade, this is airtight. Hoya is going to be the goat. You and the girl will be found dead on the tracks, and Hoya will be found here killed with your gun, which Krevel will now take away from you. Take it, Krevel!"

Krevel stepped past Larkin, who still kept his gun poked against Marty's chest. Marty's wiry body was poised, taut, but he dared not move. Larkin's finger was too ready on the trigger.

Krevel stuck a hand under Marty's armpit, took out the automatic that Marty carried there, exhibited it triumphantly. He stepped toward the unconscious Jap, put the gun to the yellow man's head, and fired. Brains and blood spattered on the floor and on the upholstery of the chairs.

Marty exclaimed: "You birds must be crazy! Some one is liable to come in here any minute."

Larkin shook his head. "Forget it, punk. Nobody is coming in. Don't you feel that we're slowing down? We uncoupled this car. We're rolling way behind the train now. As soon as we've finished with you, we get off this car, and an auto meets us. It's following us parallel to the tracks now. We drive to the nearest airport, and charter a plane—an' we're in San Félice practically before they find your bodies. How's that?"

"Swell," said Marty.

Beatriz Delcastro was swaying on her feet, looking down with fascinated, horror-filled eyes at the bloody body of the Jap.

Truswell rubbed his hands. "All right, all right. That takes care of Hoya. Now these two—"

Krevel wiped his fingerprints off the automatic, dropped it beside the body of the Jap. Then he reached in his shoulder holster and took out his own gun. "You take the dame, Larkin," he said. "I'll finish up what I started on Quade this morning."

Larkin said: "Just a minute. Quade's

got a lot of dough on him. Mr. Truswell gave him a grand, I gave him a grand, and there was a grand in the letter the dame sent him. Why lose all that? Let's take it off him."

Hackerman nodded. "Take that letter from him, too. We don't want that found on him."

Marty said mildly: "I really have four thousand dollars. Miss Delcastro just gave me another bill. It won't do me any good where I'm going. Here it is." With a gesture so innocent that Larkin never suspected him, he put his hand in his jacket pocket, gripped the gun he had taken away from the Jap and fired through the cloth at Larkin. The bullet caught Larkin in the stomach, and he went backward, his finger contracting on the trigger of his gun. It exploded. Marty had twisted to one side, and the slug tore through his left arm, instead of through his chest. He didn't even feel it in the excitement of the moment, however, for he was firing at Krevel, still from his pocket. Krevel was hurled backward, fell over the prone body of the Jap, with a bullet in his chest and another through his throat.

Carl Truswell had leaped back at the first shot, and knelt behind one of the club chairs. He was peeking out now, sighting his gun at Marty. Marty didn't have time to shoot, but dived at Hackerman, who had been standing transfixed in the aisle. Truswell fired, three times, and each of the shots entered Hackerman's body, for Marty's lunge had pushed the girl's guardian right into the line of fire. Marty went down with Hackerman, and shot from the floor at the edge of Truswell's head, which showed from behind the chair. Truswell's head disappeared, seeming to have been disintegrated by the slug.

THE booming reverberations of the gunfire filled the club car, together with the stench of cordite. Marty got to his feet, slipping in blood, and staggered over to the huddled form of Beatriz Delcastro, on the floor. Anxiously he raised her head. Her eyes were closed, her face waxen-white. Marty swore under his breath, pulled her dress open at the front, searching for a wound. Her white, soft skin was unmarred. Frantically, Marty ripped her dress further, seeking the wound.

Suddenly she opened her eyes. Her face became a deep scarlet. "I assure you, Meestaire Quade," she said, "that I am not injure'!"

Marty flushed, got up awkwardly. She sat up, and he helped her to her feet. She held her ripped dress together as best she could. "I am so vairy sorry," she apologized, "for fainting. Eet ees a weakness of the Delcastro women."

"That's what probably saved your life," Marty told her. "There was a lot of lead flying around here for a couple of seconds."

Suddenly her eyes lighted on the trickle of blood from Marty's sleeve. "Your arm!"

Marty grinned wanly, motioned to the bodies on the floor. "I bet these birds here would have liked to get away with just a scratch on the arm!"

He staggered to the rear, smashed the glass in the back door, and climbed out on the platform, began to twist the wheel brake. The car began to slow up, and soon it came to a stop.

He turned around, to find Beatriz Delcastro watching him through the broken glass of the door. She was smiling a slow, lazy smile, and her lips were soft, inviting. "I have nevair met a man like you, Meestaire Marty," she said. "I need you. Weel you come weet me to South America, and see that no other vultures take away my mines?"

Marty stepped closer to her. "Will I come? You've hired yourself a first class detective, lady!"

The type for the Introductory Essay
Was set by Ray B. Browne
On Addressograph-Multigraph 3500
At Bowling Green, Ohio
In Baskerville typeface

www.ingramcontent.com/pod-product-compliance
Lightning Source LLC
Chambersburg PA
CBHW060546310726
48982CB00007B/1037

* 9 7 8 0 8 7 9 7 2 3 5 3 8 *